BLOOD AND GUILE

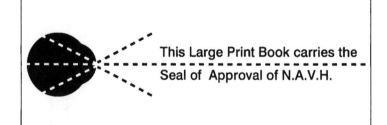

This Large Print Book carries the
Seal of Approval of N.A.V.H.

BLOOD AND GUILE

William Hoffman

Thorndike Press • Thorndike, Maine

Copyright © 2000 by William Hoffman.

This is a work of fiction. The characters, incidents, and dialogues are products of the author's imagination and are not to be construed as real. Any resemblance to actual persons, living or dead, is entirely coincidental.

Published in 2001 by arrangement with HarperCollins Publishers, Inc.

Thorndike Press Large Print Mystery Series.

The tree indicium is a trademark of Thorndike Press.

The text of this Large Print edition is unabridged.
Other aspects of the book may vary from the original edition.

Set in 16 pt. Plantin by Rick Gundberg.

Printed in the United States on permanent paper.

Library of Congress Cataloging-in-Publication Data

Hoffman, William, 1925–
   Blood and guile / William Hoffman.
     p. cm.
    ISBN 0-7862-3172-6 (lg. print : hc : alk. paper)
    1. Male friendship — Fiction. 2. West Virginia — Fiction.
   3. Large type books. I. Title.
   PS3558.O34638 B58 2001
   813′.54—dc21   00-067206

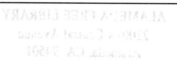

For Ben McCulloch and Bill Moore
Friends in Deed

The present works of present man —
A wild and dreamlike trade of blood
   and guile

— Coleridge

ONE

I tasted salted blood of my cut lower lip as I scrambled up from ankle-deep snow, retrieved my father's sixteen-gauge Parker side-by-side, and staggered after Drake Wingo as we climbed toward the ridge of Blind Sheep Mountain. I licked the blood and hunched my chin into my parka's fur collar.

Why am I, Walter B. Frampton II, here, I asked myself, when I could be warm and secure at my law office or apartment in Jessup's Wharf? Unlike Drake or Charles LeBlanc, I felt the urge to kill birds, deer, and bear existed only feebly in my genes. I respected the hunting tradition and the fine men who pursued it, but I would much rather have been sipping George Dickel's Tennessee Sour Mash Whisky, reading *Vanity Fair*, and listening to a Mozart quartet.

Drake had already bagged a ruffed grouse — a clean shot of the bird as it canted into hemlock shadows, which draped a dark cloak across snow. I moved obliquely through slush, the Parker heavy in my gloved fingers.

7

Drawing hard for breath, a stitch in my side, I hurried to keep pace with long-striding Drake. Kraut, his German short-haired pointer, coursed ahead.

A shot faintly heard stopped Drake and me. He peered westward along the wooded slope. When he resumed climbing, two more shots and a laggard third — three, the agreed-upon distress signal.

"What?" Drake asked, not to me, but stared toward a gauzy stratum of meandering mist. He legged downward, and I again stumbled as I dodged fluted trunks of the great hemlocks whose drooping black-green branches released shards of snow. Drake paused and raised a hand for silence. The liver pointer stood watching and waiting for command. A slow thawing caused rivulets to run unseen beneath us. I dabbed at my lip.

Drake moved into a lope traversing the mountainside. I, following, attempted to see beyond a sea of wet, glistening laurel.

"There," he said and pointed.

The figure on the steep grade waved and bounded downward, his arms flapping, his cap gone, his camera tossed about by its neck strap — Cliff Dickens frenzied, his legs looping so high his booted feet appeared hardly to touch the ground. When he reached us, he bent over, winded and retching, and I saw the blood on his hands and hunting jacket. Where was his Beretta?

"Wendell, quick," he said.

He straightened and turned to climb back along his own tracks, his steps uneven, his body reeling, his arms swinging as if deboned. He slipped to a knee, yet rose without breaking stride. Garbled words choked his breathing, and an arm curved forward weakly to gesture us upward.

"What?" Drake asked.

For an instant Cliff slowed and looked back wildly before again flinging himself at the mountain, a drunken gait, swerving and lurching back on course. Kraut, running ahead, turned to watch.

Cliff halted, tottered, and sank to his knees at the huddled figure lying on his side in the thrashed drift. Snow melting from Wendell's body heat had diluted blood that seeped through the cashmere scarf used to stanch the wound's oozing. Wendell gazed upward from his deadpan face, his set eyes now seeing far beyond any earthly vision.

Drake knelt, laid his ear close to Wendell's mouth, and lifted away the scarf. Torn, powder-burned pieces of Wendell's Woolrich jacket and bits of a plaid shirt lodged in the imploded scarlet breach of his chest.

Drake lifted his gaze to Cliff.

"I tried carrying him," Cliff said, weaving, slumped, racked. He stared at his bloody palms and pushed his hands away as if to disown them.

"But what the hell?" Drake asked while Kraut circled wanting to sniff Wendell's body. Drake ordered the pointer to stay.

"A bird flushed," Cliff said. He sank to his knees and pushed his hands under the snow to rub off blood. "I thought Wendell was on my other side. I tried to stop the bleeding and carried him down the mountain far as I could."

"You swung into him?" Drake asked as he pushed up. He helped Cliff to his feet.

"I believed he was to my right," Cliff said. "Brought up my gun, led the bird, and fired just as Wendell stepped in front of the load."

He swayed, flung snow from his fingers, and shook his head as if to cast off memory.

Drake handed me his twelve-gauge Savage and crossed to an immature hemlock, drew his sheath knife, and hacked the blade at the slender trunk. He yanked the tree loose and arranged it alongside Wendell before rolling the body onto the boughs, causing Wendell's arms to flop and his face to find rest against a mud-smeared cheek.

"The authorities won't want him moved," I said.

10

"I don't want authorities screwing around on my mountain," Drake answered.

It was like him to think of possession, of Blind Sheep's being his even when confronted by the hideousness of death. He used the hemlock as a makeshift litter to begin hauling Wendell's body feetfirst down toward the cabin. Kraut ran ahead, still hunting. The weight on the hemlock's branches left a streaked, orderly wake as if the snow were being harrowed in preparation for planting. I assisted as best I could, adjusting Wendell on the litter, cradling my Parker and Drake's Savage, guns I wanted to throw aside. The way down was softly treacherous. While Drake's strides continued long and sure, I took short, quick steps to slow my descent. Cliff wove his way behind us, head lolling, his body giving itself to gravity.

Melting snow dripped off the cabin's roof as well as the Bronco, the drops of water sliding from its black sides and puddling among slush. Drake released the litter to open the two-wheeled trailer's tailgate, cleared space among provisions, and nodded at me to lay down the guns and help lift Wendell.

We worked him onto the trailer. The body was still flexible, limbs dangling, the head thumping back and exposing throat. I tasted a vomit flake. Drake unfolded a shelter half and

11

spread it over Wendell.

"We'll go to High Gap," he said and banged up the tailgate. He chained Kraut to a papaw tree as I sat in the rear of the Bronco behind Cliff in the front. Cliff worked the Nikon's strap over his head. Drake started the engine, the Bronco pitched forward and skidded sideways, and the vehicle fishtailed along the abandoned logging road, never slowing.

I thought of Wendell, a polite, quiet little man who had willingly carried more than his share of our gear up to the cabin when we first arrived and was now himself the cargo.

TWO

The Bronco's bouncing jolted me. The air seemed to have thinned, the world to have distanced itself, and I pictured Wendell's body being tossed about beneath the shelter half. Drake drove as if to punish the vehicle. His was the gift of certainty. Rawboned and wiry, he still wore his dark hair cropped and stiff in the military mode. His direct blue eyes were flecked with gold.

The Bronco drifted sideways, its tires slinging chunks of mud-soiled snow that splattered laurel and left an ugly trail. "I can't stop seeing it," Cliff said and reached to the dash to keep from tipping as the Bronco swerved.

"Just hold tight," Drake said and twisted the steering wheel. In Slash Lick Hollow he cut the wheel to miss broken remains of a split-rail fence erected many years earlier by shepherds. Wendell had said they led their sheep down from the high sod during the first snow to allow the flocks to reach low-ground pastures.

"I can't believe this happened," Cliff said. Even during his youth Cliff had been re-

13

strained, cool, disdainful. He had become master of the arched eyebrow, and early on I had tried to model myself on him. His was a made presence during the years I had struggled to establish my own.

"It'll be okay," Drake said. A sergeant who had served three hitches in the army before mustering out, the sight of the dead had to be less stunning to him.

I couldn't stop myself from envisioning what the moment of Wendell's death must have been like — the hot blast of a high-brass 7½ load, the rupturing of flesh, the blood a red fountain finally draining away life like a faucet slowly closed.

The Bronco pounded along the hollow. Drake clicked on the windshield washers, and an arched brown film momentarily obscured the glass. He slowed for the turn onto the paved valley road. A plow had cleared lanes, leaving cindered snow piled high. We passed a marker: HIGH GAP 17M.

High Gap was the county seat of Seneca County, West Virginia, a town bound by ranges of steep, timbered mountains that clipped short the day's sunlight.

"I'm so sorry," Cliff said. He raised a hand, which dropped like a fallen bird.

"What you learn is that when it's done, it's done," Drake said. Curved forward over the

14

wheel, he kept glancing at Cliff. "Just get your story straight."

"Story?" Cliff asked and lifted his face.

"What you tell the law. He'll need to make a statement, won't he, Raff?"

"He will," I said.

"A grouse flushed, you fired swinging into Wendell, nothing more, right?" Drake asked Cliff.

For a second their eyes met and held. Then Cliff turned away and nodded. He touched his temple with long, artistic fingers that trembled.

We passed the first dwellings, a few sided with tar paper patterned like brick. Firewood had been stacked on porches, smoke rose from chimneys, and dogs barked, their voices nearly silent in the Bronco's rattling interior. The mountains' outcropping of gray boulders broke the pall of snow.

"Just an accident, nothing more," Drake said. He drove well, pushing the edge of recklessness.

"I'm due in classes Monday," Cliff said.

"The college will surely allow you time off," I said.

"So damn sorry."

Drake stopped at a Marathon gas station to ask where to find the sheriff. The attendant pointed us on along the street to the concrete courthouse that appeared squatly massive relative to the size of all structures around it, bullying its neighbors with the majesty of the law. A rectangle of lawn held a rusted cannon and a flagpole.

Drake turned in at a street beyond the courthouse where at the rear the "Sheriff's Department" sign hung over the doorway of a one-story, flat-roofed brick addition.

"Wait till I see what's what," he said and sidled from the Bronco. His boots crushed slush.

"Is this going to be bad?" Cliff asked without facing me.

"Just a procedure," I answered and hoped that would be all.

Drake returned with the sheriff, not a grizzled, potbellied lifer, but young, no more than his middle thirties, his tan uniform sharply pressed, his trooper's hat set slightly cocked. As Drake walked him to the trailer to unlatch the tailgate, I stepped from the Bronco. The fair and lightly freckled sheriff flipped the shelter half from the body and leaned forward to lay fingers against Wendell's jugular. He uncovered the clotted wound.

"You shouldn't have moved him," he said.

"His hunting partner tried to get him down," Drake said. "Panic time."

"You the one?" the sheriff asked me.

16

"No, Mr. Dickens is in the Bronco," I said.

The sheriff walked to the passenger side and opened the door.

"You did the shooting?" he asked, his accent just a touch hillbilly, the words partially filtered through his nose.

Cliff nodded, his head bowed.

"We'll carry the body to the coroner," the sheriff said. "You men follow my car."

The sheriff walked back to the building. A uniformed deputy had pushed open the storm door and stood watching. The sheriff spoke, zipped his leather jacket, and reset his hat.

Drake banged up the tailgate. He pulled out after the black Dodge cruiser that had a rack of blue-and-yellow lights bolted to its roof. Drake stayed well back to keep his windshield clean. Three crows pecking at a flattened vestige of roadkill flapped aside and settled back after we passed to continue feeding.

THREE

The Seneca County Free Clinic was a white vinyl-sided building leveled partway up the mountainside. Drake parked on a graveled lot at the front. An artificial holly wreath that hung from a hook screwed into the door looked as if it had been in place many seasons.

The bald, elderly doctor lay snoozing on the stainless-steel examination table. A stout and dark-skinned nurse whispered questions to the sheriff before gently shaking the doctor.

He rose patting himself as if to make certain he was all of a piece. When he couldn't locate his glasses, the nurse searched for and discovered them on a shelf among stacked rolls of tape, gauze, and bandages. The elbows of his brown sweater had been reinforced with chamois patches. He worked his feet into arctics as the nurse pulled on galoshes, and the two of them walked out to the trailer. The doctor's gray pants drooped around his skinny loins. He had not bothered to buckle his arctics, which flapped.

The nurse held a clipboard and pencil tied

to it by twine. Cliff stayed in the Bronco while Drake opened the trailer's tailgate. The sheriff uncovered Wendell and helped the doctor knee up inside to lay his stethoscope over Wendell's heart. The doctor's hands were palsied, and he grunted. Just holding on he was — to anything within his feeble grasp.

"All cessation of bodily functions," he dictated to the nurse, his voice rickety. "Tentative evaluation death caused by gunshot wound to the lower anterior chest cavity and upper abdomen."

The nurse checked it off on an official form and walked back inside to bring out a collapsible canvas stretcher, which she unfolded. The sheriff and Drake helped her with the body. I held the door as they carried Wendell into the building and positioned the stretcher on the examination table.

The nurse fingered Wendell's wallet from the hip pocket of his rigid new hunting britches. She drew out his driver's license, studied it, and copied information before she and the doctor began removing Wendell's clothes. When a telephone rang, the nurse answered it.

"Roof fall at the Black Eagle," she told the doctor.

"Don't it ever stop?" he asked and hastily washed his hands above the sink and again stepped into his arctics while the nurse reached him his overcoat and near shapeless fedora. Bag in hand, he listed out the door to a Chevy 4x4. At the wheel, he started the engine and, exhaust steaming, drove the pickup in winding fashion down the mountainside to the main street.

"I'll get back to you, Linda Belle," the sheriff told the nurse after he emptied Wendell's pockets of change, keys, coins, and a small wooden cross that had what looked like a tiny eye carved into the top of the upright timber. He also took Wendell's wallet.

"Won't that be a blessing," she answered.

He gave her a tight smile and we left.

"Once Old Doc Bailey was a young fellow fresh out of med school who could've practiced in Charleston or Huntington and made big money," the sheriff said. "He had this idea about serving humanity. Well, humanity's about damn near run him to death."

We drove back into the shadowed valley and to the Sheriff's Department. The white walls and green linoleum floor were brightly illuminated by overhead fluorescent tubes. He led us along a corridor and into an office equipped with a metal desk, folding chairs, and a rack of rifles and shotguns chained in place through their trigger guards. His nameplate read: *Bruce B. Sawyers.*

Coils of an electric heater glowed. Walls held tacked-up men-wanted posters, a calendar from the Appalachian Bank, and a yellow handbill listing the game schedule of the West Virginia Mountaineers football team.

"Sit," he said, indicating chairs at the front and one side of his desk. He slipped off his leather jacket and hung it along with his hat on deer antlers attached to the wall. From a drawer he lifted a mimeographed form, and from his shirt pocket he drew a white plastic ballpoint pen. "Light 'em if you got 'em."

Set on a black iron safe behind him I glimpsed the picture of a soldier dressed in battle fatigues and holding an M16. He appeared more boy than man. Drake also eyed the photograph.

"Yep, that's me way back," the sheriff said. "Lied about my age. Only job I could find those days. You all in?"

"Three hitches and an education," Drake said.

"One not taught in books," the sheriff said and hunched his chair closer to the desk, studied the form, and held his pen ready. "First thing is who should be notified. You done any of that?"

"Not yet," Drake said.

"Wife, next of kin, family, somebody's got to be told," the sheriff said. He shuffled the driver's license and other cards from Wendell's wallet, the leather slightly curved from its fit to Wendell's hip.

"I'd like to help you, Sheriff," I said, "but all I know about the deceased was that he managed a food store in Richmond as well as owned the land we hunted on."

"He had a wife, but she died off," Drake said. He pushed back his blaze orange cap and scratched his cropped hair. A sliver of scalp shone through.

"Any children?" the sheriff asked.

"Not I heard of," Drake said.

"Brothers, sisters, anybody?"

Drake and I shook our heads. Cliff looked at his drooping hands, his wrists supported by his knees.

"Which of you knew him best?" the sheriff asked. His slate-colored eyes had penetration. He would need to be smart, I thought, to survive in this rough and tough country.

"Guess that's me since I brought him along but I never knew him close," Drake said. "More like a business relationship."

"I need a name and number, though I already overspent the phone budget. Cut me to four deputies and a jailer. I'm filing to run for the legislature next term. None of you can come up with further identification?"

"You could call somebody at his store,"

Drake said. "They'd pass the word."

"Okay," the sheriff said. "I'll turn it over to the Virginia State Police and let them handle it. What's the name of the store?"

"Food," Drake said.

"Full name?"

"That's it. FOOD."

"Some name. You got a number?"

"No, just Richmond town."

The sheriff lifted the phone, dialed, and leaned back. He knew the trooper at the other end and traded small talk before listing details. "Shoot me any feedback," he said. "And my good hello to Captain Harvey."

He collected Wendell's wallet and pocket contents, dropped them into a manila envelope, and set the envelope in the desk drawer along with the mimeographed sheet. He locked the drawer before standing and reaching for his jacket.

"What say we do a look-see at your camp?" he asked, zipping the jacket and setting on his hat. "I'll trail you in my vehicle."

We drove away in the Bronco. Cliff appeared aged and bled. I glanced back to see the sheriff following in the Dodge. Each jolt of the road whipped its three antennas.

We reached the turnoff from the county road, bounced along Slash Lick Hollow, and Drake geared to four-wheel to begin the climb up the logging road. The sheriff honked, leaned from his window, and shouted. He wanted to leave the Dodge for a ride with us.

At the cabin Drake let Kraut loose, and the pointer dashed around till brought to heel. Cliff proceeded us up the mountain, his stride jarring him as if his legs had become brittle. The fragile warming continued the slow melt, the rivulets finding channels of Blind Sheep's descent. Hemlock boughs freed of snow's weight sprang upward.

We reached the drift where Cliff had let down Wendell's body. Sheriff Sawyers circled it, and voice lowered, he fed details into a hand-sized recorder held left of his mouth.

"Stay wide around this place," he directed us. From a breast pocket of his uniform shirt he slipped a small, flat camera, a Canon. He snapped pictures and worked a broken branch of a spruce pine into the ground to mark the drift's location.

We climbed on until we reached the blood-ied snow. The sheriff stepped forward alone, spoke into his recorder, hunkered, rose, and backed off. He located the over-and-under Beretta Cliff had borrowed from Drake, the shotgun apparently hurled aside, and then Wendell's Remington automatic. He didn't touch them. The guns had sunk into snow.

"Leave them lie," he ordered Drake, who

24

had started toward the Remington. Death hadn't blunted Drake's concern for guns.

"They'll rust," he said as he drew back, startled by the sheriff's tone of command.

"The department will tag and care for them," the sheriff said and faced Cliff. "Where'd your bird flush?"

Cliff had been waiting submissively, his face partially turned away. He pointed to a laurel thicket, the dark green tubular leaves cautiously unfolding to warmth. The sheriff crossed to the laurel to scan the ground.

"No bird tracks," he said into the recorder. He was definitely no hick lawman but a professional performing a meticulous investigation.

"They could've melted," Drake said.

"You swung around left to shoot?" the sheriff asked, ignoring Drake.

"It happened so fast," Cliff said.

"Wendell Ripley could've lunged past in a rush to get in a shot," Drake said.

"He could've," the sheriff said. He definitely did not care for Drake offering explanations and dictated further hushed observations, made a penciled diagram on the page of a pocket-size notebook, and again reached for the Canon. The shutter gave off precisely engineered clicks. Lastly he grouped us and snapped our picture.

"I want full names, addresses, and phone numbers," he said and wrote them in the notebook. He also asked us to show our drivers' licenses and checked our hunting permits.

"For now that'll do but you fellows stay away from this place. I'll be back with deputies and know if the scene's been compromised."

He pulled out a Buck knife, thumbed the blade open, and cut laurel sprigs he stuck in the soil to identify the area.

We hiked down to the cabin Drake had built a year ago on land leased from Wendell. Drake had chosen a bench of the mountain below the ridge, a southern exposure that used Blind Sheep itself to block the northern shriekers, which, he claimed, blew so hard they would rip the hair off a bobcat's back.

The cabin was a rectangular plank dwelling that appeared raw instead of fully weathered to the blending that nature demanded. Drake had considered restoring the shepherd's cottage on the high sod, but the roof and supporting beams had rotted and the stones fallen in upon themselves.

To the west of the cabin ran Wolf Creek, its origin mossy seepages high on Blind Sheep that fed upon themselves till they grew and gorged downward. By the time they reached the valley they had joined to become the Wilderness River, a torrent that had carved a chasm and smashed itself against boulders, the violent water grinding them over centuries to sand and sending waves to shore that created a beach and ocean clamor hundreds of miles and thousands of feet above the sea.

Sheriff Sawyers snapped pictures of the cabin and fitted the camera into his shirt pocket before looking hard at each of us as if to set our faces in his mind.

"I know all of you are from out of state but like you to stick around a few days," he said.

"Are you telling us we can't leave?" I asked.

"You're a lawyer," he said.

"I am," I answered. He had apparently sighted my Virginia Bar Association membership card when I took out my driver's license.

"Not can't," he said. "Just a request. How about a ride to my car?"

"I'll do that thing," Drake said. "You a hunter?"

"I've been known to bring meat to the table," the sheriff said.

"Knew you were a hunter," Drake said.

FOUR

I watched Drake lay out the grouse he had killed earlier, placing it on a red-oak stump he used as a chopping block beside ice-bordered Wolf Creek. Spray from the stream had laid droplets that gleamed over ferns along the bank.

"We're about ready," I told him.

"As soon as I finish," he said and with a single short chop of his ax decapitated the plucked bird. He tossed the head to Kraut and knelt by the creek to shuck out the heart and snaky red entrails. He held the grouse positioned so that the fast flow washed and emptied its body cavity.

I crossed back to the cabin to help Cliff carry his gear. He moved like a man disoriented. When I started to lift my bag into the trailer, I drew away from Wendell's dried blood that spotted the floorboard planks. I wiped them with a sheet of snow-wetted newspaper and dropped it on fireplace embers, where it drew into itself, flared, and quivered like a black winged creature expiring.

Cliff waited at the Bronco. Drake wrapped aluminum foil around the grouse before packing it with scooped-up snow in his Coleman cooler. He set the fire screen, pulled shut the cabin door, and snapped the heavy padlock through the hasp. Kraut he allowed onto the seat beside me. The dog gave me a friendly sniff and curled himself until he found comfort. No visions of the dead on his canine mind.

Drake drove off Blind Sheep and along Slash Lick to the junction where he turned south for our descent from the high country, crossed the Virginia line to Monterey, and rolled us over Whiskey Creek to Staunton, where we picked up Interstate 64 that would carry us to Richmond.

We had left our cars at Drake's house in Midlothian, west of the city. His two-story Georgian sat above a lawn shaded in seasonal weather by towering yellow poplars, their leaves now torn away by the winter's winds.

Drake had married a lovely, cultured woman named Deborah, whose first husband died of a brain hemorrhage that sent him reeling into and spilling golf trophies off the shelves of his den. A corporate attorney, he had left her a large estate as well as their twin children. She was now three months pregnant, and Drake had thrown an Indian summer cocktail party that spread over the garden and lawn to celebrate what he called his potency.

He and I helped transfer Cliff's gear to his Thunderbird. The car had a numbered decal on the rear window that entitled him to faculty parking rights at Virginia Commonwealth University.

"Stay tonight with Deb and me," Drake offered him.

"I'll be okay," Cliff said, straightening and brushing back his lank off-blond hair as well as struggling to regain poise.

While I loaded my suitcase into my Buick, they stood talking. Drake laid a hand on Cliff's shoulder, and Cliff gave slightly beneath it.

"I'll check on you later," Drake said.

"And I'll follow you in," I said to Cliff.

"I'm able to handle it," he answered.

Drake held the Thunderbird's door for Cliff, and we watched him back out, turn, and drive along the suburban street overarched by the massive bare branches of ancient elms and white oaks.

"What can we do?" I asked.

"I'll keep watch on him. Come in for a sandwich or drink?"

"I think I better move on."

"One hell of a hunt," he said.

"Poor little man, Wendell."

"When you're dead, you're not poor, just gone."

That was Drake, the attitude he had come back with from his army service. I drove away, a seventy-minute trip east to King County's Jessup's Wharf. Laughing gulls, their plumage in gray-and-white winter phase, perched on the rusting iron bridge over the tidal Axapomimi River. They had splattered the railings and faced into the wind like feathered vanes.

I stopped by my office to check messages. Oh, the sweet flow of dollars after the lean years at Jessup's Wharf, a place I had set out my shingle as a last resort. The money was partly the result of the explosion at Bellerive Plantation some four years earlier that had caused the death of John Maupin LeBlanc III and his family as well as an aged servant named Gaius.

Charles LeBlanc, John's younger brother, had been suspected of their murder, become a fugitive, and I had defended him — at first with great reluctance. After his exoneration I had sued on his behalf a life-insurance company that had been withholding payment, collected two hundred and eighty-nine thousand dollars, and administered that money for Charles, who now lived in Montana.

Moreover, he would be receiving half a million a year for seven years from the sale of Bellerive to an Arab prince named Jamir. Edward, the third LeBlanc brother, had very generously agreed to split the proceeds, the first payment of which I expected to receive in Charles's behalf any day. Three and a half million for my client, who shortly before had been a derelict. My hands on my lap beyond Edward's sight had clenched and released when he, in his precise, solemn voice, had explained the transaction.

Though I would not leave my archaic Victorian apartment at Miss Mabel Tascott's, I had moved my office over from the narrow nineteenth-century brick building once owned by a doctor who made braces for children's crippled legs. The space I leased was on the ground floor of Jessup's Wharf's River Street, the two rooms repainted, carpets installed, the electricity rewired. I now had a lavatory as well as a reception area for clients. Would I lay my copies of *Vanity Fair* on a table for them to scan along with the *Reader's Digest* and perhaps *The Farmer's Almanac*?

Behind my desk I planned to rehang my three-by-five-foot portrait of uniformed Marse Robert that I had owned since graduating from Washington and Lee. I belonged to the Society of the Lees, an organization that required proof of blood kinship as a condition for membership, and felt his unswerving gaze warded off any temptation to compromise the standards I aspired to. The revisionists were attempting to bring the general down, but in my mind he continued to stand for honor, devotion, and valor. The latter, the real test of a man, had become particularly important to me because in truth I was still uncertain of my own.

I strove to appear sober and dignified in the practice of law and felt guilt and remorse that while my life was changing so much for the better, Cliff's had been devastated by what had happened to him on our Blind Sheep grouse shoot.

FIVE

Wendell Ripley's name appeared in the obituary column of Tuesday's *Times-Dispatch*, the cause of death given as a hunting accident. The stark, two-sentence announcement listed no next of kin, funeral service, or advice as to where to send condolences.

I had worked hauling law books and files from my old office to the new one, which had been a bakery before I contracted to have it remodeled. A faint odor of bread still hung around, embedded in walls and floors. On a shelf at the rear I discovered half a dozen loaf trays gathering dust, one holding a moldy, desiccated mouse. I had arranged to have my name painted in gilt letters over the broad window that gave out onto the King County Bank's Colonial headquarters and the white steeple of St. Luke's Church beyond.

Friday morning as I left Miss Mabel's house to walk to the office, my phone's ringing drew me back. I recognized Cliff Dickens's voice.

"I'd like to drive over at a time convenient to you," he said.

34

"You bearing up?" I asked.

"I've managed to hold it together. May I come?"

"You know you can. I'm on River Street now, across from the bank."

"I ought to reach your lair by eleven."

His voice, which had shed most of his Southern accent, sounded cool and in control as of old, and I was not surprised. During our years together at John Marshall High, he had twice won the Best Actor award. Because of his talent the Dramatic Club had dared attempt *Hamlet,* a production that turned out to be a near calamity except when Cliff spoke the soliloquies. Then a rowdy young audience quieted, and some of the girls' expressions became touched by something like sexual rapture.

He remained the best student among the Marauders, a gang the membership of which consisted of Drake Wingo, Cliff, and me. We had a secret handshake and in a shack built from scrap lumber behind Drake's parents' house took a blood oath by candlelight, using the single-edge Gillette blade to cut our left thumbs and touching them so that our bloods united. Cliff supplied a motto: *nunquam trado,* which meant never betray. He excelled in Latin.

Cliff grew up the best looking among us,

five eleven, that lank off-blond hair frequently tossed both for control and effect, about him an easy physicality that never seemed hurried or baffled. He made the varsity basketball squad while Drake was second team and often benched. I too tried out for the team but quit when I realized as I loped back and forth along the court I appeared comically ridiculous.

After graduating from John Marshall, we three began to drift. For his college, Drake chose Virginia Tech, Cliff the University, I Washington and Lee. Drake dropped out after a single semester, not because he faced failure but believed all he was receiving was what he called a trainload of bull crap. He joined the army.

Cliff's grades and all-around talent had won him a scholarship. He acted in plays and became almost as theatrical offstage as on, often striding about wearing a full-flowing coat draped around his shoulders, a long scarf, and a black beret aslant his left brow. Deep thinking seemed to rack his face. He made everyday actions like the purchase of cigarettes or the dropping off of his laundry appear to be a venture of importance that demanded profound attention.

After he graduated from the University he entered Yale, where he studied drama and intended to become a playwright as well as a novelist. The few times I saw him during those years, he was so occupied we little more than shook hands and drank a beer or two together. He did most of the talking.

Lately he had taught at VCU, gotten into photography, and had some of his work featured in a daring exhibition of male nudes that shocked Richmond's gentry. Letters received by the *Times-Dispatch* demanded that the show be closed. Cliff had enjoyed the notoriety, assuming that nothing the general public approved of could have lasting value.

"And good for sales," he said. "Let the mossbacks writhe in their piety."

At five minutes after eleven I glanced from the office window and saw his Thunderbird pull to the curb. The car's sides had become crusted with chemicals road crews had spread to melt snow. He lifted out a 35mm camera before locking the door and drawing on his Austrian toggle coat. He adjusted his plaid touring cap.

I met him at my door. Other than lines of weariness, he appeared almost his usual self — detached and suffering boredom.

"Well, you must be rising in the world, Walter," he said. He never called me Raff any longer, a thoughtfulness I appreciated. His eyes stopped at the picture of General

37

Robert E. Lee, and his mocking smile reasserted itself.

"It's good to know some things in this old world never change," he said.

When I positioned a chair for him in front of my desk, he sat with a tragic sort of grace — the scene played of a man badly used. As he unfastened his coat, I crossed around the desk.

"I'm not certain whether you're insulting me or not, but I'm glad to see you, Cliff, and hope all things in your life are looking up."

"Things are becoming tolerable, as we say out on the farm. I believe I slept as much as three hours last night without waking and having to blot out certain hideous displays which attempted to invade my consciousness."

"I know you've suffered."

"I doubt you know fully, but thanks, Walter. I'm happy to see some people doing well, I mean in particular my comrades of old, you and Drake."

He was referring with the latter to "The Truth of the Grouse," a pamphlet Drake Wingo had originally given away free off the counter at Grizzly's, his sporting goods outlet. A reporter for the *Times-Dispatch* wrote an article about the pamphlet, and local bookstores started peddling the tract, each copy autographed by Drake in his bold hand. Then the paper published an interview, causing sales to increase enough to justify a second printing. Drake was invited to speak before the Rotarians.

"I've been trying for years to write only to have one story published in a magazine now defunct," Cliff said. "An ironical development, don't you think?"

I had read that story in the quarterly named *Now*. A man living in a one-room tenement stares through smudged windowpanes over roofs which have steam rising from cast-iron pipes. He sees nightmarish shapes form among the steam. Why he is looking or his identity is never explained. Frenzied fish attack and swallow each other, white snakes coil, hiss, and strike. The man's vision ends when he turns away and pours coffee grains swirling down the kitchen sink.

"Did you bring that camera to snap my picture?" I asked, evading the subject because I had detected envy.

"Not long ago I saw a man do a swan dive from the seventh story of a hotel, and I had no camera with me. Now I try never to be without. Nights I keep at least one loaded alongside the Seconal on my bedside table."

He opened his coat over a red sweater. I offered him a Winston, though I knew he had stopped smoking as had most of my friends. I limited myself to ten cigarettes a day.

"I attended Wendell Ripley's funeral," he said. "I'd been trying to get in touch with his family to express *mea culpa* and my contrition. First I drove to FOOD, where he worked. What originality for a store name. I found a handwritten sign taped to the door announcing the place was closed for the burial. Also displayed was a drawn map and directions to the cemetery. When I arrived, pallbearers were lowering his wooden casket into the ground."

I leaned back, smoked, waited. If he needed to talk, pour it out, I would give him all my time he wanted.

"A commune cemetery," he said.

"You mean commune in the present meaning of that word?"

"Out in the wilds of Chesterfield County — three long barracks, sheds, farm buildings, barns for hay and dairy cows, a simple frame church, and fields where they grow vegetables. There must have been a hundred or more people in attendance. I tried to locate family members among the crowd but found no central group of mourners, so I questioned a man standing beside me, who turned out to be an employee at the store. He said they were all Wendell's family. Apparently he meant all members of the commune, at least that's my take on it. Obviously Wendell was respected and loved. I'd not been able to make much of a judgment about him at the camp, he was so nearly mute and unobtrusive."

"I was surprised Drake invited him along."

"Wendell owned the land we hunted, and because of the grouse plenty, Drake hungered to buy it."

He laid his cap across his lap and tossed his hair, the familiar gesture I had seen many times as far back as our boyhood.

"I never thought I'd ever kill anybody," he said.

"Just a terrible break, Cliff. It could have happened to any of us."

"I've never cared to hunt. A damn fool thing for me to agree to. These Virginians and their guns."

"Let's cross over to the Dew Drop Inn for a beer and sandwich."

"Actually, Walter, I'm here to ask your advice. Sheriff Sawyers of High Gap has knocked on my door."

I visualized the neat, efficient sheriff with the slate-gray eyes.

"Early this morning," Cliff said. "While I was still in my 'jamas and brewing coffee. Invited me to come back to the highlands for a visit."

41

"He traveled all the way to Richmond to do that?"

"The man claimed he just happened to be in the vicinity — he and his wife passing through on a vacation to Williamsburg. He told me it would be a help in completing his report, that there were details that needed to be precisely delineated. It's the expression he used, 'precisely delineated.' Fancy talk from the Appalachians, don't you think?"

"Are you going back?"

"I asked whether it was necessary. He said he was merely requesting cooperation and that the county would pay mileage and put me up a night. I told him I'd think it over. The question is, should I make the trip?"

"He likely wants to depose you for the record, though I understand your not wanting to face that scene a second time."

"I don't know anybody in West Virginia. I've really never cared that much for mountains but all my life have been drawn to the sea. I sense he's up to more than he's revealed. Any chance I might become entangled in some interstate legal complication?"

"My first inclination is to think not."

"Still, with your permission, I'll notify him he's to deal with you, assuming you'll agree to represent me. I mean on a paying basis."

"I will, though I don't foresee more than

some inconvenience since hunting accidents rarely involve a charge."

"I'd feel better if I can tell him to refer any questions he has to you and then you instruct me how to respond."

"Will do," I said. "You'd never met Wendell till we went on the hunt, had you?"

"I'd never seen him, though I had heard of FOOD. He was the store manager. You require a retainer now? I brought my checkbook."

"No. You want lunch?"

"I have no appetite for food. For days I've been living off cottage cheese, Ritz crackers, and deep fulfilling drafts of Dewar's Scotch uncut by water or soda."

SIX

Tuesday morning was too windy and cold for a walk downtown. Before entering the office, I heard the whistle and chimes of saw blades starting up at Axapomimi Lumber. A flight of pigeons, their wings swishing the air, swept over on their way to feed under the loading docks at the Southern States Co-op.

Jessup's Wharf was a Tidewater town centered around the brick courthouse, the drug and general stores, the doctor's and another lawyer's offices, the moldering warehouses, two churches for whites, one for blacks, the sawmill, the Dew Drop Inn, and the King County Bank.

I unlocked my office door, hung up my coat, and switched on the coffeemaker. As I sat at my desk and checked my calendar, the phone jangled.

"Sawyers, Mr. Frampton," the caller said. "Bruce B. Sawyers, Sheriff, Seneca County, West Virginia. If you're going to be at your office, I'd like to schedule a visit. Can reach your place by midmorning."

"Where are you, Sheriff?"

"My wife and I been seeing the sights in Jamestown. According to my map, that's not far from where you hang your hat."

"Come on, Sheriff."

So Sawyers was still around. I sat wondering as I looked out the window and across to St. Luke's steeple poking into a winter sky bled of color.

At five minutes before ten, Sheriff Bruce B. Sawyers arrived not in the black Dodge police cruiser with its whipping antennas but driving a white Camry. He had left his uniform behind and unbuttoned a gray overcoat over a blue pinstripe suit that fitted nicely. His red hair appeared freshly barbered.

"Pleasure to have you in King County, Sheriff," I said, standing to shake his hand. Mary Ellen Cartwright, my secretary, had greeted and shown him in. We sat.

"It's always nice to visit Virginia. There's so much history I need to read up on it again back home to sort it all out. You people been good to me this trip. Left Annie, my wife, at an antique show. She's crazy for an old wardrobe. Hard on a man's wallet."

"Yours a working vacation?"

"Might as well get two for one, don't you think?"

"How can I help you, Sheriff?"

"Mr. Clifford Dickens tells me you represent him and has advised me I'm to speak with you about him returning to Seneca County." He drew his notebook from an inside pocket of his jacket. "Be a big help to us in High Gap if he'd assist us in binding up the loose ends in regard to events that happened during your Blind Sheep hunt."

"It seems you could depose him here in Virginia just as well."

"Could but be better to have him back. Depositions hardly ever get to all the facts. The county will pay his mileage and meals. Also bed and board him if necessary."

"Sheriff, it's natural Mr. Dickens doesn't want to go back. He was greatly affected by Mr. Wendell Ripley's death. Just take his sworn statement, and Mr. Dickens will fully and truthfully answer all your questions."

"Maybe so, and you too might be able give me a few answers. Not as his attorney but as a party on the hunt. Mr. Wingo told me you all met at his house and drove up together in his Bronco."

"I wasn't aware you had questioned Mr. Wingo."

"I talked to him like I am to you right now." The sheriff brought out his micro-recorder and set it on my desk. "You object if I copy what's spoken here?"

"I might, and if so, I'll ask you to switch it off."

"Fair enough. Just trying to fit the pieces. So let's start with the four of you leaving Richmond to go on a shoot."

"We left Thursday at noon. It is approximately a four-and-a-half-hour drive to the Blind Sheep camp. Our plan was to hunt all day Friday and Saturday and return Sunday."

"What'd you do when you reached the camp?"

"Lit a fire, laid out sleeping bags on bunks, cut cards to see who would cook and do dishes that night. The second night low guns were to catch KP."

"Low guns?"

"The two who came in with the least grouse kill. We also cut cards to pair up for the hunt."

"Okay, go ahead."

"We ate steaks, fried potatoes, and collards plus a French apple pie sent by Mr. Wingo's wife. We then made our plans for the next morning, banked the fire, and sacked in."

The sheriff turned a page of his notebook.

"This Wendell Ripley, you knew him well?"

"I had never met him till I shook his hand at Mr. Wingo's house on Thursday."

"That's what Mr. Clifford Dickens stated.

And Mr. Wingo has also said he knew Mr. Ripley only as a customer. Why was Mr. Ripley along with you?"

"Mr. Wingo wanted to purchase from Mr. Ripley the land he leased for the camp and hoped to make a deal during the hunt."

Sheriff Sawyers checked his notebook. Something had disturbed the pigeons, causing them to flap out from under the eaves at St. Luke's.

"What did you think of Mr. Ripley?" the sheriff asked.

"He was quiet, helpful, rarely spoke until spoken to, did camp chores willingly."

"Nothing out of line? Fit in with you other three just fine?"

"We were hardly there time enough to establish much of a relationship. Mr. Dickens, Mr. Wingo, and I are longtime friends. For us it was a reunion of sorts. The three of us hadn't gotten together for several years."

"None of you seems to have much information about Mr. Ripley. Think he knew anything about hunting?"

"As far as I could tell he handled his shotgun well. I saw him checking it the morning of the hunt."

"You all owned guns?"

"No, Mr. Dickens borrowed the Beretta from Mr. Wingo."

"Everybody checked his shotgun and ammo before setting out?"

"As Mr. Wingo reminded us to do."

"What other instructions did Mr. Wingo give?"

"He showed us on topographical maps the territory to be covered. Mr. Wingo and I were to hunt east of Wolf Creek, a stream that runs through the camp area."

"I know Wolf Creek."

"Mr. Dickens and Mr. Ripley were assigned the area west of Wolf. Mr. Wingo supplied maps and compasses to keep us from becoming lost. We loaded up and separated in pairs."

"You remember that Mr. Dickens stated in my office that Mr. Ripley was on his right side as Mr. Dickens brought up his gun, swung on the bird, and fired just when Mr. Ripley lunged left in front of the load?"

The phone rang. Mary Ellen in the outer office answered it. She tapped on the door.

"Taking calls?" she asked.

"Not at the moment," I said, and she withdrew.

"You're questioning his statement?" I asked the sheriff.

"I'm trying to get it exactly right in my mind."

"How about turning off the recorder?"

49

"Glad to oblige." He thumbed the switch. "Now, I been out to the scene a couple of times, and the way I recreate events by examining the tracks, Mr. Ripley wasn't to Mr. Dickens's right but following a step or so behind and below him on the slope. He was shot primarily in the lower chest and upper abdomen. Mr. Dickens was standing higher than Mr. Ripley on the slope. He would've needed to discharge his weapon with its muzzle at an angle of decline."

"A low-flying bird."

"The laurel thicket where he reported the bird flushed was to Mr. Dickens's left as he climbed. If he'd swung in that direction, it would've been high away from Mr. Ripley. And it would've taken some lunge to get up in front of the load."

"Mr. Dickens said he believed Mr. Ripley was to his right. Mr. Ripley could have shifted without Mr. Dickens being aware of it."

"No sign a bird got up."

His eyes fixed me as he waited.

"Sheriff, memory at such moments can easily be disordered. Moreover the snow was already soft and might have melted any grouse tracks by the time you reached them."

"Mr. Dickens stated that the bird was at the edge of that laurel thicket. The likely flight would've been up and over toward the hemlocks, not down along the slope."

"My understanding is that grouse are completely unpredictable in flight, a factor that makes them such excellent sport."

"That's true, but at that slope's angle any grouse on the ground to the side where Mr. Dickens stated the bird flushed would've likely been more elevated than Mr. Ripley's chest and abdomen."

"Likely is a slippery word, Sheriff. I don't think you could know without being there."

"I don't think I could either. Still it's a question to be answered, and we in Seneca County would appreciate you recommending to Mr. Dickens he return to help us clear up any possible contradictions and close the book on the killing."

"Killing. It sounds as if you might be preparing a case."

"I repeat I'm just trying to put it all together."

"And I believe a deposition would meet that requirement."

"Meaning you won't advise Mr. Dickens to come back?"

"If he finds doing so objectionable, not as things stand now."

Those penetrating eyes took me in before he stood and slid the notebook and micro-recorder into his pocket.

"Nice of you to see me," he said.

I walked him to the door as he buttoned his overcoat. Definitely no hillbilly sheriff he, but a police officer who might speak with a nasal twang, yet who used the language well. My sense of our conversation was that he knew more than he had revealed. He was truly, as Drake had observed, a hunter.

SEVEN

My first thought was to talk with Drake. When I phoned him at Grizzly's, his chief clerk, nicknamed Boomer, told me that Drake had left town and would not be back in the store till Monday.

Saturday morning to my delight I received a call from Josey Lynn. She wanted to see Bellerive.

"I'm on my way," she said.

"I'll be at Miss Mabel's," I said.

"Just your style," she said, another cutting remark in reference to her belief that I lived far behind the times. Miss Mabel was an aged spinster, her father a county judge who had left her the three-story house with pointed gables and the wraparound porch.

I phoned Bellerive to ask permission.

"Please as to wait," a man's voice I didn't recognize said. It sounded foreign with an emphasis on his *S*s. He returned. "The prince wishes to inform you that you are welcome and apologizes that the house is not yet open for inspection. You are to enjoy freedom of the grounds."

I buttoned on the chamois shirt and laced up the Bean boots I had bought for the Blind Sheep hunt. The day had dawned warmer, and goldfinches pitched down to Miss Mabel's sundial and pecked around her dormant peonies. The warmth felt as if the earth had been released and again breathed.

Josey arrived in her Lexus and veered fast around the circular drive before the house, braked hard, causing her radials to skid across the moist ground. Miss Mabel would disapprove of tire tracks.

I gathered myself, intending not to show too great a happiness in Josey's presence. Because she still continued to swim three times a week, she wore her coppery hair cut short and needed no padded shoulders as her freestyle crawl had muscled and broadened hers. Mounted on her office wall was her Sweet Briar field hockey stick, a statement she led a sporting life. Josey to me was like the freshness of morning.

"Raff, do me the dance," she said when I opened the car's door.

For Assembly in the tenth grade at John Marshall High, I had been coaxed by Josey to paint up and dress like a clown to perform a soft-shoe routine on stage — the performance my life's worst mistake. I was double-jointed, had a high waistline and unusually long legs, and had flung them and my arms about like a scarecrow and wildly rolled my eyes. I had pretended to share a lollipop with another student, who wore a gorilla costume.

Oh, the audience had applauded for my making a fool of myself. A reporter for the school paper had compared me to an inebriated giraffe. Raff had thus become my nickname and students called out to me to do the dance. I hated the memory and the name, which still followed me.

Drake, Cliff, and I had all loved Josephine, who became Josey to us. She had lived down the block from me and been a tomboy who played baseball for our team, able to slide into bases and spit long with the best of us.

During high school she had changed, still an athlete, but with her body forming new lines — startling legs and under her sweaters breasts that drew our eyes. We competed for her, and she had allowed us at one time or another to kiss her, do a little tonguing and ear blowing, but she always made me keep both my feet on the floor when we necked and never allowed me to touch anything below her waist. She had favored Cliff, and I suspected but didn't know for sure that she had allowed him a more wide-ranging freedom of her anatomy.

"Are you expecting rain?" she asked of the

tightly furled umbrella I had carried from the house. The question bore a smirk.

"Let's take my wheels," I said.

"I do have my image, and your Le Sabre, well."

I slid in beside Josey. The interior of the car smelled of perfume and burgundy leather. As I instructed her how to reach Bellerive three miles upstream, we drove through Jessup's Wharf, the Lexus scattering pigeons feeding around the loading docks of the co-op.

White posts topped by stone pineapples marked the plantation's entrance, and sunlight shimmered off the brass nameplate mortared into bricks. A Kentucky gate had been replaced by iron pickets of closed double portals. She pulled up to a speaker system installed alongside the road, and without awaiting a word from me reached out and pressed a button. We heard a click and a voice I recognized as the man's from whom I had asked permission. When Josey gave my name, the portals swung open.

The drive wound between rows of black walnut trees, and in fields on either side were barns, silos, and brick slave quarters that had been renovated as guest houses, all painted white with midnight-green trim. Snow had melted off the fields, its weight leaving the pasture grass flattened and subdued.

Josey stopped at a white plank fence beyond which horses romped. She explained their dish faces and short-coupled bodies identified them as Arabians. They didn't appear to gallop as much as to flow like swift streams over submerged rocks.

"Lovely," she said. Of course she knew about riding horses and jumping coops and oxers. She had also taken flying lessons.

We reached the serpentine wall at the rear of the house, where another gate, this one with gilded spearlike palings, opened before us as she slowed the Lexus.

"Magic," she said and drove into the courtyard surfaced with rounded cobblestones. A copper dolphin topped a scalloped fountain. The mansion had an English basement and rose three stories in courses of Flemish bond. Construction equipment surrounded the house from which came the sounds of hammers and the piercing shrill of a table saw.

Prince Jamir walked from beneath the shaded porte-cochere. Forty or so, trimly fit, his dark hair wavy and finely scissored, he appeared a sport in an orange knit sweater, tailored Levi's, and black boots.

"Enchanted," he said, and black eyes alight smiled over teeth that contrasted brightly with his tawny complexion and dark mustache as he kissed Josey's hand. That she liked what she saw was evident in a compliant softening of her body.

"I apologize for the disorder of the house," he said. "Would you like one of my people to drive you around?"

I thought he probably did own people, though I was always skeptical when those who were not British spoke the English language so well. Still his assurance was convincing, and my instinct when I had first met him was to like him.

"Thanks but we'd rather walk on a day like this," I said, careful not to be slavishly thankful. I felt he was a man who appreciated dignity, and dignity was an aspect of my life I constantly sought to achieve. I turned my head at the sound of clanking machinery north of the mansion.

"My airstrip-to-be," the prince said. He bowed to Josey. "Please make me happy by enjoying yourself."

"We'll close all gates," she said.

He walked back to the house. Josey and I strolled the boxwood-flanked path to the front terrace, where she paused to look at the portico that Edward LeBlanc had ordered rebuilt after the explosion. Limbs of mossy water oaks were so heavy they had been chained to the trunks to support their weight. At the foot of the lawn were the dock, the prince's motor launch, and a newly constructed gazebo.

"Does he have a wife?" Josey asked. "And wonder whether he'd let me shoot some landings at his airstrip?"

"The way he looked at you, I expect he'd insist on it."

"Enough, Raff," she said.

Raff, the way she always saw me. We stopped at the gazebo. The Axapomimi ran high from snows melting upstream, the water dragging at and jerking at willow branches along the bank, causing them to appear alive and frantic.

"I finally roused Cliff out of his shell," she said. "A terrible thing that shooting, but we had drinks, and he seems to be coping. His photo exhibition was naughty, naughty, naughty. He's possessed by so many inner demons. Greatly ambitious, yet nothing seems to pan out. A case of the cat-in-the-corn-house syndrome."

"Josey, you've lost me."

"A story my father related. At the farm he had opened the corn-house door, and dozens of mice scurried for cover. Our Siamese cat, named Slink, sprang among them and darted about catching the squealing little rodents, but soon as he captured one, he dropped it to chase another. Before he could make his final choice, all the mice escaped, and Slink stood baffled that he hadn't sunk his teeth into the first juicy morsel."

"That's how you characterize Cliff?"

"Actor, playwright, writer, teacher, painter, photographer — all of which he does well but no one activity that he excels in to the point of becoming a star. He carries himself as if he's intact, but he's wounded and hurting. He feels despite his many gifts he's fallen behind lesser men."

She cocked her head. "Listen. Drums?"

"The Indian reservation," I said. "Perhaps they're doing a ceremonial dance to petition the Great Spirit for a good crop or an abundance of shad when the fish return to the river. If the breeze is right, you can hear their tribal celebrations."

We left the gazebo and let ourselves through a gateway beyond the paddock and belfried stable. Josey controlled our pace across brittle, crackly grass. Ahead a flight of crows rose cawing from a dip of ground and flew toward a bordering fringe of loblolly pines.

We climbed a plank fence and walked under limbs of a leafless pin oak toward a pond on which Canada geese cruised in stately file. Josey stopped, turned her head to listen, and then we heard another kind of drumming and looked back toward the stable.

The horse, a dappled gray Arabian, rose effortlessly over the fence and raced, mane flying, across the pasture. It snorted and struck out with its hind hooves, alarming the geese, who honked and began flapping off the water. They left disturbed wakes across the pond.

"God, the beauty of it," Josey said.

The horse neighed and pranced around the pond. It flung its head, caught our scent, and gazed across the water. Snorting, it thrust itself into a gallop and pounded in our direction.

"Whoa now," Josey said.

The animal charged us, hooves slamming the ground, head lowered, neck stretched forward, teeth bared like an attacking dog. The sound it uttered was not a neigh but more a hysterical scream. Josey and I jumped aside as it swept past, eyes wild, the heat of its body a hot wind.

"Stallion," Josey said. "Let's get the hell out of here."

When we started toward the fence, the horse shifted to a high-stepping canter, his neck arched, and intercepted us. Again the god-awful scream as he flung his head. That he was a stallion was obvious by what Josey must have also noticed — his extended, stiffly flopping penis. Each time we tried to move toward the fence, he cut us off.

"The tree," I said, and we sidled back toward the pin oak. The stallion again shrieked and bolted toward us. We ran to the tree. I grabbed a lower limb, got a leg up and over, and as I reached for Josey my dangling glasses fell. She stumbled but recovered and stepped around the trunk. The horse wheeled, tried to reach and bite her. His teeth ripped the sleeve of her windbreaker. She shouted at him and scrambled to keep the trunk between herself and the stallion. He couldn't turn sharply enough to get his teeth into her.

I hollered to Josey and stuck my hand down to haul her up, but each time she reached for it the stallion struck. Warily she kept sidestepping and circling, her hands grasping the tree's trunk. I saw something beyond fear in her expression. Escape and survival were turning into a challenge and game for her, deadly but exciting. She was both frightened and elated.

A horn sounded. At the far end of the fence a man jumped from a Jeep to open a gate. As the driver sped through toward us, the stallion swerved to face it. The prince behind the wheel kept blowing the horn and gunned the Jeep past us. The stallion pawed the ground and gave chase. It galloped after the Jeep and back through the gate, which the man who'd been left behind closed and latched.

Breathless, I let down from the tree. Josey

pushed away from its trunk, exhaled slowly, and reached to remove her red brow band. With it she wiped her forehead, face, and neck. A cheek was smudged. Shaken, she stared after the horse.

"Talk about one big horny bastard," she said.

"I had my hand down for you," I said as I picked up my broken glasses. She had stepped on them.

We walked toward the fence. The prince drove back, let himself through the gate, and stopped to help Josey into the Jeep. Without my glasses, the day for me had become fuzzed.

"The groom failed to bar the door at the breeding shed," he told her. "The mares upset Grand Illustrious Sultan, our premier sire. Do you need doctoring?"

"A drink," Josey said and tucked her red wool shirt back into her tan corduroy pants.

I sat in the rear as he returned us to the mansion, where he showed Josey the way to a lavatory just inside the porte-cochere. A hefty, dark-skinned man brought out brandy and glasses on a tray.

"You know a woman in heat can arouse a stallion," the prince confided in me as we waited for Josey. He smiled.

"Lots of fun 'round this place," she said,

striding from the house. She quickly drank two brandies. The prince again kissed her hand as well and held the Lexus's door open for her.

Josey carried me back to Miss Mabel's but didn't switch off the engine.

"Thanks for one swell time," she said. Her color up, she appeared exuberant.

"I did have my hand down for you," I said.

"Of course you did, Raff. You did the best you could."

A hell of a thing to tell a man. She sped off, leaving me standing in front of the house holding my umbrella and looking after her. I believed in valor, but the truth was I felt at Bellerive Josey had acted more the man than I.

EIGHT

I drove from Jessup's Wharf to Powhatan County, where Drake Wingo now had his shop. At least a shop had been the way it had started out — a small rented space in a strip mall on Route 60 west of Richmond that announced itself by a hand-painted "Guns & Gunsmith" sign over the doorway.

Drake opened the shop after his discharge from the army and became so successful he moved farther west into Powhatan County, where he bought seven acres of undeveloped land and supervised the construction of a one-story, flat-roofed cinder-block building that appeared too small for the lot it occupied.

Over time he expanded it, adding a wing here, a showroom there, until the place became barn size and sold not only guns but also upscale lines of sport clothing and camping equipment. He never advertised and rarely offered specials, but the word spread about the high quality of his merchandise and the dependability of the repair service. He named the store Grizzly's after killing an

Ursus horribilis on a hunting trip to Wyoming.

Grizzly's sat on a grass field surrounded by a hardwood forest. At the doorway he had bolted down an outsized plastic bear reared to attack, its fangs exposed. Another attraction was a ruffed grouse in flight Drake himself had carved from balsa. It had a six-foot wingspan and was supported by an all but invisible nylon line attached to a ceiling structural beam at the center of the store. Each night after closing a spotlight played on the white bird, which seen through the display windows appeared to be luminously soaring through darkness. As people drove past, they slowed their cars to look, and parents brought children to see what had become known as the ghost grouse.

Drake often sat on a camp chair just inside the doorway to greet customers. He remembered names, shook hands, led buyers to clerks, yet there was never anything subservient about him. Rather he made people feel esteemed by the attention he gave them.

I found him at the front counter restocking his pamphlet, "The Truth of the Grouse." He had set his safari hat at its usual jaunty angle.

"And they used to be free," I said. He now charged a dollar a copy for the pamphlets.

"Raff, people never put value on anything free," he answered. "And I know why you're here. Let's go to the office."

I followed along an aisle between basketball, golf, and tennis equipment. All Drake's clerks wore blaze-orange vests and black bow ties. He stopped to straighten a pyramidal arrangement of moccasins in the shoe department.

Walls held mounted heads of deer, lynxes, coons, foxes, and bears, their glassy eyes lustrous. Shelves displayed taxidermic partridges, doves, turkeys, ducks, geese. We walked under the outsized ghost grouse that when nudged by air currents shifted slightly and drew customers' gazes.

Firearms occupied the entire hindmost section of Grizzly's. Pistols, shotguns, and rifles were racked behind locked sliding glass panels, and indirect lighting at the base of the guns caused burled walnut stocks, nickel-plated handguns, and blue steel rifle barrels to gleam with the opulence of jewelry. Young boys often stood before them and dreamt of glory in combat.

We passed through the accounting department, where two ladies worked at computers. Drake's office had a camp cot in it and grouse tails tacked to the walls, each a tagged trophy carrying a date, place of kill, and memory for him. On the desk he'd set a color photograph of his wife, Deborah, and laid across the blotter a lever-action rifle and a flat metal box, the lid open, which held compartmentalized gun-smith tools.

"This is a Winchester .44-caliber rimfire," he said and drew the rifle to his shoulder. He pressed the worn, gouged stock against his cheek. "Earliest model, 1866. The Henry 1858 preceded it but had no forearm and grew too hot to hold after repeated firing. The 1866 is a work of beauty I'm repairing and re-finishing. Comes up to you like a loving woman. It's a rifle made for joining."

He laid the Winchester on the desk gently, as if it had feelings.

"People go to art galleries and museums for their cultural highs, but I'll take a classic Win-chester or Henry any day," he said. "Guns are the real American art. They should be dis-played and admired like Rembrandts or Van Goghs. You feel their beauty where it should be felt — in your gonads."

"Drake, that's a unique aesthetic theory," I said.

"The balls never lie," he said.

"I understand Sheriff Sawyers has been to see you."

"Oh yeah. He looked over my merchan-dise."

"Did it ever occur to you to inform me?"

"I didn't consider it important. Just a law-

68

man routinely nosing around."

"He's supposed to be on vacation, not nosing."

"Some people can't stop working, and maybe he just wanted to slip away from the mountains a couple of days and used investigating as a means of getting a trip at taxpayers' expense."

The telephone on the desk rang. Drake lifted it.

"Hold the calls," he said and sat.

"Sheriff Sawyers seems to believe he needs more detail about what happened on our hunt," I said and also let down to a chair.

"I told him it's not complicated. Wendell was a hunting greenhorn. First time gunning game. His eagerness to cap the bird caused him to make a dumb move."

"How did you get to know Wendell Ripley?"

"His son Jerry used to work in my shoe department, and Wendell hung around."

"Wait a second," I said. "You never mentioned a son when the sheriff asked about next of kin in High Gap."

"No need to. Jerry Ripley no longer walks this earth. He quit the job years ago. I tried but couldn't reach him. Some weeks later, Wendell, all broken up, stopped by and told me Jerry was dead. I asked how he died.

Wendell said poisoned. In High Gap Cliff was suffering, and I wanted to get him and us out of Sheriff Sawyers's office and away as fast as possible."

"Do you have information regarding any other of Wendell's kin?"

"Not blood family," he said and pushed back his safari hat. "Wendell lived in a commune out Chesterfield County way. Call themselves The Watchers, a religious sect. When I enlarged the store and put in a shoe department, I didn't know Wendell. The boy applied for work, and I hired him. He did his job, not much more. Wendell with a father's interest stopped by. He doted on his son and was hard hit after he died. Never really got over it."

I heard firing and turned my head. Drake had an indoor shooting range where he and his clerks trained people how to handle guns.

"Then Wendell stayed around the store even after his son's death?"

"He came in one day carrying an old shotgun, a LeFever, and wanted to know if I could fix it. The gun was rusted, pitted, and had Damascus barrels. I explained that if he used today's powder, particularly high brass shells, the barrel would untwist or explode. So I fitted him with a twelve-gauge Remington three-shot automatic that had a twenty-eight-inch barrel and adjustable choke, a gun inexpensive but reliable, the same one he carried to camp."

"Did he know how to handle it?"

"Not at first. He told me he had never fired a gun. The old LeFever had belonged to his grandfather back in the mountains. I taught him to use the Remington. It turned out Wendell was a natural shot, instinctive. First just chipped the clay pigeons. I explained that if they were real birds, he'd only have winged them and the grouse would hit the ground running, bury under cover, and die, a waste."

Drake and his passion for grouse. He had been working to extend his pamphlet to book length and hoping to find a publisher.

"I showed Wendell how to bring the stock to his cheek, not take his cheek to the stock, keep both eyes open, and continue his swing past the targets. In no time at all he was shattering them. A born gunner in talent if not temperament."

"And you found out about the land he owned on Blind Sheep?"

"He happened to mention the acreage bordered the Monongahela National Forest. His family used to herd sheep in those mountains. He said he remembered plenty of what he called brown birds. I asked him whether he'd let me drive up to West Virginia and check it

71

out. He drew me a map, I took my sleeping bag, located the place, and stayed a night on Blind Sheep. He was right. Kraut retrieved me a broken hickory limb. The dog's way of telling me there were more birds than you could shake a stick over. I knew I had to have shooting rights on that place. I leased the land and built the cabin. I wanted to buy the land. He wouldn't sell."

"That's the reason you invited him along on the hunt."

"Get two for one — a reunion with old friends and let Wendell see we're decent people. I figured quality folks like you and Cliff would help me win him over and I could buy it."

"Can you tell me anything more about Wendell's son?"

"No explanation of the poison and how Jerry swallowed it. Wendell was grieving so bad I didn't push it."

"I can't figure Sawyers."

"Maybe politics. The sheriff told us he was thinking of running for the legislature. He might be looking for an arrest he can exploit, get publicity, win votes. A fishing expedition."

"It seems he ought to be able to find something more newsworthy than a hunting accident."

"Maybe there's not much happening up in High Gap, and he's got to use what's at hand."

Drake lifted the Henry and repeatedly snapped it to his shoulder to aim at his electric wall clock.

"What I want is more information on Wendell Ripley," I said. "You know anything about the store he managed?"

"I heard it's chiefly an outlet for what's produced at the commune."

"I'll stop by and ask around," I said.

NINE

I found FOOD located two blocks south of the alley where Cliff, Drake, and I had fought members of the River Rats gang — still a grimy neighborhood of garages, machine shops, and warehouses, most tainted and scarred by decline. The old King James Hotel with its twin turrets and arched entrance had long ago been razed, and spiky, winter-ravaged weeds sought to survive among the lot's scattered debris.

The store occupied a building close to the CSX railroad tracks that led past the abandoned Main Street Station. Outwardly the entrance to FOOD appeared neglected and off-putting. I made out the MORPHEUS MATTRESS CO. in flanking white paint on bricks under front eaves crusted with pigeon droppings.

So many cars filled the asphalt parking lot I circled twice to find a space. Inside, I faced a different world — a brightly lit, cavernous room lined with row upon row of long wooden bins. The place was clean, orderly, the shoppers brisk. Women in white smocks,

74

their hair bound by white kerchiefs, worked the checkouts.

"Direct you, sir?" one pushing an empty shopping cart asked.

I told her I wanted the business office.

"Up the stairs at the rear, sir. Enjoy your visit with us."

I walked past heaped fragrant bins holding cabbages, lettuce, tomatoes, peppers, cucumbers, oranges, cantaloupes, and beans as well as a battery of refrigerated cabinets offering gleaming rounds of cheeses and dairy products. Prices were cheap compared to what I paid at the Jessup's Mercantile. I found no meat displayed. Despite its roof and walls, FOOD had the feel of an outdoor country market.

The stairway rose to a loft where second-hand clothing for sale hung from pipe racks. Shelves offered shoes that had been neatly arranged and polished, the laces tied. A girl trying on a summer straw hat stood before a mirror hung from a nail pounded into a wooden column.

The office at the rear had no dividing partition between it and the merchandise. The plainly clothed women working at desks appeared out of place in the company of electric typewriters, calculators, computers, and monitors.

The nearest glanced up from a printout and smiled. Young, hardly twenty, and brightly energetic, she crooked her finger at me, and I crossed to her wooden desk — a sturdy oak model of the kind that used to be seen in federal offices and were now sold at government surplus auctions.

"Hep you?" she asked, a country girl.

I told her I'd like to speak to the manager.

"Sister Maude's right over there in the corner," she said and pointed.

I tried to remember the last time I had come across a woman named Maude, this one elderly, her creased face washed to a shine. She studied an inventory list spread over her desk. When she became aware of me, her fingers released the list and let it settle.

"Did you notice the sunrise this morning?" she asked.

"I confess I didn't," I said, slid my card from my wallet, and offered it.

"The clouds were a golden pink," she said as she took the card and reset her glasses. "When the sun touched my face, I felt the hand of God."

"Yes," I said and wondered what I had walked into.

"Nice to meet you, Mr. Frampton," she said. "I hope you're not out to sue us."

"No, ma'am, I've come to make inquiries

about the late Mr. Wendell Ripley."

"Brother Wendell," she said with no note of surprise or regret. "Our Lord has chosen him to share eternal companionship. Won't you sit a moment and rest your bones while you tell me what in particular you're asking?"

"His background," I said and drew the wooden chair to her desk. "And does he have any family I can contact?"

"Oh, he has family. Some eighty-seven of them at last count and growing. The Watchers are all family."

"But not blood kin?"

"Kin of the spirit is stronger than blood."

"Perhaps you can tell me something about The Watchers."

"Can and will. Our doors are open to anyone who'll make God's work the primary aim and purpose of their lives and profess belief that Jesus Christ is with us this very day. We accept aspirants on a six-month instructional basis. After that if they want to stay, we vote them into our family on the condition they turn over their worldly goods to be shared by all."

"An agricultural commune."

"We don't call ourselves that. We are children of God who live to serve others by feeding them. We are brothers and sisters in the Spirit. Wendell was a good, loving man who knew no strangers, a shepherd who came to us from the mountains."

"Did he have a wife? I know there was a son."

"About those questions you'd do better talking to Brother Abram. You'll find him at the farm. He speaks for us. I'll draw you directions."

She used the back of a discarded envelope to pencil the directions. Nothing was wasted at FOOD.

"You should watch the sunrise each day," she said and gave me the envelope. "It's the Lord opening His eyes upon mankind after the darkness of night as well as His promise of eternal renewal."

I drove west on Route 360 into Chesterfield County. Richmond had expanded in that direction, the malls, marts, and housing developments giving way finally to countryside and woodland. I turned on 707 and wound along a narrow paved road among shaggy cedars that bent before the wind, their branches dipping and recovering.

As Sister Maude had indicated on the envelope, the entrance to The Watchers was a mile and seven-tenths along 707. The aluminum farm gate had been latched open, and at the end of the lane the land opened before me

— fields laid out in rectangles and beyond them barns and parallel one-story buildings, all painted brown. Despite the wind and cold, bundled men and women worked using posthole diggers, shovels, and tamping bars to install fencing around a plot of fallow soil.

I stopped between a pickup and dump truck in the parking area. The sun caused me to squint as I looked for somebody to ask where to find Brother Abram. I walked to the end door of a building and knocked. I heard no sound of life inside. I opened the door onto a long corridor flanked by cots and footlockers that ran its entire length.

"Anybody here?" I called.

As I backed out and shut the door, I heard a chain saw crank up. I followed the sputtering, growling racket and came upon a man standing outside a galvanized turtle-back shed. He gunned the saw, and thin blue smoke gathered around him. His body was immense, the shoulders and hips heavy, his stomach bulging, his thighs vast as hams. He had rolled the sleeves of his brown coveralls over his hairy forearms.

The sixteen-inch Poulan appeared a toy in his huge hands. He wasn't cutting wood but carving a design on a cedar post and operated the saw with a casual expertise as chips sprayed over and gathered around his outsized clodhoppers. The rounded tip of the blade created what — an eye socket?

I stood observing until he glanced my way and used a plump thumb to switch off the saw. His beard was a luxuriant brown, and hair grew thick and curly from his head, nose, and ears as well as overflowed the neck of his coveralls.

"A blessed day," he said, his voice surprisingly soft. A smile opened over horselike teeth.

"I'm looking for Brother Abram."

"Rest your eyes, my friend." He laughed, the sound booming from the fullness of his great belly. "You may rejoice at the good fortune of having found him."

I told him my name and that I was an attorney gathering information about Wendell Ripley. I gave him my card.

"Sister Maude told me he was a member of your order and suggested I drive out to see you," I said.

"What you will find about Brother Wendell is he lies in our cemetery. Furthermore, we are not an order. That terminology is much too militant and intimidating. We are a fellowship. Anyone who comes here willing to work and live by our simple rules is welcome."

"You do own and operate the food store?"

"Yes and no. There are no owners in the usual sense of that word. This property, what it produces, all profits belong to a common fund that pays for seed, equipment, and operating expenses. We grow our edibles, make much of our clothing, wait, and watch."

"May I ask what you watch for?"

"You may. We await the end time. We believe our Savior is already among us, that He's on this earth this very instant, perhaps walking along a street, standing alone in a crowd, stopping to lay His hand on the halt and the blind. You, I, anyone may have already passed Him or He us. We won't know until we look into his eyes. One glance from Him will transform us."

"In what manner?" I asked and glanced at an old Oliver tractor hauling a wagon loaded with fence posts and rolls of barbed wire toward the fields.

"Brother, when you see into the eyes of God, all sin will be kindled to cinders and you taken up cleansed to join Him in eternity."

"Armageddon?" I asked, remembering my Sunday-school days when I had been reared as a Presbyterian and learned that at that final fiery conflict the saints would rise to meet Christ in the Rapture after which He would rule on earth a thousand years.

"Signs exist," Brother Abram said. "Wars,

81

famine, flood, blood in the streets. Read any newspaper, listen to the radio, switch on TV."

To be amiable I nodded but believed there had never been a time without such signs. He noticed me shiver in the wind and suggested we go in by his stove.

The wood burner at the center of the shed had been made from a metal oil drum and flued through the roof. Workbenches held drills, grinders, a heavy-duty vise. Tools hung in systematic fashion from hooks screwed into wood strips above the benches. Brother Abram set his Poulan on the concrete floor.

"I expect you, like many others, think we Watchers are a peculiar, even a backward people," he said. "It might be of interest to you to know that I am an educated man, attended Columbia University, spent some three years at an Episcopal seminary, and inherited a shameful amount of money from my father, who manufactured boilers and turbines — many more dollars than I could wantonly spend. I was also a drunk who drank rivers of liquor. It filled my gut and would have flooded the sea. I swam in the filth of many gutters."

We held our hands to heat from the stove. His were meaty, roughened, and callused while mine by comparison appeared slender and fair.

"They threw me out of the seminary," he said. "In my search for God and to mortify my flesh I beat my bare body with wire coat hangers. I howled on my knees in the refectory garden until they carried me to the infirmary. It was there our Lord descended to me like a flame out of swirling darkness. He lifted me away from this world and set me back. The words I heard were not spoken among thunder and lightning but in a still, small voice which said, 'Feed my people.'"

Waiting, what could I do but appear receptive and keep nodding?

"I've done so since," he said. "I bought this land and alone began tilling it. I preached God's message, sometimes on street corners, in storefront churches, or shanties where wind blew between the cracks. And people began to come, at first just one or two at a time. We worked the fields, planted potatoes, English peas, radishes, and chard as soon as the weather broke and we could work the soil."

As he talked he seemed on the verge of more laughter, a restrained whoop that was gathering in his drooping belly.

"Mr. Wendell Ripley was one who came?" I asked.

"Wendell and his frail wife joined us, her name Sarah. They had journeyed down from mountain country where he tended sheep before he found a job providing creosoted ties for the railroad. His work brought him to Richmond town, a man whose kindly nature made us love him, his wife, and the child."

He turned away from the stove to lift the Poulan and clamp its bar in the vise. Next he selected a file that had a bulb-shaped wooden handle and drew an index finger across the bite of the rasp before beginning to sharpen the saw's blade.

"Sister Sarah fell ill. Her medical bills took all their money and more. She wasted away but held on to life long enough to bear the child, the son, his name Jeremiah. Brother Wendell mourned her, but he had joy in his son. When the boy was old enough, they worked crops together and caused happiness among us."

Brother Abram's weighty hands had a delicacy upon the saw as if the blade's teeth could feel the file and understand its beneficial touch.

"When Brother Wendell came to us, we were only a dozen folks. We built living quarters, a kitchen, and our house of worship. We first sold our produce door-to-door and alongside the highway. As we grew we dickered for more land, constructed the barn, bought milk cows. We don't eat meat."

I remembered the absence of meat at FOOD and Wendell's turning down a steak at Drake's cabin.

"It was Brother Wendell's idea when we began to garner more than we could sell to utilize the old mattress factory in Richmond. He had a good mind for figures. The decaying building stood empty and was for sale. We were able to work out terms with a bank desperate to be rid of it. We gave the store its honest name and chose Brother Wendell to run it, which he did well. In fact he made it succeed. Now that entire property belongs to us free and clear, and with our low prices, fresh produce, and dairy products we do feed the people."

He continued to file in a slow, rhythmic fashion.

"Brother Wendell delighted in his boy. He gave thanks and waited for our Savior to appear among us. He sang, had a fine baritone voice, and walked with his son singing prayers through our woods."

"I knew Mr. Ripley less than twenty-four hours," I said. "To me he appeared quiet and withdrawn."

"Yes, good as he was, Brother Wendell suffered from the weakness of not surrendering himself completely during a time of pain and travail to God's judgment. Jeremiah grew to

85

be a rebellious son. At school he fell among bad company. He fled us and Brother Wendell, who searched him out in the city, but Jeremiah never returned."

"What happened to him?"

"Gone."

"You mean dead?"

"Dead, yes."

"I heard he was poisoned."

"That is true."

"In what way and by whom?"

"One among the company he kept."

"Was anyone prosecuted?"

"The police showed little interest."

"Are you able to tell me anything else?"

"Yes, brother, keep watch."

He removed the saw from the vise and gripping it made to leave the shed.

"And Mr. Ripley's buried in your cemetery?" I asked.

"With his wife, Sarah, the plots just past our church on the hillside."

I hadn't recognized the plain boxlike building he pointed to as a church, though unlike other structures it was painted white.

"Rejoice, brother, Our Savior moves among us and will bring us understanding, peace, and love," Brother Abram said as he adjusted the Poulan's choke and repeatedly jerked the cord to start the saw.

86

"What's that to be?" I asked of the cedar post he'd been carving.

"One of two to be planted on each side of our entrance," he said. "By the way we had another visitor inquiring about Brother Wendell, a sheriff from West Virginia. So much earthly distress over a man who found the most glorious good fortune of all — he resides with his Lord."

So Sheriff Sawyers had also been to The Watchers. I drove toward the cemetery — not much of a hill, merely a low rise of mowed field that grew a single locust tree from its center. I parked beside a black Pontiac.

Orderly mounds lined the field, but no gravestones or markers provided names or dates. I assumed their absence involved church doctrine, possibly the belief that those who died left nothing of their old selves behind but had put on new bodies as the apostle Paul had written.

I stopped at the church, climbed its three wooden steps to the door, and slipped inside not a narthex but a white room furnished with plain benches on either side of a center aisle. No pulpit rose above them, no curtains hung at the windows, no carpeting covered the floor. If the worshipers sang, they did so without a piano or an organ.

As I turned away, I almost missed the young woman. She sat in shadows to my left just beyond a fan of faint sunlight. Her floppy hat matched her tan raincoat. Head bowed, eyes closed, her gloved fingers steepled to her chin, she silently wept.

She abruptly realized I was watching and quickly stood and left past me. From the doorway I looked after her as she hurried toward the Pontiac in the pigeon-toed manner that women have of running. Her knee-length black rubber boots skirted frozen puddles.

Leaving the farm, I slowed to pass workers unloading posts and wire from the wagon. Again I thought of Sheriff Bruce Sawyers, who was turning out to be a watcher of a different sort.

TEN

The day before Christmas I flew to Tampa, where my mother waited at the sunny airport. In her mid-sixties, she played tennis twice a week and remained a slender, active woman. She had also been studying Italian in order to read the *Divine Comedy*.

While I was a law student at Washington and Lee, she and my father sold our Richmond house and retired to Venice and a white stucco condo that had a balcony which overlooked the intercostal waterway. My father learned to identify boats as they passed. "A Bertram," he would say, "a Hunter," or "Choey Lee." He kept score on a pad but did not count the number of drinks constantly refreshed.

"Need to put out the fire," he would say, a tic lately developed causing his right eyelid to flutter. In his attempt to protect friends prosecuted for an under-the-table land transaction with the Virginia Department of Transportation, my father got caught up in a scandal, considered his reputation forever besmirched, sold his real-estate ventures, and resigned from the Society of the Lees.

The sun-blasted Christmas seemed as unreal as the artificial wreaths tied with shiny red plastic bows. My mother roasted a turkey we ate after we opened our presents. They had bought me a wristwatch, a wallet, and two button-down Oxford-cloth white shirts. I gave perfume and books to my mother, and for my father I purchased Bushnell 7x35 binoculars he could use to watch the boats.

"The cards we're dealt," he said the morning I left. "I apologize for the heritage I've left you."

"Dad, I won't hear any more of that."

He believed himself the cause of my not being able to find a job with a prestigious Richmond law firm and ending up in Jessup's Wharf — a partial truth I had put behind me. I loved him and what he stood for.

"God the dealer," he said.

There was no breaking through to him. My mother carried me back to Tampa and my flight to Richmond.

"He's promised to take walks," she said and kissed me in sunshine so bright our shadows on the white concrete lay black as paving tar.

At Jessup's Wharf, newly hired, ginger-haired secretary Mary Ellen Cartwright sat at her desk in my office. She was aged thirty or so, formerly married to an army pilot killed in Germany, where his helicopter crashed. She had picked up quickly on legal procedures that were routine but tricky and almost indecipherable to people not trained in their use. She had laid out the mail chronologically on my desk and set a potted Christmas cactus on the windowsill.

She hummed and smiled to herself as she worked, perhaps thinking of her young son or remembering the days years earlier when she had reigned as Miss York County. Her back was to me, and her dark skirt had pulled up over her knees as she turned aside to finger paper clips in a glass dish. She had legs softly rounded in ladylike contrast to Josey's spare shanks slimmed to muscle.

"Mr. Frampton, my mama won't be home today, and is it all right for my Jason to stay here after school? I don't like him returning to an empty house. I promise he'll be no trouble."

"Fine," I said and hoped the boy's stopping by wouldn't become a habit. I liked the way she'd used "mama" instead of mother.

I fanned through the mail and list of calls. Nothing from Josey, though I'd had Talbots send her a pair of black leather riding gloves. Charley LeBlanc had phoned to wish me a Merry Christmas. Cliff had also called, but when I dialed his number I got only his answering machine. His recorded voice was the old Cliff's — curt and edging on haughty.

He rang me up just after lunch, and he sounded urgent.

"That sheriff's notified me that if I don't return to Seneca County for questioning they might seek a writ," he said. "Can they force me to go back when I live in another state?"

"Not without probable cause and a warrant."

"What do I do?"

"You might consider returning."

"I don't like it. I've told them all I know. If the sheriff has more questions, let him come to Richmond instead of inconveniencing me. Walter, the man's spoiling my days."

"I'll talk to him. Possibly the situation's resolvable."

"He didn't sound like it."

"He could be playing poker. I'll call you back."

I phoned Information for the number of Seneca County's Sheriff's Department and told the woman who answered I wanted to speak to Sawyers. She said he wasn't in his office but would give him my message.

I looked out the window. Snow had again begun falling, rare for Tidewater Virginia. These were random lazy flakes. I walked to the courthouse and the clerk's office to check out a title for Prince Jamir. Benson Falkoner was just leaving.

Benson was King County's commonwealth's attorney, a ruddy, fleshy man who talked as if he had a mouth full of molasses and made two out of one-syllable words. His eyelids hung heavy. He and Felix Bonnet were Jessup's Wharf's other attorneys.

Benson had lately become particularly cordial, hoping to share any spillover from Prince Jamir's business coming my way.

"How's life treating you, Walt?"

"Can't complain, Benson."

"A person who can't complain's not alive. Man's first utterance in this world is a cry and protest against life."

"Didn't realize you were a philosopher, Benson," I said as I drew out a heavy gray property book and opened it on the counter. Hands had been turning its pages for two hundred and fifty years. I never wanted to be standing between Benson and a dollar bill.

When I walked back along River Street, snow had collected on parked cars. I ate a bowl of spiced-up chili at the Dew Drop Inn before returning to my office. Sheriff Sawyers had called collect at two-thirty.

"I been expecting to hear from you," he said.

"I hadn't thought you'd still be investigating an accidental death so doggedly," I said.

"In the code there's no such thing as accidental death. It's manslaughter and punishable."

"There's excusable homicide."

"You contending that Mr. Wendell Ripley in some manner threatened Mr. Dickens and that provides justification for shooting him?"

"No, I'm saying what we have here is an unfortunate happenstance that is not routinely brought to trial or at most is treated as a misdemeanor both in Virginia and other states."

"Here in the mountains we don't consider any death routine, and there are details about this one that beg further investigation. Mr. Dickens alone can explain more fully what happened on that Blind Sheep grouse hunt. By not cooperating he's making problems for us and himself."

"He can and is willing to answer all your questions down here in Richmond."

"Not the same. Our district attorney, Mr. Sam Tuggle, wants him back. If your client's being up front with us, what's spooking him?"

"He's not spooked, as you put it, but has his life and work in Virginia. I believe I know all the facts and that he's told them to you."

"Let's be real, Mr. Frampton. We both

know clients don't always square up with their attorneys."

"Sheriff, how about being more specific?"

"I have a gut feeling about this one."

"Gut feelings don't count in a court of law."

"But they do before the court convenes."

I looked out the window at the snow layering the sidewalk. Women walking along the street carried umbrellas, their boots and shoes leaving imprints.

"I understand you been out to The Watchers," I said.

"Mr. Frampton, you might be surprised where all I been."

"My guess is you don't intend to tell me."

"Not at this point. Convince Mr. Dickens to return, and the district attorney will lay it all out on the table."

"Lay it out, as you put it, here in the Commonwealth."

"Okay, Mr. Frampton, I don't guess there's any need for us to continue sparring. Seneca County means to get Mr. Dickens back one way or another."

"And I might have to make the process difficult for Seneca County."

"We'll see about that. The law has a long arm. Thanks for your call."

When I hung up, I watched the snow fall

more heavily. In my mind I again went step-by-step over the Blind Sheep hunt. So Cliff in his state of shock may have described events there in a confused fashion. Surely that wasn't enough to build a case against him.

At three-fifteen a yellow school bus stopped in front of the office, and a small, pale boy stepped down to the street. Mary Ellen hurried to meet him. I guessed his age as about seven. Mary Ellen made him clean his feet on the mat and helped him off with his jacket and knit cap. His short hair was whitish blond but had no luster. She used her handkerchief to dab away snow melting on his face.

"Mr. Frampton, this is my son, Jason."

"How you, Jason?" I asked and extended my hand.

The boy didn't shake it or answer me. He kept his eyes averted. He was scrawny and maybe sickly.

"He's shy," Mary Ellen said and placed a chair by her desk, sat Jason, and fondly touched the top of his head. The boy's feet didn't reach the floor. He drew a book from his backpack and opened it across his lap.

When I offered him a peppermint from the Dew Drop Inn, he lifted his eyes. They were not honey-colored like his mother's but a much deeper brown, a bottomless hue and much too large for his small, narrow face.

Quickly he looked away but not before I'd seen a shape rise beneath the pupils like a creature from the depths. The shape's name was fear.

ELEVEN

I couldn't locate Cliff. I left messages on his answering machine and drove by his carriage house, where the gate through the stone wall remained locked. I felt he damn well should have notified me before leaving town.

I had received an embossed invitation to Bellerive for a New Year's Day hunt meet and breakfast, and though I'd never owned a horse or been a rider, I did consider fox-hunting an aristocratic sport and envied those who followed the hounds.

The snow had partly melted, but the ground firmed up from an overnight freeze. I dressed warmly and wished I owned a shooting stick. I also carried my umbrella and reminded myself to stay composed and not talk or laugh too readily.

When I reached Bellerive at eight, the entrance portals stood ajar, and along the walnut-flanked drive a farmhand directed me into a line of parked cars. Tables covered by linen cloths had been set up in the crusty, sole-deep snow. On them thermoses held hot tea and coffee. The ranks of liquor and wine bottles dimly reflected the sun's rising above the cold fog of the pine woods. Servants wearing overcoats tended bar.

Vans and trailers pulled into the pasture. As I walked among them I noted license plates from Richmond, Williamsburg, and Virginia Beach. Prince Jamir did not have to make connections. They were attracted to him like iron filings to a magnet.

I asked for a pewter mug of hot buttered rum, and its good warmth spread ease through me. Appear sophisticated, bored, and wealthy, I counseled myself.

Riders wearing hunt attire saddled their mounts — sleek animals whose manes and tails had been intricately braided. The horses' nostrils steamed, and their eyes flared at the excitement of the chase. They stomped hooves and pulled at lead lines.

The hounds arrived in a closed truck that had FOX HAVEN painted on its sides in block white letters. Their rich coats bespoke a good worming program at the kennels. The truck belonged to the Gaffneys, a couple who had moved to Virginia and King County from the north and become close friends of the LeBlancs.

The huntsman opened the tailgate to allow the hounds to boil out. They didn't run about wildly but clotted, obedient to his commands, and when two snarled at each other, he cracked his whip over them, and they cowered like reproved children.

Prince Jamir made his appearance. His hunting Pinks displayed a pale blue collar, and he moved like royalty, a hand grasping his bone-handled whip as a king might a scepter. He wound among the mounted guests offering sherry from a silver goblet. A servant followed holding a bottle in each hand to keep the goblet filled. When the prince passed, he turned back and extended the hunt cup to me.

"My local legal representative," he said and smiled. I was pleased and craved his bearing and sense of certainty.

He strode on greeting guests, nodding and receiving tips of hats until a groom brought his horse, a glossy chestnut whose leather tack gave off a deep, opulent glow. The groom joined his palms, the prince set a knee in them, and allowed himself to be hoisted to the saddle.

He conferred with his huntsman, a hook-nosed, weathered man hired from Charlottesville. The prince had ordered his carpenters to panel much of the property so that the fox could be pursued without the necessity of slowing to open gates.

As if he also controlled the climate, the sun

broke fully through thin, tearing clouds and gleamed off brass buttons, spurs, and the silver bands around whip handles. The procession did have a beauty and grandeur. I regretted I wasn't mounted on a blooded horse and part of this American nobility.

The huntsman raised his copper horn to sound a long, wavering note and moved off, the hounds trailing his heavy bay and ever mindful of his whip. The prince and members of the field dropped in behind. While I counted the riders, thirty-four in all, I spotted Josey.

She appeared elegant in her Melton, derby, and knotted stock, her gloved hands light on the reins, her shoulders curved forward slightly, her body secure in the saddle and, as always, positive of its competence. She hadn't noticed me among the crowd, and I didn't call out but stared at her black gloves. They could've been those I sent.

The hunt field moved away down toward the river and along the edge of the woods. I wished for the binoculars given to my father.

"We supposed to wait 'round here till breakfast. I'm ready to chow down."

It was Felix Bonnet, the other lawyer in Jessup's Wharf — middle-aged, his face marked with liver spots, dark glasses masking his rheumy eyes. He suffered from stomach ulcers and chewed Tums, his teeth methodically crunching them, the sound audible during court proceedings.

"We can't eat till they serve," I said. "You should have brought a horse."

"I've never ridden and don't plan to start now. Two asses on one animal."

As I was about to return to my Buick, I heard the huntsman's horn and his whooping in what sounded like a falsetto voice. I caught sight of the white-and-tan hounds racing up from the bottom after a red fox that moved in a seemingly unhurried hippity-hop fashion toward the rail fence.

The prince and the field galloped after the huntsman — all headed straight for the spectators. We scattered to the side. The fox slipped between rails, and the huntsman, the prince, and Josey jumped the fence, their horses heaving themselves upward, arching, their hooves striking and slamming the turf and throwing clods. I felt the animals' pounding weights through the ground and smelled their sweat.

Other riders took the fence, though two horses refused, and a man went over his gray to the ground. The gray leaped the fence without him while the man was left cursing and brushing dirt from his white britches. It was Harry Gaffney, and he slogged away, pulling a flask from an inner pocket of his Pinks.

The bar remained open, and I carried a double bourbon in a paper cup to my car, started the engine, and switched on the heater and radio. I wondered how Josey had worked it to be among the guests chosen to hunt. Actually she didn't have to work anything. Her presence was an automatic invitation anyplace she wished to go.

I would have driven off except for her. I became comfortable sipping, dozing in the sun, and listening to *Don Giovanni* broadcast from Tidewater Public Radio.

I roused when I heard the huntsman's horn and stepped from the car to glimpse the field straggling up from the bottom, the horses quiet now, heads drooping, their flanks foaming. I looked at my new watch to find it nearly noon.

The riders were relaxed, calling to one another, passing flasks. I meant to speak to Josey but rather than stopping among the vans she rode off at the prince's side toward his stable. I stood looking after them.

As servants closed the bar and folded tables, the guests began filing toward the mansion. I joined them and climbed the brick steps of the portico, where at the house's entrance a black domestic wearing a white jacket and bow tie opened the door for us. The prince's bodyguard, a swarthy Arab, eyed all who entered. People called him Al, I assumed short for Abdul or Aladdin, and the rumor around Jessup's Wharf was that he carried a pistol in a shoulder holster. He awarded me a cheerless nod.

Three chandeliers lighted by teardrop bulbs hung over a series of trestle tables being loaded with food by the kitchen help. China serving platters displayed hams, roast beef, partridges, shrimp, and oysters as well as an array of salads, vegetables, corn bread, and urns of coffee and tea.

A bar occupied the end of a wainscoted living room, which held a Steinway grand, Persian carpets, hunt tapestries, and a fireplace whose andirons were topped by polished brass fox heads. Above the mantel hung an oil portrait of the prince dressed as a sheik in a flowing white cloak, his legs astride a reared Arabian steed.

I looked for Josey. Those who had been on the chase had begun to join the party. They still wore hunt attire except for the caps, toppers, and whips left behind. They had also wiped their boots.

Most headed for liquor, as I had. I positioned myself beside a towering antique secretary and watched the parade of class and wealth. Hilarity opened moistened mouths wide, voices gave thrilling reports of viewing two reds and a gray as well as praise for the working of the pack, who had torn the gray to pieces as it tried to climb a tree.

"You've got to give them blood occasionally or they won't hunt," a stout, jowly gentleman remarked to an aging woman with netted yellow hair. I wondered whether she had ridden with her fingers so jeweled beneath her riding gloves.

On the second-floor landing a jazz band assembled and began to play — trumpet, tenor sax, double bass, drums, and vibraharp. I knew I should be eating but instead decided to down one last bourbon.

"Banquo got in under that fence," Harry Gaffney said, explaining his fall to people gathered around. "It was his last chance. I'm letting that plug go."

As a small-town lawyer I would likely always be an attendant to most of these people. I knew my manners and might be invited if useful and pleasing to the outer fringes of their inner circle, yet nothing more. I felt the sting of it.

Prince Jamir made his way among guests, stopped to smile and chat. He kissed the hands of the ladies. Josey entered not through the front door but from somewhere at the rear of the house, perhaps the porte-cochere. Her stock was held in place by a gold safety pin fastened through the knot. I watched her remove her net and shake out her hair.

As I moved toward her, she stepped up to stand beside the prince. She was taller than he. He kissed her not on the hand but the cheek, and for an instant his mouth lingered as he whispered at her ear.

I backed off and merged into the crowd. I meant to ease unnoticed out the door, but before I reached it a voice called my name — not Walter but Raff.

It belonged to Jefferson Burford, a student I'd known at John Marshall and Washington and Lee. A Kappa Sig, he had passed out drinking Salty Dogs and been left propped under the shower by fraternity brothers, where he almost drowned.

"Hey, Raff," he said, drink in hand, "do the clown dance for us."

Guests turned to him and me. The combo on the landing had just started playing "Take Five."

"He can do this crazy clown dance with a gorilla," Jefferson announced. "It'll break you up. Come on, Raff, show the folks."

I hated him, and I had drunk too much.

"Screw you, Burford, and I hope you've gotten the worming the vet advised you needed," I said and made for the door. I escaped down the portico steps, staggered toward the parking area, listed off course, and pushed among box bushes until I bumped the scalloped rim of the courtyard fountain, which had been emptied for the winter. I puked into it.

TWELVE

I caught up with Cliff on a rainy Thursday evening. I had been to Richmond both to carry Lee's portrait for framing to artist Phoebe Laratta and to visit my dentist for a routine checkup. When I first parked alongside the curb at Cliff's Gothic-style carriage house and rang the bell, the rain beat my umbrella, and I received no answer.

As I started to leave, he drove his Thunderbird into the service alley, his tires splashing puddles. The double doors opened on command from his remote and closed after he drove through. I walked back to the stone wall, again rang, and Cliff buzzed me in.

"I've been on a trip to the sea," he said. Rain dripped from his Irish hat onto his toggle coat's shoulders. "The humpbacks are running."

He hurried to the Thunderbird's trunk to lift out camera gear and a duffel bag. I helped carry them into the carriage house, which was cold and clammy. The first floor held his living and dark rooms plus a small kitchen, the second his bed and bathroom. I shook out my umbrella.

He switched on lights before kneeling at the fireplace to strike a match to rolled-up newspaper shoved beneath kindling and logs laid over bricks used for andirons. Smoke drifted uncertainly until the draft began to draw. The paper uncurled in flames, kindling crackled, and sparks swirled into the flue.

"I feel the need of a tod," he said. "And I've got a bottle of good rye bought in Baltimore."

From the kitchen hidden beyond a black lacquered screen decorated with a golden Chinese dragon he carried a bowl of ice cubes to mix the drinks on a battered upright piano, the top of which doubled as his bar.

He set mine before me on a black coffee table painted to resemble a white octopus, its tentacles spread over the edges and down the legs. Literary quarterlies lay fanned across it. The room's walls displayed his work, the near one studies of males, a number stripped of clothes, that must have come from his recent show.

"Some great shots of the whales," Cliff said as he checked his thermostat and removed his coat and hat before sitting on the sofa opposite me. "We boated so close their flukes wet us and I tasted the salt."

He lowered his drink to study me.

"Why don't you just go on and take an honest look at the pictures? Obviously they interest you."

"I remember you told me notoriety is its own justification in our day and time."

"Sorry you didn't attend the exhibition but not surprised. You're from another age, Walter, a living flesh-and-blood relic."

I shrugged and sipped at the rye.

"And gays bother you."

"Not they but what they do."

"What do they do, Walter? What are the mechanics?"

"You know."

"Of course I know, but they do it in privacy and it's all just too abhorrent for you to speak the words. The truth is, Walter, fucking of any variety lacks decorum or artistry. Do something for me. Say 'shit.' I've never heard you speak the word."

"No."

"Walter, it's the shit generation. Babies come from the womb using it. Everybody does."

"I don't."

"All right, I give up. Why so solemn?"

"Sheriff Sawyers is set on bringing you back to High Gap. I'm trying to turn him, but the next move's his. We will see."

"Wonderful news," he said and drank.

"Can you think of any reason why he's so

110

determined?" I asked.

"I have no answer."

"I've known you most my life, Cliff. Despite your dramatic talents, you were never the best poker player in the gang. Drake was, and this isn't a situation you can dance around."

"I was a good dancer and still am," he said, yet his reply sounded disheartened. I waited for more. He tossed back his hair. I unbuttoned my overcoat in the expanding heat. Flames of the fire lit one side of his face, the other remained shadowed.

"I want you once again to go into details of the hunt," I said.

"You were there, you know."

"I wasn't with Wendell. Maybe you overlooked something."

"I arrive home elated by whales and have to face this," he said and sighed. "All right, Walter, if it has to be. This is strictly privileged between you and me, right?"

"Correct."

"Okay, on Blind Sheep after we separated into pairs the morning of the hunt, Wendell, silent as usual, followed me up the mountain. We climbed till we reached the beech flat below the ridge. Then he surprised me by breaking the silence and beginning to talk."

"About what?"

111

" 'I wanted my son Jeremiah to learn about these mountains,' he said and told me five generations of his kin had herded sheep on the sod. He thought it a thing his boy should know but never got around to it he was so busy at The Watchers, a plan put off and never taken up. He regretted it. He lagged behind me, and I slowed so he could draw alongside.

" 'My son was in your class at the college,' he said. I tried to remember. So many students. They came in hairy droves. A vague handsome face associated with the name Jeremiah took shape in my mind.

" 'He bought a magazine with a story you wrote in it,' Wendell said. 'You'd signed your name across the top of the page for him. Kind of you.'

"I told Wendell it had been a pleasure, though most of the students were in fact sucking up for higher grades.

" 'They must look to you for more than being a teacher,' Wendell said. 'To them you'd likely seem to know the answers to 'bout everything.'

"I answered it was a sobering responsibility. He dropped back again as we hiked upward.

" 'I know you impressed Jeremiah,' Wendell said. 'For a time he talked about becoming a teacher and writer.'

112

"Before I could answer I spotted a grouse feeding near the laurel — head raised, its neck stretched high. The bird flushed, I swung and shot, and simultaneously Wendell lunged in front of my gun. That's it."

He stood to freshen his drink. I had only sipped at mine and set the glass on the coffee table. He used the poker to stir the fire, causing logs to sink into the licking aroused flames, and again sat across from me.

"Why didn't you tell me before this that Wendell had spoken to you about a connection with his son?"

"Hardly a connection. The boy might well have brought me a copy of *Now* when the magazine appeared, certainly nothing more."

"I find it difficult to believe the son being in your class and Wendell on the hunt are a coincidence. Sheriff Sawyers must feel the same way."

"Jesus, how did everything go so wrong?" Cliff asked and rubbed his face. "Why can't it be somebody just got shot in a hunting accident and leave it at that?"

"The same question I'm asking you."

"You can't defend me with what you've got?"

"No, Cliff, I need it all."

"God, to be a whale gliding majestically through blue seas. I'm so damn tired, Walter.

I feel I've been punctured, the air let out."

He drank, let his head fall back, and talked toward the ceiling, his eyes half-shut.

"When I spotted the grouse, I told Wendell not to fire unless it flushed.

" 'You'd never shoot a bird on the ground, I reckon,' " he said. " 'I sure admire your high standards.'

"There was a harder edge to Wendell's voice, and I would've faced him except for the grouse. It didn't flush but footed away making trilling sounds as it peered back at us.

" 'We'll step up the pace,' I told Wendell and lengthened my stride to close the gap and force a flush.

" 'Maybe that bird's so young it don't know it should be scared,' Wendell said.

" 'I'll give it further motivation,' I said and scooped up a handful of wet snow, patted it into a ball, and threw it. The grouse flushed and angled up and over the laurel. We watched it curve around and glide downward, its shadow skimming the snow.

" 'Gone away,' Wendell said.

" 'We didn't exactly respond with the killer instinct,' I said.

" 'Killing's new to me,' he said.

"I looked at him, but he continued to gaze off in the direction the bird had flown. As we began to work around the laurel, I turned to

114

Wendell and found him watching me.

" 'Something?' I asked.

" 'Hate dirtying clean snow,' he said and used his gun barrel to indicate the tracks left by our boots. They had stirred up mud from the thawing ground.

" 'I feel the same way,' I said.

" 'Like something good made bad,' he said, and those pale eyes leveled at me. 'You consider yourself a writer or teacher first of all?'

" 'I don't think it's an either-or proposition,' I said over my shoulder.

" 'The minds of the young,' Wendell said. 'Like bread dough. Pat them into all kinds of shapes.'

" 'A great responsibility,' I said.

" 'Drop the wrong word, and it might lodge in the brain of a boy, take seed, set him off bad the rest of his life.'

" 'I try to be guarded in the sensitive areas about what I tell my classes.'

" 'Jeremiah told me you always went the extra mile for your students.'

" 'I attempt to,' I said.

" 'A man and his wife grow a beautiful child,' he said. 'They give him the fullness of their days, their toil, and their love. They clothe and protect him from hunger and cold. Then he's thieved away and corrupted, lured

115

into sin by an older man he admires, his teacher.'

" 'You're accusing me of that?' I asked, again turned. Fury had transformed that deadpan face. He raised his gun barrel.

" 'I seen your exhibition,' he said. 'Walked through that place. Naked men on walls. Sodomites.'

" 'Those photographs were no moral statement but an exercise and study in black-and-white,' I answered him. 'And I'm in the dark why you're talking to me like this.'

" 'You in the dark all right,' he said. 'You belong to the dark.'

" 'Wendell, we've gotten off wrong here somehow, so let's forget the hunt and straighten this out,' I said.

"He drew back the Remington's bolt, released it, and aimed the gun at my genitals.

" 'I been trying to do right,' he said. 'I asked God for release, but the Lord's not granted it. You got to provide me that.'

" 'You're actually meaning to use that gun on me?' I asked.

" 'I am,' he said and clicked off the safety.

" 'Mr. Ripley, for God's sake let's be rational here.'

" 'God and rational don't come into this,' he said. 'I studied it out.'

" 'How will killing me help you or any-

116

body? Consider the consequences.'

" 'I been living with consequences long enough. Time to wipe the slate.'

"The Remington was still aimed at me. I watched his index finger snug to the trigger.

" 'You'll end up in prison or worse,' I said.

" 'Maybe not. During hunting season you can hardly pick up the paper without seeing somebody's been shot. The authorities expect it.'

"I was trembling," Cliff said. "Everything was quiet except for the sound of water trickling under the snow and calls from ravens up toward the ridge. I swore to him I'd never had any relationship with his son.

" 'No jury'd convict me,' he said.

"I turned away and glanced down over rounded contours of the white land before I again looked behind me. He'd lifted his shotgun to his shoulder and was squinting along the barrel. He meant to do it. I saw the hate. I had no doubt, took a step away, pivoted, and fired. Oh, Jesus, the blood, all that red blood spurting out over the white snow."

His head hung forward, and his eyes clenched against seeing it.

"Why haven't you told the truth about what happened?"

"I thought I could keep it simple. Wendell was right about hunters often being killed. I

117

would avoid being charged and possibly taken to court."

"Tell it now."

"Who'd believe it? And he called me a sodomite. The furor caused by my exhibition would resurface and stamp me forever in the public's eye as a deviant. Walter, I've been seeing a girl in Baltimore. We're serious about each other. She was with me and the whales. Her father's a prominent doctor who doesn't approve of me as it is."

"There's no way you could have been mistaken about Wendell's intent?"

"I saw the contorted loathing on his face. He meant to kill me all right."

I tried to make sense of it and waited for Cliff to give me more. He sat holding his glass in both hands, his eyes open now but still directed to the past.

"You know nothing more about Wendell's son, Jeremiah?" I asked.

"Nothing."

"You haven't heard he was poisoned?"

"It's news to me, and I've told you all I can. See Drake."

"See him about what?"

"The son worked for him."

"I know."

"Well, Drake can help, and will, and that's all I have to say."

THIRTEEN

I drove to Grizzly's and walked past the plastic bear, which had a loudspeaker inserted inside its belly that produced a low cyclic growl, the result both frightening and delighting children. They drew toy pistols to aim and shoot at it.

The chief clerk, a muscled Virginia Tech ex-football player named Boomer, told me Drake had driven to his Blind Sheep cabin for two days hunting. Boomer had been selected second-team All-American but was slipping into a softening, settling body, though you could still see muscled remnants from his days of gridiron eminence.

"He go alone?" I asked.

"Un-huh, Drake likes solo hunts. He told me he gets his best ideas by himself up on Blind Sheep."

"Boomer, were you here when Wendell Ripley's boy Jeremiah ran the shoe department?"

"Sure was, though we never called him Jeremiah. Just Jerry."

"Why did he quit his job?"

"Can't help you there, Mr. Frampton. He upped and left without telling anybody. I worked the stockroom back then. Jerry never said good-bye or collected his last week's pay."

"You hear anything about his being poisoned?"

"I did but got no details. Lots of talk, nothing nobody could pin down."

A customer entered, bringing along wind with him, and the ghost grouse stirred on its nylon line. Boomer signaled a clerk to wait on the man, who carried a pair of ice skates.

"You knew Jeremiah's father?" I asked Boomer.

"I sure did. Mr. Ripley liked being around here near his son. Came in and hung out even after Jerry left. He never talked much, though he eyed everybody who walked through the door."

"Why would he do that?"

"Lonely, I guess. Maybe hoping for somebody. He was bad tore up."

"You able to tell me anything else about Mr. Ripley?"

"Well, he was kind of country, you know, the sort that'll sit around for hours without needing to talk. I guess he had nothing much else to do. He did ask me and others if we knew a sailor named — hold it a second, I got

120

it — Leonard Dawson. I told him I didn't. I think he hoped to see that fellow."

"He never explained why?"

"No, sir, he never explained hardly anything."

"What did you think of Jerry?"

From the back of the store came the sound of grinding. The clerk was sharpening the man's ice skates.

"Nice, clean-cut boy, had a way with women customers who came in to buy for their men. More citified than his father. I liked and missed him around here."

Again I drew on what Cliff had told me. Wendell had used the word "sodomite" and talked of a youth lured and defiled by a man trusted and admired. Possibly the sailor Leonard Dawson was in some way connected to Jeremiah's poisoning?

I thanked Boomer, drove off, and in Richmond stopped by stockbrokers Bunker, Rose & Diggs, where I left my umbrella beside the entrance and glanced after the fleeting market tape. At her desk Josey studied the monitor as she scribbled on a pad. Her white seashell earrings set off her tan. I pushed my new glasses higher on my nose before I made my entrance. A pearly conch shell served as a doorstop.

"I've been missing you," I said as I watched her slim, proficient fingers move rapidly over the keyboard, the nails clear and shiny from a natural polish. The sun had bleached downy hair along her wrists.

"Just returned from Grenada and blue waters," she said and had only a glance for me.

"I've always wanted to go to Spain."

"Not Spain. Long *a*. The Grenadines and scuba diving. I looked a sand shark right in the eye and stared him down. The guy turned tail."

Her phone sounded a musical tone, and she lifted it. I listened to arcane talk about expiring options. She had dated lots of men, a couple from the first flight of Richmond's blue-blood society.

I started to light a Winston. I was careful not to hold it in the thumb-and-finger reversed palm style I preferred. She and others had made fun of that as they did my umbrella. She waved a hand side to side in front of her face and shook her head. I returned the pack to my pocket.

"You live an active sporting life," I said when she finished talking.

"You should too, Raff. Take care or one of these days you'll become portly and look like a lawyer. You're already just a tad short of being a stuffed shirt."

A man stepped through the doorway, one of many who worked for the firm, a nearly total enterprise of eligible males, most if not all more physically attractive than my thin, reedy height.

"The Flannigan account again," he said.

"Tighten the screws on those turkeys and no compromise," Josey said, and he left nodding. Command came naturally to her.

"How you abuse me," I said.

"Loving abuse."

"I saw you chasing the fox at the prince's hunt breakfast."

"You didn't speak to me," she said and turned away from the monitor.

"You appeared fully occupied."

A second time her phone sounded. Again I adjusted my glasses. I continued to wear them because contacts irritated my eyes and during the fall term I had lost the left lens during a traffic case before the General District Court, the resulting disruption causing the bailiff and everybody else except the judge himself to help find it. The clerk on his knees had located the lens beneath the defense table and come up with it atop a fingertip.

"Actually I witnessed a bit of your exit," she said as she set the phone down.

"I had to leave but noticed you and the prince hit it off well."

"He's now doing business with Bunker, Rose and Diggs. The fact is he asked me to execute a significant order."

"You go to Grenada with him?" I asked, though I had not meant to. The question formed and was spoken before I considered any loss of aplomb.

"We flew in his plane."

"And looked sharks in the eye."

"Raff, I believe it's time for you to leave. I'm very busy. Visit me when the market's not rollicking."

She again turned to her monitor. I had wanted to talk about the stallion, the pin oak, and the hand I held to her. Well, not this day, if ever.

"I'll do that," I said and started off.

"And stop thinking those bad thoughts about me," she called.

As I walked past the ironfronts to the parking garage I passed a specialty store that sold toys. Through the display window I looked at a simulated American Indian village — scattered red-and-yellow autumn leaves, a te-pee, birchbark canoe, bow and arrow, calu-met, feathered headdress, and stones of a circular fireplace.

Children's books had been upended among them, one titled *Blood Brothers.* On the cover a buckskin-clad frontiersman shook hands with a bare-chested, war-painted brave. They solemnly eyed each other. In the background stood an Indian maiden, who held a clay cooking vessel. I bought a copy for Mary Ellen's young son, Jason.

My thoughts of Josey pictured her and the prince together, two beautiful people, their sun-toasted bodies entwined. I created pictures that aroused, angered, and shamed me.

FOURTEEN

Before heading for Jessup's Wharf, I again thought of Wendell's son, Jeremiah. If he were poisoned, there should have been an investigation. I drove to the Department of Public Safety building located behind Richmond's white, tombstone-style City Hall — the police like poor cousins housed in the older, shabbier structure.

I told the uniformed deputy at the desk I wanted to speak to a detective.

"The purpose of your visit?" he asked through a circular two-way speaker set into bulletproof glass.

I explained who I was, gave him my card, and told him I needed information concerning a missing person.

"See what I can do," the deputy said and lifted a phone. "Citizen here on a look, anybody open?" he inquired. He listened and set the phone back. "Through the door and ask for Detective Bush."

He pointed me to a locked double door and buzzed me through. I walked along the beige corridor until I saw the "Detective Section"

126

sign. The windowless room was filled with cubicles and resembled more what one might see in the office of an insurance agency than the jumbled disorder of a squad room as represented on TV. The detectives wore shirts and ties and might have been salesmen or executives except for handcuffs and snub-nosed pistols holstered at belts. There was, however, a certain weighing and sharpness of eye.

A female officer directed me to Detective Bush at the rear of the room. Thin, with graying hair, he appeared resigned and weary. I introduced myself as I gave him my card. He studied it before looking me over and indicating a chair. On the desk he'd set a color photograph of a border collie jumping to catch a Frisbee.

"And the person you're looking for?" he asked, his voice unhurried, yet not so much relaxed as fatigued, his body posture defensive and suggesting he expected nothing that could bring happiness into his life.

"His name is Jeremiah Ripley. I have no middle initial."

"Is this a criminal matter?"

"At this point I have little information about him."

"Spell his name for me."

I did, and he methodically two-fingered the name into a computer and scrolled the monitor. The lobe of his left ear was gone. Shot or bitten off? He exhaled and shook his head slowly.

"No wants on him," he said. He continued to scroll, pulled up a page, and scanned it. He was not a man to speak without laboriously ordering his thoughts, and his weariness seemed to gray the atmosphere that surrounded him.

"A Jeremiah Daniel Ripley reported missing by his father some three years ago. He was never located."

"Were there any leads?"

"None." He waited passively. I had the feeling he would never speak again.

"Do you have anything else?"

"The monitor has a description."

"Is he presumed dead?"

"We don't presume in this department."

I considered a moment.

"What about a sailor named Leonard Dawson?"

"His name's here, an inquiry about him. Again no record or other information and no description."

"If something turns up on either man, would you please get in touch with me?"

"I'll make a note," he said and did with a resigned effort. He looked at me out of faint blue eyes that surely belonged to a much older man. They were hooded as if peering from a burrow. He carried his burrow with him. "Your father Walter Frampton?" he asked.

"I'm his son, yes."

"Thought you resembled him."

I waited for more but no words came. Was he recalling my father's troubles? He opened a drawer and lifted out an amber Smith Brothers cough drop he placed on his grainy tongue. A good man, I thought of Detective Bush, who had likely encountered so much of humanity's mayhem and vileness that they had seared and withered all emotional responses and left him bound and deadened by scar tissue.

I headed to Jessup's Wharf and parked in front of my office, where I looked out the window. The snow had become slush along River Street, and water ran along the gutters into storm drains. I watched the red-tail hawk circle in and make a pass at the St. Luke's church steeple. The pigeons flung themselves into flight and escape. The red-tail didn't give chase but sat at the base of the steeple knowing he could take one for a meal anytime he wanted.

FIFTEEN

I needed to talk again to Brother Abram, but it was too late for me to drive back through Richmond to Chesterfield. The next morning, a cold misty day, I drove out to The Watchers. No workers sowed or reaped in the gray fallow fields. The ground had frozen again overnight, and a pond grew a dull, gray skim of ice.

I found Brother Abram not at his workshop but in one of the barracks-like buildings, from which I heard clattering. When I opened the door at one end, I faced two rows of Singer sewing machines with both men and women sitting before them. They were making brown coveralls of the type they wore themselves and I had seen for sale on the second floor of FOOD.

Brother Abram ambled among the workers until he noticed me, then approached in his heavy, rocking gait. Sewers' eyes had lifted to take me in. The place was so noisy Brother Abram led me into a small office whose desk was a section of half-inch plywood laid over sawhorses. I avoided looking at the hair growing so thickly from his nose and ears.

"I can make you a good price on a pair," he said as he closed the door. Again he seemed on the point of laughter. "Or is it you're thinking of joining us? You're surely welcome."

"Not yet, but thanks for the gracious invitation. What I'd like is to ask a few more questions about Wendell Ripley."

"Dead to this world but alive in the Lord."

"His son Jeremiah also?"

"I seem to remember I told you he was poisoned."

"And died from it?"

Brother Abram hesitated, and the corners of his merry mouth leveled slightly.

"In the spirit, yes."

"You're insinuating not the body?"

"The body is a flimsy garment."

"Brother Abram, it's important I know for certain."

"He's gone from us. We prayed for him and still do."

"Why pray for him when he's dead?"

"We pray for all the damned. Surely you've heard of Hell."

"Rarely lately. How was he poisoned?"

"Evil is a poison in the bloodstream," he said and lifted a large pair of tailor's shears from the desk to snip at an irregular scrap of discarded cloth.

"It seems what you're telling me is the poison was spiritual, not actual."

"Spirit is actuality, the most enduring gift God grants us."

"I won't dispute that, Brother Abram, but who did the poisoning?"

"Jeremiah became enticed and perverted," he said, and I saw he was fashioning a small star out of the scrap of cloth.

"Please help me by being more specific."

"Why should I?" The shears stopped snipping.

"Because I think you're a good man who believes in justice."

He laid down the star, and his cinnamon eyes lifted to mine. "Jeremiah became enticed by and consumed with the desire for the bodies of other men."

"Who did the enticing?"

"An evil one."

"Are we talking about Satan?"

"Who else but the father of all evil?"

"Yet not a flesh-and-blood person in the here and now?"

"In the guise of one such. The devil can assume any shape he wishes except that of Our Savior."

"Does that shape have a name?"

"Most people do." The shears clicked away at emptiness.

"Is the name Leonard Dawson?"

"I have heard that name mentioned by Brother Wendell. I know Mr. Dawson not."

"But Jeremiah, his body, might not be physically dead?"

"To those of us here he is whatever the nature of his present state."

"Brother Abram, I very much need to know his whereabouts if he's alive."

"I can't be of help to you, sir. He left us and never returned. We would have taken him back and washed him in the blood, but sin conquered and defiled him. We have not closed the book on Jeremiah Daniel Ripley. He closed it on himself."

As I then turned to leave the office, I thanked him. He saw me to the door, which he shut behind me over the din from the rhythmic clacking of sewing machines. I walked to my car and driving out had to stop for plodding cows being herded across the road by a scowling, albinic man whose long colorless hair swung around his neck. He turned furious and swept an arm about in a gesture meant for me to leave.

"Sir?" I called to him after I lowered my window.

In a long-legged country stride, he moved

away after the cows and gave me a fierce look while he again swept his arm as if to wipe me off the land.

I drove to Jessup's Wharf, where steam from Axapomimi Lumber's black stack flattened out over the river, the sign of a falling barometer. I fretted how to find Wendell's son, Jeremiah, whether he were dead or alive. On the slimmest chance I had overlooked the obvious and he might still live in Richmond, I checked his name in the phone directory. No such luck.

I dialed Grizzly's to see whether Drake had come back, and he answered the phone.

"I'm on my way," I told him.

I drove through the city on the Expressway to Powhite and cut over to Route 60. A tractor at Grizzly's pushed aside the last of the snow, the blade leaving black swaths across the wet asphalt. I spoke to Boomer, who stood among basketball equipment where he had fixed a hoop to a roof-support column. With a balled-up sheet of paper he made what appeared to be a delicate shot for such a large man into the center of the hoop.

"Two," another clerk called out.

I found Drake in the stockroom using a knife with a curved blade to cut open large cardboard boxes that contained fishing rods and brightly colored artificial baits.

"Preparing for spring," he said and laid the knife on the box. "I expect you'd like to talk in private."

He walked to his office. On his desk this time lay not a 1866 Winchester but an unframed oil painting of a grouse drumming atop a mossy log shaded by a hemlock forest. He lifted the canvas and examined it.

"In the larger edition of 'The Truth of the Grouse' I'm hoping to get published, I want illustrations included," he said. "The chances are I can push sales beyond the local area, maybe even interstate."

"I've been talking to Cliff," I said as I sat. "He told me what really happened between Wendell and him during the hunt. At least I'm working on that assumption as regards the truth."

"Yeah, he told me too," Drake said and laid the painting back on the desk.

"And you just went along with the story of a hunting accident without telling me?"

"Raff, it seemed the simplest way out for him and everybody concerned. I didn't want scandal any more than he did. Dangerous for him and bad for Grizzly's and my proposed book. The story would've worked except for that sheriff and still will if Cliff hangs tough."

"But you should have told me."

135

"Agreed and I'm sorry."

"I can't defend Cliff if he's lying."

"Sure you can, Raff. Lawyers do it all the time. Make those shitkickers in West Virginia bring a charge and prove it. They can't now with what they got."

"Maybe they know something we, or at least I, don't."

"No," he said and sat. "And without Jerry Ripley they lack the evidence for conviction."

"What could they do if they had Jerry?"

"Who knows?" he said. He again lifted the oil to gaze at it.

"Drake, how about saying what you mean?"

"All right, what I keep thinking of is Cliff's faggy downtown exhibition. Why the hell did he have to get into that?"

"I think I don't like where you're heading."

Without comment, Drake again laid the painting on the desk.

"Cliff's one of us," I said. "And has a girl he's serious about who lives in Baltimore."

"You seen her, Raff? No? Me neither. Look, nobody's been charged yet, have they? I believe the sheriff's bluffing and this thing will blow over if everybody stays cool."

"I think you're wrong about Cliff."

"That would make me happy."

"And I need to find something definite on what happened to Jeremiah Ripley."

136

"Wasted effort, Raff. Jerry's gone for good one way or another, and my bet he's six feet under and wearing a grass skirt."

"You ever know any of his friends or acquaintances?"

"Jerry drove here to work from the city, did his job, and left. He never spoke about himself."

"And quit with no explanation or asking for his last week's pay."

"As I told you before, I tried to find him. I had his phone number, but he never answered, and the phone was disconnected a couple of days later. I sent his check in the mail, and it was returned by the post office, no forwarding address."

"It never occurred to you there might be trouble bringing Wendell along on the hunt?"

"It was his land. How could I know he had anything against Cliff? And Wendell wanted to come."

"He manipulated you into the invitation?"

"Looking back on it, that could be. When he heard I was going, he said he'd like to see his home place once again. The land now belongs to The Watchers. I'll never get it unless they put it up for sale. Maybe kick my tail off Blind Sheep when my lease runs out."

"I'm not certain what to do next?" I said and reached for a Winston.

"Play it cool, Raff. It's the only way. The sheriff's got nothing substantial on Cliff."

"He was at The Watchers snooping around."

"Doesn't mean he found anything. As I said before, maybe he enjoys traveling at tax-payer expense." He lifted and turned the painting to me. "So you like this picture?"

"That picture I like," I said.

SIXTEEN

Driving away, I thought about Drake and his book. People around Richmond and increasingly elsewhere had begun to call him "the Prophet of the Grouse." That appellation had its origin in Letters to the Editor columns of the *Times-Dispatch* when the shooting and resulting death of a jogger along a suburban road aroused the antigun, antihunter factions. Their protests filled mailbags, and voters petitioned the General Assembly for more severe firearm and game regulations. One letter read, "It is time mankind sheds his barbaric atavisms and joins the twentieth century."

Drake composed his own reply and posted it. He wrote: "What's so wonderful about the twentieth century? Many of its years we've been at war and buried tens of thousands of young men.

"Face it, to eat is to ingest something that has been alive. We live on life. Which is better, to award wild game a sporting chance or to herd cattle into a slaughterhouse and hit them with an eight-pound sledge between their eyes? Can you respect a slab of cow or hog meat on your plate? It's just food. I believe God provided man fish in the sea and game in the forests not only for his use but also his guidance. True hunters in the pursuit of game learn respect for this created world."

Drake's bringing God into the argument caused more letters. One correspondent wrote, "Sure, the Lord's trekking through the woods with a .45 strapped to His hip." Another stated that "God holds out His hand to offer life, not death."

When the General Assembly at its fall session debated a law that would further restrict gun ownership and use, Drake closed himself in his office and wrote the pamphlet explaining what hunting grouse meant to him. The hundred copies he ordered printed he laid out on Grizzly's front counter for customers to carry home and read. By the end of the week all the copies were gone, and he ordered two hundred additional ones printed. Moreover he began to receive requests over the phone and by mail for the pamphlet as well as invitations to speak before private and civic organizations.

I attended a debate at the Public Forum held in the St. Jude's Episcopal Church's auditorium. A sincere, collared young priest took the affirmative on the proposition that

"Hunting Is a Dangerous Historical Vestige, a Nostalgia for a Time That Will Never Return." He spoke well and convincingly and ended with the words, "Let us share the goodness of this earth with our fellow creatures and rejoice in living together at peace."

Drake rose from his chair on the stage and crossed to the podium. He appeared professional and distinguished in his charcoal business suit, vest, and maroon tie. He showed neither nervousness nor discomfort.

He had brought no notes. After a pause that allowed the talking and shifting about of the audience to die, he rested his hands lightly on the podium and spoke. He kept his eyes raised and moving over the assemblage to make contact. His voice was conversational, yet authoritative. He did not seem to debate as much as to share indisputable truths of life.

"Some years ago after I returned from the service, I was unemployed, near broke, and felt I walked alone on this planet," he said. "Oh, I heard people talking, but they were distant voices across gaps from another land. I spoke just enough to get through the day and also slept a lot. The fact is the bed became the biggest part of my world.

"When I was on my feet, I drank with the same intent as a man looking down off a bridge into the invitation of dark water. I thought of slipping away from this life, just letting go and drifting off like flowing out with the tide.

"What changed me was a hike I took, this one on a mountainside in northwest Virginia, up in the high country around Monterey and across the state line into West Virginia and the uprearing of Big Allegheny. I'd been invited to a hunt by a friend. We had served in the Second Armored Division together. He'd built a shack on the mountain — one room, two bunks, a potbellied stove. We dressed in darkness by lantern light and stepped into a cold January morning. That sharp forest air cleaned out the lungs, and our boots crunched ground rime as we climbed into a hollow named Sawmill Run on the chart.

"As we hiked, a stream narrowed and divided around an island of birches. My friend instructed me to take the left fork and he took the right. We'd meet again higher up where the water junctioned. Ferns, moss, and running cedar grew along banks of the stream. Laurel glinted as frost thawed on the leaves. I walked under a hemlock gloom that had never known a full thirst.

"I had bird-hunted but never yet met a ruffed grouse and seen only pictures in sporting magazines. I knew that compared to partridges they were larger, rarer, and more difficult to bring down. My friend Mike told me hunters were lucky to gun all day and carry home a single bird.

"As I passed under a hemlock that dripped moisture, a grouse flapped from the tree. Because of the loud batting of its wings, I believed it a turkey till I saw it had a shorter neck extension and smaller body. I lifted my shotgun, but the grouse banked low and put big laurel between itself and me. Too late to shoot.

"I climbed on. I was accustomed to lowland hunting, and my calves ached. As I stopped to rest, a second grouse flushed behind me. I'd walked right by him. He flew not away but at me. I ducked, saw his dark glinty eyes as he passed, felt the fanning of his wings. By the time I righted myself and lifted my shotgun, he'd become a shadow within shadows and gone.

"Such energy and rocketing into life. These birds gave their all at full throttle. I now hiked up the hollow with no thought for aching calves. A third bird flushed. I glimpsed him and fired. The load blasted into an ironwood bough and caused it to swing broken.

"The stream narrowed as it angled to the junction. A fourth grouse busted up beyond a stand of alders. I got off a snapshot, and the bird dipped but kept going before setting down from an awkward crippled flight ahead of me.

"I marked the spot and hurried to it, my Savage at the ready. The bird was running, dragging a wing. He left drops of blood on the leafy ground cover. I tracked him twenty or thirty yards until he toppled and lay watching me from his fully opened, shiny eyes.

"Calmly he waited for death, no whining, bitching, no panic or begging, the grouse way, all or nothing, live high and die without flinching. Fly hell bent and measure life not by extent but intensity.

"The bird gave up the ghost in my hands, a last faint flutter and gone. I felt saddened and loving. The intricate beauty of its bronze feathers and its will to survive in such rugged country inspired me. I drove back to Richmond thinking I could at least give life all I had left. I borrowed money to start a gun shop, a business where I not only repaired and sold firearms but also tried to teach the truth of the grouse, which is bravery and endurance, no compromise with surrender.

"I hope the theologians don't become upset when I say on Big Allegheny I refound the God I'd lost. The grouse became my communion. I mouthed its white flesh with reverence and tasted the forest and goodness of creation. From that day to this my God runs the ridges with me, lives and breathes in high clean air and beside the pure water and mighty hemlocks.

"Some men are barbarians during hunt season. They are pigs, meat hunters, hogs for the kill. They are lawless and in no way will be changed by acts of the legislature. But there are others who are ennobled by what they hunt and honorably kill. They are first to come to the aid of an endangered species, to spread feed during the heavy snows, to save the ducks by building breeding grounds, to care for the wounded fawn or the eagle that has taken shot. They are law-abiding men who shouldn't be penalized for the sins of others. They preserve more than they kill.

"I give thanks for the grouse and honor the gallant bird. I feel I'm a brother to him. There are nights when I wake in the dark and think of them perched on thrashing limbs of wind-whipped hemlocks in the high country. I lie hearing in the pumping of my blood the birds' drumming and beat of their wings. I give thanks for the grouse to the only place it can be awarded, to God, the Master Architect of all things."

Drake paused a moment before walking back to his chair on the stage. A single clap of hands started applause that built to a standing ovation.

"To say the least a very out-of-left field theological position," the young priest spoke in rebuttal. But he had lost the debate and knew it.

SEVENTEEN

As I walked back along River Street, Prince Jamir sped through town on his sun-dazzled Harley, its engine speaking rumbling, bridled horsepower. He appeared dashing in a visored black helmet and awarded me a wave.

At the office Jason sat in his chair beside Mary Ellen's desk. He held *Blood Brothers* open across his knees.

"It's his favorite book," Mary Ellen said. "And kindly of you to give it to him."

"Would you rather be the Indian brave or the frontiersman?" I asked Jason.

He didn't look up or speak, but his small index finger moved slowly and touched the war-painted Indian.

"Me too," I said and glanced at Mary Ellen. At least his response was to me directly, meaning I had made progress in our relationship. Mary Ellen was pleased.

That afternoon as I worked at my desk with the door closed I raised my head, then stood and moved quietly to the door and listened. She was singing softly to Jason. I peeped through to see him sitting on her lap, her arms

147

around him, her lips close to his ear:

There is a land not far away
Where children love to run and play,
Where trees are hung with lemon drops
And all the clouds have ice cream tops.

When she glanced up and caught me watching, she placed Jason on his chair and handed him the book. His delicate hands took hold of it. She came into my office.

"Mr. Frampton, I didn't know you could hear us. And we won't disturb you again."

"I never heard the child's verse you were singing."

"It's one I made up. They reassure him."

"Mary Ellen, I've noticed he doesn't arrive with the other children but is let off by another bus earlier."

"He's enrolled in special education and has a shorter day," she said.

"I seem to scare him," I said.

"Not you, Mr. Frampton, but all men. He won't talk to them. The women, yes, a little, but not the men."

She turned away quickly with no further explanation and hurried into the outer office, where she kept her back to me. I sat uncertain what to do next. Apparently I'd disturbed her. Then she again walked into my office and closed the door.

"The night my husband Ben died in Stuttgart, the German TV showed his crash on camera — the helicopter hitting the power line, exploding, falling in flames. They had a close-up of his body black and steaming, his face bloody and agonized."

She stopped and drew breath. She was trying not to cry.

"The hospital called me while I was playing cards with other servicemen's wives. When I left the hospital and reached our living quarters, I heard Jason screaming and the baby-sitter trying to quiet him. She had been in the kitchen and hadn't realized what he was watching on the TV. He had seen his father on fire and screaming. Jason too screamed, for hours, until he dropped asleep exhausted, and when he woke he wouldn't talk or look at anyone. Not a word or glance. He kept his eyes shut and felt his way around his room as if blind."

Fighting to maintain control, Mary Ellen swallowed and lifted her chin.

"It's taken two years for doctors, psychologists, and special teachers to bring him to where he'll speak, and that for a time just to me. Not until last spring has he spoken to others, but only women. He can read and count, do his written exercises, but he won't talk to men. The psychologists believe this will pass, but he should be protected from further traumatic experiences. There are times during the night he still screams."

She again turned, opened the door to walk to her desk, and sat by Jason. I stood, stopped behind her, and touched her shoulder. Again about to break, she bowed her head and gripped her hands, squeezing the blood in her fingers to their tips.

"I have business in the clerk's office," I said and left her.

Valor, I thought. During the heat of battle it displayed itself chiefly in men, but long term and over the wear of years the women owned it.

"A Mr. Sam Tuggle called," Mary Ellen said when I reentered the office.

Jason was still reading and didn't look up.

"Mr. Tuggle identified himself as the Seneca County, West Virginia, district attorney and requested you contact him. I have his number."

If he wanted me, I thought, let him pay the bill, and I considered calling collect. No, better to stay on the best terms possible with all legal authorities. Oil over the waters.

"Mr. Tuggle," I said after I was passed through to him by his secretary.

"Call me Sam," he said, his voice husky,

deep, energetic. "Get that out of the road."

"Fine. I'm Walter."

"What's the weather down your way?" He sounded expansively genial.

"Sunny, cold, wind from the northeast," I said, thinking he was talking on my nickel. "Twenty-nine degrees."

"Don't tell me about wind. Blowing hard enough 'round here to scalp you. People carrying weights to keep their feet on the ground."

I wasn't about to trade small talk about the wind or weather and waited.

"It's my understanding you represent Mr. Clifford A. Dickens," he said.

"That's correct."

"We'd appreciate it here in High Gap if you could persuade Mr. Dickens to pay us a visit."

"Sam, traveling back out to those mountains would cause Mr. Dickens both anxiety and great discomfort. He is more than willing to offer himself here in Virginia for deposing at your convenience."

"Afraid that just won't buy it, Walt. We want him here with us one way or another."

"You're thinking of charging him?"

"We may feel compelled to do that very thing."

"On what count?"

"Involuntary manslaughter. Now, I know

you're going to tell me the shooting was just an accident, but I'd like to remind you that under the code in your state and mine that there's no such thing as accidental homicide."

"I'm aware of that, yet believe it's pushing the code to bring a charge in this instance."

I had raised my voice a bit, and Mary Ellen looked through the doorway at me. She held the green can with a long spout she used to water her African violets.

"Your client killed another man in the negligent and reckless use of his firearm. Prima facie case."

"At worst a misdemeanor."

"A misdemeanor under the code of West Virginia that's punishable at the discretion of the court by fine or imprisonment or both."

"Why inflict either in this case?"

"Because we're clamping down out here and trying to put a stop to the taking of human life. Too many good people dying needlessly. We investigate all homicides. We want the word to get around that Seneca County won't put up with the careless use of firearms."

"My opinion is that such a procedure can be carried too far," I said and glanced out the window to see the pigeons flying around St. Luke's steeple.

"Saving a single life justifies lots of prosecu-

152

tion. Of course the court can also just repri-
mand and fine a man, put him on probation,
turn him loose. But that's up to a judge or
jury. They good people around here and not
out to stick it to anybody from out of state. I'd
like you to believe that, and we'd appreciate
you advising your client to come on up and
see us. We'll treat him in a manner that could
benefit him in any further legal action. You're
also invited."

"You would appreciate it?" I said, thinking
that the correct plea if necessary should be
self-defense but that I could not use it without
subjecting Cliff to an investigation leading to
Jeremiah and the possible allegation and
airing of a homosexual association. I also
thought of Cliff's relationship to his girl and
her father, the doctor who already disapproved.

"Save everybody time, sweat, and money,"
Sam said.

"It would save more if you just took his
sworn statement here in Virginia."

"We don't seem to be getting very far down
this road, do we?"

"I believe any charge is excessive under the
circumstances."

"Well, if Mr. Dickens doesn't comply, I got
no alternative than to request a Seneca
County magistrate to issue a warrant for his

arrest, such warrant to be forwarded to the commonwealth attorneys office, city of Richmond, Virginia. But I'll hold off awhile. Action won't be necessary if Mr. Dickens presents himself to my office within three days."

"I will get back to you."

"That'd be real nice," he said and laughed. "Let's do all we can to keep everybody happy and full in the belly."

When I hung up, I immediately phoned Cliff's carriage house. No answer except the reply from his damn answering machine. I called every hour as I sat working and fidgeting at my desk.

Just after three that afternoon he lifted his phone during the recorded message. I explained my conversation with District Attorney Sam Tuggle.

"If I go to High Gap voluntarily and they try me, I'll receive just a slap on the wrist?" Cliff asked.

"Likely, but no guarantee. It's your decision."

"No way, I'm not doing it. What if I take a vacation for a while?"

"Cliff, I can't be a part of your evading arrest if it comes to that."

"It hasn't come to that yet, has it? Give you time to work things out for me and get them off my back. Walter, my thanks and talk to you later."

He hung up, and I tried raising him again, but he wouldn't answer. I laid my legal tablet before me on the desk and in For and Against columns listed all the facts I knew about what had happened on Blind Sheep. I definitely wanted to cut this thing off before it reached the indictment process. The fact was that even if we were forced to use a plea of self-defense in court, it would not hold up without collaborating evidence.

The missing link was Wendell's son, Jeremiah, probably dead but no verifiable facts about his death, and if alive, where would he now hang his hat? I reviewed what I knew about him: brought up among The Watchers, a Virginia Commonwealth University student, apparently an admirer of Cliff, a shoe clerk at Grizzly's, from what Brother Abram told me involved in homosexual liaisons. Wendell, according to Cliff, had used the word "sodomite."

I considered hiring a private detective. Costs would be substantial, and though I was doing all right financially, I didn't want to spend the money if I could find another way. I thought about Richmond's gay community. At least the possibility existed that someone in that community had associated with Jeremiah

155

and could answer the question whether or not he lay in his grave. Might I ask around in the right quarters and find answers? I didn't know how or where to start? If I frequented the homosexual bars and their other haunts, who would talk openly to a prying attorney?

A thought emerged. Philip Garrow. I'd known him at John Marshall and liked him, though he'd never been as close as Drake and Cliff, my blood brothers.

EIGHTEEN

I knew what had become of Philip Garrow. He had attended Dartmouth, lived for a time in New York, and returned to Richmond where he opened the Left Bank Café in Shockoe Bottom, a once seamy section of Richmond where Confederate deserters hung out during the Civil War. The Left Bank had done so well he had bought an old saddlery in Shockoe Slip and turned it into a classy restaurant named Le Gallic. I had never eaten there. He had also been seen in the front rank of those marching during Gay Pride Day, an act which had disconcerted me, yet I conceded his leaving the closet so openly demonstrated valor of a different sort.

I couldn't get away from the office till noon and at Richmond found space in an underground municipal garage eerily lighted by mercury vapor lamps that cast spectral shadows on dingy yellow walls. I walked along Cary Street to the Slip, a deteriorating commercial area during my youth that in more recent years had transformed itself into a region of style and fashion. An elegant hotel rose among smart shops, bistros, and art galleries. Youth, money and as yet undaunted hope created excitement and vibrancy.

The entrance to Le Gallic appeared modest, a single door with a large brass knob, and unlike other eateries along the street, no menu had been posted. A carelessly penned note announced that Le Gallic would not open until six o'clock.

Using my car key, I tapped on the door's frosted glass. No one answered, though I heard voices inside. I rapped more loudly. Still no response. I walked up the street to the Windsor Arms Hotel, located Le Gallic's number in the directory of a public booth, and called.

"We're taking no reservations until Tuesday," a voice told me before I asked.

"I'm phoning to speak to Philip Garrow," I said, thinking business had to be good. I remembered Philip always accented the second syllable of his last name.

"The nature of your business, sir?"

"That's confidential."

"Your name, *s'il vous plait?*"

I told him.

"I'll see whether Monsieur Garrow is available."

I had heard the waiters spoke with French accents but that only a few could converse in the language. Reportedly the service was flaw-less, yet if you failed to leave an adequate tip, you might receive dark looks and insolent re-marks on your way out.

"That you, Walter?" Philip asked, no French accent, just softly Southern and cul-tured. "It's been such a very long time."

"I knocked but nobody answered."

"Le Gallic's found it sound business to be difficult to reach and that impertinence pays." He laughed. "What can I do for you? Any-thing, just ask."

"I'd like for us to talk."

"I'll be waiting."

At Le Gallic he opened the door and shook my hand. His white bow tie contrasted brightly against a dark blue shirt. He had taken on weight since college days, a glow to his skin, a bemused expression about his eyes and mouth.

"So good to see you, Walter," he said. "I've often thought of you and heard you've be-come a barrister. Life's treating you well I hope."

"Well enough. I read in *Richmond After Dark* about Le Gallic's success."

"The public loves a bit of fakery along with food, and our fare is honestly good," he said and raised a hand as if to present his restau-rant on his palm to me. Milky globed lights illuminated the high room and dark paneling relieved by alternating gilt-framed mirrors and prints by Matisse, Picasso, and Rouault. The bar had a speckled marble top. White linens covered round tables set at the center with crystal carafes.

"Impressive," I said.

"Come eat as my guest," he said. "We serve a rack of lamb so delicious it would melt hearts at the IRS."

"I'll do that," I said, though I knew I wouldn't. "Spare me a moment in private?"

He smiled, raised a finger, and led me to his office off the kitchen, where a white-clad chef and assistants darted about among steam from simmering pots. Philip closed the door against rattling and clashing.

His desk held a French telephone set beside a silver inkwell on a green blotter. As we sat, I faced a shelf behind the desk on which was displayed a piece of sculpture that had been made from painted tin and twisted copper wire — the representation of a naked tightrope walker who held not a pole to balance himself but a fire extinguisher in one hand and flames of his burning palm in the other. The implication was that if he tried to put out the fire he would fall into a chasm beneath.

"Fetching, don't you think?" Philip asked.

"Who or what's the figure?"

"You could say mankind perhaps, or possibly Job, or take your choice. The artist gave it no name. The point is it resonates in the mind. You know him by the way, your friend Clifford Dickens."

Cliff. Of course he would have an acquaintance with Philip and others here in the Slip. There had been the exhibition, and his work necessarily meant he moved among artistic people. Was there a closer association with Philip?

"He is still your friend?" Philip asked.

"I spoke with him only yesterday."

"Clifford's an authentic genius but needs focus. Always hopping around from one project to another, different genres, a little of this, a little of that. I read about the hunting accident and trust it hasn't shaken him too greatly."

"He's surviving, though stressed."

"And your father? I felt terrible about all that publicity created by the ravenous wolves of the press and media. You haven't married, have you?"

"I have designs on a lady," I answered, wondering whether his question had subtle implications.

"Designs, a good word. Like blueprints for a structure that needs to be built brick by brick and not on shifting sands. Well, I wish you luck. Look, Walter, you're not uncomfortable with me, are you? You seem, well, a bit fidgety."

"No," I lied.

"I have no designs on you if that's what you're worried about, but I am fond of you and wish we could have a drink and converse now and again about the old days."

"That's generous of you, Philip."

"All right, now what's on your mind? You're not after money, I hope. I'm very close with it."

"Do you see Cliff from time to time?" I asked, again looking at the gaunt tightrope walker.

"He's been in to dine occasionally, but not for months. When he does come, I send a good bottle of wine to his table. I paid him twenty-five hundred for that piece. Really an artist of the first degree."

"My interpretation of the figure on the wire is that he's desperate but doesn't have a chance," I said.

"Very good, Walter. Man, or mankind, is desperate — also brave, at times pitiful, heroic, a coward, a survivor, weakling, giant, himself a work of art."

"It's one man I'm looking for. I thought perhaps you could help."

"Connected to one of your law squabbles? I

162

won't be drawn into any sort of litigation."

"I'm not asking that but attempting to find what's become of a youth named Jeremiah Ripley. You've heard of him?"

"Why should I have done so?"

"I was told he used to live around the area."

"You're suggesting he's of a certain persuasion?"

"I think he is or was."

"And of course that means I would know."

"Please, Philip, not you personally. Just a chance shot you could put me in touch with someone who might remember him."

"You're very sure you're not dragging me into a legal thicket?"

"You have my word."

"Good enough for me. Fact is I do know a little something about Jeremiah. He was quite a handsome, sought-after young man. Heads turned when he passed. He had beautiful blond hair and an aristocratic nose like the Prince of Wales."

"What's happened to him?"

"I have no idea. He hasn't been seen around the Slip for several years. He applied for a job at Le Gallic, was hired, yet never arrived for his training."

"Would you ask about for me?"

"I'm not to be involved?"

"I'm just after information. And what

about a man, a sailor, named Leonard Dawson?"

"There I draw a blank."

"I would greatly appreciate your help."

"I'll do what I can. Humanity, Walt, members come and go."

I didn't know whether that was another innuendo or not and drew a card from my wallet to give him.

"Jessup's Wharf," he said. "Quaint village. Are you happy there, Walter?"

"I'm doing all right, thanks."

"The roads we travel, eh? A curiosity. What do you think the good Lord had in mind when He started it all?"

"Philip, I haven't worked that out."

"Sometimes I believe it's entertainment. Celestial follies. He and the angels draw chairs to the brink of the firmament and watch the show. I'll do what I can for you."

He escorted me to the street. I looked back at waiters moving among tables and setting napkins they shaped like a pope's miniature white miter. Again Philip shook my hand.

I walked into the world, my mind still relaying the vision of the naked man on the tightrope, his palm burning and the destruction that waited beneath.

NINETEEN

Since I was in the city, I walked from Shockoe Slip up to East Main and past Richmond's contradictory mixture of antiquated iron storefronts and contemporary steel-and-concrete towers of the banking and financial district. At Bunker, Rose & Diggs I found Josey leaned back in her chair, her hands joined behind her head, a posture that lifted her breasts beneath her yellow knit sweater. She looked, well, victorious.

"What's happening, Raff?" she asked and cocked an unshod, nylon-encased, beautifully arched foot on an opened lower drawer of her desk. A black leather pump lay toppled on the mouse-gray carpet.

"I'd like to take you to dinner."

"Can't tonight, old buddy of mine. I'm full to busting anyhow. Digesting a good day on the market. The Dow's up — a fine seventy-points-and-change meal."

"You made a killing?" I asked and sat carefully so as not to entangle my legs. I had come close to stepping on her conch shell doorstop when I entered.

165

"Oh, I made some bread this day. When you bringing me your dollars? I just happen to know of a situation I believe has tremendous potential."

"Tremendous is quite an enormous word," I said.

"Well, admittedly a bit overstated. As you know it's part of the trade. At Bunker, Rose & Diggs, we live on a diet of adjectival superlatives."

"This situation have a name?"

"No mon-ee, no tick-ee," she said and flexed her arms.

"You and the Prince Jamir still doing business?" I asked.

"None of your concern, but, yes, I receive a nice order from him now and again."

"And I assume you continue to pursue the fox and engage in other sporting events."

"Raff, let's not drop into your haughty mode. Indeed we, along with the Gaffneys, chase Reynard from time to time. We ran a red fox into the outskirts of Jessup's Wharf, and the little beastie turned at the river, where he escaped through a culvert. Buckshot, our lead hound, got stuck, and the Rescue Squad had to sledge the pipe to save him. The prince intends to pay them and the Virginia Department of Highways the cost."

"You ever going out with me again, Josey?"

"Old buddy, you're my lifelong friend. Of course I'll go out with you but not to bed. It would be an unnecessary complication to both our lives."

"I'm all for complication."

"You're sweet, I love you, and wish it had worked out for us, but it's not to be."

"I may go home and shoot myself," I said as I stood.

"Wait, I can make you some money. It's pretty nearly a sure thing."

"Put me down for five thousand," I said.

"Five's the best you can do?" she asked and made a wry face.

"Well, ten."

"Afraid this investment trust has a twenty-five-thousand entry."

"Too steep for me at the moment," I said and thought if Charles LeBlanc had not been spending his insurance money so freely I could have made the investment for him.

"Alas," she said, dropped her arms before standing, and fitted her foot into the fallen pump. "Kiss my cheek."

"I would prefer other regions but can't refuse even such a meager portion," I said and brushed her cheek while at the same time inhaling the full womanly scent of her to carry along with me.

I was back in Jessup's Wharf and my office

by three. Mary Ellen had left a note which read: "No calls." She had left early to take Jason to a female Richmond orthodontist. Rain pelted the window. I had neglected to bring my umbrella from the car.

I'd not eaten lunch and considered crossing to the Dew Drop for a bowl of hot vegetable soup before settling to work. As I stood and reached for my hat, Cliff called.

"They're holding me under arrest," he said.

"Who's holding you?"

"The police in the city's Detention Section. Two detectives were waiting at the carriage house."

"I'm coming," I said, thinking District Attorney Tuggle had jumped the gun. I bundled up and drove through rain to Richmond's modern John Marshall Courts Building on Ninth Street, where I explained to the receptionist that I represented Cliff and wanted to see the charge listed on his arrest warrant. She had dark eyelashes so long they resembled antennae and told me Gerald Horner, the commonwealth's attorney, had gone for the day.

"But I believe I can line you up with Mr. DeVan, his assistant," she said. She too was ready to leave.

I sat on a leather chair waiting to see Mr. DeVan. Except for a large, decorative Virginia state seal on the wall, the carpeted anteroom could have belonged to a dentist and lacked only outdated magazines and elevator music, yet from this place the process began that sent men to prison and occasionally death.

Mr. DeVan — black, intense, and harried — asked me into his small, first-floor office that had semitransparent gauzelike drapes over the lower half of the ceiling-to-floor window, its glass tinted a pale green.

"Give me a minute to find what's transpiring," he said as he sat at his computer keyboard.

I waited. People walking past on the street appeared like apparitions moving through an aqueous world. I wanted a cigarette.

"We received an extradition warrant delivered by fax, the demanding state West Virginia, specifically Seneca County," Mr. DeVan said as he turned from the monitor. "The charge is voluntary manslaughter."

I stared unbelieving. Not involuntary but voluntary, its definition a felonious taking of life without premeditation, conspiracy, or malice. The cause was typically great provocation. What could they know in Seneca County that I didn't?

"How do I arrange bail?" I asked.

"Bail's denied at this time by our magistrate since Mr. Dickens is a fugitive from another state."

"He's no fugitive. He hasn't fled this jurisdiction."

"He was arrested on a fugitive warrant, so in terms of the law he is. Moreover Seneca County requests that bail not be granted."

"That is not Seneca County's or West Virginia's province."

"Agreed, it's not binding, but the magistrate in that jurisdiction can request whatever he wishes."

"When's the hearing?"

"Nine in the morning, General District Court. The Commonwealth's practice is to bring a fugitive before a judge as quickly as possible to inform him of his rights. We do it for other states, they for us. At the hearing a detective will be present with a prepared waiver of extraditon in the event your client chooses to execute it."

"Might Mr. Dickens surrender himself to Seneca County voluntarily?"

"That can't be decided by this office or at this juncture in the process."

"I want to see him."

"I'll call over to the lockup," he said, lifted his phone, and spoke into it, his chair swiveled away from me. Droplets of rain streaking the window had a greenish hue. He again faced me. "They know you're coming."

"May I use your *Michie's Jurisprudence* a

170

moment?" I asked, eyeing the law books on his shelves.

"Be my guest."

I stood, looked up the penalty for voluntary manslaughter in West Virginia, and thanked Mr. DeVan. The city lockup was across Ninth Street in the same Department of Public Safety building where I had talked to Detective Bush. Rain splashed in puddles, and I hunched under my umbrella tilted against a wind that flapped patrolmen's yellow slickers.

I knew that Richmond's Sheriff's Department operated the Detention Section and took the escalator down to the lower level, where I showed my identification to a desk officer. He turned me over to a deputy who led me through a corridor at the end of which we passed through two electronically operated steel doors of a sally port, the second one opening onto the lockup. Prisoners wearing either tan or orange coveralls stood in line under guard waiting their turns to arrange bail before a magistrate who sat behind what reminded me of a movie theater's ticket window except if those under arrest had the money, their admission costs would provide them tickets out rather than entrance in.

Everything in this lower level was painted the same dingy beige — the brick-and-mortar walls, the floors, the bars of the holding cell that the deputy showed me to. A fluorescent light buzzed, the tube protected by a ceiling cavity. Cliff waited, his clothes disheveled, his long hair in need of a comb.

"I thought you'd never reach here," he said, wiping at his hair. "They've fingerprinted, photographed, and strip-searched me. Look at the bunk." He pointed. "It's steel and has no mattress. Am I supposed to sleep on that? They told me they don't allow prisoners to have anything they can set fire to. They've emptied my pockets. Where would I find a match to start a fire? It's inhuman, Walter. Spring me from this loathsome place."

"Easy, Cliff," I said and touched the back of his hand that gripped a bar. "We'll get it worked out."

"Don't I have rights?" he asked and looked about him, his expression agitated and frightened. "What are they accusing me of?"

"Essentially that you provoked Wendell or he you, causing tempers to flare and a resulting death."

"I wasn't provoked into hot temper. I acted to save my life."

"The charge indicates their belief they have proof of a dispute or conflict between you and Wendell."

"That's insane."

"My guess is the sheriff suspects your past

relationship with Jeremiah is the basis for the warrant."

"There was no relationship. I had him in class and signed his magazine. Nothing more."

"Still it's a connection from which a relationship might be inferred."

"They must be desperate to pursue that reasoning. Christ, you smell the fear in this place? It's in the walls. There's no other stink like it. Help me, Walter."

"I intend to, but we'll have to wait for the hearing in the morning. Extradition's been requested by Seneca County. Nothing can be done until that's decided."

"Walter, this thing's gotten grossly out of hand. Make Drake do something."

"Do what?"

"He can come testify for me," he said and ran fingers through his hair.

"I'll call him soon as I leave here."

"What happens in High Gap if I go back and am convicted?"

"In West Virginia voluntary manslaughter is punishable by confinement in the penitentiary for not less than one or more than five years."

"You hear what you're telling me? They're ruining my life."

"Do you want another lawyer? I can recommend good ones but none that can get you out before the hearing."

"It's not you." He stepped away from the bars and then back. "I mean you do realize I am actually here in a jail and facing prison?"

"I realize it. You want to tell what else happened up on Blind Sheep between you and Wendell?"

"Nothing else happened."

"Sheriff Sawyers has apparently convinced Seneca County's district attorney that you're lying."

"Get Drake over here."

"What will he do for you I can't?"

"I need to talk to him."

"Why would you want to talk to him and not me?"

"Just please do it, Walter, and don't ask questions."

I started to refuse, but even if he were keeping the full truth from me, a meeting between the two of them should bring it all out, and I could assess the situation from that point forward.

"Okay, Cliff. I will seek him out."

TWENTY

I left Cliff looking miserable, frantic, and lost under the harsh, unforgiving cellblock light. Back through the sally port I used the pay phone in the corridor to phone Drake at Grizzly's. Boomer said Drake had gone to a Lions Club meeting in Petersburg to give his grouse talk.

I drove through the dark to Jessup's Wharf and Miss Mabel's. As I hung up my overcoat, she tapped on the door that separated her side of the house from the section I rented. She often did so at odd hours. Though I'd been living with her some three years, I'd never been in her quarters. She was a spinster, a protector of the old bygone ways and manners I considered better than those of my own generation. She apparently believed it would not appear proper for her to have the company of a single man in her parlor without another lady being present. Often her small mouth rounded as if awaiting a kiss, yet at the same time she had the look of a graying, erect women who for many years had faced into a stiff wind.

She remained concerned about my health, telling me I looked pale and puny. Often she brought me oatmeal, fried liver, greens, grits, beaten biscuits, and slices of rare beef. "You should eat more meat," she instructed me. "Don't listen to the voguish nonsense on TV about calories and fat. For women yes, perhaps, but all the great men of this nation were meat eaters."

As she stood at our joint doorway she would also try to peer around me. I believed she suspected I kept liquor and was attempting to sniff out where I hid my Old Crow and George Dickel. So far I'd been able to foil her. If she sneaked into my apartment to look while I was away at work, I'd never found evidence of it. Actually I believed her too honorable to commit such a deceitful act.

"You'll catch your death running around in this weather without your overshoes," she said and offered me a plate of fried pork, snap beans, applesauce, and a glass of milk. I thanked her, and again she tried to look over my shoulder before pulling the door shut and locking it.

I ate, had my bath, and as I buttoned on my pajamas found among the covers I'd left tossed that morning the library copy of *Moby Dick* that I had been reading. As usual I lifted the color photograph of Josey in her slick

176

black bathing suit posed to dive off the three-meter board, one knee raised, her arms leveled before her, drops of water glistening on her skin. Cliff had snapped and enlarged the picture for me.

I gave myself to the bed, reviewed events, and sank into sleep trying to decide my next move in Cliff's behalf. At seven minutes before midnight my phone rang, and I flung covers aside to reach it. I recognized Charles LeBlanc's voice, but didn't complain about the hour. The time was earlier in Chinook, Montana, and he was a person I greatly admired, a former felon and outcast who had the aspect of a rawboned man that had endured long suffering and become stoically ennobled by it.

"How much in my bank account?" he asked, no opening pleasantries, his voice sure of the words, no trimmings. Music thumped in the background — a twanging guitar, fiddle, and whacking banjo.

"You're taking it down fast," I told him. As of now he had only what remained of his insurance money. "According to the last statement from the King County Bank, you've reduced your balance to some thirty-seven thousand dollars."

"What about the half million?"

"Your first payment's in escrow until the

prince exercises the lease-option agreement and it becomes a seven-year amortized loan. According to your brother Edward, that should be by February fifteenth at the latest."

"I'm fixing to buy a ranch, and I'll want the money."

"I'll notify you as soon as it's available, and I strongly recommend you put aside ten percent of all income you receive in a retirement account."

"Not yet, Walt. I been needing a touch of the high life. Bought another Cadillac car, a remuda of cutting horses, and a diamond ring."

"Charles, I can't see you wearing a diamond ring."

"Not for me, Walt."

I waited for him to tell me about the woman, but he didn't.

"You're still at the Buckskin Motel?" I asked.

"Till I get the ranch."

"Charles, you were a hunter. You ever shoot grouse?"

"No grouse — partridges, duck, geese, turkey, and deer. You thinking of doing some gunning?"

"No, but I'd like to pass something by you, get your opinion, if that's okay."

"You got to be pretty hard up for advice to

178

consult me if that's what you're doing."

I told him in detail about the Blind Sheep hunt, Wendell's death, and Cliff's story of what had happened.

"How does it all strike you?" I asked when I finished.

"Don't see how the man could've been shot in his chest if he lunged past the shooter. My thinking is one big thing's missing and somebody has to be lying — maybe two or three lies going 'round at the same time."

"My thinking too. Charles, I wish you were here."

"That it, Walt?"

I told him it was.

"Send me another couple of checkbooks," he said and hung up.

TWENTY-ONE

At six-thirty my alarm clock woke me. The rain had stopped, but wind ruffled water in Miss Mabel's birdbath lit by a streak through the window from my ceiling light. I drank a cup of hot tea, smoked, and waited until seven before phoning Drake's house. He answered, and I told him the police had Cliff locked up.

"He wants to see you," I said.

"I heard," Drake said. "I got a collect call from him not twenty minutes ago."

"Tell me what's going on between you two."

"Don't get your drift, Raff."

"When I saw Cliff yesterday, he was extremely anxious to speak to you."

"We've talked on the phone. I just hung up. No big secrets. I told him to tough it out."

"Why is it I'm not convinced that's all there is?"

"Look, we're the Marauders, *nunquam trado*, never betray, aren't we?"

"I don't like it."

"Just cool it, Raff. Make them prove the

charge, isn't that an attorney's job? Maybe we can turn this whole thing around during the hearing. I'll be there."

At eight-fifteen I entered police headquarters and waited in the corridor for a deputy to bring Cliff out. As the sally port door opened, a voice from back in the lockup called, "One day the lawyers gonna be in here and us out there."

"Give me a minute with him?" I asked the pug-nosed deputy whose plastic name tag read *Leo.*

"Maybe two," he said and stood by.

"I need a shower, a shave, and clean clothes," Cliff said. He was pale and red-eyed, his face stubbled by a sandy beard. They had fastened no cuffs or restraints on him. "Will this take long?" he asked.

"I don't know but straighten up and get hold of yourself. Body language counts.".

"I feel I have bugs crawling on me," he said. He tightened his belt and smoothed down his sweater.

"We fumigate the bugs," Leo said. "Time to move."

I followed while he escorted Cliff on the escalator up to the General District Court. Again I was reminded of theater because the seats were fold-up red plush, had armrests, and faced the lofty judge's bench front and center, which in its way was a stage flanked by flags of the United States and Virginia. They formed a proscenium arch topped by the state seal depicting the foot of Justice on the prostrate neck of Tyranny. Let, I thought, the show begin.

Leo seated Cliff between us on the front row. A housefly that had survived the winter in the courtroom was revived by the warmth and buzzed around a ceiling light. A brisk young brunette walked in and sat in the clerk's box beside the bench. She held a bundle of warrants bound by a thick, brown rubber band. She checked and adjusted the tape machine before flipping through the warrants as one might a deck of cards.

Next Drake appeared carrying his overcoat and hat. He reached out to shake Cliff's hand.

"Don't touch him," Leo said, causing Drake to step back.

"It'll work out," he said to Cliff, who was staring at him.

A dark-suited man carrying a document folder introduced himself as Detective Norman Hale. He had a deeply furrowed forehead and the drained, soulless eyes of men who had seen too much war, combat, and death.

"You and your client made a decision

about extradition?" he asked me.

I told him no.

"I have the papers if you decide to waive," he said and moved away from us to sit and open the folder, which he centered on his lap.

"All rise," a bailiff called. "Judge Augustus P. Oliver, presiding."

The portly judge's black judicial robe swept behind him as he made his entrance. More theater, I thought.

"All right, what do we have here?" he asked, settling himself in the high-back regal chair. He adjusted his bifocals. The clerk switched on the recorder and arranged warrants before him. The judge studied them and handed the first to the bailiff. People entering the courtroom seated themselves in rows behind us.

"Clifford Arehart Dickens," the bailiff called.

Cliff and I stood and walked through the bar to stand at the defense table. Detective Hale crossed through to the prosecution's side.

"You're Mr. Dickens?" the judge asked. The fly buzzed around him, and he slapped at it.

"I am, Your Honor," Cliff answered.

"I have before me an arrest warrant issued in response to an extradition demand from the state of West Virginia asking for your return to face a charge of voluntary manslaughter." He focused on me. "Who are you?"

"Walter B. Frampton, sir, representing Mr. Dickens."

"All right, let's get through this. Mr. Dickens, the purpose of this proceeding is to explain to you your rights. First of all you have a right to counsel, which I see you have retained.

"Secondly the State of West Virginia has requested this Commonwealth to extradite you back to that jurisdiction to undergo judicial process. Now let me tell you about extradition. Its implementation is not determined by this court's weighing of evidence but solely upon the fact that you are charged with a crime in another state. Therefore, any attack on these proceedings based on the claimed innocence of the accused, which is you, is immaterial. We are not having a trial here. Follow me?"

"Yes, sir," Cliff said.

"Now, you can waive extradition. If you do so, the waiver and consent are executed before me, after which a copy is sent to the governor and the accused is held for delivery to authorized agents of the demanding state. We in effect turn you over to the West Virginia authorities. Their people have ten days to take you into custody. It is that simple and results in a more expeditious resolution of all accusations against you whether you are innocent or guilty."

He again slapped at the fly.

"Or you can defend yourself against being extradited. You have the right to counsel, the right to the issuance and service of a governor's warrant of extradition, and the right to seek habeas corpus to test the legality of your arrest. If the above rights are exercised, the court shall rebail or recommit you.

"I must call to your attention, however, that extradition proceedings can involve an extended period of detention. The accused may be kept in jail thirty days, but in the event the governor's warrant of extradition does not arrive within that time limit, the judge may recommit the accused for an additional sixty days during which period you will be incarcerated in the city jail to guard against your fleeing either state. Got me?"

"Your Honor," I said.

"Mr. Frampton, why do I expect to hear from you a little song and dance?"

"Your Honor, Mr. Dickens was on a grouse hunting trip among friends. He accidentally shot and killed a companion. The proper charge, if any, would be involuntary manslaughter. I believe the warrant is incorrectly drawn."

"You're telling me it was a misadventure?"

"There was no provocation, no *furor brevis*, simply an unfortunate action on the part of the deceased, who moved impulsively in front of Mr. Dickens's gun in an effort to get a shot at a grouse."

"Apparently Seneca County, West Virginia, disagrees. No bad blood between you and the deceased, Mr. Dickens? No past history of dispute or controversy on the day of the homicide?"

"None, sir."

"But you did shoot him?"

"I didn't mean to, sir."

"Still the fact is you held the gun, pulled the trigger, and he died in Seneca County, West Virginia. Probable cause in and of itself."

"Your Honor," Drake said and stood. "My name's Wingo and it was my grouse hunt. I can testify to the shooting being just an accident, no bad feelings involved."

"You the man who wrote the pamphlet getting all the attention?"

"Yes, sir."

"I've read it. Inspiring piece of work. And you are telling me what?"

"Mr. Dickens and the deceased didn't even know each other till the day of the hunt. The shooting was just ordinary human error."

"You were present the moment it happened?"

"Not the exact moment."

"It's the exact moment that counts, and death is never ordinary. Some word or misunderstanding could have ignited provocation, perhaps whose gun brought down a bird, an inflammatory remark, politics, a woman."

"Sir, there was no bad feeling between them."

"Bad feeling can spring up in an instant from a multitude of causes, Mr. Wingo. But even if that were not the case, as I said earlier, an extradition hearing does not weigh evidence or judge innocence or guilt. The only question is whether or not you, Mr. Dickens, will waive the proceedings."

"Your Honor," I said, "would you consider a stay of a week to give Mr. Dickens time to put his affairs in order?"

"I would not, Mr. Frampton. A life has been lost, and we must allow for some inconvenience."

"Will Your Honor grant a recess to allow me to talk to my client?"

"Ten minutes, Mr. Frampton. No more. Deputy, you will remain with Mr. Dickens and his counsel during their consultation."

The judge stood and left through a door

187

which opened behind the bench. The clerk switched off the recorder as Detective Hale stood to chat with the bailiff. People in their seats whispered, yawned, stood to stretch.

"You all talk," Leo said. "I'll stand by but won't listen." To Drake, "Remember, no touching or exchange of anything."

He backed off, folded his arms, and spread his legs to balance himself comfortably — a man used to waiting.

"Ninety days?" Cliff asked, his voice lowered. "They can keep me locked up for ninety days and then send me to West Virginia and put me in a cell all over again if we don't waive?"

"It's how the law reads," I said.

"What are the odds he'll have to go back if he fights it?" Drake asked.

"A near certainty. Extradition is chiefly a time-taking formality during which the governors treat each other politely and rarely refuse one another's petitions."

"What do I do?" Cliff asked. He was looking at Drake, not me, when he asked the question.

"You talking to him or me?" I asked.

"Will he be able to get bail up there?" Drake asked.

"Only a slim chance since he's not a resident and could become a fugitive."

"I can't believe this is happening," Cliff said.

"You can be acquitted," Drake said. "Mountain people are used to hunting accidents. They'll understand."

"My chances?" Cliff asked me.

"Without a bill of particulars I can't predict."

"How can they prove provocation?" Drake asked. "They're bluffing."

"I don't know," I said. "Maybe something Sheriff Sawyers dug up. Without it they'd need to reduce the charges to involuntary manslaughter, a misdemeanor there, but still open to jail time, though rarely invoked. Either of you have anything else to tell me?"

Again Drake and Cliff faced each other.

"I'm waiting," I said.

"If my back's to the wall, can't I tell the Seneca County district attorney what really happened on Blind Sheep and plead self-defense?" Cliff asked.

"It's doubtful you could prevail without a witness," I said.

"Drake?" Cliff said.

"Your call," Drake said. "I'd go back, take my chances, get it over one way or another. We'll stick by you."

"I'm not licensed to practice in West Virginia and would need to find an associate there," I said.

"But you'll go?" Cliff asked.

"I'll go."

"Bring me a change of clothes. They emptied my pockets, and you have to get the key from the lockup's property clerk."

"And?" I asked.

"We'll waive," Cliff said.

TWENTY-TWO

"Let the record show that Clifford Arehart Dickens has responded affirmatively," Judge Oliver ordered as he rapped his gavel. Detective Hale allowed me to look over the waiver of extradition before it was signed in triplicate by Cliff and the judge.

"Just like that," Cliff said and raised his hands to look at the steel cuffs Leo had fastened on him. "Incredible what a few words before a judge can do to a man's life."

"I'll bring you clothes," I said.

"This will work out, old friend," Drake said. He hugged Cliff and patted his back. "Just believe it."

"Let's go, fellow," Leo said and held Cliff's left elbow to return him to the lockup. I followed down on the escalator to get his keys from the property clerk. I watched the sally port's door close behind Cliff.

The deputy clerk had me sign a release. I drove to the carriage house and switched on lights in Cliff's bedroom, which had once been a hayloft. The windows on both gabled ends were Gothic-shaped — one offering a dismal view to the wet narrow street where a trash can had been overturned, the other to an elm from whose scaly limb a child's swing dangled and swung, prodded by the wind.

I opened his bureau for shirts and underwear, drew slacks and a jacket from his louvered closet, and stuffed socks into a pair of loafers. I glanced at the cluttered cove he used as a darkroom, then turned back to examine a photograph hanging from a drying clip of a dark-skinned girl with bare shoulders and frizzy black hair. His Baltimore girlfriend and perhaps a black herself? Just like Cliff to go against all conventions. A reporter had written that if you threw Cliff in the James River, he would float upstream.

"He won't be able to use them out Fairfield Way," the deputy at the lockup told me as he inspected the clothes. Fairfield Way was the city jail's location. "All inmates required to wear prison garb, but I'll see these get tagged through to West Virginia."

I talked to Cliff in the same holding cell of the Detention Section.

"How long before they come for me?" he asked.

"As the judge explained, they have ten days."

"Just don't leave me hanging."

"I'll check daily. Anything else you would like to tell me?"

"No, and I guess for a while I'll be catching up on my reading."

"I can bring you books."

"*War and Peace*," he said. "I never got around to finishing *War and Peace*."

I left recollecting Drake's embrace of him. Cliff had stood passively and allowed it. Like a tape my mind rewound to the day of the hunt when we returned to Richmond, and the frame stilled at the memory of Cliff's shoulder sliding out from beneath Drake's hand and the private look that had passed between them. Somehow I had to break into the confidence they shared and were withholding from me.

Using a public phone, I first tried to reach Drake at Grizzly's, then his house. Deborah told me he had left town.

"It's his book," she said. "He's talking to a publisher."

I asked her to have him call me soon as he returned.

"I'll do that, but you've been neglecting us. The portrait I had painted of Drake is back. Promise you'll come see it and have a drink — and I mean soon."

I promised, drove to Jessup's Wharf, and worked at my desk reviewing the homicide laws, a generic term that covered manslaughter and murder. Luckily the West Virginia and Virginia codes aligned because they had formerly been one and the same state.

I also used the *Attorney Directory* to look up names of lawyers in High Gap and found seven listed. Hiring one as an associate would mean more expense for Cliff, or me if I had to pick up the tab.

At five Mary Ellen readied herself to go home. She drew on her coat and hat as well as zipped up Jason's jacket.

"You like Brunswick stew?" she asked at the door. "We have a plenty if you'd like to break bread with us."

"I'd better stick around here awhile longer," I said.

"We'll hold dinner for you."

"Don't do that but thanks. I need to be alone with my thoughts."

She left, Jason beside her, his book bag strapped over his slender shoulders. I wondered whether Mary Ellen was just being gracious or trying to move us onto a more personal footing. Already darkness had settled like a veil along River Street. I stayed at my desk till seven-thirty, ate beef Wellington at the Dew Drop, and in case Cliff called, walked back to my office to check the answering machine before driving to my apartment. The red light blinked. The message was not from Cliff but Philip Garrow. I dialed him at Le Gallic.

"You might try around Grizzly's," he said.

"Try what?"

"An acquaintance informs me Jerry Ripley had what might best be termed a special friendship with somebody in the vicinity of that bizarre gun store."

"Philip, give me a name."

"I wasn't able to close on that. My source claims that he heard Jerry while in his cups allude to it."

"What does vicinity mean?"

"I really have no idea."

"Anything else?"

"Nothing substantial but still delving into the matter."

"I need to know bad."

"Bad can be used as an adverb," he said, "but I prefer badly, which has a more harmonious tonality."

TWENTY-THREE

Who in the vicinity of Grizzly's and did "vicinity" define just the store itself or a wider range? I thought of Boomer. Despite what he had told me about his casual association with Jeremiah, they could have been lovers.

First thing in the morning I headed for Powhatan County. The early sun caused frost on Grizzly's roof to steam as it thawed. The spotlighted grouse mobile at the center of the store gave off its white gleam as I walked to the entrance to find the doors locked. I peered through glass to see clerks wearing their blaze-orange vests moving about organizing wares. Boomer stood at a cash register, noticed, and allowed me to enter.

"You early, Mr. Frampton," he said. "Drake's not here yet."

His football linesman build had given way to pliant shoulders, but his bulk still suggested inherent power. I asked when Drake was expected.

"This morning sometime," Boomer answered as he closed the cash register's drawer by pressing his stomach against it.

"No matter. The fact is I came to talk to you further about Jeremiah Ripley."

"Sure, old Jerry." He leaned against the counter.

"You told me you two worked together," I said and watched for a reaction of consternation or evasion.

"Not with him. He was in shoes. I sold mostly football and baseball stuff, other gear in season."

"But you were close?"

"Just here at the store, the way everybody is."

"You didn't consider him a special friend?"

"We spoke and helped each other out during rush times, sometimes ate lunch together. That's about it."

"How did Jerry get along with the other clerks?"

"We all got along good. Anybody that doesn't fit the team is out at Grizzly's. Drake sees to that."

"Was Jerry particularly drawn to any particular one of them?"

"Nope, not that I remember. Friendly and all, but stuck to himself, though not standoffish. A nice kid."

"You know anything about his life outside the store, for example, in the immediate vicinity?"

"Not much immediate vicinity 'round here and never talked with him about himself. His running and stocking of the shoe department was a classy act. We got a good man now, Eddy Turner over there, but Jerry was hard to replace. He talked Drake into starting the department and built it into a profit maker. Designed the display shelves and lighting. Drake didn't want to go along with the idea at first, couldn't see money in shoes."

"It was Jerry who convinced Drake?"

"Sure and it was Jerry who came up with the idea of hanging the ghost grouse, making it the store's emblem," Boomer said and glanced at the mobile. "Drake paid him a bonus."

I remembered my conversation with Drake and his telling me that Jeremiah had been no more than ordinary help, certainly nothing special. Drake had also taken credit for the shoe department and the ghost grouse. That was unlike him. He was not small minded or given to envy.

"Are you able to remember anything you haven't told me about Jerry?" I asked.

"Like I said, his father used to come around looking, but nobody seen Jerry after he quit us here. Hey, there's Drake now."

Drake crossed the parking lot and entered the store. He must have come straight from the airport, for he carried an attaché case and could have passed as a downtown attorney.

"Raff, something happening?" he asked. "Come on along."

I followed him through the store to his office. He laid his attaché case on the desk, removed his hat and gloves, and began flipping through mail as he unbuttoned his overcoat.

"I'm assuming you're here to talk about Cliff and how we can best help him," Drake said. "Listen, my checkbook's open. Spend anything you need."

"I wish this were just about money," I said.

"If not, what?"

"You and Cliff leaving me out of the loop."

"Who's got a loop? Grizzly's can sell you a lasso. Sit and rest your bones."

"Something's going on between you two that you're keeping from me."

"Raff, nothing you need to know."

"I insist on knowing."

"All right," Drake said as he tossed his overcoat to the camp cot. "It is the money situation. Cliff doesn't like people learning about his financial problems, but for the last year he's been one hop ahead of the bill collectors. I been assuring him I won't let him sink no matter the cost."

"That's generous of you."

"He'd do the same for me or you if he had

it," Drake said, again at the mail. "Now, I continue to believe this whole situation is overblown. At the worst Cliff will get off with probation and a fine."

"I don't like the feel of it."

"I don't either, but if we stand by him, everything will come out right. Have a little faith. When's Cliff leaving?"

"As soon as the West Virginia authorities send deputies to take him back. They work in pairs."

"Nothing more we can do at the moment?"

"No," I said, unbuttoning my own coat as I sat.

"Okay, we're on instant standby to help him. Now I'll tell you the good news. I got a publisher for 'Truth of the Grouse.' " He patted the attaché case. "Been negotiating since November. It'll be a hardback edition with illustrations, an advertising budget, a book tour."

"I'm happy for you, Drake."

"Things are definitely breaking my way. I hate to be feeling so good when Cliff's having troubles. But it'll be okay if he just stands tall, which I keep advising him. Anything else on your mind?"

"I'm still trying to track Jeremiah Ripley, who his friends were, what finally happened to him."

"In his grave," Drake said and sorted through envelopes.

"Where's that grave?"

"On that I got no idea. Lots of ground to lie under in this old world."

"You worked close with him. Can you think of any way that might help me find out for sure?"

"I worked close with him?"

"Helped him start his shoe department and spotlight the grouse."

"Hold it, he was helping me, not me helping him."

"Those weren't his ideas?"

"Hell no, I planted them, made suggestions, allowed him to ride shotgun. He was proud of his work, bragged about it, but they were my concepts. He didn't know a grouse from a turkey buzzard."

"But you paid him a bonus."

"Sure, him and others earned overtime working nights. I didn't want to interrupt business while installing a new department. We had to reorganize floor space."

"You're not able to add anything that would help me discover specifically what happened to him?"

"Raff, we going in circles here. I've told you all I can. I never got into Jeremiah's personal life while he was my employee. He could sell shoes, a high markup item and very profitable to Grizzly's. I have no idea why he left and didn't collect his last week's pay. You know as much as I do about the rest. Anything else?"

"No," I said and again congratulated him on his success with the book before I walked from the store.

TWENTY-FOUR

I drove off reviewing the contradictions between what Boomer and Drake had told me about Jeremiah. Boomer was a man I hardly knew, and there was no way I could trust his word more than my friend Drake's, whose nature was direct and devoid of deception. We were Marauders and had joined our blood.

I wanted to pick up my portrait of Marse Robert reframed for me by Phoebe Laratta, a second-generation Lebanese, dark of eye, her skin olive, her straight black hair hanging long and low over a back often bared.

A reckless child of the sixties, she had carried all that wanton baggage with her until she finally crashed and the police found her wandering at night naked and sobbing on Church Hill during an Easter snowstorm. First committed for treatment and rehabilitation by the court, after her release she survived day to day. A number of years ago, prior to Phoebe's fall, and before Drake met Deborah, he had lived with Phoebe until they fell out and he was replaced by a series of other men. Her slinky body and libertine ways drew them.

She now worked for Très Chic, a downtown store, as an illustrator and window decorator, yet had always considered herself a serious artist, her studio and home a narrow ivy-covered house that provided a view to the red-brick American Tobacco factory, its lettered "Lucky Strike" smokestack, and a ravaged flow of the James.

I stopped at an Amoco station, bought gas, and phoned first the store, then her house. We had come to know each other during her days with Drake when I attended one of the bohemian parties that took place among an ambience of guitars, drink, and pot, plus clutches in a shadowed hallway. She had allowed her blouse to slip and reveal a breast, her nipple's aureole the color of Burgundy wine.

"Bring your checkbook," she said.

I drove up the hill and parked beside a honeysuckle tangled fence of broken iron pickets around a small, neglected yard. To a porch post Phoebe had tacked a black palette, her street number painted on it in blue letters. The door had an oval glass panel that rattled loosely when I knocked. She opened it and kissed me full on my mouth. It meant nothing. In her late forties, her slanted eyes often seemed to be sighting objects far distant beyond where she stood.

"Come with me before you freeze your vitals," she said and drew me into the house. The paint-splotched denim shirt over a black leotard reached almost to her knees. Her worn and mottled face was a startling contrast with her still-shapely body of a much younger woman.

"I expected you to be at the store," I said.

"I've taken leave. Weary of lingerie displays and repairing mannequins, and I've been given a promise of an exhibition down in the Bottom."

What had been the parlor she had transformed into her studio. A bay window let in a northern light, and tables and shelves held tubes of paints, brushes, tools of the craft. Several easels stood about, all empty except one that held an oil of what appeared to be two glittering red eyes peering up from a darkened pit.

"Hell?" I asked.

"Daily life," she said. "Want a drink? I have Lebanese wine and a slab of goat cheese."

Canvases placed around represented mostly conventional and commercial scenes, evidence that she needed money — a willow-draped pond, a fading sunset, kerchiefed black women selling daffodils, Laurel Street's Sacred Heart Cathedral under a misting rain.

The sad fact was her true talent and curse lay in producing conventional art.

I told her no, and she sat me on a ratty green divan to wait while she brought and displayed General Lee bordered by a two-inch beveled Confederate-gray frame.

"Exactly what I wanted," I said, honestly pleased.

"One hundred fifty dollars," she said and began taping brown wrapping paper around the portrait. "Tax included."

I wrote a check knowing no tax would ever be paid. She slipped the check under an Aztec ceramic jug on her mantel before coming to sit by me, sighing, and drawing away her hair in a distracted fashion. A strand fell back aslant her cheek. She smelled of turpentine.

"You used to be afraid of me," she said. "That the reason you stopped coming around?"

"No, with you I could have become desperately overwrought and lost my bearings."

"You believed I would devour you?"

"The problem was I hoped you would."

"Liar. You were shocked and very much disapproved."

"I was also envious of Drake," I said, though not the whole truth. I had been aroused by her but knew better than to return.

"You fled me." Again she drew at her hair, her face saddening. "And Drake too. Raff, I finally figured what love's all about. It's a brew God supplies to drive us mad."

Her eyes became unfocused, seeing or not seeing what?

"Well, I'll go," I said.

"No you won't," she said, rousing. "Not without telling me about him. You can skip the part about his being married to a rich bitch who's a member of the DAR."

"Drake's doing fine."

"Of course he's fine. You've seen him recently?"

"Little more than an hour ago."

"My bold, hot-blooded lover who now flourishes not only in the realm of commerce but is also becoming a celebrity."

"His grouse book's going to be published."

"Will it have illustrations?"

"I believe so."

"Raff, do me the favor of suggesting to him I'm available for the job."

"Of course, Phoebe."

"The sonofabitch," she said. "Everything was always his show. I gave him all the loving a man could ask for, anything he wanted. I lived for Drake. For once during my life I thought more of someone else than myself. I did until I found he couldn't keep his prick just for me."

"I don't think I want to hear this," I said.

"You will anyway. I became suspicous when his heat slackened suddenly, and he spent more time at the store. I became convinced when I put on some rather fancy shows for him, garter belt, fishnet stockings, a silk chemise, the works, and his response was less than rapturous. I put the question to him. He told me it was the pressure of business."

Her fingering back of her hair was like the drawing aside of a curtain from her oval face.

"I took pressure under consideration. I also thought maybe my hygiene wasn't as sweet as it should be. I devoted myself to appearing alluring. He was somewhat less inflamed than the moment called for."

A phone on her worktable rang, the old-fashioned sort that had a rotary dial. She stood and crossed to it. The floppy heels of her mules slapped the floor.

"Later," she said and dropped the phone back to its cradle. She crossed her arms and began slowly circling a worktable on which lay soiled rags and a paint-encrusted putty knife. "I shadowed him on nights when he called to tell me he had to work late. I drove out and parked not in Grizzly's lot but across the highway on the shoulder of a secondary intersecting road. I used his army binoculars to watch the store's entrance and that damned spotlighted grouse. No lie, he was working late. I'd beat him home and be waiting when he walked in the door."

Again the phone rang. She ignored it.

"I believed he was exhausted from running the store till the October night he drove away early and got ahead of me. I nearly panicked he'd reach the house before I did. I planned to tell him I'd gone out for cigarettes. But he didn't take the home route, and as I followed he crossed the river south of the city to the Shady Spring Motel, a place that had seen better times, its neon sign missing an O. There he met her."

"Met whom?"

"No one I knew. She had already parked. It was windy, and there'd been a quick cold shower. He registered and got the key. She was a cheap, trashy young thing, I could see that, and her spiked heels made her ass stick out as they walked from their car to the room. He stood aside for her, followed her in, and closed the door."

Phoebe came to sit beside me.

"They stayed ninety minutes in the room. When they walked out, I snuck away and drove off. Back here in the house I helped myself to a drink, not wine, but Drake's bourbon.

" 'I know you're tired,' I said to him when he came in.

" 'Sort of,' he answered.

" 'Ain't fucking hell?' I asked.

"He just looked at me. Didn't get mad or make excuses.

" 'Yeah,' he said and climbed the steps to the bed.

"I slept that night on this divan and waited for him to come down in the morning. We drank coffee, and he told me he was sorry. I said we had a chance if he gave her up. He agreed to but didn't. I kicked his ass out. 'Couldn't help it,' he said. All the loving I was giving him, and he had to have more. He claimed it was a sickness. What shit."

"I better be going, Phoebe."

"Sure, I didn't mean to dump on you. Just can't cut Drake out of my mind. The truth is I once wondered what it would be like for you and me to make love. Where would all the arms and legs go? We might find ourselves tangled up in a knot and have to call the fire department to get untied."

She managed a one-bark laugh, we stood, and I lifted the portrait. We walked to the door, she holding to my arm.

"I'll speak to Drake about the illustrations," I said.

"Don't tell him I asked you to."

"You have my word."

"I trust you, Raff, but I don't much take words any longer. The human race would be better off if words had never been invented and all we had was the sign language. Words are more dangerous than bullets and bombs."

I had expected her to ask me about Cliff. There had been a short account of his arrest in the *Times-Dispatch*. Maybe she didn't read the papers. She opened her fingers and released me.

TWENTY-FIVE

If not Boomer, the possibility still existed that someone else at Grizzly's might have been intimate with Jeremiah. I could ask Drake for a list of people who had worked at the store during the period Jeremiah was employed there, trace and question them, though a daunting procedure that would possibly require more time and expertise than I possessed.

I also continued to be nagged by the incident of the fierce-looking herdsman at The Watchers who had waved me off their farm. He had not appeared to be the sort to belong to a pacifist, vegetarian sect that lived humbly to serve God.

I was desperate enough to drive out to Chesterfield, a calm day, the sky covered by gauzy clouds that let through a pale lemony light. Again Watchers toiled in the fields, and a tractor pulled a plow whose blade curled up rolling waves of dark moist soil.

I parked and first checked the building where they made coveralls and found rows of sewing machines waiting silent, the chairs vacant before them. I next tried the corrugated work shed where I'd first seen Brother Abram. It too was empty. I continued on to the barn and located stalls of the milking parlor bedded with fresh straw, the ammoniac odor of urine strong.

"Anybody around?" I called.

Through an unlatched open door I glimpsed Holstein cows in a pasture circling and feeding on rolled hay. I left the barn and walked toward a garage where I heard tapping and found Brother Abram sitting on a stump of wood before the wheel of a jacked-up John Deere gleaner. He dipped a dabbing stick into a can of grease and packed the bearing.

"Well, looka here," he said. "You becoming a regular visitor to our acres."

"It's a pleasure to see a well-run farm," I said. Again his sleeves were rolled above his hairy arms. His knees flanked his great belly as if they supported it.

"Making ready for spring planting," he said, and when he sneezed his breath rippled his long curly nose hairs. "Generally put in our first crops early as February if God has it on His calendar. Do something for you, Mr. Frampton?"

"I'm still attempting to find what finally happened to Jeremiah Ripley."

"Finally's a long time. Finally's forever in a

place where there is no time."

Using a rubber mallet he tapped the bearing cap in place and twisted the lid on the can of grease before using a rag to wipe his hands and heave himself to his feet.

"What about the here and now?" I asked.

"Puff and it's gone," he said. He moved around to another of the gleaner's wheels, set the stump of wood before it, and sat to remove the cap. "Leaves blown on the wind."

"Is there a chance Jeremiah could be in your cemetery here?"

"Not unless somebody snuck in after dark and buried him."

"You're suggesting that's a possibility?"

"No, sir, and if he's occupying ground, it's somewhere else. Don't let me get this grease on your overcoat."

"Brother Abram, the last time I was here a man herding cows ordered me off the property. He acted angry, though to my knowledge I'd never seen him before."

Brother Abram stopped, again sneezed, and looked up at me from his ruddy, bearded face.

"That's Brother Lucas," he said and rumbled into laughter. "He's our unofficial sin sniffer."

"Your what?"

"As a young man he used to work high steel

214

down in Norfolk town. Up eleven stories he fell off an I-beam and broke his back and most of his bones. He did a lot of talking with the Lord, and the Lord spared him and gave him a gift. Lucas can walk around a man and scent the sin on him — a smell he describes is like sulfur rising off rotted flesh."

"You don't believe that?"

"With God anything and everything's possible. Sure, why not? You think sin don't stink?"

"Did he smell it on Jeremiah?"

"Claims he did. Lucas appears scarier than he is. He's never hurt anybody and has a way with animals. You can't fool animals. They're the best judges of character."

"How well did he know Jeremiah?"

"Everybody at The Watchers knows everybody else. No secrets."

"I'd like to talk to Brother Lucas."

"All right, Mr. Frampton," Brother Abram said, set the dabbing stick on the grease can, and strained to lift himself. "We'll do that very thing."

Legs straddled, his drooping belly pushed ahead, he moved forward and began whistling "Bringing in the Sheaves" as we crossed the road back to the barn and a stone building that adjoined it at the far end. Brother Abram opened a door onto a room that had a concrete floor. A small man stood at a deep laundry sink washing a galvanized bucket with soap and a brush. Ranks of electric milking machines and a stainless-steel storage tank shone with surgical cleanliness.

"Brother Lucas, Mr. Frampton here would like a word with you," Brother Abram said.

Lucas turned to me warily. The albino's coveralls hung loosely from his leprous body, and stringy blanched hair coiled around his neck. He set the bucket and brush in the sink, stepped away, and moved slowly toward me in short, shuffling steps of a man much older than he appeared.

"Do him?" he asked, his voice surprisingly deep.

"Sure, go ahead," Brother Abram told him.

Brother Lucas's head wove side to side as he approached like a setter winding game.

"Don't you move," he commanded.

He stopped in front of me and peered out of pink aqueous eyes set so deep his colorless brows shadowed them. He leaned forward and began sniffing at me as a dog might a bush, tree, or fireplug. I resisted drawing back. He began circling slowly and continued to sniff. I looked at Brother Abram, who smiled, rocked side to side, and nodded.

Brother Lucas reversed the circle, closer

now, his nose almost touching mine as he passed. I felt his breath on my cheek, ear, the back of my neck. I smelled milk, soap, sweat, and sweet feed on him. Again he stopped in front of me, his face bony, his expression hawklike. I thought of Old Testament prophets preaching in the wilderness.

He stepped back, his eyes now hooded.

"Got me a score?" Brother Abram asked.

"Four," Brother Lucas answered.

"Four's not hopeless, in fact it's about average," Brother Abram explained. "On Brother Lucas's sin scale, the grading goes from seven, which is the highest good of man, and descends to one, the lowest. Four means you have a way to go yet to be beyond the reach of redemption."

"One is Satan," Brother Lucas said.

"Lawyer Frampton wants to ask you a question or two and would appreciate you helping him out."

Brother Lucas's eyelids raised, and he glared.

"You knew Jeremiah Ripley?" I asked.

"Started out seven," Brother Lucas said. "He'd sunk to three when he left."

"Can you tell me what happened to him after he left?"

"Three is a slippery slope and nigh a sure path to destruction."

"You believe he's been destroyed?"

"It's the road he chose."

"A road to where?"

"The bowels of Hell."

"Do you know where he might be?"

"Hell is a place," Brother Lucas said and turned away to cross back to the sink. He lifted and began washing another bucket, the water from the spigot splashing inside and causing soap suds to foam over his long, glimmering hands.

"Then you don't know?" I asked.

He didn't respond, and I looked to Brother Abram. He shook his head and gestured me toward the door. Just as we reached it, Brother Lucas spoke again.

"Jeremiah 17:9," he said.

I followed Brother Abram out, and he walked me to my car. His expression continued to be one of restrained merriment.

"You take him seriously?" I asked.

"He's often been right. Frequently those like him who seem out of step with the mass of mankind are given special talents. It's the Lord's way of compensating. Look at the amazing variety of His creatures, each a miracle of invention. God does what He wishes. He is the Master Creator and Magician."

I thanked him and drove off. At the apartment I looked up Jeremiah 17:9 in a King

James Bible Miss Mabel had left on my bed-side table. It read, "The heart is deceitful above all things and desperately wicked: who can know it?"

TWENTY-SIX

As I drove toward Richmond, I decided to detour and keep my promise to Deborah by stopping at Drake's and her Midlothian house. Despite cold and the wind that had stripped the poplars, winter jasmine grew down over the terrace, the yellow blooms' freshness startling in dappled shadows laid by the trees' limbs and trunks.

Deborah and Drake reared the twin girls fathered by her first husband, a corporate attorney and Richmond's amateur golf champion named Louis, and she dressed them like princesses of the realm. Drake carried them in crooks of his arms, danced them around, and lifted them high and squealing above his head. I wondered whether or not the woman he had met at the Shady Spring might have been Deborah. No, Phoebe had said that girl was cheap and trashy, and I could never believe Deborah would become part of anything as sleazy as an affair in a rundown southside Richmond motel.

Behind the house Drake had built a pool used during summers to keep fit and give the twins swimming lessons. Deborah provided a pony cart to drive them over the bluegrass lawn and through the sheltering woods. Everywhere you turned in the house — the parlor, library, den — photographs of the twins had been placed to greet the eye.

I saw Drake and Deborah several times a year, always on his birthday, usually for a cocktail party during the Christmas season, and at Easter when we all attended Grace and Holy Trinity to hear the music and afterward ate a long, leisurely dinner in the garden, weather permitting. Cliff was ritually invited but of late had made excuses, offering prior commitments, his absence vexing Deborah and causing Drake's face to tighten.

"He's not doing anything that's so damn important," Drake had said. "You'd think he was in demand all over the country."

Deborah's Volvo station wagon turned into the driveway just ahead of me, and I followed. She stopped before a bay of the three-car garage, inched the car forward, set the brake, and stepped out. She was a stylish woman who made an ordinary gray down jacket and plaid skirt appear elegant. A gust of wind that roused her dark blond hair seemed in league with her grooming. When she turned, the closeness of my Buick startled her, and I legged out to apologize.

She embraced me, presented her cheek, and because of my height, I needed to bend over to kiss it. Her complexion was fair, with a touch of color. The first time I met her I had expected to hear the languid accent of the satiated rich, but her voice was always warm, lilting, and enthusiastic.

"What's all this about Cliff?" she asked. "I can't believe they put him in jail. I want to visit him, but Drake says Cliff would hate for his friends to see him that way. Drake's terribly upset. What can I do?"

"Nothing at the moment. I check with Cliff daily and look after him."

"But he's imprisoned, and it's barbaric," she said. "How could such a thing happen?"

"An overzealous sheriff and district attorney are my best explanation."

"All right, I won't press you. I just want him to know I'm here and concerned. Please tell him that. Now, you come in the house with me this instant."

"I should have called first," I said as I lifted groceries from the rear of the Volvo.

"You never have to call. Around this place you're one of us."

A door led from the garage to a covered walkway connected to the kitchen. Ivy entwined the square white columns, and I glimpsed the covered pool, a sliding board, and a log playhouse, a window of which was cracked and needed replacing.

Lotte, their aged, shrunken black maid, opened the kitchen door to help with the groceries. I wiped my shoes on a mat just inside as Deborah toed off her boots and slipped her feet into Docksides. She clicked the counter's automatic coffeemaker before leading me into a paneled den where over the fireplace Drake's oil portrait hung.

His leather armor-corps helmet removed, his goggles hanging loose around his neck, he held binoculars as he stood in the command turret of the sand-colored Abrams tank. His skin was sun-bronzed, his cropped hair sweat-soaked, his gold-flecked blue eyes fixed as if to make out the enemy in the distance. Behind the tank the shattering glare of dunes receded in parallel descending contours. I thought of Prince Jamir on his Arabian steed at Bellerive. Each man in his own way a desert warrior.

"What's your opinion?" Deborah asked. She had removed her jacket and insisted I turn my coat over to her. Her pregnancy was just noticeable — an ultrasound had revealed that Drake would father a son.

"He's an up-to-date Lawrence of Arabia."

"You're not mocking me, are you?" she asked and raised fingers to her chin to study the painting. The chin had a cleft that appeared decorative. "Drake scoffs at it. He claims it glamorizes him and that war is organized butchery."

"No, I'm envious," I said and was. I had once dreamed of becoming a fighter pilot, of flying F-16s and after battle zooming down the conqueror onto aircraft carriers. The hope had been vain because of my poor eyes and lack of coordination. Nor did I have the temperament and character of a warrior. Despite my love of valor, particularly after the incident with Josey and the stallion at Bellerive, I had come to doubt even more forcefully that such a heritage had been bequeathed to my genes.

"You're a dear friend who doesn't visit us enough. I tell Drake he ought to bring you more often. You want to keep on the good side of me, you better not stay away so long."

She sat gracefully on a love seat, a person prepared for charm through breeding and expensive schools, also provided a life of money and ease laced with the responsibilities of charities and good works that go with being a Richmond lady. She gave off sexuality, not raw and up-front like Josey, but with a refined suggestiveness seen in the brushing of graceful fingers along her lap to straighten her skirt or the way she positioned her body in demure invitation.

I told her I was sorry, promised to reform, and asked about the twins.

"Come along with me," she said and stood. I followed her up the carpeted steps to the second floor and the nursery, where the three-year-olds lay sleeping in miniature white beds, each covered by a white canopy. Dolls had been arranged on window seats and colorful Humpty-Dumpty tiles fixed along the pale pink walls. The twins were lovely children, their mouths opened slightly in sleep, their small fingers curled on top of quilted counterpanes, their golden hair spread over lacy pillows.

"There's nothing more beautiful than the innocence of children," she whispered as we left and pulled the door quietly to.

I loved being with Deborah. She made me feel like a person of consequence — the manner in which a true aristocrat treated everyone. I thought of General Lee.

"It's great news about Drake's book," I said downstairs. "I expect an inscribed copy."

"It's marvelous for him. Except from me he never received much encouragement on the project — that's what he called it, a project — and to be frank I wasn't certain anything would come of it. 'The Truth of the Grouse,' a means for a man to pattern his own life on the habits, bearing, and courage of a wild bird. Who would have believed such an idea could catch on?"

"Not I."

"Drake's always been a man to choose his own path," she said and looked at the den wall where she had mounted and encased in a shadow-box frame his silver star and other medals. "And he saved me, Walter. After my Louis died, I sank into a seemingly hopeless and bottomless depression. Drake reached out and brought me back to life, really a modern-day resurrection."

Lotte carried in coffee on a silver tray.

"I know people believe he used my money," Deborah said. "It's not true, never a cent for Grizzly's or the book. And talk about being proud, his becoming a father is all but popping the buttons off his shirt."

She served my coffee not in a mug but a delicate porcelain cup that I stirred with a small silver spoon. For me her gentility mixed with the elusive sexuality was an exciting combination. Drake might be rough and profane at camp or work, but when with Deborah he acted the gentleman, knowing all the moves of the socially elite.

"Walter, I have a lady friend I'd like you to meet. She's a docent at the Poe Museum. I think the two of you would enjoy each other's company."

"Don't tell me you've gotten into match-making."

"I worry about you. This is a delightful woman, a master gardener, and she loves books, art, the ballet."

"I don't think so, Deborah. Not at this time."

"You're still seeing Josey?"

"Only occasionally."

"Ah," she said, turned her head slightly, and gave me a tender look which I interpreted to mean that any chance of my ever turning Josey to my cause was not only misguided but also futile.

I finished my coffee and told her I had to leave. She fussed, insisted on holding my coat for me, and walked me back through the connecting walkway to the garage and out to my Buick. She pressed my hand in her special way, a touch signifying *I cherish you.*

"You were kind to come," she said. "Drake will be pleased."

"I always leave here feeling good, and it's never just the liquor."

"You take good care of our Cliff, you hear? Carry him my love. How long will they hold him?"

"It shouldn't be but a few more days."

"Will they allow me to send him a cake and magazines? Surely I can write a note."

I promised to find out, and she again embraced me. As I left, she stood on the terrace, her hair and skirt blowing in the wind. I held that picture in my mind while I drove away to Jessup's Wharf and felt both jealous of Drake and downcast at the loneliness I was returning to.

Though it began to rain, I stopped by the office. Somewhere I had misplaced my umbrella. Mary Ellen had locked up and left no messages on my desk. I sat and looked out the window to the illuminated steeple of St. Luke's. If there were pigeons, they huddled in shadows of the eaves.

I nodded, almost dozed, and rallied myself to retire to Miss Mabel's. Though the iron radiators warmed my fingers, my rooms felt cold and damp. Light from the converted gas chandelier that had once been a dining room fixture seemed feeble, casting a faded yellowish tint on things, like old paper or linens brought up after lying long years in a basement trunk.

A plane flew low over Jessup's Wharf, possibly the prince returning to or leaving Bellerive. More rain tapped the roof. The temperature of my window thermometer was just above freezing. Wearily I surrendered myself to the sound of a gutter dripping and its final overflow.

TWENTY-SEVEN

At mid-afternoon the next day as I was about to phone Drake and ask him for the names, addresses, and the terms of service of his ex-employees, I received an agitated collect call from Cliff, who told me that two sheriff's deputies from Seneca County had arrived to take him into custody and transport him to West Virginia.

"They're carrying me off in ten minutes," he said. "You know what belly cuffs are?"

I did, a chain with handcuffs attached to its links locked around a prisoner's waist.

"And shackles," Cliff said. "They've fastened them on me as if I'm a slave to be deported to another continent."

"Cliff, it's just a procedure."

" 'Just,' huh? You know how it feels to walk past people who gawk at and whisper about you as if you're monstrously depraved?"

"I'm on my way to Seneca County. Soon as I get myself together and can pack a bag."

"They signed me over like meat to be delivered to the market."

I tried to reach Drake at Grizzly's to give

him the news, but he had left town on a buying trip. I told Mary Ellen I would stay in touch by phone and also explained to stately, gray-haired Miss Mabel I needed to be away a few days.

"Turn down the heat in your apartment," she said. Though far from poor, she often repeated the adage that if you watched your pennies, the dollars would take care of themselves.

I gassed up before starting out. By five o'clock it was dark, and with my eyesight I hated driving at night. Moreover, the weather report announced a storm watch. I reached Staunton before the first flakes flattened against the windshield. My wipers labored to swipe them away in clean arcs, but they rapidly reclotted.

I sensed the mountains before I made out their looming darkness within darkness. The car's six-cylinder engine shifted down to pull harder. Still I made good time till I crossed the border beyond Monterey and headed toward High Gap. Yellow and red lights of road crews' trucks and plows flashed over mounds of snow, creating a grotesque landscape. I thought of Dante's *Inferno* and the concurrent presence of ice and fire.

Though two lanes had been partially scraped, snow again covered them. I braked behind an eighteen-wheeler logging truck, the tires of which flung up cinders that rapped my windshield. The cleaning fluid sprayed from the engine compartment's reservoir couldn't handle the job, forcing me to stop and use my handkerchief to wipe the glass. When I finished, I tossed the soiled handkerchief to the rubber floor mat.

Rolling again at only twenty miles an hour, the tires hit a patch of black ice, and when I braked, the car did a leisurely spin near the edge of the road before straightening and continuing on course. Sweat collected under my armpits.

By the time I reached High Gap I had been driving six hours. I felt tired, my eyes burned, I was nauseous. The fuel gauge's needle hovered toward empty. Under the snow nothing about the town appeared identifiable, and I lost my sense of direction until I recognized the Marathon Station where we had stopped the morning we carried Wendell's body in from Blind Sheep. The same attendant, his cap pulled low over his ears, took my money.

"Reckon winter'll ever turn us loose?" he asked.

I reached the courthouse, the lighted windows of which were steamed to opaqueness, and found the parking lot. Heat swept out to me as I opened the door of the Sheriff's Department. The green tile floor had been sullied by snow melting from shoes and boots. I found Sawyers's office locked and walked the corridor until I reached a glass window behind which a uniformed, overweight woman with full rosy cheeks sat at a console on which tiers of green and red lights blinked from a control panel.

The name tag pinned to her breast pocket read *Bess*. Behind her were file cabinets, a computer, and radio equipment. The large wall-mounted electric clock read 11:57. She had been flipping through *Cosmopolitan*.

"I'm Mr. Clifford Dickens's attorney," I said. "He is being held here?"

"Sure enough and can I see some identification?"

I slid my Virginia Bar Association card and driver's license through the slot at the bottom of the window. She held them at half an arm's length under the concentrated light of the desk.

"I want to see him," I said.

"Mr. Frampton, it's way too late for visitor hours."

"I'm no visitor but an attorney who has a right to confer with his client."

"Now don't get all hot and bothered," she said and swiveled her chair aside to pick up a phone, finger a button on the control panel, and wait to speak. "Hey, Bruce, lawyer fellow here by name of Frampton wants to see prisoner Dickens. Un-huh, tall, thin, wears glasses. Don't make a bit of difference to me."

She held the phone and touched another button. "Gilbert'll be here in a sec," she said to me.

"Gilbert?"

"Our jailer. Like a cookie?" From a small round tin she removed the top, which was painted with yellow tulips, and pushed it through the slot. "Chocolate chips I made this afternoon."

I took one so as not to offend her, nibbled it, told her it was delicious, and received a matronly smile. She glanced through a second window at her side and pressed another button on the control panel. The lock of a black steel door released with a clank.

Gilbert limped out. His tan uniform shirt was open at the collar, his holster emptied. He dragged a foot and surprised me by offering to shake my hand and apologizing for having to pat me down and look through my briefcase.

"I wouldn't ordinarily do that to a lawyer," he said. "But we don't know you 'round here yet. Okay, if you'll come on along with me, Mr. Frampton. Bad night to be out 'less you got polar bear blood."

He led me through the doorway, which Bess relocked after us. She watched from the second window that gave her a view of the block. The ten cells were numbered and equipped with peephole and waist-high portals that could be slid open. The walls had been painted sky blue.

I couldn't tell how many cells were occupied. Two carried the designation WOMEN, meaning not only the inmates were of that sex but also the cells were to be entered only by female deputies. I was not surprised that Sheriff Sawyers ran a modern, efficient jail.

Gilbert stopped before No. 5. He looked back toward Bess, and she released the lock. He opened the door onto an antechamber furnished with a metal table and two metal stools, all bolted to the floor. Behind bars Cliff swung his feet from a fold-down bunk that had a brown blanket over a thin, plastic-covered mattress. The stainless steel sink and toilet reflected light from a caged bulb. The cell had no window.

"We want a conference room," I said to Gilbert.

"No need, Mr. Frampton. I can just shut this outer door here, and you got all the privacy a man needs."

"Is this cell wired for communication?" I asked and looked at the ceiling and walls.

234

They too were sky blue.

"It is, but neither me or Bess'll be listening. Come morning, you can speak to the sheriff about other arrangements. Holler if you need me."

I started to demand a conference room but then thought I shouldn't cause any bad feeling with a jailer when Cliff, not I, might have to pay for it.

"They took my clothes," Cliff said after Gilbert shut us in. The laces were gone from his shoes, and he sadly fingered out his oversized orange coveralls. "Tommy Hilfiger, right?"

"They treating you okay?" I asked. He needed a shave, his hair was disarranged, the skin under his eyes puffy.

"Wonderfully. You ever taken a tour in the backseat of a patrol car enclosed with rat wire? And they've been at me with questions. I've refused to answer and told them they had to talk to you. Walter, my head's about to bust, and I'm living a nightmare."

"I can do nothing till I see the district attorney. Have you eaten?"

"I turned down food. I'm unable to swallow."

"Anything I should bring you?"

"My freedom."

"I'll be working at that first thing in the morning."

"Does Drake know I'm here?"

"I tried to reach him. He's away on business."

"It's important he finds out."

"I'll see to it, but give me a reason, and don't tell me it's so personal you can't reveal it to your attorney and friend."

"Walter, you've come with me this far, please, I implore you, stay one more step."

"All right, Cliff. I don't like it, but we'll wait until after I visit the district attorney. Try to sleep."

"Oh sure, sleep, what's that?"

I rapped the door for Gilbert to let me out. Our feet echoed along the cell block. I asked Bess where I could find a room for the night.

"The Mountain View Lodge," she said. "Want me to call for you?"

I thanked her. She rang up the lodge and gave me directions. I drove away from the jail, through the silent, ghostly town, and up a grade so steep my tires slipped. The motel's red sign emerged through snow like a fogged beacon at sea. Only a few blanketed cars were parked in the lot. I walked across the heated lobby to the desk and signed the registration card for the polite young clerk who looked no more than high-school age and had been studying a Spanish textbook. His radio played beneath pigeonholes that held keys. I recognized Willie Nelson's voice.

"I could use some food," I said.

"The kitchen's shut down but can fix you a sandwich and a glass of milk."

My room was comfortable enough, a queen-sized bed, TV, and a balconied window that overlooked High Gap. No cars moved. The snow fell with a quiet hiss and caused the town's solitary lights to appear hazed, their beams broken.

I sat on the bed and phoned Drake's home number. When Deborah answered, I apologized for calling so late.

"He's attending a gun show in Kentucky," she said. "Is this an emergency?"

"No emergency but important. Soon as you hear from him, ask him to reach me at this number."

"It involves Cliff?"

"He's jailed here in West Virginia."

"But not hurt or being mistreated?"

"He's all right, but we need Drake."

"Let me write down that number. Oh, God, look after Cliff, Walter."

When I hung up, I stood at the window and watched the snow fall into the night. The clerk brought my grilled-cheese sandwich, two sweet pickles, a glass of milk, and a paper napkin on a tray.

"Gracias," he said as he left after I tipped him.

I munched the sandwich and watched the snow smother the town's lights, reducing them to erratic embers.

TWENTY-EIGHT

I was so exhausted I sank into a hard sleep that left me more drained than refreshed. Waking, I felt addled, unsure where I lay in the first unearthly white light of morning. I held my watch over my eyes, the time 7:27.

I showered, shaved, and sat in a leatherette booth of the motel restaurant, where I ordered tomato juice and coffee. I was the only customer. I bought a copy of the Seneca *Register* as well as *USA Today* that I would carry to Cliff. The headline on the *Register* read COUGAR REPORTED KILLING SHEEP.

I left word at the desk I could be reached at the courthouse if calls came for me. Wind blew curling wisps of snow over the town. I scraped the Buick's windshield, and the car slithered along the road driving down the hill to the courthouse, its stone facade snow-blasted. A trustee wearing tan coveralls used a blower to clear parking spaces. A second trustee shoveled off steps.

I studied the lobby directory to locate the district attorney's office. The elevator to the third floor felt slow but determined. Mr.

Tuggle's young secretary was eating a glazed doughnut as I entered, biting at it daintily, her purple fingernails carefully positioned to protect them. She laid the doughnut aside and licked at her thumb.

"He's waiting for you," she said and with a small, pinched mouth announced me through her intercom.

Sam Tuggle met me at the door, a ruddy, vigorous man as tall as I and a good seventy or eighty pounds heavier. The grip of his hand edged on being painful. As he showed me in, he took my overcoat, patted my back, and pulled out a chair for me beside his desk.

"We glad to have you here in our fair state, Mr. Frampton. Hope everybody's been showing you a friendly face. If not, you just point 'em out and we'll nail their hides to the barn door."

On walls hung diplomas, glossy snapshots of himself with politicians, commemorative plaques, and over the window behind his desk the mounted head of a wild boar, its fangs exposed. There was also a large color photograph of him as a coal miner, his face blackened except around the eyes, his teeth gleaming in a minstrel's mouth. The helmet held an attached lamp, and an insulated wire ran from it to a battery pack at his side. Knees of his filthy, baggy jeans were protected by strapped on leather pads. His grimy hands held a lunch pail and thermos.

"Way I started out," he said. "Dug black diamonds eight years before I went to night school and passed the bar. Was near born under a lump of coal."

"It's a good picture," I said.

"The voters like it," he said, unbuttoned his gray double-breasted jacket, and sat. "Sorry about the snow. Well, part sorry 'cause we encouraging skiing around here. Got us a good slope up the road with a lift and half a dozen runs. We hoping lots of Virginians coming our way and bringing money. You ski?"

"I never got around to it."

"Be glad to give you a complimentary pass for the lift. Ten-dollar value. Had your breakfast? Gail'll bring you a doughnut and a mug of battery acid."

I declined. The fullness of his face, the florid good-ol'-boy manner, failed to mask his sharply focused hazel eyes. He struck me as being a fit, energetic man with a swift brain behind a broad brow, his folksy language a smoke screen.

"Mr. Tuggle —"

"Call me Sam. Thought we got that out of the road over the phone."

"And me Walter."

"Everybody 'round here calls me Sam. Even the felons."

"Yes, sir, well, Sam, as you know I represent Mr. Clifford Dickens, who at this moment resides in your jail."

"Not my jail. I don't own any jails. It belongs to the county, and the sheriff runs it."

"Right. I guess what I want from you first is a bill of particulars."

"Well now, I try to be accommodating to my fellow officers of the court, but as to a bill of particulars, you see, Walter, there's this question about you."

"You're going to ask whether or not I'm licensed to practice law in this state. The answer is no, but I intend to take on a local attorney as an associate if necessary."

"It will be necessary."

"I'm hoping, however, you'll extend the courtesy of talking to me at this stage of the process."

"Always try to be a good neighbor to my fellow man." He leaned back in his chair, his hands settled on its arms.

"Thank you, Sam. I confess I continue to be somewhat mystified at the trouble your office has gone to in bringing my client all the long way from Richmond to High Gap."

"Mystified? How so?"

"By what appears to be an all-out press

against Mr. Dickens. You are sticking with a charge of voluntary homicide?"

"That's how it's marked up."

"And carrying it to a grand jury?"

"Already done, and they brought forth a true bill of indictment."

"You didn't waste time."

"Justice swift is justice served."

"At the heart of the matter as I see it, Mr. Wendell Ripley's death was caused by human error, and I find it a far stretch to make a case for voluntary homicide, which requires disagreement, provocation, and anger between the parties."

"The heart of the matter," Sam said, his thick fingers tapping the chair's arms. "Wonderful phrase. Get down below the skin, the fat, the muscle, the bone, and you find a heart pumping out blood and beating like a tom-tom. Got to figure what message the tom-tom's sounding."

"I don't see where you're headed."

"You wouldn't be trying to fool around with this old country boy, would you, Walt?"

"I'm here to advise my client to agree to a charge of involuntary manslaughter subject to what punishment will be imposed for that plea. I assume you would rather save your taxpayers money by not going to trial."

"Sorry to have to break the news to you but

things are turning out more complicated than they first appeared."

"Sam, voluntary manslaughter is a felonious homicide committed in the heat of passion, *furor brevis,* the bloodshed growing solely from incitement to conflict."

He grinned and pointed at the wall.

"Don't you suppose I know that? There's a diploma right up there that proves I been to law school."

"What happened on the Blind Sheep hunt doesn't meet the definition."

"We don't happen to agree with you around here. Something else went on up on Blind Sheep."

"What else?"

"You don't need to know at this point since we thinking of nol-prossing voluntary manslaughter."

"You're dropping it?" I asked, surprised and relieved.

"If we do, we'll go back to a grand jury for an indictment of murder two."

I sat stunned and attempted to order my thinking. Murder in the second degree was different from murder one that required willful, deliberate, and premeditated killing. Rather, murder two involved the sudden transport of passion that the law called *furor brevis* plus malice. In Virginia it was a class three felony punishable by confinement in the penitentiary for a minimum of five to as much as eighteen or twenty years. West Virginia law would likely impose a similar penalty.

"I don't believe what my ears are telling me," I said.

"Believe, Walt. It's no joke 'round this office. We hold the law in great respect in these parts despite what you might think down in Virginia of us backward hillbillies."

"You brought my client here with a charge of voluntary manslaughter while all the while you meant to go for murder two?"

"Irrelevant at the moment since we do have him in custody and that being the fact a grand jury can charge him with anything they want once we nol-pros the voluntary charge. It won't, however, be a frivolous move on this office's part."

"There has to be malice. You can't have murder without malice."

"Walt, I'm not giving away my case till the time is nigh, but let me say that there's evidence which don't square with either involuntary or voluntary manslaughter."

"Would you be more specific?" I asked, attempting to appear composed.

"Look in my ear," he said, leaned forward, and again grinned. "You see anybody in there listening?"

"Sam, please, I've had a hard trip," I said. His large ear looked as if it had been battered and did resemble cauliflower.

"I can be more specific but don't feel compelled to at this point, and you'll have the full right of discovery in due course. On the other hand you look like you done been run over by an eighteen-wheeler, and as I said I want to accommodate my fellow officers of the court. Let's see if we can get Sheriff Sawyers to drop by." He thumbed his intercom and tilted sideways to speak into it. "Gail, how about asking Bruce to pay us a visit." He again faced me. "So you a hunter too?"

"No, I came to Blind Sheep for an outing with friends."

"And more than grouse got bagged, huh? I'm fixing to have myself another mug of coffee. Sure you don't want some?"

I shook my head. He walked out, and I looked through his window to the top of a snow-covered mountain that to a lowlander like me seemed like a white tidal wave about to sweep over and smash the town. Tumbling gray clouds sliding eastward gave the mountain an appearance of falling.

Sam, holding a yellow mug decorated with the blue initials WVU, came back followed by the sheriff, who had taken off his trooper hat and unzipped his leather jacket. Snowflakes melted on the fur-lined collar. Had the two men conferred? Sam sat and drank his coffee. The sheriff appeared freshly shaved, his uniform as before sharply pressed, his red sideburns precisely leveled. He nodded to me.

"Bruce, Walt here wonders why we paying so much attention to his Mr. Dickens. We want to be hospitable 'cause we Virginians too, though not Tidewater born and bred. You been fretted by your findings up on Blind Sheep. Mind telling Walt a thing or two about why without giving away the henhouse?"

"I checked the scene out from all angles and studied my photographs," the sheriff said. His slate-gray eyes fixed me. "First, Mr. Dickens reported that Mr. Ripley lunged to the left just as a grouse flushed. If Mr. Ripley had lunged past Mr. Dickens as Mr. Dickens has stated, he would have been shot in the side or back, not his lower chest and upper stomach. Second, his boot prints don't confirm a move either left or right. Mr. Ripley was downslope and behind Mr. Dickens. Mr. Dickens would've had to fire at an angle of decline, the barrel of his shotgun lowered fifty degrees or more to strike Mr. Ripley in those areas of his body. If a bird flushed, as has been stated by Mr. Dickens, though we found no tracks, it would've flown up, not down. I've diagrammed it."

"The bird could have flushed and flown low," I said.

"Had not Mr. Ripley been there to intercept, the load would've gone into the ground not more than thirty-six inches in front of Mr. Dickens's feet," the sheriff answered. Did he ever blink?

"And Mr. Dickens might have triggered his shotgun involuntarily during the excitement of the moment," I said.

"He stated he swung left on the bird, not down."

"You're basing your conclusions primarily on the reconstructed scene of a shooting that is surely subject to varying interpretations," I said.

"My deputies and I acted it out. What we found doesn't square with what Mr. Dickens has testified to."

"But it's still only what you believe could have happened, not enough for a conviction."

"Well, that just got Bruce started," Sam said and set his mug on his desk. "Roused his interest enough he spent his own time checking things out while down in Virginia on vacation. We can't keep Bruce from working. He talked to people, like those folks out at that place called The Watchers where Mr. Ripley had his domicile till he departed this vale of tears. Mr. Ripley was a deeply religious man, but Bruce here learned things about Mr. Ripley's son, what's his full name, Bruce?"

"Jeremiah Daniel Ripley," the sheriff said.

"Name of Jeremiah and Daniel in the fiery furnace. Bruce learned the youth was a homosexual known to other men of that predilection in the city. Learned Mr. Ripley was mighty upset and despondent about his son's behavior. Learned Mr. Dickens had a photo exhibition that pictured such men showing everything except them doing it to each other. Learned the boy had been Mr. Dickens's student. Began to appear that while Mr. Ripley and Mr. Dickens were up there on Blind Sheep hunting together they had reason to get into a heated disagreement that ended with Mr. Dickens shooting and meaning to kill Mr. Ripley, and that intent supplies the malice. They could have fought but nobody had to die. Malice plain and simple. The fight might have started when Mr. Ripley tried to break up the association his son had with Mr. Dickens or maybe Mr. Dickens feared the truth about him and the boy coming out."

"Too many mights and maybes," I said.

"But enough we could use," Sam said. "That about it, Bruce?"

"About," the sheriff said.

"All theory, not evidence," I said.

"We'll see," Sam said. "Haul it to the grand

jury and let them carry the ball."

"And grand juries most often provide what prosecutors request of them," I said. "But it doesn't mean your case will hold up in court."

"Prosecutors don't like to waste their time any more than anybody else," Sam said.

"For the sake of our talking here," I said, "if Wendell Ripley believed he had cause to be angry at Mr. Dickens, any shooting by Mr. Dickens could have been self-defense."

"But your Mr. Dickens never told it that way," Sam said. "He lied. He's been lying all along."

I needed to be careful not to reveal what I did and did not know.

"He has never given a sworn statement on any charge," I said.

"We have his taped account I recorded the day of the shooting," the sheriff said.

"His account claims it was an accident," I said.

"And can be used against him if we present testimony or evidence that contradicts it," Sam said.

"I'd like to suggest to you that if inconsistencies are found, they might well arise from Mr. Dickens trying to save pain and heartache to others. He has friends as well as his professional reputation to protect."

"What I understand, his reputation around

Richmond town is he kept company with the limp-wristed and sweet types," Sam said.

"He's an artist. They frequently move in that circle. I've known him all my life, and he's not like that."

"Lord God, you think you know people," Sam said. "You sit in this office, you find you never get down to the final layer of what a person really is. You can peel all the way through to the core and find you grabbed only air in your fingers."

"If there was anger between the two of them, I still maintain it could be self-defense on Mr. Dickens's part."

"I wouldn't advise you to go for self-defense. No sign of a struggle. Neither man had a fight mark on him. Odds are it was hot blood and hate. To justify self-defense Mr. Dickens would need proof his life was endangered."

"Mr. Ripley held a loaded twelve-gauge shotgun," I said. "A threat in and of itself."

As Sam leaned back, he drew his hands from the desk and looked away from me to the sheriff.

"What you think, Bruce?"

"I never believed in ambush," the sheriff said.

"Discovery'd kick it out anyhow. Oh hell, go on and tell him."

"We're holding the guns for evidence," the

sheriff said. "The Beretta over-and-under used by Mr. Dickens and belonging to Mr. Wingo as well as the Remington automatic that Mr. Ripley carried. Those were the fire-arms they hunted with, correct?"

"Correct," I said.

"I wrapped the guns in plastic and drove them to Charleston to undergo a State Police Lab examination. Received a report back that surprised me. While Mr. Dickens's Beretta had a fired shell still in a chamber, Mr. Ripley's Remington was empty."

"He could have shot at the bird a second before he died," I said.

"But he supposedly had lunged past Mr. Dickens, and he would have needed to shoot three times to empty the Remington if fully loaded. He didn't. The Remington hadn't been fired and the bolt was closed instead of locked open."

"Mr. Ripley might've forgotten to load. It happens. To me once in a duck blind. Or maybe he shucked the shells by mistake during the excitement of the flush. That happens too."

"Maybe with a pump gun, not an automatic. As to forgetting, Mr. Dickens's statement made after the killing, and you and Mr. Wingo agreed, you all four had stopped to load at the same time before splitting up to

252

hunt in pairs. Mr. Ripley was bound to notice you other three thumbing in the high brass."

I hesitated, running my mind back to the hunt. Had I seen Wendell loading like the rest of us? I believed so, but I'd been an attorney long enough to know that even the most honest memory could deceive.

"And his safety was still on," Sawyers said. "If he meant to fire, wouldn't he have pushed off his safety?"

"I don't know. Things happen on hunts."

"We found something else," the sheriff said after a glance at Sam, who nodded. "Mr. Ripley had no shells in his hunting vest. It's the reason when the snow melted we backtracked down the mountain from the homicide site. We used a metal detector to find ten twelve-gauge high brass 7½s, 1¼ ounces of shot, 3¾ drams of powder, lying on the ground."

"Mr. Ripley never hunted before," I said. "A case of confusion, fumbling, buck fever."

"He might've fumbled a shell or two but what about the others that fit tight in slots of his shooting vest. He dropped them at approximately fifty-foot intervals, like counting his steps as he climbed. No way they could've just fallen. They had to be pulled out and turned loose of."

I sat silent.

"Sure suggests malice on Mr. Dickens's part," Sam said. "He was facing a man holding an empty shotgun."

"He wouldn't know that."

"Maybe yes, maybe no, but there could be no intent for a man with an unloaded gun to do harm to another individual unless he used it as a club. It don't pan out, Walt. What we got here is a homicidal stew with lots of bad meat. Now you understand why this office just can't let go of this thing?"

"I understand," I said, though still trying to set it straight in my mind. "When's the preliminary hearing?"

"Before the magistrate, ten this morning. Hate to treat a guest in the county poorly but now you know the lay of the land around here."

I walked fast down the steps and to the jail. This time Gilbert let me use a conference room at the far end of the cell block, a space not much larger than a closet furnished with two metal chairs, a wall desk, a telephone, and a directory. He brought Cliff cuffed and locked him in beside me.

Cliff seemed smaller now, shrunken, his eyes a larger part of a tragic face.

"I feel I've been shat upon and stink," he said and rubbed his throat. His palms rasped his beard, and his fingers left his eyebrows ruffled. "Why you looking at me like that?"

"I'm waiting for you to tell the rest of it."

"The rest of what?"

"The game you and Drake have been playing with me."

"There's been no game."

"Listen, now that they have you here, they're thinking of upping the charge to — are you ready for this? — murder in the second degree. There will be no bail. If convicted, you will receive years of hard time."

"Murder?" He paled. "Just a ploy to make me plead to voluntary, right?"

"No ploy, Cliff."

"They can bring me here under one charge and switch it to another?"

"It's their ballpark, and they're able to do pretty much what they want now they hold you. Prosecutors have enormous powers."

"What can you do?"

"At this point not a lot. There will be a hearing, the preliminary before a magistrate during which you'll be able to plead not guilty. While you're held, however, the district attorney can quash the voluntary manslaughter charge and bring in a new indictment of murder two. You'll face trial, I'll need a local associate, and the two of us will defend you. Even if we succeed in clearing you of murder two, a jury might still convict you of the lesser voluntary charge."

"You shouldn't have let them do this to me, Walter. What kind of lawyer are you?"

"Run-of-the-mill variety, and what kind of client do I have that keeps withholding the truth from me?"

"What truth? I told you how it happened on Blind Sheep."

"You told me Wendell threatened you. It's difficult to believe a man using an unloaded shotgun could do that."

"Unloaded? You and I saw him load that Remington."

"The sheriff discovered all of Wendell's shells dropped along the slope up toward Blind Sheep ridge."

"I didn't know his gun wasn't loaded. How could I? I heard him working the bolt and believed he was just checking his load as we all do. Why would he empty the gun?"

"I've been thinking hard about that. My guess is it means Wendell never had any intention of shooting you but maneuvered you into shooting him. True or not, there's little possibility your attorneys will be able to make a plea of self-defense prevail in court."

Cliff again rubbed his face, started to speak, licked his lips.

"Cliff, they're convinced you and Wendell's son Jeremiah had a homosexual relationship, that hostility between you and his father arose from it, and that's the reason you shot him."

"That's not so."

"I'll believe you only if you tell me what you and Drake have been holding back. Otherwise I'm resigning the case."

He turned his face aside, his expression tormented, and again ran fingers along his throat.

"Drake needs to be in on this," he said.

"On what? Tell me or I'm gone."

He inhaled as if he had come up from holding his breath long underwater.

"I thought no charges would be brought if I claimed Wendell's death was accidental. I wanted to avoid a media event and the possibility of a scandal. I had a girl whom I intended to marry. There was a chance I'd lose her along with any career left me in Richmond if what really happened came to light. And there was Drake."

"Drake what?"

"I don't want to tell you."

"Cliff, you tell me or I walk."

"There's got to be another way."

"No, no other way."

He stared at his hands before looking at me.

"Oh Christ, it happened almost three years ago when driving to a New Year's Eve party. I passed Grizzly's and spotted his delivery truck and two cars parked in the lot. It was just like him to be working. The lights at the front of the store had been switched off, the ghost grouse floated in darkness, but I knew Drake used a rear entrance when he opened and closed the place. I walked around the building and found that door unlocked."

We heard Gilbert's foot dragging along the cellblock. He paused before the conference room, checked us, and withdrew.

"Go on," I said.

"I opened the door and stepped into the stockroom," Cliff said. "A ceiling bulb burned, enough light for me to find my way among the shelves and crates. I walked toward the office where the door was partly open. Walter, I hate doing this."

"Don't you stop on me now."

"There's a cot in the office."

"I've seen it."

"They were in his office on the cot."

"They?"

"Drake."

"Drake and who?"

"Another man."

"You have proof?" I asked when I could speak.

"No."

"I thought you always carried a camera."

"I left it in the car but wouldn't have used it if I had."

"The other man was Jeremiah Ripley?"

"I think so but can't swear to it. They were lying in shadows."

"But you're certain you saw Drake."

"He lifted his head and looked at me."

"All this time you've been protecting him?"

"Trying to protect both of us. We thought it would work. Now that you know, what will you do?"

"Shoot myself," I said.

TWENTY-NINE

The hearing at ten charging Cliff with the voluntary manslaughter was only a formality in the small first-floor courtroom that had mingled scents of dust, tobacco, and body odors. The oak benches could have been church pews, and the hanging light fixtures gave off an essence of a distant time, as if the electricity had been wearied by far travel from another age, maybe 1936 when the WPA courthouse had been built according to a plaque screwed to the corridor's wall.

The magistrate, a thin, elderly man whose skin was like white parchment, appeared incongruously dapper in a tattersall vest, a polka-dot bow tie, and a linen handkerchief folded to three peaks sticking from the breast pocket of his tweed jacket.

"How do you plead to the indictment, Mr. Dickens?" he asked Cliff in a fatherly voice.

Cliff answered not guilty. I requested bail.

"Your Honor, the accused was a fugitive, and there's risk he'll flee this jurisdiction," Sam Tuggle countered.

"Your Honor, Mr. Dickens has no criminal

record and would have gladly surrendered himself voluntarily to this court."

"I believe we best hold your client a spell while I review the pertaining data," the judge said and tapped his gavel delicately as if it were as infirm as he.

Before a deputy returned Cliff to his cell, I told him I was on my way to see Drake.

"I'm so damn sorry," Cliff said.

I shook his hand, watched the deputy lead him away, and returned to the Mountain View Lodge for my things. The weather had let up, and a faint sun laid a sheen on the snow. I drove cautiously along the slick road between the plowed, sooty banks. A jackknifed trailer truck held up traffic for ninety minutes. It had spilled tomatoes grown in Florida, and many of the people stalled picked them up to carry to their cars.

The snowbanks gave way as I crossed back to Virginia and were gone before I reached Powhatan County. When I stopped at Grizzly's at a few minutes before seven the parking lot was empty except for the Ford delivery truck that on its side panels portrayed an aroused bear rampant above a pair of Kentucky flintlock muskets. The store's doors were locked. The mobile grouse ghosted eerily within the showroom's darkness.

I was not about to confront Drake at his

house, where he would be with Deborah and the twins. I had never gone to the expense of installing a cellular phone in my Buick and used the public booth in front of a Winn-Dixie at a Route 60 shopping center to make the call.

"I need to see you immediately," I said when Drake answered.

"Come on to the house, Raff."

"You meet me at Grizzly's."

"Deb and I are just finishing dinner."

"I'll be waiting in the lot."

"Well damn it, Raff."

"Right now," I said and without waiting for him to speak further hung up and drove back to the store. I pulled in beside the truck. The night had become still, and ice of refrozen puddles reflected a gleam from the ghost grouse. The heater running, I left on my gloves. I felt worn, queasy, and a thick, dirty taste coated my mouth.

At twenty minutes after seven the Bronco slowed, the headlights flashing as it turned in, and Drake drew alongside. He stepped out and crossed bareheaded around to the passenger door of my car.

"You in some kind of sweat on a night like this?" he asked as he opened the door and bowed in beside me.

"A cold sweat," I said.

"I don't readily give up nighttime with Deb and the twins."

"They've got Cliff jailed in High Gap. He faces a possible murder charge."

"Sonofabitch," Drake said, turning to me. "How can they do that?"

"They're convinced Wendell's shooting was deliberate and malicious."

"Malicious meaning what exactly?"

"That the force used was not justified by the provocation that arose between Wendell and Cliff."

"It's bullshit."

"They're dead serious."

"Politics then. The sheriff and DA are putting on a show for the voters. Keep their names in the papers."

"They have Cliff for lying and are able to make a connection between him and Jeremiah Ripley."

"What kind of connection?"

"A liaison is the kindest word I can use."

"I been afraid of that," he said and leaned back in the seat.

"Of what?"

"You know how Cliff's changed and become, well, hell, the crowd he runs with these days, plus the Shockoe exhibition."

"I don't like what you're suggesting. He has a girl he wants to marry."

"You ever seen her?"

"I've seen her picture."

"Not the same. Why hasn't he had her around?"

"She lives in Baltimore, and she may be black."

"Damn him, I don't care if she's got red-and-yellow stripes, the fact is she's not been seen in the flesh."

"Why are you so angry at Cliff?"

"I'm angry for what he's done to us, the position he's put us in, not only himself, but me, my family and business, and you think you're going to help your reputation by being associated with him?"

"You believe he and Jeremiah Ripley had that kind of relationship?"

"I believe it's possible. We haven't been close to Cliff of late. He's gone his own way and left you and me behind."

"This thing could ruin his life."

"Cliff hasn't had much life lately, but I'll keep my word and stick by him. Look, maybe it was a onetime thing between him and Jerry, a weak moment. I already told him and you I'd support him financially and otherwise."

"It's the otherwise that interests me."

"Don't follow you, Raff."

"What about you and Jeremiah?"

"Me and Jeremiah what? He sold shoes for me, nothing else."

"Cliff claims there's more."

"Let's hear it."

"Two bodies on your office camp cot New Year's Eve, 1991."

Drake again turned to me. Lights of a passing car slashed across his face, causing him to look bloodless and spectral.

"Poor Cliff's got to be scared shitless to make up a story like that."

"You think he'd do that to you?"

"I think he's reaching out for anything he can grab to save himself. Look, Raff, I'll stand by him. You want to hire another lawyer, F. Lee Bailey, I'll underwrite the expenses and do anything else you ask. How'd Cliff get himself into this fucking mess?"

"It was you who encouraged or persuaded him not to tell the sheriff about what actually happened on Blind Sheep."

"I told you I did that for him as well as myself. It had nothing to do with murder."

"Why was Wendell on the hunt?"

"As I explained before, because I wanted to buy his Blind Sheep land. I never knew anything about a connection between Cliff and Jeremiah."

"Drake, ask yourself why if Wendell believed Cliff had corrupted Jerry and meant to kill him, he never fired his gun."

"How the hell can I answer that? If they had a fight, maybe Cliff got the drop on him. Remember, I was with you, not them."

"I picked up a little piece of information while talking to the sheriff and district attorney in High Gap. Wendell's Remington was empty."

"Say again."

"No shells in the gun."

"Wrong. I saw him loading up."

"And the shells from his vest dropped in the snow along the way. Wendell was a Watcher. They are conscientious objectors and believe in nonviolence. My guess is he never meant to hunt, to shoot, or to kill anything."

"Your guess?"

"I think he tricked Cliff into believing he had to fire in order to save himself. How else do you explain it?"

"I can't 'cause I repeat I wasn't there. Cliff could've had reasons we don't know about."

"Can you think of one?"

"Maybe Wendell told Cliff he meant to expose him. They had an argument, Cliff panicked."

"No shells in Wendell's gun. That's what I keep coming back to. No need to shoot."

"Cliff wouldn't've known that."

"It's the main thing they have on him," I

said. "He shot and killed an unarmed man."

"Just tell me what it is you want."

"I want to be convinced you've been completely honest with me."

"How long you been knowing me, Raff? You think I'd go queer and do that with a man?"

"I think either you or Cliff's lying."

"You ever heard me tell a lie?"

"Not before this."

"Take your choice, Cliff or me."

"That's not enough," I said.

"It wasn't me on the cot, but if there was anybody it had to be Boomer and Jeremiah. They volunteered to help take inventory that New Year's Eve, and we worked till after dark but didn't finish. I left early, they offered to keep on, and I paid them double overtime for doing so."

"There were two cars and your delivery truck in the lot according to Cliff."

"Any cars would've belonged to Boomer and Jerry. The delivery truck stays here."

"Where were you that night?"

"I'll pretend you didn't ask that question but give you an answer just the same. I'd taken a young redheaded gal named Rosemary Palmer to a New Year's Eve party."

"Where was the party?"

"The Chesterfield Country Club."

"And Rosemary, where's she now?"

"Last I heard she's married and lives in Atlanta."

"Anyone see you two there?"

"Let me think, sure, Josey. She and her tennis pro sat at the table with us. And I guarantee you if there's any truth to what Cliff claims, Boomer's ass will be out of here faster than shit shat from a goose."

He cocked his finger as if it were the hammer of a revolver, pointed it at the front of the store, and mouthed the word "bang."

THIRTY

I drove to Jessup's Wharf, slept, and when I reached my office sat trying to think how I could check out what Drake had told me. I decided to start with Boomer and at mid-morning called Grizzly's.

"He's left us," a woman's voice told me, I assumed one of the two ladies who worked in billing and accounting.

"Does left us mean he quit or was let go? And I'd like his full name and telephone number."

"I'm sorry, sir, I'm not authorized to give out that information. Would you care to speak to our owner, Mr. Wingo?"

"No," I said and hung up. Whatever Drake told me, rightly or wrongly, would absolve no one but himself.

I had known Boomer only by that name. I called the *Times-Dispatch*, asked for the Sports Desk, and talked to a reporter who identified himself as Bucky Ruff. He remembered Boomer from his glory days at VPI.

"Boomer's in the phone book, listed as Ernest B. Mosely," Bucky said. "The B's for

Bartholomew. I looked it up."

I found the listing and drove to Boomer's Oregon Hill, South Pine Street address, a Richmond neighborhood of closely spaced frame houses built during the 1850s and lived in originally by German blue-collar workers. His small, one-story cottage was freshly painted a pale orange, had a crepe myrtle bush in a tiny picket-fenced yard, and was shuttered. Nobody answered the bell.

Next door an elderly hunchbacked woman, her hands gloved, her long black overcoat reaching almost to her ankles, her frizzled white hair wind tossed, stopped sweeping her porch.

"Ernie drove off early," she said and sucked at her toothless mouth as if tasting her pink gums. "Told me he'd be gone a spell."

"Did he say where he was going?"

"Texas. Told me he'd always wanted to see Texas and the Alamo."

"Do you know when he's coming back?"

"Can't tell you that, bud," she said and resumed sweeping. "I'm to feed his cat, and I never seen the first one of them animals I liked."

I drove back to Jessup's Wharf assuming for whatever reason that Drake had sent Boomer packing. I should have tried to reach him earlier. His leaving was inconclusive — either

Drake had confronted him and discovered Boomer had been on the cot with Jeremiah or to protect himself had fired Boomer to be rid of him.

I sat at my desk unsure what to do next. Mary Ellen answered the phone and from her chair raised a finger. When I picked up, it was Josey.

"Please come see me," she said. "It's important."

"I'm up to my neck in work, but have I ever been able to refuse you anything?"

"Start the meter running," she said.

I drove to Richmond, no meter running. I hadn't charged Cliff anything yet either, not even expenses. When I entered the trading room at Bunker, Rose & Diggs and started toward Josey's office, the receptionist intercepted me.

"Miss Lynn's occupied," she said.

I asked her to tell Miss Lynn I had arrived. The receptionist fingered her switchboard, spoke into her headset, and listened before motioning me past. Josey's door was closed. She opened it as I lifted my hand to knock.

"Let's get the hell out of here," she said. The skin of her face appeared waxen and tightly drawn. "The goddamn phone's about to drive me out of my skull."

She buttoned on her camel's hair overcoat.

The receptionist called after her to ask when she would be back.

"Sometime," Josey answered, and her heels clicked on the lobby's terrazzo floor.

We walked out onto East Main and turned at Ninth Street down toward the James. I liked being seen beside her. She stuck her hands deep into her overcoat pockets as the buildings channeled the wind against us. Her stride was fast and hard.

Past the towering Federal Reserve edifice we crossed the pedestrian bridge over to Brown's Island. The James flowed full from snows in the mountains, the water dirtied by the flotsam and a stirred-up bottom. The river, seemingly wrathful, swirled around bridge piling. She stopped, put her hands on the rail, and looked down at the water coiling viciously beneath us.

"I'm in trouble, Raff," she said. "Prince Jamir's bolted and carried away the ton of money people invested with him."

"Where's he now?"

"The sonofabitch is beyond reach, believed to be in an Arab country, Dubai or elsewhere along the Persian Gulf, but it's no certainty. We discovered only this morning he's gone. Raff, I put hundreds of thousands of my clients' dollars in that investment trust as well as all my own and a big chunk of Drake's. I went

272

on margin to buy shares."

Her eyes closed, and she leaned over the railing. I thought of Charles LeBlanc's escrowed money from the Bellerive transaction that I might have invested with the prince had it been available to me. I felt cold and shivered.

"He's left a mountain of bills unpaid," Josey said. "Most of Bellerive's construction costs, the furniture, his plane, all rented or leased. I may be sued, investigated by the SEC, even go to jail. Raff, help me."

"I'll do all I can."

She drew away from the railing and looked at me out of those chestnut eyes that made me feel weak and helpless, stepped to me, circled her arms around my waist, and cried against my chest. I felt her body's trembling.

"I'm so frightened," she said.

"Just don't panic and give me time to look into the matter and get back to you. Make no statement to anyone unless you clear it with me."

"You're a good man, Raff."

"And you're the woman I'm stuck with loving."

"Oh, God, don't talk to me like that at this minute when I'm terrified everything in my life's falling apart."

She continued to cry, the first time I had

273

ever seen her tears, even to way back when she was a young girl who could spit as far as Drake, Cliff, and I. I held her, and the water poured under the bridge, causing the sensation that the river stood still and we were moving upstream together.

"All right, enough," she said and touched her eyes.

I walked her back to Bunker, Rose & Diggs. Wind snapped the colorful banners that fluttered over us. I thought of what Drake had told me and stopped her in the building's lobby.

"Josey, I need to ask you something. A New Year's Eve, some three years ago, were you dating a tennis pro and did you sit at a table with Drake and a girl during the party?"

"The shape I'm in, you're asking me about a fucking party three years ago?"

"It's very important. Do your best to remember."

She touched fingers to her forehead, bit her lip, then raised her face to me.

"Let me think," she said. "Oh, God, yeah, the Chesterfield Country Club, and her name was Rosemary. She wore a slinky red dress that was slit almost to her pudendum."

"Thanks, that's what I was after," I said and held her arm as we moved on to the boisterous trading room, where I left her. She breathed deeply, braced her shoulders, and walked toward her office as if ready to fight and take on all comers.

THIRTY-ONE

Objectively considered, Cliff's situation was more pressing than Josey's, though it was difficult for me to place anyone else's troubles ahead of hers. I couldn't honorably suspend his defense even temporarily to take up hers.

Mary Ellen had left for home, and the day grew late as I sat staring not at lighted St. Luke's and the pigeons but at the office's yet-to-be-decorated back wall in an effort to clear my mind of all distractions and choose how best to proceed.

The phone rang. Wearily I reached for it and recognized the cultured, unhurried voice that belonged to Philip Garrow.

"Concerning Jeremiah Ripley and your problem locating him, I have a ragtag of information," he said. "It is completely unreliable, and I promise nothing. I picked it up from a new employee who claims to have been a friend of a friend sort of thing. If you're still interested."

"Give it to me, please," I said as I drew a pencil from my W&L mug in which Mary Ellen kept half a dozen sharpened and waiting for my use.

"Nirvana Tours, Fort Lauderdale, Florida. I repeat I can't and won't vouch for its accuracy. So many names these days coming and going. We live in a fluid society, nothing permanent."

"The phone number."

"Which I don't have. You might try Information."

"Thank you, Philip."

"Likely a dry well, but the best I can do. Come eat with me soon."

"One day," I said, meant it, and as soon as he hung up phoned Information. I had no difficulty obtaining the number. On reaching Nirvana Tours, I listened to a recorded announcement that the travel agency was open eight to five Monday through Friday and ten till four Saturdays.

At exactly eight o'clock in the morning I called from my apartment and got the recording. I waited five minutes before again trying. The same male voice answered, but this time it was live, and I asked to speak to Jeremiah Ripley.

"Sorry, no one here by that name," he said and hung up.

I called a third time.

"Do you know where Jeremiah Ripley can

be found?" I asked.

"No."

"What's your name?"

"Raoul."

"Have you ever heard of Jeremiah Ripley?"

"Sir, this is a travel agency. You want to go somewhere, we'll plan your trip, okay?"

"You haven't answered my question."

"Don't have to," he said and hung up.

A lost cause, I thought. Philip's employee had probably given him information picked up from gossip heard along the Slip. I looked at St. Luke's steeple, where the pigeons gathered on the lee side. But suppose Jeremiah had fled Richmond and was using another name? Raoul had sounded defensive and been rudely abrupt cutting me off.

I considered hiring a private detective to follow through with an investigation. There was no time. Though I had other cases backed up, making a day trip down to Florida to find out for certain would be both faster and less expensive.

USAir was able to provide me a reserved coach seat at 10:51 that morning which after a change at Charlotte would put me into Fort Lauderdale at 2:43. I booked a return flight at 8:23, again with a change at Charlotte.

I left the office to Mary Ellen, withdrew two hundred dollars from the King County Bank, and drove fast to Byrd Field. A light cold rain rolled across the runway. On the plane I sat next to a man whose nose was almost gone and right hand missing at the wrist, the stump covered by a leather cup. He told me he had been a soldier.

"I saw God's almighty power in the hot pinwheeling blast of a mortar shell," he said. "You can't hide. God searches you out. You hearing me?"

"I'm thinking it over."

"You don't have to think. God'll do your thinking. Mortar taught me that. Mortars speak a universal language that everybody understands — Japs, Chinks, A-rabs, don't make no difference, you know right on the spot. You believe in anything?"

"I believe in yesterday," I said.

"Ha," he said and turned away, hunched in his seat, and slept.

I thought of yesterdays and how Cliff, Drake, and I had grown close during our youthful adventures. The three of us went way back to a Richmond neighborhood called Wellsby Park, an area of houses that sat as snugly comfortable on mowed and tended lawns as hens on their nests.

Up the street rose the stone seminary buildings, and their antiquated, lichen-coated elms dropped a deep shade on uneven brick sidewalks along which theological students strolled, their hands lifted in doctrinal discourses. Drake, Cliff, and I had sneaked onto campus one September night and sewed a jockstrap on the bronze erect figure of John Calvin, who stood gazing upward with arms spread as if conversing with God.

As boys our parents sent us to Wicomico in Westmoreland County, Virginia, a summer camp on the broad tidal river that emptied into the Chesapeake Bay. We learned to shoot with .22-caliber rifles at bull's-eyes of paper targets and used twenty-gauge shotguns to break clay pigeons flung by a trap out over the lapping water. Oyster spat clung to sunken, shattered pieces and reproduced bountifully.

Sun-blasted, we fished for spot, croaker, and flounder. The black cook and his wife served us so many fried softshell crabs that we complained. The camp's main activity centered around sailing in twenty-foot wooden sloops built by native shipwrights along the river's shore. The sloops were open, no cuddy cabins or lazarettes, no compasses or running lights, and held to course by slablike centerboards located amidship. We bumped our knees on their protruding wells.

Across the Wicomico the girls had a camp named Hiawatha. We spied them at a distance in their bright canoes, the colors reflected in the water. A southern breeze carried their shouts and laughter as paddles dipped up flashing sunlight.

Drake, Cliff, and I got into trouble on a July Fourth because we broke rules by sneaking away a boat at night to intersect with a spit of land near Hiawatha, where the hull ground across sand as we beached her. Hiding under drooping cedars, we spied on the girls dressed like Indians who whooped it up around a campfire, their hunched-and-reared shapes silhouetted against the sparks of the swirling flames. When we returned to the boat, the rising tide had lifted and carried her off. We hiked seven miles to a bridge and worked our way back to Wicomico late that night, where all the cabin lights were switched on and Captain Tom and the counselors waited.

Captain Tom, a craggy man with skin like rawhide from years of boating on the Chesapeake, called our fathers to tell them to come after us. We caught it hot because our parents received no refunds, but passing through tribulation together set Drake, Cliff, and me apart. Mine had been a lesser daring, not really wanting to take the boat and trying to talk Cliff and Drake out of it, yet I had gone along, and to use the military parlance, we had all three shared the action and bonded.

★ ★ ★

After the change in Charlotte I watched the earth transform itself beneath the plane, a patchy fabric of snow giving way to slowly emerging green, and finally the sun cast the Airbus's shadow onto a sweep across blue water as we made our approach to Fort Lauderdale. The ocean, as if a vast broken mirror, reflected silver shards all the way to the horizon.

At the Fort Lauderdale terminal I stored my overcoat, hat, and umbrella in a locker, used the phone book to find Nirvana Tours' address on South Mahia Boulevard, and hailed a cab. The Hispanic driver drove us along a tropical avenue flanked by royal palms and white houses with red tile roofs, many behind walls overgrown with flowering bougainvillea. Wishing I had brought my sunglasses, I squinted against the glare. In Florida's warmth, my flannel suit felt scratchy and oppressive.

Nirvana Tours turned out to be the first floor of a stucco building in the Mermaid Plaza Mall. Shimmering heat rose from an expanse of dazzling concrete. Atop a fountain a plastic mermaid sat — rouged, her breasts covered by strands of golden hair, her enormous eyes looking astonished at her navel from which water spurted and splashed into a pool at her feet.

The window at Nirvana Tours held a smirking plaster Buddha with raised arms who offered an airline ticket in one hand, a tiger lily in the other. Around him were coconuts, seashells, and colorful brochures offering cruises to the Bahamas, St. John, and Aruba.

I opened the agency's door and stepped into the cooling relief of air conditioning.

"Got a letter here to mail," a young man said. He had a Latino appearance, and when he stepped around me to leave, I smelled aftershave lotion. His voice belonged to Raoul.

I glanced at wall posters of a Hawaiian beach and Gauguin's Tahitian women. Small clocks displayed the times in Australia, Berlin, London, Buenos Aires, and a ceiling loudspeaker gave out sounds of waves softly splashing a shore.

The door behind the desk opened, and a blonde holding a pencil stepped out. In her hair she had pinned a pink hibiscus which coupled nicely with her white sleeveless blouse.

"Raoul?" she asked.

"I believe he's mailing a letter," I said.

"May I help you?" she asked as she crossed to the counter. Her bare, tanned legs contrasted prettily with her white linen skirt. Before I answered, the yellow desk telephone rang. She reached for it, identified Nirvana Tours, and cocked her head to listen. Her earrings were tiny ceramic pelicans, and around her neck hung a thin gold chain that held a tiny bleached and lacquered starfish.

"I'll send a schedule of events," she said and let her eyes drift upward as if long suffering. They were a greenish-blue turquoise and striking. "Yes, charges include breakfast."

She hung up, penciled a note, and stuck it on the monitor before again facing me.

"Now," she said and smiled.

"I called earlier today and talked to Raoul about locating a man named Jeremiah Ripley who I was told works at Nirvana Tours."

"He doesn't, and to my knowledge never has. Afraid you made your trip for nothing."

"How do you know I made a trip?"

"You're typical of a tourist right off the plane."

"Help me," I said.

"Help you how?"

"By cooperating with me."

"I believe that's exactly what I'm doing at this moment."

A whistling Raoul walked in carrying mail. He stopped to glance at her and me.

"Raoul, how long have you been working here?" she asked.

"You know, Phyllis."

"Tell the man."

"Couple of years," Raoul said.

"Did a Jeremiah Ripley have a job here?"

"Not in my time."

"You've never known a Jeremiah Ripley?" I asked.

Raoul shook his head and gave his attention to the mail.

"Enough cooperation?" Phyllis asked and turned away. Thongs fastened leather sandals to her ankles, and her toenails too were pink. She walked into her office and closed the door.

"Something else?" Raoul asked. He began sorting mail on the counter, slapping down envelopes as if dealing cards to different poker players. He sailed an advertisement into a wastebasket.

"You ever heard of a Jeremiah Ripley?" I asked.

"Only Jeremiah I heard of's in the Bible," he said. "Big-time prophet."

"I've traveled a long way. If you have any information at all about him it could be of great assistance to me."

"Just don't know your guy. Sorry."

Something nagged at my memory. The office door opened, and the woman, Phyllis, looked out.

"I hope you're not becoming a nuisance," she said.

"I don't mean to be, but I have this feeling that things here aren't altogether what they seem."

"Will you leave or do I call mall security?"

"Why won't you talk straight with me?"

"Call them," she ordered Raoul.

Raoul crossed to the desk, lifted the phone, and punched in the numbers with a middle finger that looked meant for me.

"All right, I'm gone," I said.

I walked from coolness into the pain of sunlight flashing and reflecting off this great white city. To have come so far for so little. A breeze caused fronds of coconut palms to rattle dryly but brought no relief. Children played around the splashing pool on the bottom of which lay pennies. The water, like the blonde's eyes, was turquoise.

Three ancient, white-haired men guiding battery-powered and flagged wheelchairs passed like ducks in a row, the rubber tires making a hiss across the hot concrete. I felt sadness at the plight of the old, the sick, the failing, these chasers of the sun's warmth who could generate little heat of their own. I remembered a line from *Moby Dick*, ". . . tearless Lima the strangest, saddest city thou canst see. For Lima had taken the white veil; and there is a higher horror in this whiteness of her woe."

I had hours to kill before my flight to Richmond. I could eat, perhaps ride a cab to the beach, push off my shoes, and walk at the edge of the surf, allowing it to wash and foam around my pale ankles.

As I stood by the pool and watched the spreading ripples, I thought of the cold rain or worse back in Virginia. I looked upward to the astonished mermaid. Phyllis's striking eyes lodged in my mind. I tried to call up a face briefly seen where and when. While I strolled along South Mahia Boulevard, I passed the incongruity of a Baptist church built after the flamboyant Moroccan style. The marquee read, ARE YOU PREPARED FOR ETERNITY? APPLICATIONS ACCEPTED INSIDE.

I reset my glasses and recalled being at The Watchers and seeing the hillside graveyard that had plots but no markers. A girl wearing a raincoat and slouch hat had been sitting in a rear pew of the church weeping. I couldn't be certain, not in the few seconds I had glimpsed her that day. I might be forcing memory, in effect composing it.

I walked back to Nirvana Tours, where Raoul typed at the computer keyboard. Through the partially opened office door I saw Phyllis seated in a leather-and-chrome swivel chair. She uncrossed her legs and leaned forward to peer at papers on her desk before becoming aware of me.

"Security," Raoul said and again reached to the phone.

"I believe you were in Virginia," I called to her. "At The Watchers' cemetery and church."

"You have lost it, mister. Never heard of anybody named Watchers."

"Ring security," I said to Raoul. "I'll go with the police and ask for their assistance. I'm an attorney and officer of the court. Better for you to talk to me now than later."

She gazed at me, stood, and walked to Raoul's desk where she laid a finger to click off the connection.

"Identification?" she said.

I showed her my Virginia Bar Association membership card. She read it and my driver's license before passing them back.

"Why are you here?" she asked.

"I'd appreciate your allowing me to come in for a talk."

She hesitated before making a listless motion with her hand, a half turn of her palm, and returned to her office. I walked around the counter and entered. She closed the door, sat, and adjusted her skirt across her knees.

On her desk she had set a color photograph of a mustached, bare-chested man holding a fishing rod and standing beside a blue marlin hung by its tail from a dockside pulley, the fish's eyes seemingly widened in shock and astonishment at its situation.

"Talk," she said.

"Wendell Ripley," I said, and looking into her face I pictured a quiet little man in Drake's Blind Sheep cabin whose bleached turquoise eyes had met mine over the pale yellow flame of a kerosene lamp.

"That name means nothing to me."

"You resemble him."

She shrugged. "So?"

"He and his wife had an only child, a son named Jeremiah."

"I know nothing of him or them."

"I believe otherwise," I said, though still unsure. "I intend to pursue it fully with the police."

She delayed speaking.

"There is no Jeremiah Ripley," she said. "He's gone."

"But then it turns out you do know of him."

"Did. He's dead."

"The cause of his death?"

"His was a suicide."

"Can you tell me where he's buried?"

"At sea. His ashes were scattered at high tide from a powerboat off the city."

"You're certain of that fact?"

"Yes, I am, I was there."

"My belief is that you're kin."

"We were. Wendell Ripley was my uncle."

"I've been told Mr. Ripley had no other family."

"You were told wrong."

"Not according to Brother Abram. You remember Brother Abram out at The Watchers?"

"No."

"I'll find out. Believe me, there will be no place you can hide."

She tightened her mouth, ran the fingers of one hand over the back of the other, and looked at the photograph of the man on her desk. He was sandy-haired and clamped a congratulatory cigar in teeth of his grinning, sun-darkened face.

"Did you come to hound me?" she asked.

"I came because a man in jail will go to prison unless I gather evidence that will resolve the charge against him. Now just tell me what you know about Jeremiah Ripley."

She touched the tip of her tongue to her upper lip, removed the hibiscus, and laid it on her desk. The shadowed lids of her eyes heightened their color.

"Jeremiah Ripley's dead. Laid to rest in this world. Phyllis Duke supplanted him."

"Supplanted?"

"Look at me." She lifted and profiled her face. "Look at me good. Am I a woman?"

"Obviously you are."

"Ashes dropped into the sea."

"You're telling me you're — ?"

"Say what you're thinking."

"A transsexual?"

"What a loaded word. I'm what I've always been inside."

"Your operation was when?" I asked.

"Two years and four months ago. When I first fled to Florida. I had saved money and borrowed more. The operation cost twenty-seven thousand dollars. God, if you could feel the liberation and freedom I felt. Like a bird released from its cage. All those years at The Watchers, that grim life forced on me. I loved my father but had to break loose. For nineteen years I lived in a prison. I almost died there — like a plant denied sunlight."

There was no lingering male huskiness in her voice, and she was lovely, anguished, and very definitely appealing.

"Jeremiah Ripley's gone," she said. "I changed my name legally and started work at Nirvana as a clerk for the lady who owned it and wanted to retire. She's allowing me to pay for the purchase out of profits."

She glanced at the photograph.

"I'm to be married," she said and held up the diamond on her finger. "I'll answer the question you want to ask. Does the man understand about me? He does. We live together. He thinks I'm wonderful."

"It's your past relationship with Clifford Dickens and Drake Wingo I need to know about."

"Clifford Dickens was my teacher for one English class at Virginia Commonwealth University, nothing more. Drake Wingo employed me at Grizzly's."

"Why did you leave Grizzly's so abruptly?"

"I saw no future in selling shoes."

The telephone rang. We heard Raoul's voice in the front office. He knocked on the door, stuck in his head, and said, "Allan."

"Tell him I'll call soon as I can," Phyllis said, her every action womanly. Raoul closed the door.

"How did it happen?" I asked.

"What happened?"

"The sex you had with either of them or both."

"What makes you believe I had sex with anybody?"

"You and Drake Wingo were seen on the camp cot in his office," I said, presenting it that way, though not at all certain that's the way it had been. "New Year's Eve three years ago."

She was shaken. Her body softened, and her hands gave way to her lap.

"Do you absolutely need this information? It could cause me great and enduring harm."

"Without it the wrong man will go to prison."

"Goddamn you for doing this to me. I have a new life."

"Believe that I don't like doing it."

"From the first day at Grizzly's I was attracted to Drake. He didn't know. I didn't want it to be that way and hid my feelings. He used to lay his hand on my shoulder as we talked about stock and displays. His touch made me fall apart inside."

She moistened her lips, and her hands continued to lie but had begun to quiver palms upward.

"Drake and I worked late New Year's Eve taking inventory. The others had gone home. When we finished, he brought a bottle of bourbon from his desk and invited me to share a drink. It had been a good year for the store. 'Some way to celebrate,' he said. 'No bands or whistles, just a toast to Grizzly's.' "

She swallowed, raised her face, but averted her eyes.

"We kept drinking. We walked around the store holding insulated glasses taken from camping equipment. While we started switching out lights, he put an arm around my shoulder, a man-to-man gesture. On a drunken impulse, I turned and kissed his mouth."

I didn't speak or move.

"He hit me. He knocked me down, stood above me, cursed and kicked me. I covered my face. He walked off, returned, and knelt to help me stand. I clung to him. He tried to shake me loose, but I wouldn't let go. He stood with me holding to him, my face pressed against him until the fight went out of him and, as the saying goes, one thing led to another."

"That the only time?" I asked. I felt sick and had difficulty steadying my voice.

"Over several weeks we met, but not at the store. He became terribly confused and tormented, yet kept coming back for me. He hated himself for it, and that's why I left. I escaped, no forwarding address. In Miami, Jeremiah gave way to Phyllis."

"Did you dress as a female back in Richmond?" I asked, remembering Phoebe's telling me about shadowing Drake and a young woman to the Shady Spring Motel.

"Whenever I could. I was already considering the change, gathering the money, taking injections."

The phone again rang, and Raoul talked, yet didn't disturb us. Phyllis set both feet on the floor, sat straight in the chair, and ran fingers along the skirt covering her thighs.

"You had no sexual relationship with Clifford Dickens?"

"None. Isn't there any way you can keep me out of this? I've made a new life for myself."

"I don't see how altogether. I'll do my best to hold it to depositions and expose you as little as possible. What about a sailor named Leonard Dawson?"

"There was no such person. I made him up and used him to deflect my father from Drake."

"You won't run?"

"I'm through running. I'm ready to lead a normal life as odd as the word may sound to you."

"I'd like to see your Social Security card."

"So you can track me down?"

"I don't want to have to use it."

"You won't need to," she said and reached to a drawer to lift out a wallet. "I'm through running."

The number and the name Duke were on her driver's license. I copied it and handed the license back. I also asked for her home phone number.

"And I believed I'd become free at last," she said.

THIRTY-TWO

In the airport's sandwich shop, I ate a hot dog at the stand-up counter, smoked, and rubbed my eyes during the flight back to Virginia. I kept shaking my head and received inquiring looks from a stewardess, who passed out pillows.

I let my head fall back against the pillow and remembered how Drake had been our leader the autumn evening we fought three members of the River Rat Gang who accosted us as we sneaked past the twin turrets and arched stone facade of the old King Arthur Hotel. Only a few naked bulbs, one of them red, burned dimly behind begrimed panes beyond which were mysterious and threatening shapes. The hotel's upper windows were as vacant as gouged-out eyes.

We had heard stories that prostitutes paraded around the hotel, and we wanted to see them in their actual painted flesh. We caught only a glimpse of a single dusky woman who wore tight shorts and high heels that cracked against the sidewalk as she diminished into an embracing darkness. As we left disappointed, three River Rats stepped from the reddened alley and mauled us against the hotel's sooty bricks until a blue-and-white cruiser arrived, and two patrolmen broke up the melee and sent us home.

During the fight I had been shocked and sickened by the pain from the fists and mostly just covered my face and ducked around behind Drake and Cliff while they valorously attempted to slug it out. I had shared the glory of conflict and survival but secretly felt they had somehow left me behind and was greatly relieved they still accepted me as their equal and friend. It had been the next night we swore triple oaths of allegiance by candlelight, the words ratified by our shared juvenile blood. *Nunquam trado.*

The plane landed in Richmond at 12:14, too late to go directly to Drake's house and see him without alarming Deborah. That confrontation could wait until morning when I would also begin procedures for releasing Cliff from jail.

I drove to Jessup's Wharf, had a bath, and plopped into the bed. Half a dozen times during the rest of the night I stood to smoke. I finally drifted off listening to the wind and woke startled by the Axapomini Lumber's shrill seven-o'clock whistle. A thick, nasty taste continued to gum my mouth. While still in pajamas, I made the call to Drake.

"He's at his camp," Deborah said. "He never misses the last week of grouse season. He tried to reach you."

I thanked her, thought of conferring with Cliff, but decided to wait till I had it all straight with Drake. My window thermometer read thirty degrees, and I pulled on my hunt britches, Bean boots, and jacket. When I stopped by the office to leave Mary Ellen a note telling her where I'd be, I saw she had logged Drake's call.

I drove west under a scarf of clouds draping a pale cold sky. At New Kent I drove up the ramp to Interstate 64 and four hours later stopped for gas at Monterey before turning north into the Wilderness River Valley. The sides of the road were still flanked by partially melted humps of blackened snow.

Drake would be wary, sure to figure I had not come for the hunting. I couldn't force him to return with me and considered changing plans and detouring to High Gap and a conference first with Sam Tuggle. No, I owed Drake more than that, at least hearing his side of events I didn't yet understand.

At one-thirty I crossed the Seneca County line and twenty minutes later stopped the car at the foot of the logging road that led up Blind Sheep to the cabin. My Buick lacked four-wheel drive and would likely become stuck in the rutted road or bang its oil pan. I locked the car, tightened my belt, and hiked the slope coated with hoarfrost.

Wolf Creek ran full, smashing its way among rocks, the spray misting along the bank. The ground was caught in a partial thaw that caused my boots to lose their grip.

I spotted Drake's mud-caked Bronco beside the cabin. Thin whitish smoke drifted from the chimney. The door's hasp had been swung aside, and the padlock dangled from its chain. I knocked as I stepped inside.

Drake stood lifting his Savage from the gun rack. A plucked and gutted grouse hung from a leather noose attached to a nail pounded in a roof beam. Kraut stood beside Drake, the liver pointer's docked tail wagging, his amber eyes alert and alight.

"I got tonight's meal up Ash House Hollow," Drake said of the grouse. "We'll leave him to ripen. You just in time to join me for the afternoon shoot. Where's your artillery?"

"I'm not here to hunt, Drake."

"Well, I am and mean to," he said and moved around me.

"Stop and talk to me."

"No, man, not now. You too solemn. Only birds on my mind the last week of the season. Everything else is against the rules and off-limits. The last days belong to the grouse."

He fitted shells into his jacket slots, reset his cap, and walked outside.

"If you're staying, I won't lock it," he called back.

"I have serious stuff on my mind, Drake."

"Me too. Brown birds, and I'm hitting the trail."

He circled away around the cabin.

"I'm asking you to wait," I said as I followed.

He ignored me, and I hesitated. Go for the sheriff? Drake moved up the mountain with his determined stride. Kraut stayed at heel, wanting to leap ahead, the restraint stiffening his legs. The small bell attached to his leather collar tinkled.

"Listen to me," I called as I hurried to catch up.

"We'll climb to the ridge and hunt till we reach Sugar Camp and then cut down to Laurel Fork and along Burnt Cabin and back to Slash Lick."

"Don't do this to me, Drake."

"I'm not hearing you," he said and jerked back the bolt to thumb three shells into the Savage. When he pressed the release, the bolt clanged forward.

"And to Cliff," I said.

He hiked on without answering. A swirl of

wind caused hemlock branches to stir and wa-
ver. Snow still draped shadowed depressions
of the mountain, and a damp coldness moved
off them.

"I love wind," Drake said. "It wants its
meal. Give me something to tear up, the wind
says. A spruce, sumac, or ironwood, my
belly's never full. Wind's music to the
grouse."

"I've heard your talk," I said and climbed
behind him.

"Worth repeating. Hold the grouse in your
mind, you won't go wrong."

"Is that what you're doing?"

"Got to hie to the mountains to get right,"
he said and increased his pace.

"Let's stop the performance," I said as I
struggled to keep up.

"Raff, you're too grim. Not allowed on
Blind Sheep. And the pollution of words can
befoul the air. Just listen to the mountain's
language, take it in, let it clean your blood."

We reached a stand of laurel, not catalpa,
but large-leaf rhododendron, which Drake
skirted. He had warned Cliff, Wendell, and
me we could become exhausted trying to
bully our way through. The leaves had partially uncurled in the increasing warmth. Our
boots dislodged pebbles, maybe former boulders ground down by the relentless creep of

glaciers. A dip of land gathered mist like a drifting pool of unearthly water.

Drake's motion of tossing a softball under-handed released Kraut, who bounded forward and coursed ahead along the trail.

"With this wind the birds should stick to the lee side of the mountain," Drake said. "They could be gathering on the beech flats."

"Stop evading me, Drake."

"I'm not hearing you," he answered, and at that instant a grouse burst into flight from laurel and banked left. Drake didn't hurry. He lifted the Savage with seemingly leisurely grace, fired, and the bird dropped in an arc to crash through laurel leaves.

Again the sweep of a hand, and Kraut twisted in for the retrieve. The leaves clacked, the bell sounded, and Kraut emerged holding the grouse. He stood on his hind legs to place his front paws on Drake's chest. Drake patted him and took the bird in hand. Kraut dropped back to the ground, excited, proud, tongue out panting.

"Hen," Drake said, his fingers stroking its feathers, a reverence in his touch. The grouse's dark eyes closed as if entering sleep. Drake slipped the bird gently into his game pouch, where it would cool and stiffen.

"Rockets," he said and reloaded. "Some university pointy head figured they reach a speed of forty-five miles an hour. Maybe that's increasing as the slower birds get shot out. How'd you like to be a grouse, Raff? Live it all to the full? Life not by extent but intensity?"

"Cliff's waiting in jail," I said.

"Grouse don't question the life allowed them. Live hard and die cleanly."

"I know about your relationship with Jeremiah," I said.

Not answering, Drake signaled Kraut forward and moved upward to eerie thorn apple trees growing in the wild tangled grass that had once been land used by shepherds to feed their flocks. Like sheer, torn rags the mist clung to the bare twisted branches.

"Birds dine on the hard bitter fruit," Drake said as if I'd asked. "Tough and bitter to man but to grouse it tastes of the mountain and freedom."

"I talked to Jeremiah."

"Sure," he said and didn't slow.

Kraut pushed up a bird among the thorn apples. It flew low and canted down the slope. The dog slunk back guiltily. Drake called him in, rubbed his chest, and said, "It's all right, fellow. It spooked long. Hie on."

Kraut resumed coursing ahead of us. A feeble sunlight broke through and glimmered on the wet grass and shiny limbs of the thorn apples.

"No more evasion, Drake," I said.

"Bird," he said and slowed to raise his Savage. With the gun's muzzle he indicated the faint tracks — a dainty stitching across a shadowed patch of snow. "Close. Searching for cover."

He whistled to Kraut, and the bell quieted as the pointer approached softly. His tail signaled interest but not conviction. The Savage held high, Drake stepped forward. No grouse flushed, though Kraut nosed in. Drake squatted to examine the tracks and their abrupt disappearance.

"Didn't get up or we'd heard," he said. "A ghost bird."

He stood to climb on, acting as if I were no longer behind him, then stopped, knelt, and fingered chalky round pellets.

"Droppings but not fresh," he said and smelled them. "Around here we don't call them fresh unless they still rolling."

"Jeremiah told me about the two of you," I said.

"Raff, you're fucking up my hunt."

"Who were you fucking?"

He looked at me hard, then again strode upward toward the ridge at the same time shifting the Savage to the crook of his left arm.

"Not hearing you," he said. "Got brown

birds on my mind. The sunshine'll bring them out to feed."

Kraut went on point. The grouse flapped up from under sumac, its wings beating the bush, its neck stretched long, and its gleaming eyes took me in as it curved left away. When Drake fired, the load hit the bird so squarely it went limp, spun into a drooping fall, and bounced against the ground, where it left a sprinkle of blood across snow.

"Poleaxed him," Drake said and stroked the bird before handing it to me. I drew fingers over the beautiful and marvelously complex design of brown and bronze. The black stripe across its tail feathers appeared a masterful touch of creation. I felt the warmth of the bird's breast and the last lingering tremor of departing life.

"That stripe identifies a male," Drake said.

"About Cliff in jail," I said. "This is your chance to explain before I drive to High Gap and tell the authorities what I know."

"I might give up life in the lowlands and stay on the mountain full-time," Drake said, again climbing. "Sometimes I feel I can fly off Blind Sheep to the Ram's Horn. Up to the top of the world with the ravens in the mist. Hunt my own food. Like a bear graze the land. You want to hear some real poetry, Raff, not the crap the arty crowd laps up."

"What I want is for you go back with me."

"Persimmons, papaws, fiddleheads, cattails, mountain rice, ramps, wild hyacinth, Indian cucumber, wild onions, walnuts, sheep sorrel," he recited. "The real poetry."

"Your best chance is to come in with me."

"Here's more: pokeweed, sassafras, beechnuts, shepherd's purse, chokeberries, wild plum, black cherry, Kentucky coffee, sweet cicely, wild parsnips, watercress. You'd grow fat, Raff. No chemicals in the system. All mountain food unspoiled by the human touch. Lowland shit can't reach this high unless you bring it with you."

We heard the batting of wings but saw no bird. Kraut stopped to listen before nosing on before us.

"Kraut knows in his genes that before putting down the bird will flair to one side or the other," Drake said. "Tough scent, the feathers air-washed."

Again he stopped to check droppings.

"J-hooks," he said. "Not grouse, but male turkey. Hens don't have the hook."

"I can bring Jeremiah to High Gap," I said.

He kept on without answering. A bird fluttered from a limb of a shelly bark hickory and barreled directly at us, its head lifted above the plane of its body, seemingly intent on collision. I ducked but Drake stood upright and waited for the bird to pass before turning to shoot him cleanly, causing the grouse to shed feathers and tumble across the trail.

"I love them," he said, taking the retrieve from Kraut. "For me it's spiritual."

"Who else have you loved?"

As he fitted the grouse into the game pouch, he spat and stepped to the top of the ridge. Combers of mountains rolled away westward, a gray, whitecapped sea. Beyond rose the Ram's Horn, the snow-crowned peak dazzled by sunlight that broke through rampaging clouds.

"Indians believed the Great Spirit lived up there," Drake said. "They smarter than us."

"Jeremiah will testify."

"Next Sugar Camp," Drake said and strode fast along the ridge to a cleavage of land where the hollow intersected it. The way down was steep, the footing loose shale, but he didn't slacken his gait. Under a canopy of hemlocks a creek made up and began its descent to the valley. He stopped, dipped a hand in the water, and drank from his palm.

"Have a swaller," he said. "Tastes of the mountain. The pure stuff that moves down so fast it bashes all the germs. No bacteria can take the beating. Living in cities you forget what real water tastes like."

"Jeremiah will reveal your relationship with him," I said.

Drake didn't respond but jumped the creek to a needle-strewn deer path that wound down among the hemlocks. Again I followed. We walked past the grouse, which flushed to my right. Drake fired, the bird shuddered and fought to keep flying, lost altitude, and drifted into shadows.

"Winged him good," he said. "Kraut'll run him down."

Kraut skirted the side of the hollow, moving fast, his nose low to the ground. He stopped on point as if he'd crashed into an invisible wall. Drake stepped in behind. No bird. Drake circled. Still Kraut didn't break. He trembled, and his eyes bulged. Drake raised a finger. As I looked to the spot he indicated, the bird seemed to materialize and take shape among the moist, leafy mast. Drake reached down and lifted it.

The grouse's eyes were open, watching, seemingly not so much frightened as waiting and accepting whatever the hand would bring.

"Cock in the red phase," Drake said, examining it. He held it close to his eyes. "Just grazed him, one pellet across his skull knocked him silly. He ought to be able to shake it off and fly."

He kissed the top of the bird's head and lifted it on his palms as if presenting an offering to the sky. The grouse dipped almost to the ground before its wings took hold of air and it sped low and away down Sugar Camp.

"Have a good life," Drake called after it before turning to me. "You know anything better than this?"

"I know you're in terrible trouble."

He drew a Winesap from the pocket of his jacket and bit into it. His teeth crunched the bite.

"All right," he said, chewing. "We befoul the high country with words."

THIRTY-THREE

As Drake munched the apple, his blue eyes locked on me. Kraut loped back and stood beside him to wait and watch.

"You're telling me you've been with Jeremiah?"

"Just yesterday," I answered.

"You see, Raff, I don't happen to believe that."

"You'd do well to, Drake."

"What I believe is he's long gone."

"No, I found him."

"Got your proof?"

"He told me about your New Year's Eve celebration at Grizzly's and said among other things that you knocked him down and kicked him."

Drake with one last deep bite finished the apple. He tossed the core down the slope, and Kraut raised his head, alert and ready to retrieve.

"Where is he?" Drake asked.

"Where I can find him."

"So you claim."

"He won't run this time."

"And you won't tell me?"

"Not at the moment."

"I'm not falling for this."

"The best thing you can do is come in with me."

"You told anybody yet?"

"I wanted to talk to you first."

"How can I be sure you got him and he's not lit out somewhere else?"

"I'm looking you straight in the eye and telling you."

Drake spat out seeds, reset his cap, and started down along Sugar Camp Run. He looked at me.

"You think I wanted this?" he asked. "That I meant to hurt Cliff? I'm no fag, Raff. You know it. I been more man than any of you. I just got into a craziness during a moment of liquor and heat. And he was more girl than guy. Had curves on him, ways of moving like a woman. Little bitch knew the buttons to push. I couldn't shake him or live with it."

A plane gleaming like silver flew over high. Through a break in the clouds I looked up among the rustling hemlocks and saw the white contrails it laid behind uncurl and warp slowly in the wind.

"You have to come back," I said.

"Look, Raff, even as things stand now, there's still a chance Cliff won't be convicted and serve jail time. We hire the best lawyers and fight it to the wall."

"And if he's found guilty?"

"I'll set him up, deposit money to his account every month, invest it in his name. He'll be released with deep pockets and can play the artist the rest of his life."

"That won't do."

"You got to see things been going right for me. This shit comes up just when I'm getting all I ever wanted in the world. I'm not turning it loose."

"You'll need counsel," I said.

He took off his cap and wiped it across his face. Crows cawed, fussing and diving at a hawk that flew on unconcerned.

"Your way it can't be kept quiet," he said. "The word'll get out and ruin me. Raff, try to understand I didn't mean for it to turn out how it has. I burned with shame, fired Jerry from the store, but I'd be hit with this call of the wild, and the dirty thing would build up. This last couple of years all that's over. Jerry was gone, I believed dead. I'm a good husband and father. You concede that?"

"I do, Drake."

He set on his cap and shifted the Savage from one hand to the other.

"Wendell was trying to track down Jeremiah," he said. "Biblical name for a slut.

Dressed up like a woman, all the intimate paraphernalia. And the sonofabitch could be beautiful, wearing earrings, lipstick, eyeliner, heels. Jerry'd tease you with a nylon thigh that you'd swear belonged to a chorus girl. After he left, Wendell was searching for him and the person he believed seduced his son. Nobody ruined Jerry. He was what he wanted to be."

A shadow slid across broken sunlight on the ground — a buzzard flying over, wings set, wobbling in flight, searching.

"Wendell never suspected you?" I asked.

"He did but Jerry laid a false trail about a man named Dawson, supposedly a sailor from Chicago. Wendell tried to find Dawson, paid a private detective to do it. Wendell considered it wrong to hate, yet hate ate him up. He wanted vengeance, a mortal sin, and at the same time to forgive, and the contradiction tore him apart."

"Why did he suspect Cliff?"

"Wendell received a phone call from a stranger. He began checking, asking questions around. He hated himself for hating."

Drake again started down the mountain, following the stream's flow. Thin, fragile ice along the bank was giving up to warmth and breaking away.

"While hanging out at the store Wendell discovered I knew Cliff," Drake said over his

314

shoulder. "No way I could deny it. He questioned me, and I believed I'd persuaded him Cliff wasn't his man but that it was Dawson."

"Why did you take the risk of having Wendell on the hunt?"

"I didn't consider it a risk. Wendell appeared convinced it was Dawson. I'd been organizing the hunt for you, Cliff, and me anyhow as well as trying to buy the land. Seemed a time to get two for one. How could I know he'd blame Cliff?"

He lifted a hand and pointed. The shadow within a shadow was a white-flecked doe slipping delicately among hemlocks. She stopped to look at us before bounding off, her flag lifted.

"I never believed Wendell would cause trouble," Drake said, moving on. "Not with his religion. That first evening at the cabin, he and Cliff got along. You were there and saw it."

"Any idea who the stranger was that called and put Wendell on to Cliff?"

"No."

"But Wendell did for a time suspect you?"

"He suspected everybody."

"He grew to trust you."

"As much as he trusted anybody."

Sugar Camp Run had deepened and was flowing faster as we descended. Ice slabs bobbed and broke against rocks.

"It must have been tough for you to face Cliff knowing he'd seen what you and Jeremiah were doing that night at Grizzly's."

Drake stopped, and his eyes searched mine.

"The picture of you Cliff carried in his mind," I said. "Every time you faced him, you'd wonder what he was remembering. He had to be a reminder you couldn't escape, mocking the life you presented to the world."

"You got a smoke?" Drake asked.

We lit up my Winstons. It was the first time for years I had seen Drake with a cigarette. He liked to center them in his teeth, breathe and talk around them.

"Be difficult in such a situation to put up with a person like that, thinking he was recalling memory pictures each time you met," I said.

"So?"

"I'm just trying to put it all together and thinking of Sheriff Sawyers checking Wendell's Remington and finding the safety on, no shells in the gun, slots of his hunting vest empty."

"We been over that."

"My guess is after our talk you got in touch with Josey and asked her to lie for you about your being at the Chesterfield Country Club's New Year's Eve."

"Something like that."

"She believed she was helping Cliff by lying for you."

"She didn't and doesn't know the whole picture. We've always been close. She's also into me for a bunch of my money she invested."

"And you fired Boomer before I could reach him."

Drake shrugged.

"I told you my theory. Wendell never meant to kill anybody, that he maneuvered Cliff into thinking he had to shoot to save himself," I said.

As I spoke the words, a sickening option formed in my mind, and for a moment I faltered. Drake's eyes probed, and they saw that I saw.

"Something?" he asked, blowing smoke.

"I'm again wondering how Wendell's religious convictions would have held him in check. He couldn't bring himself to kill, yet still would want retribution for what happened to Jeremiah. What about this — he could resolve the dilemma by compelling Cliff to shoot him, resulting in the end of Wendell's suffering as well as the prosecution and punishment under the law of the person he believed was his son's corrupter?"

"Anything else?" Drake asked. "Come on,

Raff, I see it on you."

"All right, another scenario. Picture the situation. A man of standing fears a hideous secret might be revealed. Only one person is left living who shares it, he believes, and our man of standing is haunted by the danger of the secret's ever being revealed and is desperate to be rid of the anguish it causes him. To do so he manipulates a third party full of an obsessive rage into solving his problem."

"Fancy theory," Drake said. "What's the point?"

"Why I guess you're the point, Drake. You said Wendell suspected you. You could have led him on as he grew close by creating false leads. You might have made a telephone call from a stranger. You taught Wendell to shoot and arranged the time and place for it. As I remember, you also cut the cards that paired us for the day's hunt. You had me alongside as a witness to prevent your being implicated in the killing."

Drake drew the cigarette from his teeth, snuffed it with his fingers, and field-stripped it as soldiers learned to do. I dropped mine and ground my heel on it.

"That it?" he asked.

"But Wendell deceived you. He arranged his revenge by bluffing Cliff into protecting himself. You meant for Wendell to kill Cliff and thought he would. How's that so far?"

"Makes a good story."

"A well-constructed plan — Cliff goes to the grave carrying the secret, Wendell is likely to escape prosecution, and you're safe. Except Wendell turns out to be more devious than you considered possible."

"I didn't kill Wendell. There's no way they can put that on me."

"You can be indicted for accessory to murder."

"It's still my word against Cliff's."

"Except for Jeremiah."

"Goddamn you, Raff."

"Is this a confession?"

"You really expect me to turn myself in?"

"Drake, what's happened to you?"

"Survival's what's happened."

"No matter how the law judges you, your affair with Jeremiah will come out. You'll not be able to dodge the media muck."

"You think I haven't considered that? I got the most to lose. Simple, an elementary equation, you do the numbers, like a body count in the military — one casualty lost, Cliff, against another man, his wife, twin daughters, his son about to be born, and 'The Truth of the Grouse.' I can't give those up."

"Come back with me. I'll stand by you and do all I can to negotiate and devise a plea that'll hold publicity to a minimum. There's no alternative."

"Maybe one," he said. "You told me you found Jeremiah. My guess is you're the only one who knows where he is."

"A very bad guess," I said and steadied my eyes.

"You're lying, Raff. You were never a poker player."

"You think I'd come up here alone without telling anybody?"

"Yeah I do."

"I left word and directions with my secretary," I said and started around him down the slope.

"You can't even find the trail back," he said.

"You told us on the hunt if we ever got lost to follow the water, which is what I'm doing now."

"Hey, Raff, I just can't let you go like this."

"What will you do?" I asked. He was following me.

"We'll hike to the cabin and figure out something. Maybe persuade you to go to Cliff with a deal."

"And Jeremiah?"

"No Jeremiah."

"Got to be, Drake."

"Then I advise you to stop right there."

I heard the Savage's safety click off and stopped to face him. Drake held the shotgun at the ready.

"You'd go so far as to kill me?" I asked.

"Have to do what it takes. Just hang around awhile."

"No," I said and continued on down.

"Raff, don't make me do this."

"They'll come after you."

"No sure thing and if so what evidence will they find? I could bury you and your Buick, the car in a certain deep slough I know about. You're leaving me no choice if we can't deal."

"Best to you, Drake," I said, moving on.

He fired the Savage, and I felt the load's heat, tripped, lost my glasses, and for a second believed I'd been hit. The high-brass shot had shattered hemlock boughs, causing them to fall across my shoulders and back.

"No farther," Drake said. "We'll go to the cabin, have us a drink, think up a solution. I mean it, Raff."

I worked out from beneath the branches. I was so damned scared and felt my sphincter release and warmly wet my undershorts and leg. I lifted my broken glasses.

"Last chance," Drake said.

I staggered on.

"I got to admire you, Raff," he called.

" 'Course you're about to crap your pants, yet with style."

I kept moving and waited for the shot, my eyes half-blinded, my throat choked, my body shaking and giving itself to gravity's pull. But Drake didn't shoot. He allowed me to totter on down beside Sugar Camp Run.

"You did good," he shouted. "You did just fine, Walter."

I looked behind me. He had lowered the Savage, and Kraut stood beside him. Drake waved once before turning to climb back among the hemlocks. I stumbled into a jog only half realizing the last word I had heard from him was not Raff but Walter.

THIRTY-FOUR

Sugar Camp Run fed down into what I recognized to be Slash Lick Hollow. Afraid that Drake might be lying in wait if I tried to circle back to my Buick, I followed Wolf Creek to the paved county road and hiked the shoulder till an International twin-axle loaded with saw logs stopped and the driver offered me a ride.

"Look like you been gnawed on by a bear," he said, a long-faced youth with black hair bound into a ponytail by a thick rubber band. "You lost?"

"I was," I said, feeling weak and light-headed. I smelled my urine and hoped he didn't.

"It happens. Mountains turn people around. Hunting brown birds?"

"Yes," I said, easier to lie than explain.

"Not enough meat on 'em for the cost of ammo you shoot up."

"I need to reach High Gap."

"Where we headed. I figured you was lost. Hard time finding your way out?"

"I followed the water."

"That's the way my old daddy taught me," he said and tapped a palm against the steering wheel as he hummed a tune heard beating only through his head.

I tried to quiet my mind. The sun shone directly into the windshield, and I shaded my eyes. The road seemed to wind on forever until at High Gap the driver stopped at the timber loading yard beside the railroad tracks. I thanked him and walked to the jail.

I wanted to talk to Cliff before I saw Sam Tuggle or Sheriff Sawyers. Bess and Gilbert at their glassed-in control center eyed my clothes. Gilbert unlocked the cell where Cliff sat on the bunk reading a newspaper, his back against the wall.

When Gilbert left us, I explained what had happened between Drake and me. Cliff slowly released the paper, which settled across his lap. He didn't speak till I finished.

"Drake meant for Wendell to kill me?"

"He believed it the only way to protect and save what he has, and he has a lot."

"But Drake," Cliff said, his voice lingering on and sliding off the name.

"You tell the district attorney the whole truth after I talk to him. Jeremiah will need questioning. Once that's done, we move for your release."

"And Drake?"

"That's up to Sam Tuggle, who'll charge him at least with inciting homicide unless Drake can bargain a lesser plea."

"Then what?"

"The worst part. Blood sport in the papers and on TV."

"Poor Drake. What happened, Walter? What's happened to us?"

I had no answer, but I caught the note of genuine sympathy and sorrow that Cliff felt for Drake instead of a justified anger and loathing.

"I'll do some talk-talk," I said and whistled for Gilbert to let me out.

I crossed from the jail to the rear door of the courthouse and climbed the steps to the third floor and Sam Tuggle's office. Gail wiggled her fingers in greeting.

"He's in court," she said, looking at my clothes. She raised her nose slightly. Maybe she too had winded me. "You shoot anything?"

I told her I hadn't and sat across the room by the window. The full sunlight melted snow, causing water to collect and run along the street, and the drab houses and buildings appeared as if they had just been released by the earth. Of all things I remembered the long, lazy swims Drake, Cliff, and I had made in the ocean off Virginia Beach during our last summer before college, the languid strokes, the sun drunkenness, our bodies tanned, our hair bleached. We had become denizens of the water — sea creatures.

Sam entered the office, his face flushed and smiling, both signs of victory in legal joustings.

"Sentencing March seven," he told Gail. "Calendar it."

"Don't I always?" she asked.

"You the best, darling," he said and shook my hand. He gestured me into his office, where he closed the door. He thumped his stomach as if he had eaten well.

"A weasel-eyed car dealer selling hot items from Alabama," he said. "He'd changed the serial numbers. There's going to be lots of unhappy buyers around here who believed they got the bargains of their lifetime."

He adjusted his body in the chair, leaned back, and entwined his fingers behind his head.

"Got something for me?" he asked and sniffed.

I began uncovering details on how and why Wendell died. Sam listened, his expression skeptical, but he didn't interrupt until I was through.

"Quite a tale," he said, pursed his lips, and looked at the ceiling. "You, of course, can provide substantiation for any and all of this?"

"I have more than enough for you to drop the charge against Clifford Dickens."

"He's been lying to the law."

"To protect a friend. I expect you understand how to value that quality."

"Some friend," he said, sitting straight and drawing himself to the desk. "And you know the whereabouts of this Jeremiah Ripley who'll give testimony he had a homosexual relationship with Mr. Wingo?"

"I know where and how he can be reached. He's reluctant but has agreed to cooperate."

"Looks like the first thing is to bring in Wingo. He's still at his Blind Sheep camp?"

"He was when I left little more than ninety minutes ago."

"I'll fetch the sheriff," he said and reached to the intercom.

Sawyers arrived holding his trooper hat. In sunlight from the window, his freckles stood out.

"You think Mr. Wingo will resist," he asked me.

"I don't know. It's possible."

"Maybe you could give us help."

"I'd prefer to stay out of it."

"Not a case of prefers. You'd be doing him and the law a favor."

We rode in his Dodge cruiser. A stripped-down Chevy followed carrying two deputies, their names Louis and Belcher. The sheriff kept to the posted 55 mph speed limit. If he detected my urine's odor, he gave no indication.

"I ran these ridges when a boy," he said. "Killed my first buck less than half a mile from here — a seven-pointer. The deer fed with sheep on the sod."

My Buick was still parked at the foot of Blind Sheep. Sawyers stopped beside it and cut the Dodge's engine. The Chevy pulled up behind. Sawyers set on his hat, took the keys, and unlocked the cruiser's truck to lift out a lever-action Winchester. He slipped his walkie-talkie from its holster to report his location to High Gap.

"Wingo at the cabin?" he asked as he picked cartridges from an army-issue ammo box to load the rifle.

"I've no way of knowing," I answered. He saw me looking at the rifle.

"Lock the cars and stay with them," he told Louis. "Belch, you tail us keeping a twenty- or thirty-yard interval. We don't mean to spook him. Mr. Frampton, let's you and me go up together."

The sheriff and I climbed toward the cabin. Drake's Bronco had not been moved. We slowed as we drew closer. The sheriff was watching everything, his moves seemingly casual but his body gathered to react.

"Get you to call out if you will," he said. "Tell him we just want to talk."

I cupped my hands at my mouth and shouted Drake's name twice. There was no reply. The sheriff motioned me to stay back and approached the cabin from its windowless western end. He held the Winchester ready as he worked around the cabin, ducked under the front window, and stepped to the door. He used the rifle's butt to nudge it open. He pulled back and waited before peering inside.

"Mr. Wingo, you in there?"

No answer from Drake. Sawyers looked in my direction before rushing through the doorway. Expecting a shot, I closed my eyes. None came. Sawyers appeared and waved to me to join him. He stood inside looking at the hanging grouse and then Drake's gun rack.

"Any missing?" he asked.

"His Savage."

"Okay, we'll go on up. You stay behind me. Belch will follow. Where you think Wingo might be?"

"There's a trail to the ridge," I said.

"Let's move out."

Sawyers radioed another report while we climbed. He remained cool and observant, holding the Winchester lightly by fingers of his left hand at its balance point as he studied the chain-link treads left by Drake's boots. He stopped to look around him, gazed into laurel and hemlock cover, and licked at the air as if to taste its flavor.

"The dog's stayed with him," Sawyers said. He checked Kraut's paw prints in the softened ground.

When we reached the ridge, we squinted against the sun. Sawyers doubled back twice but had lost Drake's tracks.

"What now?" he asked.

I looked toward the Ram's Horn. Its crown of snow seemed to give off its own shimmering light instead of reflecting the sun's. Drake had said that was where he wanted to live. I told Sawyers, who nodded, radioed in his third report, and looked back to make certain Belcher was in place.

The day warmed as we climbed down from the ridge into what I remembered was named Burnt House Hollow. I felt winded and sweat slicked. Snow ebbed in deep hemlock shade, the melting causing a runoff that trickled. I hoped Sawyers would slow but he kept his steady pace and used the tip of his rifle to indicate Drake's rediscovered boot prints.

"I could use a rest," I told him.

He stopped, and we palmed up water from

a pool that had formed beneath a dripping boulder. I patted wetness against my face and neck. Sawyers gave me three minutes. On the go again we reached the foot of the Ram's Horn and began another ascent.

"Sheep laid this trail a long time back," Sawyers said, speaking softly, his slate eyes never still. "Mostly deer and bear use it now."

We climbed until I sucked for air, my calves ached, and my feet felt heavy and clumsy. The pull of the mountain worked stabbing pains into my thighs. Let it end, I thought.

Sawyers stopped and gazed up the slope. I'd heard it too, a dog's bark. The sheriff studied the wooded path before turning to me.

"Hail him," he said.

I collected my breath, shouted Drake's name, and identified myself. Croaking caws answered from on high.

"Ravens," Sawyers said. "The high sod's their country."

We waited as he radioed in a report of our position.

"All right, we'll let Belch come on and you follow us," he said. He signaled the husky deputy, who trudged upward puffing. Belcher wiped the back of his hand across his mouth and drew his .38-caliber revolver.

They climbed ahead of me. The tree cover of oaks, hickories, and spruce thinned. I glimpsed a blue-sky opening in the forest. Sawyers advanced slowly, the rifle now held in both hands, his steps softly exact.

A shot sounded close. I dropped to a knee and thought, Oh Christ, he's going to shoot it out with them. Sawyers and Belcher had crouched. Sawyers pointed at his own mouth and then at mine.

"Drake, don't shoot again," I called, my voice breaking. "Let's talk this out."

No answer.

Sawyers left the path and worked his way aslant the slope. Belcher trailed him, and I followed Belcher. We reached the tree line beyond which lay the sea of grass sod that had once been used for high pasture.

Sawyers shaded his eyes to study the terrain. We might have missed Drake had we not heard another distant bark from Kraut. The sheriff again pointed at his own mouth and mine. I hailed Drake, and my voice caused more barking.

Sawyers stepped back from the tree line and skirted the sod's edge. Belcher and I stayed with him. They stopped, whispered, and motioned for me to wait. I watched them move warily onto the sod and slip out of sight.

Sweat stung my eyes. What the hell were they doing? The ravens fussed. Belcher reappeared and motioned me to come on. He and the sheriff stood at one of those antiquated lengths of fencing shepherds had left. Kraut waited beside Drake's body sprawled among a broken section of rails. The Savage lay just beyond the outstretched fingers of Drake's right hand. The shot had smashed his chest, and blood thickly scarlet under the sun's brightness had found and flowed along channels of his hunting jacket. His blue eyes flecked with gold were opened upward, his face splattered with bits of blood and of flesh. Already the green flies had found feast.

"A sheepfold here once," Sawyers said, the Winchester hanging loose in his fingers as he circled Drake's body. "Locust posts and chestnut rails, they last forever. Funny Mr. Wingo would try to climb the fence when he could've easily slid between the rails."

"It had to be an accident," I said and looked up to the snow-shrouded knob of the Ram's Horn.

"Sure," Sawyers said and patted Kraut, who whined and whose amber eyes beseeched like my own. "Wouldn't you know?"

THIRTY-FIVE

Old Doc Bailey, the coroner from Seneca County's Free Clinic, was too frail to climb the Ram's Horn and examine the body. Sheriff Sawyers radioed High Gap, and a helicopter belonging to Appalachian Power brought the doctor to the sod. The rotating blades caused grass to wave and cower. Two members of the Rescue Squad strapped Drake in a metal basket, loaded him, and the helicopter carried him to High Gap. When I reached the clinic, they had laid him out on the stainless-steel examination table and covered him with a sheet.

From the courthouse I used a phone to notify Deborah. I heard her draw her breath. "Bring him to me," she said, her voice little more than breath itself.

"As soon as I can arrange it," I told her.

After I registered at the Mountain View Lodge, showered, and changed into underwear, shirt, and chinos I bought at High Gap's Dollar General, I sat with Sheriff Sawyers and Sam Tuggle in the district attorney's office. Darkness filled the window. Sam and I smoked as the sheriff remained impassive.

"The fact is you have no case now," I said. My strategy was not only to have all charges dropped against Cliff, but also to protect Deborah and her children from the media by saving Drake's name.

"So you keep telling us," Sam said. He liked to blow smoke rings that coiled lazily from his fleshy mouth and then poke his cigarette through their centers.

"A deposition from Jeremiah Ripley will attest that no intimacy existed between him and Mr. Dickens."

"Attesting's not always the same as truth telling," Sam said. "You got to do better."

"He has nothing to gain by perjuring himself and you'll cause unnecessary pain and suffering to people by pursuing the case farther. I can't believe you want that."

"No deposition," Sam said. "You produce Ripley in this office, where we see for ourselves."

"I request cover for him and that you make no announcements to the press."

"I could law you and make you reveal his location to the court."

"And needlessly create a lack of cooperation and understanding."

"We'll see about that. You bring him in or we go after him. We want him here in person, don't we, Bruce?"

"The best way of nailing it down," the sheriff said.

I advised Cliff where we stood. He paced the cell and held his throat one-handed as if he would choke himself.

"You're certain Jeremiah will appear?"

"I believe so, yes," I said. "I'll keep you informed."

From the Mountain View Lodge I phoned Phyllis's home number and received no answer. I next tried Nirvana Tours, heard Raoul's voice on the recorded message, and Phyllis, screening calls, picked up.

"I've been hoping I'd never hear from you again," she said. "Do you have to do this to me?"

I explained about Drake's death. She was silent on the other end.

"If you won't return voluntarily, the authorities will come after you with a warrant. Our best chance of avoiding the press is for you to appear voluntarily."

"Can anyone ever avoid anything?"

"Make your reservation and I'll pay for the ticket. Bring your birth certificate and the court order authorizing your name change."

"Please no," she said.

"I apologize, Miss Duke, but it has to be," I said.

I met her the next afternoon at the Roanoke airport. Her gray overcoat had dark piping around the lapels and collar. Men eyed her as she rode the escalator up from the passenger gate and tapped across the lobby where I waited. Her blond hair was curled under and bounced slightly with each step.

"I've never liked planes," she said. "They make me feel I'm enclosed in a coffin with dozens of people and we'll all be buried together."

"I know the feeling," I said and carried her leather suitcase to the car. She sat beside me and adjusted her skirt.

"I'm sorry for Drake," she said. "The madness love can cause."

"Atomic power," I said.

"Is less destructive," she said.

I gave her the details of what had happened on Blind Sheep as we drove to High Gap. At the courthouse Gail blinked. She had believed I would be bringing a man to the office. Her expression quizzical, she buzzed us through.

Sam stood and refocused at Phyllis. He was confused, yet recovered his gallantry as he walked around his desk to be introduced. He shook her hand, took her coat, and positioned a chair for her. He also helped himself to a look at her legs as she crossed them.

"I was expecting someone else," he said,

giving me a searching glance. "But I'm delighted with Miss Duke."

"And Jeremiah Ripley," I said.

"Is?" Sam asked.

"Here with us."

"The name I used to bear," Phyllis said. She stripped off her thin black leather gloves and flattened them on her lap. Her nails were rose-tinted.

Sam stared at her and at me.

"Jeremiah Ripley was her former name," I said. "After her operation she had it legally changed. We have papers."

"Whoa now," he said and pulled at his porous nose. His bushy brows rose and lowered. "This a first in my office."

Phyllis sat calmly. She returned his gaze, her composure not the least defensive. Sam reset his face to the business at hand.

"Miss Duke, is that what I call you then?"

"Yes."

"The essential question here involves your relationship with Mr. Clifford A. Dickens. Would you care to enlighten me?"

"There was nothing personal between us. He taught a college class I attended. I asked him to sign a magazine, which had published his story."

"You were never alone with him?"

"No."

"Not in his office?"

"He signed the magazine at the campus bookstore."

"He didn't touch you or you him?"

"No."

"It was Mr. Drake Wingo you were intimate with?"

"For a time, yes."

"You're a homosexual?"

"I'm a woman about to be married."

Sam backed off a step with another glance at me.

"Did your father, Mr. Wendell Ripley, know about you and Mr. Wingo?"

"My father was distressed by the life I lived in Richmond. It's one reason I fled."

"What's another reason?"

"I wanted to protect Mr. Wingo from himself."

"You believe Mr. Wingo conspired to manipulate your father in ways that resulted in his death?"

"I do now."

"Mr. Wingo's motive being an attempt to prevent his past relationship with you from being discovered?"

"We can't be sure how much Mr. Ripley was manipulated by Mr. Wingo," I said. "Possibly Mr. Ripley had his own agenda and acted keeping it to himself. Whatever the truth there, Mr. Dickens had no meaningful association with Miss Duke and no reason to kill Mr. Ripley other than acting in what he believed was self-defense."

"I'll study about that one," Sam said. "Miss Duke, we'll need to see your papers and ask you to give a statement affirming what you've told me here. The statement will be taped as well as transcribed and sworn to under oath by you before a notary. It subjects you to a charge of perjury if the law finds any point of truth contradicting it. We will investigate thoroughly and woe the misery you will suffer if you're playing with the legal processes of Seneca County."

"I'd like to get this over with as quickly as possible," she said.

"I'll have the sheriff join us," Sam said and spoke into the intercom.

Sam introduced Sawyers to Miss Duke. On learning who she had been, the slate eyes took her in without reaction. Sam used a recorder as well as a male stenotypist named Alvin, identified himself, the sheriff, Phyllis, me, and Gail, who was a notary, as being present. Phyllis spoke calmly into the microphone and answered the questions directed at her without flinching.

"You have never as either Jeremiah Ripley or Phyllis Duke had a sexual affiliation with

Mr. Clifford Arehart Dickens?"

"None."

Alvin twisted up the telescopic tripod legs of his stenotype machine and left the office to transcribe Phyllis's statement. Sam examined her birth certificate and court-ordered name change adjudicated in Florida. When Alvin returned, Phyllis again took the oath, this time before Gail, who affixed her signature and notary seal.

"Now, about Clifford Dickens?" I asked.

"Hang around for another day or two," Sam said.

"There's sufficient evidence to release him on bail as of this minute."

"Just humor us poor mountain folk. We got to let all this sink in."

"I have a nine-o'clock plane in the morning," Phyllis said.

"We'll do all we can to help you make it," Sam said.

I drove Phyllis to the lodge, where she registered. We ate dinner together, and again she drew eyes. She refused a drink and ate only a small portion of her tossed salad. She remained cold and removed.

"I go to church these days and pray," she said. "The preachers talk of eternal life. I can't really fathom it. Eternal rest is what I ask for. The final, peaceful darkness. Have you ever read the poet Robinson Jeffers? He wrote, 'How shall the dead know the deep treasure they have?' Thanks for helping me as best you could."

She would not allow me to pay for her meal, and I walked her to her room, told her good night, and saw her inside. I heard the click of her door's lock.

My room phone was ringing.

"Man, what a day, and Phyllis is enough to make a man doubt his gonads," Sam Tuggle said. "Well, the circuit judge's going to release your boy on bail pending a final motion. Your client won't be one-hundred-percent sprung but we no longer got any essential reason to hold him. If we find something else, we can come after him with hoe handles and pitchforks."

Deputy Belcher drove Phyllis to the Roanoke airport enabling me during the late afternoon to attend the private hearing held in the judge's musty, badly lit chambers, those present his clerk, Cliff, Sam, and me. Bail was set at ten thousand, Cliff to appear in court on an indeterminate date if so notified. Cliff owned no property except his cameras and Thunderbird, the latter bound by a lien. I paid the bail.

"You think this court ought to accept a Virginian's check?" the judge asked and smiled to show his question a jest.

I drove Cliff to the lodge. He showered fifteen minutes and shaved before we walked down to the bar. We sat at a window that offered a view of High Gap, the lights looking lonely and shattered in a bluish night. He downed two Scotch on the rocks fast.

"I don't believe I'll ever get the smell of jail off me," he said. "And look at my hands."

He raised them to show their tremors.

"You were great to hold out long as you did for Drake," I said.

"Yeah, thanks. What's happened to Kraut?"

"I'll carry him back to Deborah. Right now the sheriff's feeding him."

"Maybe the sea will do it," Cliff said. "Cleanse and make me whole. I want to travel to Italy and might apply for a job on a cruise ship, take photographs, paint portraits."

"Your Baltimore fiancée?"

"Damage repair required. Her father knows about my arrest, so I'm tainted."

He ordered a third Scotch.

"Drake," I said.

"He did the right thing finally, as I believed he would. Walter, I still see him like in the old days, the times we had together, the three of us, the Marauders."

"So do I," I said.

THIRTY-SIX

In the coffee shop of the Mountain View Motel as I ate a Danish and drank my breakfast coffee before leaving High Gap with Cliff, Sheriff Sawyers, trooper hat in hand, entered and crossed to my table.

"Okay to join you?" he asked, adjusting his holster.

"Of course, Sheriff."

He did and shook his head no at the waitress who was on her way to take his order. He eyed me in his intimidating fashion a moment before he spoke further.

"I knew you didn't tell it all," he said and ran fingers through the crease in the crown of his hat.

"I don't know what you mean."

"I smelled your piss in the cruiser when we went after Mr. Wingo. Now, that indicated to me something scared you real bad, something you haven't told. I drove back up to Blind Sheep to revisit the scene, picked up some of yours and Mr. Wingo's tracks. I also found an empty high-brass shotgun shell casing just short of where the hemlocks give way to the

344

slope down into Slash Lick."

"Are you interrogating me, Sheriff?"

"I'll get to that in a second. I picked up the shell casing and noted hemlock branches that had been broken off not by wind or weather but number 7½ shotgun pellets. Under and around the branches I found the boot tracks, yours and Mr. Wingo's. I checked them out. He shot at you, didn't he?"

"Not at me."

"Well, he shot to stop you, but you didn't, at least not for more than a waffling step or two. You kept on down into Slash Lick, and the shot explains the piss. Am I right?"

"I have nothing to say on the matter."

"Look, I've been in combat, and some of the best soldiers I ever knew wet their GI drawers or a hell of a lot worse but also stood and fought. Now, I admit I didn't like my first impression of you, you seemed too fussy, but I've changed my thinking. I figure you're all right, Mr. Frampton. Since I left the service, I haven't come across many brave men. My thinking is you qualify. For what it's worth I wanted you to know that before you left High Gap."

"It's worth a great deal to me, Sheriff, and I thank you."

He stood, shook my hand, and left to drive his Dodge cruiser down toward the courthouse. I thought of Charles LeBlanc. Each of these men should've been a rawboned Texan out west of the Pecos, Winchester cocked in hand, squinting at Apache smoke signals among the scorching buttes. For a moment the sheriff had made me feel I stood among them. Maybe I'd write to invite him down to Jessup's Wharf for a tour of Tidewater Virginia or a day of fishing when the shad were running in the Axapomimi.

A phone call from Sam Tuggle authorized Doc Bailey to release Drake's body for ambulance transport to Richmond. At the eleven-o'clock burial Cliff and I served as pallbearers. The afternoon turned mild, and a light southwest breeze bore scents of warehoused tobacco as well as the alluvial James. Our hands gripped the casket's hinged steel handles as we carried it from the hearse to the grave, and I felt the weight of Drake's body so close beyond my clenched fingers.

The breeze blew across the cemetery's grass and caused wreaths to stir and the scalloped green canopy to flap softly. Seagulls dipped from thermals, their cries seeming not so much quarrelsome as forlorn. The army's Honor Guard raised their rifles and fired three volleys heavenward.

Hundreds attended the service, both

friends and those drawn by Drake's celebrity. A garland of cut flowers shaped like a grouse was laid on the casket, the black roses forming a band across the spread tail. I remembered Drake had told me such markings identified male birds. Deborah stood bravely taut, her moist eyes catching glints from the sun.

Father Everett, the Episcopal priest, quoted Drake's words:

" 'When I hunt the misty high country of the grouse, God runs the ridges beside me.' "

After the service, Cliff and I drove to the house. Deborah hugged and thanked us for loving her Drake. We looked at the fireplace portrait of him standing in the turret of the sand-colored tank — the wind-and-sun-bronzed warrior.

"It helps to know he died among mountains he loved best," she said.

Josey entered, her black hat, dress, hose, and heels bringing high style to a death gathering. She and I, holding drinks, were able to find a moment alone in the den. I would never reveal to her I knew she had lied for Drake.

"I think you might slip by any charges from the government," I told her. "Since you lost your own money, you can't be accused of fraud. The worst you have to fear is a civil action."

"I'm still hanging on to my job and a few

loyal customers," she said and looked at the portrait. "Oh, God, he was the best of us," she cried, and I wondered whether it had been Drake not Cliff to whom in our teens she had given her first love.

The three of us stayed till two o'clock before taking embracing leave of Deborah. On the lawn above the fading yellow winter jasmine we told each other we would get together. Cliff and I walked Josey to her Lexus and watched her pull away under the leafless, overreaching oaks.

"Tears become her," Cliff said.

I drove him to his carriage house and turned down his offer of a drink.

"Maybe I'll visit Greece as well as Italy," he said. "Learn the language, sip the wine, swim in the languid Aegean, revive in the pure white light. I want to thank you, Walter. You're a stout fellow in the breach."

We shook hands, he left my car, and I watched him walk to the walled entrance. I waited till he passed through and closed the studded wooden door before I moved on along the street.

I returned to Jessup's Wharf. At three the yellow school bus stopped in front of my office to let Jason off. He scampered across the street, his book bag strapped to his back, his red billed cap pulled low over his brow. His skinny legs appeared so fragile out there among the stopped cars and panting diesels — a lamb among wolves.

He removed his cap and jacket and sat on his chair. Mary Ellen left for the courthouse to record a deed of trust. Jason slid a book from his bag and opened it across his lap. I recognized *Blood Brothers*, the slim volume I'd bought him that pictured the war-painted Indian brave and buckskinned frontiersman facing each other in friendship. When Jason went to the lavatory, he left it on the chair.

I turned away and looked out the window. A conclave of pigeons moved restlessly on the ledge of St. Luke's steeple. Likely the hawk lurked around. All at once the sorrow I had been holding back welled in me. I thought of Josey, Drake, and Cliff, what life had done to us or we to life. I sagged and felt I lacked the strength to straighten my body or lift my head until I realized that Jason had returned, stood at my side, and for the second time since I'd known him was looking directly at me. I saw the fear surface in his enlarged and anguished brown eyes like a predatory shape from the deep.

I gathered myself, forced a smile, and began my double-jointed clown dance, my legs crisscrossing, my eyes rolling, my tongue lagging out. I soft-shoed across the floor and flung my arms about. I envisioned the gorilla approaching and pulling a giant yellow lolli-pop from my hand. As we snatched it back and forth, I croaked out a hee-haw.

Mary Ellen entered the office and stopped bewildered. The dance became crazy, like a deranged Indian among tom-toms seeking to invoke the Great Spirit, except this dance was for the past — the good, the love, the loss, and above all the humanity.

Jason's expression didn't change, but his devouring eyes stayed lifted to mine, and the shape sank away beneath them — perhaps a portent, a viewing of promise, and something worth reaching to and drawing forth.

THIRTY-SEVEN

At Miss Mabel's I tossed my clothes aside and attempted to sleep, but mostly I smoked and paced my rooms. The dawn's sunlight worked around edges of the blinds, and for once no frost coated the grass and peonies of Miss Mabel's garden. Her washer-woman named Lucinda came Mondays to pick up laundry, and my plastic bag waited bulging full. I also inserted two suits into the chute of the cleaner's drop-off at the Jessup's Mercantile. All items were carried to Williamsburg for the job.

Miss Mabel tapped on the door that separated her side of the house from mine. I'd never been in her living quarters but had glimpsed tasseled carpets, Victorian furniture, and a grandfather clock whose pendulum no longer swung its arcs. I suspected she had stopped the clock, for she herself seemed stuck in time. I had never seen her when she wasn't wearing hose or bleak unfashionable dresses closed at the throat by a cameo brooch. Her gray hair appeared as stiffly set as stove wire, and she held herself rigidly erect, a soldier on parade. Though small of frame, while a teacher at King County Elementary School she had terrified many a hulking oaf or bully with her stern expression and the swift application of a pussy willow switch to their bared calves. I thought of her as being the essence of brave spinsterhood and the old bygone values.

I'd been about to fix myself a drink and before answering her knock hurried to stick my bottle of George Dickel's Tennessee Sour Mash Whisky behind the peacock fan that covered the living-room fireplace.

"I heard you walking again last night," she said. She held a paper bag. More beaten biscuits, I thought. She also attempted to peer past me into my pantry. So far I'd still been able to hide my liquor supply from her alert and prying eyes.

"Miss Mabel, I'm sorry if I been disturbing you."

"No ifs about it. You do disturb me. You're not sick?"

"No'm, just fine."

"You need sleep. It's as important as food."

"I know."

"I used to have difficulty sleeping, but I now take a little tonic every night before retiring to the bed."

"Tonic?" I asked.

"In moderation," she said and presented the paper bag to me. I carefully opened it. Inside I uncovered a fifth of Black Jack Daniel's. I stared at her.

"I heard about the death of your friend," she said. "You can keep this bottle along with your others in the fireplace. Remember, the good Lord gave us alcohol to be used wisely. A drink before bedtime is a gift from Him to those of us who have trouble sleeping. I often feel there must be times He has the need of a tonic because of the fret we human beings cause Him."

She turned away abruptly and closed the door before I could thank her. I stood holding the bottle until I placed it alongside my George Dickel behind the peacock fan. I tried to envison her on the other side of the door. She would never be the type who slapped her knees laughing, but a smile yes, maybe even a tightly controlled grin.

At my office I looked over calls Mary Ellen had listed on my legal pad. The first was from Charles LeBlanc's brother Edward at Boone and Massey.

"No one's located Prince Jamir," he said, his voice as toneless and regular as a metronome. He was a man who when walking constantly kept his eyes on the ground for either what might be found of use or missteps that would endanger his footing.

"Thus far we're not hurt and of course still hold his first payment for Bellerive in escrow along with the accumulated and accumulating interest," he continued. "Furthermore, we are receiving inquiries from interested parties, chief among them a Charlotte syndicate with a proposal for converting Bellerive into an English village complete with upscale homes, pools, golf course, marina, stables, and use of the airport, while the mansion itself is to become the clubhouse. Stop by and I'll show you their initial presentation."

I sat brooding how it had come to pass that Bellerive with its centuries-old Huguenot heritage would be transformed into a housing development, a splendid one yes, but instead of family and the grandeur of ancient blood belong to a procession of carted, newly rich golfers hitting balls across grass that had once sustained the hoofbeats of Thoroughbreds.

I called my mother in Venice, who told me she and my father were taking daily walks along the beach bordering the Gulf of Mexico. Occasionally my father picked up seashells and studied their configurations and identities by using a book she had bought him. She had started translating Dante.

"A wonderful way to see the universe," she

said. "Everything laid out systematically, no questions unanswered. I'm becoming a Catholic."

"And Dad's fine?"

"He's wearing Bermuda shorts now," she said. "In public."

I finally reached Charles LeBlanc late at night in Chinook, Montana.

"Hope you're not telling me I'm out of dollars," he said.

"No, you have some twenty-six thousand left, but you might need to put off buying that ranch for a time. You will receive Bellerive money eventually, possibly even more than first calculated."

"Better than dirt in the mouth," was his response. "Just keep taking your cut."

Nothing more, and I again admired and envied his stance in the face of adversity.

Mary Ellen helped me hang my portrait of Marse Robert. I often sat at my desk looking at him instead of working. Mary Ellen had quickly realized I wasn't acting myself. She brought a Jerusalem cherry plant to place on my window's ledge. I remembered when I'd first interviewed her for the job she told me she had once been Miss York County. There were moments when I gazed at her that I could see the phantom beauty of a pretty, bare-shouldered eighteen-year-old girl in a shimmering white gown riding on a parade float covered with full-flowering gardenias.

"Country ham and red-eye gravy you can sop up with my buttermilk biscuits," she said, again inviting me to dinner with her and Jason.

"I'll try to get by," I said.

"We'll wait for you," she said.

I drove out to visit Deborah, the late afternoon warm and sweet with a fleeting scent of the looming spring. I found her in her garden, where she knelt planting tulip bulbs to provide the borders for her box bushes. A straw hat shaded her face, and suppressed grief made her appear beautifully and nobly wounded. She removed her gloves, and we drank tea under the trellis strung with bud-swelling wisteria vines. Following my advice, she had hired movers to drive to Blind Sheep and bring Drake's belongings from his cabin.

"It's empty now," she said. "I have no idea what to do with his guns. Would you care for them?"

"I'm no hunter. Why not let Boomer sell them?"

On my recommendation she had rehired Boomer, and he was temporarily at least running Grizzly's.

"And I don't know what to do about the

store. I'll need your continued help there."

"We can always find a buyer if it comes to that."

"The one good thing is 'The Truth of the Grouse' will still be published. I have that assurance from Drake's editor."

When I finished my tea, I stood to leave, and after I kissed her cheek she straightened my tie.

"Please come see me often," she said.

I promised I would and drove not directly back to Jessup's Wharf but in order to have a look at Grizzly's headed westward to Powhatan County and into a blasted red sunset that shattered the horizon. Though the store was closed for the day, the ghost grouse had begun to emerge through a gathering twilight.

I sat in the car watching the ghost grouse's luminous whiteness dawn fully in the converging darkness. As of itself or perhaps because the spirit of Dante Alighieri had taken hold of me, my arm raised, and my hand made the sign of the cross.

The employees of Thorndike Press hope you have enjoyed this Large Print book. All our Large Print titles are designed for easy reading, and all our books are made to last. Other Thorndike Press Large Print books are available at your library, through selected bookstores, or directly from the publishers.

For more information about titles, please call:

(800) 223-1244
    or
(800) 223-6121

To share your comments, please write:

Publisher
Thorndike Press
P.O. Box 159
Thorndike, Maine 04986

Dumping Billy

*Also by Olivia Goldsmith
in Large Print:*

Fashionably Late
Marrying Mom
Pen Pals

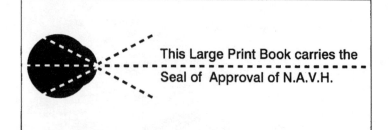

This Large Print Book carries the
Seal of Approval of N.A.V.H.

Dumping Billy

Olivia Goldsmith

Thorndike Press • Waterville, Maine

Published in 2004 by arrangement with Warner Books, Inc.

Thorndike Press® Large Print Basic.

The tree indicium is a trademark of Thorndike Press.

The text of this Large Print edition is unabridged.
Other aspects of the book may vary from the original edition.

Set in 16 pt. Plantin by Ramona Watson.

Printed in the United States on permanent paper.

Library of Congress Cataloging-in-Publication Data

Goldsmith, Olivia.
    Dumping Billy / Olivia Goldsmith.
        p. cm.
        ISBN 0-7862-6643-0 (lg. print : hc : alk. paper)
        1. Brooklyn (New York, N.Y.) — Fiction.   2. Bars
(Drinking establishments) — Fiction.   3. Dating (Social
customs) — Fiction.   4. Rejection (Psychology) — Fiction.
5. Female friendship — Fiction.   6. Large type books.
I. Title.
PS3557.O3857D86 2004b
    813'.54—dc22   2004047924

To Nina

AND TO

Ethel Esther Brandsfronbrener Schutz
A lover of books, mangoes, oranges, and me

As the Founder/CEO of NAVH, the only national health agency solely devoted to those who, although not totally blind, have an eye disease which could lead to serious visual impairment, I am pleased to recognize Thorndike Press* as one of the leading publishers in the large print field.

Founded in 1954 in San Francisco to prepare large print textbooks for partially seeing children, NAVH became the pioneer and standard setting agency in the preparation of large type.

Today, those publishers who meet our standards carry the prestigious "Seal of Approval" indicating high quality large print. We are delighted that Thorndike Press is one of the publishers whose titles meet these standards. We are also pleased to recognize the significant contribution Thorndike Press is making in this important and growing field.

Lorraine H. Marchi, L.H.D.
Founder/CEO
NAVH

* Thorndike Press encompasses the following imprints: Thorndike, Wheeler, Walker and Large Print Press.

Acknowledgments

As this is my tenth novel, I'm a little late in acknowledging the gratitude I have for my readers. Writers have a lonely job, and the kind notes, the warm reception at bookstores, and the fact that you continue to buy enough books to keep me employed is a wonderful thing. There are not many writers privileged to not have a day job and I am grateful to everyone who has picked up and read one of my novels. I hope they have given you much enjoyment and diversion.

Special thanks to Jamie Raab for her belief in me and wonderful nurturing; thanks to Larry Kirshbaum for laughing at my jokes and feeding me lunch; thanks to Nick Ellison just for being Nick; thanks to Onieal's Restaurant, my unofficial office, and the wonderful staff, including: Chris Onieal, Nicole Blackham, Kristen Collen, Kristin Prinzo, Jaqueline Hegarty, Anna Schmidt, Stuart Bruce, Lauren Reid, and Jodie McMurty.
Special thanks to John Claflin of Colours

who has not only built (and painted!) my home but has gotten me out of hot water time and time again. Thanks also to Jed Schutz for all his help; Roy Greenberg for his good humor and legal expertise; PG Kain for his creativity and input; and as always, Nan Robinson for her enormous contribution. For anybody else I left out, you know who you are. Thank you.

Chapter One

Katherine Sean Jameson sat behind her desk and looked at her client. Being a therapist was never easy, but with a client who needed this much help and had this much resistance, it was really tough. And heartbreaking. To the casual observer, Kate was just a mildly pretty twenty-four-year-old (though she was actually thirty-one) with long curls of wild red hair.

Now, as she looked at Brian Conroy, she unconsciously twisted those curls into an impromptu bun at the nape of her neck with a practiced motion and pushed a pencil through it to hold it in place.

"So what do you think?" Kate said, and almost bit her tongue. Despite what laypeople believed, a good therapist didn't sit around all day saying, "What do you think?" She'd have to try a different approach. She was wasting her own time as well as Brian's. Why was it the clients she loved most were so often the ones she could help the least?

9

It was warm. Kate's office was not air-conditioned, and the breeze from the open window felt good on the back of her neck. Brian, looking at her intently, was sweating, but it could just as easily have been from nerves as from the early spring heat.

Kate sat silently. Silence was an important part of her work, though not something that came naturally. But she had learned that at times stillness and space were all that were needed.

Not today, apparently. Brian pulled his eyes guiltily away from her own and looked around the office. The walls were filled with pictures done by children — some of them very disturbing. Kate watched to see if Brian's attention focused on one.

Kate stifled a sigh. She was trying to wait Brian out but was conscious of their time ticking away, and for his sake she needed immediate results. Brian was obviously in crisis. She looked with compassion at her eight-year-old "client." His teacher said he was constantly disrupting class and showing signs of obsessive-compulsive or maybe even schizophrenic behavior.

And disruption simply wasn't allowed at Andrew Country Day School. A private school in the best neighborhood in

10

Manhattan, it accepted only the best and the brightest — of students and staff. Every amenity was provided, from an indoor swimming pool to a state-of-the-art computer center to language lessons that included Japanese and French for six-year-olds. That's why there was a school psychologist. Kate had gotten the plum job only recently, and Brian, like other kids who showed the slightest "difficult" behavior, had been immediately remanded to her office. Nothing was to disrupt the smooth daily ingestion of information by the children of the elite.

"Do you know why you've come here, Brian?" she asked, her voice gentle. Brian shook his head. Kate rose from her desk, moved around it, and sat on one of the small chairs beside the boy. "Can you guess?" He shook his head. "Well, do you think it's for eating gummy elephants in school?"

He looked at her for a moment, then shook his head again. "There's no such thing as gummy elephants."

"Gummy rhinos?" Kate asked. Brian shook his head again. "Eating peanut-butter-and-raccoon sandwiches at your desk?"

"It wasn't for *eating* anything," he said.

11

Then he lowered his voice to a whisper. "It was for talking. Talking in class."

As Kate nodded, the pencil fell out of her bun, and her hair cascaded over her shoulders while the pencil clattered to the floor. Brian smiled and actually let a giggle escape before he covered his mouth. Good, Kate thought. She leaned closer to her little patient. "You're not here just for talking in class, Brian. If you were just talking in class, then you'd be sent to the principal's office, right?"

Brian's adorable face gazed up at Kate with terrified eyes. "Are you *worse* than the principal?" he asked.

Kate felt such empathy for the boy at that moment that she was tempted to take his hand in hers, but he was so anxious that she feared he might shy away. This kind of work was so delicate — like dealing with Venetian spun glass, where the slightest jar could shatter it — and she often felt so clumsy.

"Nobody is worse than the principal," Kate said. Then she smiled and winked at Brian. None of the kids at Andrew Country Day liked Dr. McKay, and — as so often was the case — their instincts were good. "Do I look as bad as Dr. McKay?" Kate asked, feigning shock.

Brian shook his head vigorously.

"Well. Thank goodness. Anyway, I do something different. You aren't here to be punished. You didn't do anything wrong. But everybody hears you talking — even though you're not talking to anybody." She watched as Brian's eyes filled with tears.

"I'll be quieter," he promised. Kate wanted to scoop him up onto her lap and let him cry as long as he needed to. After all, his mother had just died of cancer, and he was still so very young. Kate's own mother had passed away when she was eleven, and that had been almost unbearable.

She dared to take one of the boy's hands in hers. "I don't want you to be quiet, Brian," she said. "You do what you need to. But I'd like to know what you're saying."

Brian shook his head again. His eyes changed from tearful to frightened. "I can't tell," he whispered. Then he turned his face away from her. He mumbled something else, and Kate managed to hear only one word, but it was enough.

Go slow, she told herself. Go very, very slowly and casually. "You're doing magic?" she asked. Brian, face still averted, nodded but didn't speak. Kate was already afraid

13

she had gone too far. She held her breath. Then, after a long moment, she lowered her own voice to a whisper and asked, "Why can't you tell?"

"Because . . . ," Brian started, then it burst out of him. "Because it's magic and you can't tell magic or your wish won't come true. Like birthday candles. Everybody knows that!" He got up and walked to the corner of the room.

Kate actually felt relieved. The boy wasn't schizophrenic. He was caught in a typical childhood trap: total powerlessness combined with hopeless longing and guilt. A toxic cocktail. Kate gave him a moment. She didn't want him to feel trapped. Yet he shouldn't be alone with this pain. She approached him slowly, the way you might move toward a strange puppy. She put her hand on the little boy's shoulder. "Your wish is about your mother, isn't it," she said, her voice as neutral as she could manage to keep it. Brian didn't need any of her emotions — he needed space for his own. "Isn't that right?"

Brian looked up at her and nodded. His face registered a cautious relief. The dreadful burdens of childhood secrets always touched Kate. Though she was a long-lapsed Catholic, she still remembered

14

the power and release of the confessional. She had to serve this child well. "What are you wishing for?" she asked, her voice as gentle as she could make it.

Brian began to cry. His face, usually so pale, flushed deep rose. Speaking through his tears, he said, "I thought if I just said 'Mommy, come back' a million times that she would be back." He sobbed and put his face against Kate's skirt. "But it isn't working. I think I've said it two million times."

Kate's eyes filled with tears. She took a deep breath. She could feel the heat of Brian's face through the thin fabric of her skirt. The hell with professional detachment. She scooped Brian into her arms and carried him over to one of the chairs. The boy nestled against her. After a time he stopped crying, but his silent neediness was even sadder. They sat for a few moments, but Kate knew their session was nearly completed, and she had to speak. "Oh, Brian, I am so sorry," she told him. "But magic doesn't work. I wish it did. The doctors did everything they could to help your mommy. They couldn't fix her, and magic can't fix that. It's not your fault that the doctors couldn't save her." She paused. "And it's not your fault your

15

mommy can't come back." Kate sighed. Breaking children's hearts, even to help them, had not been part of her job description. "But she can't, and your magic can't work."

Brian suddenly pushed against her, wriggling his way out of her embrace. He stood up and looked at her angrily. "Why not?" he demanded. "Why can't my magic work?" He glared at Kate for another moment, then pushed her hard and barreled out of the room, nearly knocking over the dollhouse. The office door crashed and rebounded open. From down the hall, she heard a voice — Elliot Winston's — try to stop Brian. "Shut up, you stinky dick!" Brian shouted. Kate winced and listened to the little boy's footsteps recede.

A moment later, Elliot stuck his head around Kate's door. "Another satisfied customer?" he asked, his eyebrows raised nearly to his receding hairline. "Perhaps you should have stuck with French."

Kate had majored in French as an undergrad. For a while, she had even considered continuing her language studies in graduate school. She had never regretted not doing so, because her work with the children was so satisfying, but occasionally, particularly at moments like this, Elliot —

16

one of the math teachers and her best friend — teased her about her choice.

"As I recall, the German for 'stinky dick' would be *riechende Steine*. What would you say in French?"

"I would say you are very annoying," Kate told him. "That's good enough. And I would also say that Brian and I are making some progress. He expressed some of his true feelings today."

"Well, he managed to express his feelings about me and my genital odor. Congratulations on your progress." Elliot stepped into the room and sat beside the dollhouse in an overstuffed chair — the only piece of adult-size furniture in Kate's office aside from her own desk and chair. Elliot was dark-haired, average in height, slightly overaverage in weight, and possessed of a much higher than average IQ. As usual, he was wearing wrinkled chinos, a baggy T-shirt, and a clashing open-necked shirt on top. Putting his feet up on the toy box, he opened his lunch sack.

Kate sighed. She and Elliot usually had lunch together. But today Elliot had had the dreaded cafeteria duty and was just now, at nearly two-thirty, getting a chance to eat. She delighted in his company, but she was melancholy from her session with

17

Brian. Elliot, fresh from the horror of the lunchroom, was blithely unaware of her mood as he pulled out several items and tore into a sandwich that smelled suspiciously like corned beef.

"Brian's in Sharon's class, isn't he?" Elliot asked too casually.

Kate nodded. "Poor kid. His mother dies, and his teacher is the Wicked Witch of the Upper West Side." She had to smile. Neither she nor Elliot had much use for Sharon Kaplan, a truly lazy teacher and a deeply annoying woman.

"So aside from a recently deceased mom, what's bugging Brian?" Elliot asked.

Kate felt too fragile for their usual badinage. "You have mustard on your chin," she told him, but as Elliot reached up to wipe it away, the glob fell onto his shirt.

"Oops," he said, and dabbed ineffectually at his shirtfront with one of the hard paper towels from the school's bathrooms. The yellow splotch looked particularly hideous against the green of his shirt. Watching him eat, Kate often thought, was a spectator sport.

"He believes that magic can bring his mother back," she said, sighing wistfully.

"See? See what I mean? They're all obsessed with witches and wizards. Damn

18

that Harry Potter!" Elliot said, and took another huge bite of the sandwich. "So what's your prescription?" he asked, forcing the words out while chewing his food.

"I want him to give up the magic and get in touch with his anger and pain," Kate answered.

"*Oy vey!*" Elliot said with the best Yiddish accent a gay man from Indiana could manage. "When will you give up on this quest to get every little boy at Andrew Country Day in touch with his true feelings? And why discourage magic in his case? What else does the kid have?"

"Oh, come on, Elliot! Because magic won't work, and he mustn't think it's his fault when it fails." She shook her head. "You of all people. A trained statistician. A man who could trade this job in, triple your salary, and become chief actuarial at any pension fund. *You're* telling me to encourage magic?"

Elliot shrugged. "Haven't you ever had magical things happen?"

Kate refused the bait. Elliot, raised in the Midwest and stoic to the bone, had once told her, "The unexamined life is the only one worth living." He often challenged her about the efficacy of psy-

19

chology. Now, just to annoy her, he was going to take a perverse stand on magic. "If you think you're going to start an argument today," she warned him, "you're out of your mind." Then, to annoy him — as well as for his own good — she added, "I didn't think corned beef was good for your cholesterol."

"Oh, what's a few hundred points one way or the other?" he asked cheerfully, swallowing another mouthful.

"You've got a death wish," Kate said.

"Ooooh. Harsh words from a shrink." He winced mockingly as he opened a Snapple.

"Look, I'm leaving," she told him, gathering some notes from her desk and putting them into her file cabinet. If she left now, she'd be able to do a bit of shopping before meeting her friend Bina. She took a lipstick and mirror out of her purse, dabbed the color over her mouth, and smiled widely to make sure she didn't have lipstick on her teeth. "I'll see you for dinner."

"Where are you going?"

"None of your beeswax."

"A secret? Come on. Tell! What if I threw a tantrum like Brian?" Elliot reached into the toy box at his feet. Then he hurled a stuffed bear in Kate's direction. "Would you tell me then?" The plush missile hit her squarely in the face. Elliot curled up in the chair, held his hands in front of his face, and started to beg rapidly. "It was an accident. I'm sorry, I'm sorry, I'm sorry."

"I'll show you sorry," Kate warned. She threw the bear back at Elliot, but it missed him.

"You throw like a girl," Elliot taunted. Then he picked up another animal and threw it at Kate. "Duck!" he called as he reached for yet another toy to throw. It was indeed a duck, yellow and fluffy.

"Duck this, you math nerd," Kate almost shouted as she grabbed a fuzzy rabbit and pummeled Elliot's head. It felt good to blow off some steam.

"Abuse! Abuse!" Elliot screamed in delight as he rolled off the chair to protect himself. "Teacher abuse! Teacher abuse!" he continued to yell.

"Shut up, you idiot!" Kate told him, and rushed to close the office door. She turned from it just in time to get a stuffed elephant right in the face. It stunned her for a moment, then she grabbed the pachyderm and lunged at Elliot. "I'll show you abuse, you sniveling cholesterol warehouse," she threatened as she fell on top of Elliot and beat him repeatedly with the toy.

Elliot fought back with both an inflatable flamingo *and* a stuffed dog. He might be gay, but he was no wussy. When both he and Kate were exhausted, they sat panting and laughing together in the big chair, Kate on top. The door opened.

"Excuse me," said Dr. McKay. Despite his words, he wasn't the type to excuse anything. "I thought I heard a ruckus in here."

George McKay, the principal of Andrew Country Day School, was a hypocrite, a social climber, a control freak, and a very bad dresser. He also had a knack of using words no one else had used for several decades.

"A ruckus?" Elliot asked.

"We were just testing out a new therapy," Kate said quickly. "I hope we didn't disturb you."

"Well, it was certainly loud," Dr. McKay complained.

"From the little I know of it, AAT — airborne animal therapy — can frequently be noisy," Elliot said, poker-faced, "although it's having significant measurable success in schools for the gifted, where it's being pioneered. Of course," he added, "it might not be right for this setting." He nodded at Kate. "I'm not the expert," he said as if he

22

were deferring to Kate's professional judgment. She smothered a laugh with a cough.

"We'll put this off until after three o'clock, Dr. McKay," she promised.

"All right, then," he said primly. He left as suddenly as he had arrived, shutting the door with a firm but controlled click. Kate and Elliot looked at each other, waited for a count of ten, then burst into giggles that they had to stifle.

"AAT?" Kate gurgled.

"Hey, straight men love acronyms. Think of the army. He'll be on the Internet in less than ten minutes, searching for 'airborne animal therapy,'" Elliot predicted. He stood up and began collecting the stuffed animals. Kate got up to help him. The irony of the situation was that Elliot had helped Kate get hired, and since then George McKay had told several teachers that he suspected them of having an affair. Ridiculous as that idea was, the sight of the two of them in the chair was not one to instill confidence in Dr. McKay, who had frequently announced at teachers' meetings that he "discouraged fraternizing among professional educational co-workers."

When Kate and her "professional educational co-worker" finished laughing, she stood up, smoothed her skirt, and put her hair back up, this time with a barrette she found in her drawer. Elliot was standing still, looking down at the chair. He heaved a dramatic sigh.

"Oh, shit!" he told her. "You crushed my banana." He held up the mangled fruit from his lunch bag, which had slipped under them during the battle.

Kate turned, struck the pose of a femme fatale, and rasped, "How times have changed. You used to like it when I did that."

Elliot laughed. "I'll leave all banana handling to you and Michael."

Kate and her new boyfriend, Dr. Michael Atwood, were going to dinner with Elliot and his partner, Brice. It was Elliot's introduction to Michael, and Kate felt a little flurry in her stomach at the thought. She hoped they liked each other. "If I don't leave now, I'll be late tonight," she told him.

"Okay, okay."

She grabbed her sweater from the back of her chair and moved toward the door.

"So you like your work so far," Elliot said, watching her. As she passed by, Kate nodded. But she kept moving: She knew what was coming. "And even though I

24

helped you get the job, you're still not going to let me know where you're going?"

Kate didn't bother to answer as she sailed out of the room, Elliot scrambling to hurry after her. Elliot was what people in Brooklyn called "a nudge."

Chapter Two

In all the years Kate had known Elliot — over ten now — he'd always managed to cheer her up when she was sad and support her in her successes. Now, as they walked down the corridor to his classroom, she glanced at him affectionately. The stretched-out orange T-shirt, the ugly green overshirt decorated with mustard, the slight love handles, and the wrinkled chinos didn't make him look like much, but he had a keen mind and was a loving and generous friend. She felt a swell of gratitude toward him. As always, he had cheered her up and helped her make the break from school.

Kate was proud of the work she did with these kids. She had learned a lot from them, too. For one thing, the school catered to the children of the rich and successful, but Kate saw that money, privilege, and education brought on as much misery as had her own deprived childhood. She had lost her resentment of those with money, and she was grateful for that. She had not picked her calling for the money it earned; in fact, she regarded her work as a kind of vocation. It was one thing she never made light of, and she often found it hard to leave her work behind at the end of the day. But tonight she had to, to help Bina prepare for her big night and then, later, to introduce Michael to Elliot and Brice at dinner.

She waited just inside Elliot's classroom as he chucked the offending lunch sack in a bin and started messing about in his untidy desk.

"You know, it's very hard not to keep thinking about Brian. He's so adorable, and has had a really difficult time. And I think the disappointment when his magic doesn't work, which of course it won't, could cause real problems later." Kate sighed. "Boys are just so much more fragile than girls."

"Tell me about it." Elliot sighed deeply, too. "I'm still getting over the time Phyllis Bellusico told me I smelled."

"Did you?" Kate asked, ready to be either his straight man or his audience. She was used to Elliot's shticks. Since college they had been amusing each other with dark humor from their childhoods.

"Well, yes," Elliot admitted reluctantly,

27

"but I smelled *good*. I should have. I'd dumped an entire bottle of my mother's White Shoulders into my underpants."

"Pee-yuw," Kate said, imitating any one of her school "clients." "Maybe Brian has a point. I'd have to agree with Phyllis. And this happened . . . ?"

"In third grade, but with a little more therapy and Brice's love and support, I expect to get over it in the next decade."

Kate loved it when Elliot got going. She had to laugh. "Boys. They always break the thing they love."

"Not if they can kill it," Elliot replied bitterly. He had been tormented by kids in school. After a moment he said, "I have to go to Dean and DeLuca to get rice for our dinner tonight. Brice is making his world-famous risotto. You can tell Michael it's your recipe. The way to a man's heart . . ."

Kate looked up with a suspicious glance. "Yeah, and please be on your best behavior. Elliot," she began, "can't you just —"

"No," Elliot retorted, "I can't just anything." He walked over to her and gave her a quick hug. "I don't want to discourage or criticize you. I just want to make sure you know what you're doing."

"Oh, God! Who knows what they're doing when they try to find a soul mate?"

28

"Well, you have a point there. But I don't want you to be hurt again, Kate." He paused.

Kate knew where he was going, and she didn't want him to. Her last entanglement had ended so badly that she didn't know how she would have gotten through it without Elliot. She had invested a lot of time and emotion in Steven Kaplan, all of it worse than wasted. It had left her more suspicious and distrusting of men than she liked to admit. One of the good things about Michael was that she could trust him completely. He might not have Steven's banter and easy charm, but he had substance and achievement and sincerity. At least she thought so.

"That's why you're meeting Michael."

"Ever since Steven, I get to meet your *new* boyfriends. I'd like you to just find the right one and make him an *old* boyfriend."

"He's thirty-four. Old enough?"

Elliot rolled his eyes. "I worry about you."

Kate looked directly at Elliot. "This one is different. He's got his doctorate in anthropology, and he's very promising."

"Promising what? You always think they're different, and you always think they're promising, until they bore you, and then —"

"Oh, stop," Kate interrupted. "I know: I won't pick losers on account of my father, and I won't pick winners on account of my father. Yadda, yadda, yadda."

"Don't leave out your fear of commitment, yadda."

"I'll have you committed if you bring that up one more time. How come for thirty-one years you're allowed to be a gay bachelor — in both respects of the phrase — and then one day you hook up with Brice. Bingo! But since then I'm neurotic for not doing the same."

"Hey, I don't want you to hook up with Brice," Elliot cried in mock protest. "We're both strictly monogamous."

"I can't tell you how relieved I am to hear that," Kate retorted. "But don't project your fears onto me. It isn't easy to find a kindhearted, dependable, intelligent, sensual single man in Manhattan."

"Tell me about it!" Elliot exclaimed. "I had to try almost every guy on the island before I met Brice."

"Try not to be bitter, Elliot. I try so hard not to be." She reached up and wiped off a remaining bit of banana from his mouth with her thumb, then gave him a little peck on the lips. "Do you really have to be gay?" Then she smiled. Elliot was everything to her except her lover. And sometimes she thought that's what made her love him the most. Elliot was safe. Unlike the other men in her life, Elliot would always be there.

"What makes you think I'm gay?" Elliot asked with wide-eyed innocence. "Is that your professional opinion, doctor, or just a guess? Is it my spectator pumps?"

In fact, Elliot was not a flamboyant homosexual. He didn't look or act like what Kate's old Brooklyn crowd might have called "a fag," and like most of the young gay men in New York, he didn't go in for the high-maintenance *GQ*. Elliot looked and acted like a grade school math teacher — no, what he looked like, she thought affectionately, was a classic nerd: The only thing missing was the broken glasses held together with tape.

"How did a little queer kid from Indiana get to be so well-adjusted?" Kate asked him, also not for the first time.

Elliot reached over, took one of Kate's hands, and held it in both of his. "Listen closely," he told her, "because I am going to tell you something from Indiana about getting in touch with your true feelings." He looked at her intently and asked, "Are you listening? Because I am *not* going to repeat this." Kate nodded, and Elliot continued. "I got in touch with my true feelings by learning how to mask them very early in life. When you realize that your true feelings are most likely going to get the shit kicked out of you, you learn how to hide them and nurse them inside of you for as long as you have to until you find a safe place to express them." He smiled and gave Kate's hand a gentle squeeze. "You and Brice are where I can express them. And I don't recommend kids try to find a best friend and lover when they're in Andrew Country Day."

"I hear you," Kate agreed, and thought of poor Brian again.

"So, what *are* you doing now before dinner? Feel like making the trip to Dean and DeLuca with me?"

Kate noticed the time — she'd have to hurry now — and gathered up her backpack and cotton sweater. "No can do. I must run. I have a date."

"You're meeting this early with Michael?" Elliot asked, surprised. "You have a date with him *before* he's coming to dinner with us?"

"It's not with Michael."

"You have another date with someone else before Michael? And I don't know about it?" Elliot's voice rose with shock

32

and offense. "How could that happen? On average we speak six point four times a day in person and two point nine times by phone. A date I don't know everything about is a statistical improbability."

Kate rolled her eyes and decided to put him out of his misery. "It's just a date with Bina. Barbie's told her Jack is finally popping the question tonight — they're going to Nobu because Jack wants to make it really special — and to help prepare her, I'm taking her out for a manicure." She wiggled her fingers in the air. "They should look good for the ring," she said in an accent similar to Bina's Brooklynese.

"You're kidding! And you didn't tell me?" Elliot asked.

She shrugged, slipped on her jacket, shouldered her bag, and started toward the door. "I guess not."

Elliot followed her to the school door. "The fabled Bina and the much-sought-after Jack. Together at last."

"Yep, wedding bells have broken up that old gang of mine," Kate said. "Bye-bye, Bitches of Bushwick. It's only Bunny and me left unmarried." She looked down at her Swatch, refusing to acknowledge the depression this thought gave her. "Gotta go."

"Where are you and Bina getting together?" Elliot demanded.

"In SoHo," Kate answered as she pushed against the bar of the school safety door.

"Oh, good. I'm going that way. Just let me pick up my stuff."

"Forget it," Kate told him sternly.

"No. No. Wait for me!" he begged. "We can take the subway together, and I can finally meet Bina." Kate tried to keep her face still. Elliot had waged a year-long campaign to meet her old Brooklyn gang. But Kate didn't need it. In fact, as she'd made it clear more times than she could count, she loathed the idea. She'd tried in the dozen years since she'd left home to erase most of the dark memories of her troubled background, and though she was still close friends with Bina Horowitz and occasionally saw her other old pals, she didn't need Elliot's jaundiced eye appraising them.

Kate gave him a look. She disappeared out the door, then called back, "You need to meet Bina like I need another unemployed boyfriend."

She thought she was safely away and down the steps of the school when she heard Elliot behind her. He had on a madras hat and was clutching his backpack with one hand while he ran in a crouched posture that was a cross between Groucho's walk and a begging position. "Oh, come on," he pleaded. "It's not fair."

"Tragic. Absolutely tragic. Just like so many things in life," Kate told him, and kept on walking while he flapped at his other backpack strap.

"How come I never get to meet any of your Brooklyn friends?" he demanded. "They sound so fascinating."

Kate stopped in the schoolyard and turned back to Elliot. "Bina may be a lot of things, but fascinating is not one of them." Bina Horowitz had been her best friend since third grade and was still, in some ways, the most dependable. Kate had spent every holiday and most summer vacations at Bina's, partly because the Horowitz house was so clean and orderly and Bina's mom was so kind, but mostly because it allowed Kate to avoid the empty apartment that was her home or, worse, her father, who was too often drunk.

If Kate had perhaps outgrown Bina, who'd dropped out of Brooklyn College and worked at her father's chiropractic office, it didn't stop her from loving her. It was just that they had different interests, and none of Bina's would appeal to Elliot or any of her other Manhattan friends.

"Elliot," Kate said sternly as they made their way down the street. "You know your interest in Bina is only idle curiosity."

"Come on," Elliot coaxed. "Let me come. Anyway, it's a free country. The Constitution says so."

Kate snorted. "Unlike the U.S. Constitution, I believe in the separation of church and state."

"No," retorted Elliot, "you believe in the separation of gay and straight."

"That's not fair. You had dinner with Rita and me a week ago." She wasn't going to let him manipulate her with his politically correct blackmail. "You're not meeting Bina because even though she's my oldest friend, you have nothing, absolutely nothing, in common with her."

"I like people I have nothing in common with," Elliot argued. "That's why I like you and live with Brice."

"Don't be greedy, you're getting to meet Michael tonight," said Kate. "Isn't that enough for two yentas like you and Brice?"

"Yeah," Elliot conceded, giving in. "It will have to do."

Kate laughed and said, "Come on, I'm going to be late for my girlie date. Let me give you the same advice I gave Jennifer

Whalen, my student, a few hours ago. 'Try to make your own friends, dear.'"

They were at the IRT subway entrance. She gave Elliot a big smile and then hugged him good-bye. He shrugged, admitting his defeat. As she descended into the shadow of the subway, Elliot shouted after her, "Don't forget; dinner's at eight!"

"See ya there!" she yelled back, and ran to get the train.

Chapter Three

Kate and Bina walked down Lafayette Street, gazing in the windows of the fashion boutiques and art galleries that lined the SoHo strip. Kate looked and felt at home in SoHo. She would have liked to live in the neighborhood, but it was far too pricey for a school psychologist's salary. Her apartment was in Chelsea, but Kate could pass as a downtown hipster. Bina Horowitz, on the other hand, was still all Brooklyn: her dark hair too done, her clothes all "matchy-matchy," as Barbie used to say back in high school. Short, a little dumpy, and wearing too much gold, Bina stuck out like a sore thumb among the modelesque shoppers converging in one of the coolest sections of downtown Manhattan. That didn't stop Kate from loving her friend dearly, but she was grateful for all she herself had learned about style from Brice, college, Manhattan boutiques, and her current New York friends. She'd left her Brooklyn look far behind, thank goodness.

"My God, Katie, I don't know how you live here," Bina said. "These people in Manhattan are the reason girls all over the country go anorexic." Kate just laughed, though Bina wasn't far from wrong. Bina continued to crane her neck at every opportunity, slowing them down to look at a pedestrian painting of a nude, or a dress shop window where the clothes were torn into strips, and to marvel at the boutique called Center for the Dull. Kate had to explain it was just a clothing store like Yellow Rat Bastard — a store Kate didn't shop in, although she had one of their shopping bags.

"Why all the confusing names?" Bina asked. "And isn't it hot?" she added, fanning herself frantically with a flyer for a failing Off-Off Broadway show that some guy had just shoved into her hand as they walked by. He hadn't tried to palm one off on Kate, but then she didn't look like the kind of person who accepted garbage.

"Just calm down," Kate said. She tried to quicken their pace — the salon was notorious for demanding promptness — but Bina was Bina, and she simply couldn't be rushed or silenced. The Horowitz family had taken Kate in when she was eleven, and Kate knew practically everything about Bina. Kate had once done the math and realized that Mrs. Horowitz had fed her more than five hundred meals (most of them made with chicken fat). Dr. Horowitz had taught her to ride a two-wheeler bike when Kate's own father was too drunk or too lazy (or both) to bother to do it. Bina's brother, Dave, had taught the two of them to swim in the municipal pool, and Kate still swam laps whenever she could.

Back in Brooklyn, when Kate had had no other outlet and longed for more sophisticated friends — like Elliot and Brice and Rita — with whom she could banter or talk about books, Bina had sometimes annoyed her. But now that she had a circle of intellectual, cosmopolitan pals, she could give up the frustration over Bina's provincial interests and conversation and simply love her good heart.

"It's really hot," Bina repeated — a habit she had when Bina was paying no attention to Kate's response.

"Is it hotter in Manhattan than it is in Brooklyn?" Kate asked her, teasing.

"It's *always* hotter in Manhattan than it is in Brooklyn," Bina confirmed, completely missing Kate's irony. Bina definitely had an irony deficiency. "It's all these damned sidewalks and all this traffic." She

40

looked up and down Lafayette Street and shook her head in disgust. "I couldn't live here," she muttered, as if the choice were hers and million-dollar lofts were an option she and Jack could consider. "I just couldn't do it."

"And you don't," Kate reminded her, "so what's the problem?"

Bina stopped fanning herself abruptly, looked at Kate with a wide-eyed appeal, and meekly asked the question that she always asked midway through one of her anti-Manhattan tirades. "Am I being horrible?"

Kate felt a rush of affection overcome her annoyance and, as always, remembered why she loved Bina. Then she gave her the answer that she always did: "Same old Bina."

"Same old Katie," Bina responded in the litany they'd used to make peace and settle differences for two decades.

Kate grinned, and the two of them were right back on track. Kate could neither imagine introducing Bina to her Manhattan friends nor envision life without Bina — although she sometimes tried. Bina absolutely refused to grow, and that was both irritating and comforting to Kate — and sometimes downright embarrassing.

Just as they crossed Spring Street, Bina, as if reading Kate's thoughts, virtually shouted, "God, look at him!"

Kate turned her head, expecting at the least to see a mugging in progress. Instead, across the street she saw a pierced and tattooed guy going about his business, not the slightest bit fazed by the local wildlife. Kate didn't even comment; she merely looked down at her watch. "We can't be late," she warned Bina. "I have something special reserved." And to change the subject, "So have you picked out a manicure color?"

Bina dragged her eyes away from the local sideshow with obvious difficulty and focused instead on Kate. "I was thinking of a French manicure," she admitted.

Kate felt distinctly unenthusiastic, and it must have shown. Bina had been having the tips of her nails painted white with the rest a natural pink since high school.

"What's wrong with a French manicure?" Bina asked defensively.

"Nothing, if you're French," Kate retorted, having conveniently forgotten her teenage days when she, too, thought a French manicure the height of sophistication. Bina looked puzzled by Kate's remark. Kate had forgotten Bina's irony deficiency. "Hey, why not just try for something a little more up-to-date?"

Bina held out her hands and studied them. Kate noticed she was still wearing the Claddagh friendship ring Kate had given her for her sweet sixteen. "Go for something . . . daring," Kate suggested.

"Like what?" Bina asked, again defensively. "A tattoo on my fingernail?"

"Oooh, sarcasm. The devil's weapon," Kate said.

"Jack likes French manicures," Bina whined, still looking at her left hand. "Don't push me around like you always try to." Then she dropped her hands to her sides. They were both silent for a moment. "I'm sorry," Bina said. "I'm just a little nervous. You know, I've been waiting for Jack to propose for over —"

"Six years?" Kate asked, forgiving her friend. She had to start remembering to stop giving unwanted advice, which was difficult for a woman with her temperament in her profession. She smiled at Bina as they continued to walk down the street. "I think that on your first date with Jack, you started designing the monograms for your towels."

Jack and Bina had been going out for so many years. He had been her first and only real love. He'd made her wait while he finished college, got his degree, and became a CPA. Bina giggled. "Well, I knew right away he was the one. Such a hottie."

Kate reflected on the wide variation of people's tastes. To her, Jack was so far from a hottie that he left her ice cold. Of course, she'd never, ever, in all the six years of their courtship revealed that to Bina. And Bina had thought Steven was sour and gaunt, while to Kate he'd been —

"I just can't believe that he's leaving for Hong Kong for five months tomorrow, and tonight's the night," Bina chattered on, interrupting Kate's thoughts. Kate smiled at her.

There were few secrets among Kate's old Brooklyn posse, so when Jack had consulted with Barbie's jeweler father to get "a good deal" on an engagement ring, the news had traveled faster than e-mail among them. The day Bina had waited for for so long had finally arrived, but when Kate glanced at her friend, she noticed something odd: Bina seemed anything but happy. Surely she couldn't be having second thoughts. But Kate knew Bina well enough to see that something wasn't right.

Oh, my God, thought Kate. Bina has changed her mind, and she's afraid to tell anyone. Her parents — especially her mother! — will be beside themselves if . . . "Bina, are you starting to have doubts?" she asked as gently as she could, stopping to look at her friend. "You know, you don't *have* to marry Jack."

"Are you crazy? Of course I do! I want to. I'm just nervous that . . . well, I'm just nervous. Normal, right? Hey, where is this place, anyway?"

"Just to the left on Broome," Kate said. And if Bina didn't want to talk about her nerves, it was fine, she told herself. Give the girl a little space. "This is the Police Building," she said as a diversion while they passed the domed monument that Teddy Roosevelt had built when he was chief of police. "It's condos now," she went on, "and they found a secret tunnel from here to the speakeasy across the street, so —"

"So the Irish cops wouldn't be caught getting drunk," Bina said, then stopped in embarrassment. Kate just smiled. Her father, a retired Irish cop, had died three years ago from cirrhosis of the liver, and Kate couldn't help but consider it a release for both of them. It was the Horowitzes who couldn't get over it.

"No harm, no foul," Kate told her. "We're almost there and we're only four

45

minutes late. You're going to like this place. They have great nail colors, but just in case, I brought a few alternatives for you." She scrambled around in her Prada bag — the only purse she owned, and she carried it everywhere. It had cost her an entire paycheck, but every time she opened it, it gave her pleasure. Now she pulled out a little bag. It contained three nail polishes, each one a wildly different seductive shade.

Bina took the bag and peeked into it. "Ooooh! They look like the magic beans from 'Jack and the Beanstalk,'" she said. Then she started to giggle. "Get it? Jack and his beanstalk?" she asked, raising her eyebrows suggestively.

Kate gave Bina her "I'm not in the mood" look. Clearly her moment of nervousness had passed. "Hey, spare me the details of Jack's beanstalk or any other part of his anatomy," she begged. "Consider that your bridesmaid's gift to me." She took Bina's arm to get her around the guy selling used magazines on the sidewalk and across to their destination.

Just then, as they crossed the street, Bina stopped — as if the Manhattan traffic would wait for her — and pointed to the corner. "Omigod! That's Bunny's ex."

Kate looked in the right direction as she simultaneously pulled Bina's arm down. She was about to tell her not to point when she caught sight of one of the best-looking men she had ever seen. He was tall and slim, and his jeans and jacket had the perfect casual slouch. As a cloud moved, light from the west fell on that corner and reflected off his hair as if he had a halo around his head. He had stopped for the light, and before he began to cross the street, he fished in his inside pocket. Kate couldn't help following his hand, and as he crossed the street she turned her head to get a look at his buns. She always had a weakness in that area, and this guy was . . . well, his buns must have come from the very best bakery.

"He went out with Bunny?" Kate asked. Of her posse, Bunny was probably the most garish and certainly the dimmest bulb.

Bina nodded. Kate could only see that in her peripheral vision, because she couldn't tear her eyes off the man just twenty feet away.

"Are you sure that's him?"

To Kate's good luck, the guy stopped at the corner across from them and turned downtown in their direction. Kate stood rooted to the spot, although it was a few steps off the curb. She thought that he looked at her. Just then a taxi honked, the driver deciding he would warn them before he ran them over. At a shriek from Bina, Kate pulled her eyes away, and the two of them scampered across the street. By the time they had walked single file between parked cars and gotten to the sidewalk, the Adonis had put on sunglasses and was striding away.

"What color do you think I should do for bridesmaids?" Bina asked.

Kate suppressed a groan. Bev had had them all in silver, and Barbie had picked a pistachio green that not even a blonde could wear without looking sallow. "How about basic black?" Kate asked, but she knew there wasn't a hope in hell. She sighed. She and Bunny would be the last of their high school crowd not to be married — at least there was still Bunny. Kate would try not to mind, but everyone else would. No one at Bina's wedding would leave the naked state of her left finger unnoted. "Please, Bina! Don't make me walk down that aisle again. Why not just make me wear a sign that says 'Unmarriageable'?"

"Kate, you have to be my maid of honor. Barbie was always closer to Bunny, and

Bev . . . well, Bev never really liked me."

"Bev has never liked anyone," Kate informed Bina, not for the first time, and took her arm. "Hey, I'm really touched." The pair came up to the door of the salon. Kate held the door open for Bina, who nervously stepped inside.

Chapter Four

Kate knew the spa was unlike any place Bina had ever seen in her life — a sort of postindustrial French boudoir with Moorish touches. That was exactly why she had chosen it. Not to show off, but to make it very special for her friend. "This is," she informed Bina in a dramatic stage whisper, "the most expensive spa in the city of New York." She studied Bina's face to make sure what she was telling her was sinking in. "And I mean the *entire* city," she continued.

"Wow," was all Bina could manage, looking around at the sheer curtains, the concrete floor, and the Louis XVI bergere armchair.

Kate smiled and walked up to the counter. A chic young Asian woman smiled back and, without speaking, raised her perfectly shaped eyebrows. They did a good brow wax here. "Kate Jameson," Kate announced. "There are the two of us here," she added, because Bina had disappeared shyly behind Kate. "For manicures, pedicures, and toe waxing."

From behind, Bina whispered, "Toe waxing?" but Kate ignored her. "We have a reservation. I have the confirmation number."

"It will be just a moment," said the beautiful receptionist. "Please, have a seat."

Of course, that was difficult with just the one antique armchair, but Kate motioned for Bina to sit and she did, albeit gingerly.

Then she looked up at Kate and grabbed her hands. "Oh, Kate. I'm nervous. What happens if I go through all this and it jinxes me? What if Jack doesn't —"

"Bina, don't be silly. You can't 'jinx' things." Kate sighed. "I just spent an hour trying to convince an eight-year-old that magic won't work. Don't make me repeat myself."

"Look, I know all about you. Little Miss Logic. But I'm superstitious, okay? No black cats, no hats on the bed, no shoes to friends."

"Shoes to friends?"

"Yeah. You give shoes to a friend and she walks away from you," Bina said. "Don't you know that?"

"Bina, you are truly crazy," Kate said. "Anyway, this is your big day, and I want to be a part of it. So relax and enjoy. Everything will be fine, and tonight with Jack will be wonderful."

Bina still looked doubtful. She craned her neck and looked around again. "It just must be so expensive," she said. "You know, I can have all of the same things done in Brooklyn at Kim's Korean place for about one-quarter the price. And I bet it's every bit as good, too."

Kate smiled. "Maybe — maybe not. But here you have ambience."

"Well, my mother would say, 'Ambience, schmambience, paint my nails.' "

"You know I love your mother, but sometimes she's not exactly au courant." Bina looked perplexed. "And by the way, how do you spell schmambience?" Kate asked with a smile.

"You don't," Bina told her. "It's Yiddish. It's a spoken language."

Kate laughed. This was typical of the verbal exchanges she and Bina had been having since Kate first entered the Horowitzes' household and Mrs. Horowitz pronounced that Kate's father knew *"bupkis"* about raising a *"sheyna maidela."*

At the time, Kate didn't know that *bupkis* meant "virtually nothing" or that *sheyna maidela* meant "pretty little girl," but she figured it out from the context. She learned what *putz* and *shnorrer* and *gonif* meant, all of them words that sounded better and more accurate than their English equivalents.

Kate had celebrated every holiday at Bina's house — even if they weren't Kate's holidays — and learned to love sweet noodle kugel. When the time came for Kate's first Holy Communion, Mrs. Horowitz sewed up Kate's white dress and bought a headpiece. (When Bina wanted a white dress and headpiece, too, she got one, though Dr. and Mrs. Horowitz drew the line at allowing Bina to get on line with the little Catholic girls for the ceremony.)

Kate, told by a priest in her catechism class that trick-or-treating on Halloween was a mortal sin, felt tremendous disappointment. When she shared this with Bina's mother, the reassurance Kate got was, "Sin, schmin! Do your best with that *meshugene* in a dress and go out to get your candy. Don't worry about it."

"But I don't want to go to hell after I die," Kate told her tearfully.

"Hell, schmell," Mrs. Horowitz responded. "Trust me, there's no such place except here on earth." She drew Kate onto her lap and held her close. "There's only heaven, honey," she whispered. "And that's where your mama is."

Somehow, Mrs. Horowitz's complete conviction sank in. A few months later, after catechism, when Vicky Brown told Kate and Bina that Bina's Jewish mother was going to hell after she died, Kate turned to Vicky and declared, "Hell, schmell! What do you know?" After that, Kate and Bina made a pact to stick up for each other.

Maybe it was from that day they became known as the "Witches of Bushwick." As teenagers, their posse grew, with Bev and Barbie and, later on, Bunny, but they stayed the same, though in the neighborhood their nickname changed to "Bitches." Then Kate drifted from the group.

Bina was still holding on to Kate's hand. "Oh, Kate," she said, and squeezed hard. "I'm so excited! Tonight's the night I get proposed to by the man I love."

"Don't forget to act surprised," Kate warned her. "You don't want Jack to know you already knew."

"I wish Barbie hadn't told me that he bought the ring." Bina sighed. "I'm so nervous. Why couldn't she just have let it be a surprise for me?"

"Oh, honey." Kate laughed. "You don't want surprises. You want to look your best."

Just then another Asian woman even more beautiful than the receptionist walked into the waiting area. "Kate Jameson?" she asked. Kate nodded. "We have your room all ready. Follow me, please."

Kate and Bina followed her into a small room, and Kate sat in one of two facing chairs. Each was thronelike, with a built-in foot Jacuzzi already filled with delightful-smelling bubbling water. The softly lit room, all in soothing sea blue, also had two glass tables on wheels prepared for hand pampering. Two young Asian women knelt on blue silk pillows on the floor beside the foot baths. They helped their clients out of their shoes and indicated that they should plunge their feet into the fragrant Jacuzzis in preparation for the pedicure. Bina looked across at Kate in amazement. Kate merely smiled at her. The air smelled of freesia, and Kate took a deep, appreciative breath. If she had to pay half her salary check for the "ambience, schmambience," it was *so* worth it. The second beautiful Asian woman came back into their blue heaven and asked the pair, "Would you like bottled water, coffee, tea, juice, or champagne?"

"You're kidding!" Bina almost squealed.

"Champagne, I think," Kate replied as if

Bina hadn't reacted. Bina didn't usually drink, but, "This is a big celebration," Kate told her.

In the moment of silence that followed, Kate closed her eyes, and the image that came to her, unbidden, was the long, lean jeans-clad guy whom Bina had pointed out. She must have been wrong. Bunny could never have dated someone like that. She mused about it for a moment or two and, guiltily, compared what she had seen to Michael. Michael was just a little too broad in the beam, and there was something about his walk. . . . Kate shook the thoughts from her head as unworthy. "What's his name?" she asked Bina.

"Whose name? Jack? His name is Jack." Bina gave her a look, then laughed. "You're so funny." Kate blushed and decided to forget about the guy on the corner.

"Kate, this is so nice of you," Bina began as one of the two pedicurists began to massage her feet. She giggled, pulled them away, and giggled again.

"Oh, just relax, Bina," Kate told her. "Breathe." For a moment the two were silent. Kate closed her eyes and let herself feel the strong hands work her heels and instep.

Bina leaned forward to whisper across the small room, "Is this really where Sandra Bullock, Giselle, and Gwen Stefani get their manicures?"

"Yup," Kate said. "And it's where Kate Jameson and Bina Horowitz have their manicures, too."

"Soon to be Bina Horowitz Weintraub," Bina reminded her. "Oh, Kate, I love Jack so much. I'm just so . . . so happy today, and so glad I'm sharing part of it with you. I just want you to find your Jack and be as happy as I am."

Kate laughed. "As your mother would say, 'From your lips to God's ears.' " Before Bina could speak, the door opened and the woman entered with a tray holding two flutes of champagne. She offered one to Kate and one to Bina.

"Enjoy!" she said as she glided from the room.

Kate felt a slight change in her emotional landscape. There was a time when she thought she might be drinking champagne to celebrate something with Steven, but she had been very wrong. She wondered if the time would come when she and Michael . . . She pulled her thoughts away and focused on the moment.

Bina looked at her glass. "I don't think I

should start drinking this early in the afternoon."

Kate rolled her eyes. Bina never wanted to drink. "Oh, come on, Bina. Live a little," she said, lifting her own flute. "To your wedding!"

"Oh, Kate!" Bina was clearly touched. Both girls took a sip of their champagne. Then Kate started looking through the polishes. "Boy, I bet Bunny wishes she were in my chair," Bina said, leaning back.

"How *is* Bunny?" Kate asked. Bunny was a dental hygienist whose record with men was admittedly poor. Again Kate thought of the delicious-looking man they had seen outside. Bunny's ex? It was hard to believe.

"You don't want to know," replied Bina.

Bina was right. Kate *didn't* want to know. Bunny was really more Bina's friend. She'd entered Kate's life in junior high, taking the Bitches to five and changing her name — Patricia — to begin with B so she'd fit in with the gang. Kate had drifted from the group by then. She spent more time studying and reading. While the others were worrying almost exclusively about hair, makeup, and boys, Kate was focused on SAT scores and college scholarships. And when graduation day came, the other Bitches set their sights on nondemanding jobs, good marriages, and babies, while Kate declared that she was not just going to "sleep-away" college, but also intended to become a doctor of psychology.

As Bev put it, "She thinks she's who the fuck she is." If it hadn't been for Bina, that would've been the end of Kate's association with the Bitches and everyone else in Brooklyn. But Bina made friends for life. At first Kate had resented what she had considered Bina's "clinging." Then she realized that there was no one who knew her the way Bina did. And while she'd prefer to forget much of her other "backlash" from Brooklyn, for Bina's friendship she was grateful.

She finished her glass of champagne and was immediately brought another. Bina was still talking about Bunny.

". . . so the guy drops her like a rock. You saw him. I mean, Bunny should have known he wasn't for her, but she took it hard. And now she's on the rebound. She's already going out with another guy — Arnie or Barney or something — and she's telling Barbie they're getting serious."

Big news flash. Bunny picked one inappropriate man after another, always insisting they were "serious" and always being disappointed. Classic repetition compulsion, Kate thought, but what she said was, "Denial ain't just a river in Egypt."

"What?" Bina paused for a moment. "Oh! I get it!" She paused again, then made her voice falsely casual. "How are things going with this Michael?"

"All right," Kate said noncommittally, and shrugged. She liked to keep a low profile on her dating life with Bina and the others, or else the Horowitz family would be sending out engraved announcements. "He's very smart and seems promising. We're going over to Elliot and Brice's tonight for dinner."

"Who's Brice?" Bina asked.

Kate sighed. When it came to Brooklyn, Bina remembered what day of the month each of her friends had their periods, but outside Brooklyn . . .

"Elliot's partner."

"Elliot who?"

"You remember, Elliot Winston. My friend from Brown. The guy I teach with."

"Oh, yeah. So if he's a teacher, how does he have a partner?"

"His *life* partner, Bina," Kate said, exasperated.

Bina paused, then dropped her voice. "Are those guys gay?"

Yeah, and so is your unmarried uncle Kenny, Kate thought, but all she did was smile tolerantly. So what if Bina's gender politics were way behind the times. She decided to change the subject. "So what color are you going to go with? Remember, every shade goes with a diamond!"

"I don't know. What have *you* picked?"

Of course the question was completely irrelevant, but Bina was like that. Before she selected anything from a menu, she had to know what you were having.

"Same old Bina," Kate said, smiling at her irrepressible friend.

"Same old Katie," Bina said, slurring her words a bit. The champagne was clearly starting to get to her, and looking at her friend, ready to take such a big yet inevitable step, Kate shivered. Jack had never been her cup of tea — and he certainly was no glass of champagne — but he seemed loving to Bina, her family liked him, and . . . well, looking across at Bina, Kate had to admit that Jack was probably a good match. She was torn between bursting into tears and laughing out loud. Bina smiled at her, slightly cross-eyed. "I love you, Katie," she said.

"I love you, too, Bina," Kate assured her, and it was true. "But no more drinks for

61

you. You've got a big night ahead of you."

Bina took a last sip of champagne. Then she leaned over, close to her friend. "Kate," she whispered. "There's something I'm dying to ask you."

Kate steeled herself. "Yes?"

"What's a toe waxing?" Bina inquired.

Bina's tone made it sound obscene. Kate laughed. "You know how sometimes there is a little bit of hair on the knuckle of your big toe?" she asked.

Bina pulled her foot out of the Jacuzzi and studied it. "Wow," she said. "Look at it. Eeuuyew." One of the Asian women turned to look at the other, and both started to giggle. Bina's face turned a bright pink. "It's kind of icky," she admitted. "Like Bigfoot. God, Katie, you're making me feel like a freak. But I never noticed it before."

"Well," Kate continued, "after it's waxed off, Jack won't, either. You can let him kiss all your little piggies with pride. So, what color have you picked?"

Bina turned her attention to the gift bottles from Kate and the others arranged beautifully along the wall shelf at her elbow. "They don't have most of these colors in Brooklyn," she admitted.

"Just one more reason why I live in

Manhattan," Kate declared. "Step up to the plate. What's it going to be?"

Bina looked down at the Asian girl already working on her left hand. "Do you do French manicures?" she asked.

Chapter Five

Kate's Manhattan apartment was undeniably small. Still, she had been lucky to find it. It was in a brownstone on West 19th Street, on a tree-lined block close to the seminary, a very desirable location. The apartment was on the first floor, above street level, and consisted of a large room that had once been a parlor, a small bathroom and smaller kitchen behind it, and then a cozy bedroom.

The main room faced the back garden, which unfortunately belonged to the apartment below. But at least she had quiet, a green view in summer, and a chance to watch the snow in winter. She hadn't had much money to spend on furniture, but Elliot, always alert for bargains, had helped her find and carry home the sofa — a small one with blue-and-white awning stripe. She had found an old wicker rocker in a thrift store, and after it was sprayed blue, it made a comfortable, if slightly rickety, seat.

Max, who lived upstairs, had recently

helped her put up bookshelves that now filled in the recesses on either side of the fireplace. Max was a friend of Bina's brother and he worked on Wall Street with Jack, his cousin. He'd introduced Bina to Jack, so when Kate had heard that he was searching for an apartment, she'd let him know about the one about to become available in her building. Max, who would be forever grateful, had also been interested in her, but Kate couldn't get up any enthusiasm. He was nice and good-looking, but they had nothing to talk about, although Max didn't seem to mind that. And though her father had given her precious little advice about life, he had expressed his philosophy to "never crap where you eat." She had managed to handle Max diplomatically, though, and they were friends as well as good neighbors. Though Max would never need to stop by to borrow a cup of sugar, he might well ask for a cup of coffee, a shot of vodka, or, less frequently, a fix-up with some girl Kate knew.

Kate opened the curtains. It looked like rain. She threw her purse on the sofa and hurried across to her bedroom. The beauty treatment with Bina had taken more time than she'd expected, and she had only a half hour before Michael came over. Although she had been cavalier about it with Elliot earlier in the day, Kate was actually a little nervous about bringing Michael over. Introducing a boyfriend to Elliot was like taking him home to meet her family, and she wanted everything to go smoothly.

Kate's bedroom was really just a part of the larger room that had been partitioned off. Its biggest disadvantage was the smallness of its closet.

But she lived with it, as most New Yorkers did. Kate decided she didn't have the time to shower, so she selected the Madonna blue sleeveless dress she'd just bought and ran into the bathroom. She had enough time to wash her face, take her hair down, brush the cascades of wavy red that fell below her shoulders, and pull out her makeup bag for a quick fix.

She never wore much makeup. Her skin was pale, and she'd finally outgrown the tiny freckles, no bigger than pinpoints, that used to dance across her cheeks and the bridge of her nose — a sort of Irish trail. Now her face was simply creamy, and most of the time she only bothered with lipstick so that her hair didn't overpower the rest of her face.

She had only ten minutes before Michael was supposed to arrive, though he was often a little late. That, she'd come to understand, wasn't because he was disrespectful — Kate hated lateness as a pattern and thought it a narcissistic trait — but because he was often so wrapped up in his work and thoughts of his research that he occasionally forgot to get off the subway or he overshot the bus stop.

She smiled at the thought of him. He had a good mind, good hands, and a strong jaw. She liked his silver-rimmed glasses, his earnest eyes peering through them, and his dedication to his work.

She had only recently begun sleeping with him: She wasn't usually so prim, but her affair with Steven had left her more cautious than she had been before. They had met at her friend Tina's; Tina and Michael worked at the same university. Tina hadn't "fixed them up" because she hadn't thought that Michael was Kate's type, but since Steven, Kate wasn't sure what her "type" ought to be. Michael's courtship had been slow but steady. When they had finally taken the plunge, Kate had been delighted to find he was caring and generous in bed. And it seemed as if he were just as taken with her. But this was the point of the relationship where things could go on for a long time without actually moving forward. Kate had spent nearly two years with Steven, a writer, and had been hurt when she realized that he would never want to marry her or possibly anyone else. She didn't want to spend another year only to have that happen again.

She sat on her bed and looked down at her painted toes. For a moment she could even imagine being envious of Bina, who had her life settled. But she reminded herself that Bina had put in her six years with Jack. She knew she wanted children but wouldn't marry just for that. The work she did with Brian and the others at Andrew Country Day would hold her until she was ready to have a normal family of her own.

And Michael seemed like a possibility. They had not yet discussed exclusivity, but, as he called her almost every night and since they saw each other regularly, Kate thought the talk would be only a formality. She wasn't in a rush and wouldn't make ultimatums. Still, deep down, she wanted to know her goals were shared.

Kate slipped into the silk dress and scrambled under the bed for her high-heeled sandals. Black and strappy, they would show off her newly painted toenails. They were killers to walk in, but she didn't have to walk far to Elliot's.

When there was a knock at the door a few moments later, Kate was ready. She clicked across the floor and opened the door. But it wasn't Michael. Max was there, holding a bouquet of snapdragons and statice. "Hey," he said. "You look great."

"Thanks." Kate smiled briefly, trying to show she didn't have the time to chat. Max held the flowers without moving. He had an adorable smile; one of his incisors showed because it had moved up onto the tooth next to it, and Kate found that appealing. But Max was a bit like his incisor: He often tried to push in where he didn't belong. There was no harm in him, though, and no denying he was a likable guy.

"Are those for me?" she asked.

"You betcha," Max said. "The green market was open when I walked by. The snapdragons reminded me of your hair. You can't say no."

Kate didn't. But as she took the bouquet, she worried that Max might still have a crush on her. She didn't want to encourage him, nor did she want to be rude. She tapped across the living room floor to the tiny excuse for a kitchen and fumbled for a vase. Max followed her and stood in the doorway. Kate filled the vase and couldn't help but smile when she saw the red snaps with the orange centers. "I wish I could wear two of these as earrings," she joked.

"You don't need any earrings," Max said. "You look perfect. And as cool as a cucumber."

Kate took the flowers and set them on her small dining table. They did make a pretty spot of color. "Thanks, Max," she said, and kissed him on the cheek, leaving a small imprint of lip gloss.

"Where you off to?" he asked.

"Oh, just dinner at Elliot's." Max, an accountant and actuarial, occasionally enjoyed talking higher math with Elliot. She hadn't yet told Max about Michael.

"Well, that dress is wasted on him," Max said, and to Kate's dismay, he sat down. It wasn't that she had any reason to feel guilty, but she didn't want Michael to arrive and find another man in her apartment or to have to introduce them to each other. Michael didn't seem overly possessive. On the contrary, he seemed a little nervous. But Kate wanted him to feel secure, so she also wanted Max to get up and go, although she didn't want to have to ask him.

Max shifted position on the striped sofa

and pulled some envelopes and a rolled-up magazine from his back pocket.

"Oh, here. I picked up your mail."

Kate smiled and tried to hide a sigh. There were no separate mailboxes for the four tenants of their brownstone, and mail was left on a radiator in the vestibule. "Are you being so nice to me because you wanted to borrow a bottle of Absolut?"

"No, I try not to rustle booze until it's Absolut necessary."

Kate gave him another obligatory smile. He was a nice guy, but a little tiresome. "Well, hey, I've got to go."

Max got up and ambled over to the door. "Whatever." At last she saw his back and closed the door. She took the mail he had brought and walked over to the wastepaper basket beside her desk. She tried to smooth out *The New Yorker*; picked up a catalog from Saks, tore it in half, and threw it into the basket before it could tempt her; filed a bill from Con Ed next to her checkbook; and threw away all the junk mail. Then, at the bottom of the small pile, she found an almost square envelope addressed to her in gold calligraphy. Oh, my God, she thought, has Bina jumped the gun and sent out wedding invitations before the proposal?

71

She turned over the ominous communiqué and saw Mr. and Mrs. Tromboli's address written across the back. Kate's hands began to tremble. She slit open the envelope and accidentally tore off the corner of the enclosed pasteboard. She pulled out the inevitable: an invitation to the wedding of Patricia (Bunny) Marie Tromboli to Arnold S. Beckmen. For a moment, Kate felt dizzy. How could this have happened? What had Bina been saying earlier about that Brooklyn guy who had broken Bunny's heart? Now Kate felt her own heart quiver. With Bina engaged and Bunny about to get married, she would be the last of her old friends to be single. When they started having children, she would really be alone. And Bev was already heavily pregnant; inevitably, young mothers got involved with playgrounds, preschools, play dates, and pregnancies — the four Ps. Four peas in a pod, the Bs would be busy reproducing, and Kate would be closed out of the circle completely.

She put down the invitation, feeling a little dizzy. Then the buzzer rang. She and Michael had no time for a drink now, and she had no desire for one, either. She hit the intercom as hard as the wedding invitation had hit her, and when he said hello, instead of inviting him upstairs she told him she'd be down in a minute. Stuffing the stiff card into her purse, she told herself she wouldn't think about the Bunny situation; but on her way down the stairs, careful not to trip in the sandals, the idea of Bunny reproducing like a rabbit came to her. As much as she loved the children at school, and as dedicated as she was to them, Kate felt mournful. She knew she would always make do if she didn't have a child of her own to raise and love.

Michael was standing in the vestibule. He was wearing pressed chinos, a white Oxford shirt, and a tweed sports coat. It was a little heavy for the season, but Kate had noticed that he was always careful to dress conservatively and just a little "scholarly." He was both a good-looking and a nice-looking man, just slightly taller than Kate was in her heels, and she liked his abundant curly brown hair. "Hi," she greeted him, trying to put away her concerns the way she had stuffed Bunny's wedding invitation into her bag. They kissed, just a peck on the lips. "You've had a haircut," she said.

"Nope, just had my ears lowered," he replied.

Kate wished he hadn't cut his hair, especially just before meeting Elliot and Brice. It made him the tiniest bit geeky looking, but she put that thought out of her mind as well. Michael looked fine, and he was a decent human being. He had put himself through undergrad and graduate school on scholarships and various jobs. He'd already published papers in important journals and was poised for a brilliant career in academia. He was well-read, well-informed, and well-intentioned, as far as she could tell. The fact that he'd been married — but for only one year, when he was too young to know any better — made him look even better in her eyes. He knew how to commit, even if it had been to the wrong woman.

Now he looked at Kate, and his deep brown eyes sparkled behind his glasses. "You are breathtaking," he said, and Kate smiled. The cost of the dress was well worth it.

"We'd better go," she said. "Brice hates late guests when he's cooking." Despite her words, Michael pushed her gently against the doorway and kissed her. He was a good kisser, and Kate let her tongue and mind wander. Then Max, clothed for the gym, came bounding down the stairs. They pulled apart, but Max, of course, had seen them. He raised his eyebrows as he walked past them, Kate's lip gloss still on his cheek.

"Dinner at Elliot's?" he asked as he walked by and down the stoop. Kate felt a twinge of guilt. Of course, she *was* going to dinner at Elliot's, but by withholding the information that she was going with an escort, she now looked like a liar. Michael, unaware, took her hand and they walked outside and down the steps.

Kate couldn't help but think of her two years in Catholic school. Sins of omission and sins of commission: She thought she remembered they were equal. She promised herself she would find some way to apologize to Max later.

Now she took Michael's arm as they walked down the shady street. Chelsea was very pretty west of Eighth Avenue. "Let's walk through the seminary garden," Michael suggested. Kate smiled her agreement. At this time of day, the block-size park enclosed by the church and seminary buildings was at its most lovely. They walked arm in arm.

"Kate, stop for a minute," Michael said. "I have something for you."

He fumbled around with his briefcase

straps for a moment. He had given Kate a gift before — an out-of-print English psychology book by D. W. Winnicott. It had been very thoughtful, and just now she expected another book. But instead he took out a small, oblong box wrapped in silver paper. Unmistakably a jewelry box. "Do you know today is our three-month anniversary?" he asked. Kate actually hadn't, and she was really moved that he had. "I saw this and thought of you," he said. He handed her the box, which she unwrapped. Once she opened it, a thin silver bracelet with a tiny K hanging from it was revealed. She looked from it to the expectant expression on Michael's face. It wasn't anything she would have chosen for herself, but it was very sweet nonetheless.

"Oh, Michael. Thank you." They kissed again, and this time there was no interruption.

"Do you like it?" he asked.

For a moment, Kate thought of sins of omission again, but even Sister Vincent couldn't believe they would extend to this. "Yes. It's lovely. Would you fasten it for me?"

Michael leaned forward and fiddled with the tiny clasp. It took a moment, but at last he had it around her wrist. She stretched out her arm. "It looks very nice," she said.

"It looks great!" Michael said, and tucked her arm in his.

Kate felt better than she had all day.

Chapter Six

Brice and Elliot met three years ago but had moved in together only in September. Brice's stylish retro furniture in orange and lime green had taken precedence over Elliot's collection of thrift shop purchases and off-the-street finds. Their two-bedroom apartment in a Chelsea brownstone near Kate's had large windows in the living room overlooking a tiny backyard. An old refectory table was set before the windows, and despite their protests, Michael and Kate were given the chairs that faced the garden view.

"The tulips are just over and the roses haven't started, so it's not at its best," Brice said apologetically as he seated them; then he excused himself to bring dinner in from the kitchen. Kate noticed they were using Brice's good glassware and Havilland china, and she was touched. Elliot brought in a wine cooler and set it on the oak credenza.

"A coaster! A coaster!" Brice exclaimed,

and slipped one under the crystal cooler. Kate suppressed a smile.

In a few moments, dishes were being passed around. Elliot, standing, began to pour wine into the waiting goblets. Michael picked up his glass and almost ostentatiously set it upside down. "None for me, thanks," he said.

Kate winced. She should have seen this one coming. Michael didn't drink at all, just said he didn't like it. Given her father's bad habits, it seemed a good trait to Kate, but she knew it wouldn't go down well with Elliot. He prided himself on his wine cellar — even though it was actually in the linen closet — and he must have taken pains selecting this Pinot Grigio.

"Don't you drink?" Brice asked, his brows slightly raised. Kate could imagine the talk afterward: "Is he an alcoholic, is he in AA. No? Then he's a control freak or a born-again Christian." Oh, it would be endless.

"I prefer to keep a clear head," Michael answered.

"Yeah. You never know when someone might need to see through it," Elliot muttered beside Kate's ear as he reached for her glass.

Once all their plates were filled and the

drinking crisis was past, they began on Brice's famous appetizer: a beautiful, multi-colored vegetable terrine. There was some cursory conversation, but the tension seemed thick in the air, especially between Elliot and Michael. Of course, Elliot was always very protective of Kate. And he had already registered his dislike of this accomplished and nice-looking new boyfriend. The fact that Michael was a bit priggish and overly fastidious wasn't lost on Kate, but he did have other, compensatory traits.

"There's a good chance I'm going to get that Sagerman grant," Michael said to Kate as they finished the first course. "I saw Professor Hopkins, and he told me that the committee discussions seemed to be very . . . well, promising." Kate saw Elliot and Brice exchange a look. It was rude of Michael to ignore them, even briefly, but he was a single-minded academic.

Kate held back a sigh. Even when she and Michael were alone, it was sometimes difficult to remember all the cards in his academic deck. Now, to make the conversation general it would be necessary to explain to the others about the Sagerman Foundation, Michael's interest in a postdoctorate appointment, and his complicated relationship with his mentor, Charles Hopkins. It was the kind of thing that made a difference to a couple but didn't make for good dinner talk.

"Great," Kate said.

No one else spoke. Elliot refilled their glasses, and Brice passed around the second course. Kate looked at it and knew that her friends had spared no expense to impress Michael. This was Brice's risotto with truffles, and she knew what truffles cost. They all took a bite of the steaming rice. As the awkward silence stretched out, Kate turned to Brice in an attempt at light conversation. "Brice, this risotto is really delicious."

"Very good," Michael agreed.

Brice beamed at the compliments. He was proud of his cooking, his design sense, and his extensive collection of pristine Beanie Babies arranged meticulously on a series of long floating shelves over the credenza. Kate had watched Michael notice them and avert his eyes. He was not, she had to admit, very playful in his attitude to decor or dining chitchat.

"So, what happened at the salon this afternoon?" Elliot inquired of Kate.

She smiled. She knew him so well: He was taking pity on her and trying to make the dinner less painful. And he also figured she'd spill her guts more readily just to keep the conversation going. Nice try, she thought, but it wouldn't work.

"Oh, I just had my nails painted," she said. She showed ten gleaming fingertips and still managed to hold the fork. "Do you think Dr. McKay will feel they're subversive?" The previous semester, the principal had declared toe rings subversive, and all the kids had to remove their socks and shoes to have contraband foot jewelry confiscated.

"That and cock rings," Elliot said.

"Elliot, please!" Brice reprimanded. "Not in front of the Havilland." He flashed a smile at Kate and Michael.

Their conversation continued in fits and starts, but Kate knew Michael was not a hit. Of course, Elliot had really liked Steven and that hadn't worked out, so . . . perhaps Elliot's first impression was not as important as she had thought it was.

"Salad or cheese and fruit before dessert?" Brice asked. "I have lovely Bosc pears."

"No thanks, Brice," said Kate.

"None for me," Michael agreed. Across the table, Elliot stood up and began to clear away the dishes. "It was very good," Michael added.

Even to Kate it seemed a bland thank-you. "Wasn't the terrine terrific?" she prompted. She looked at Michael, who in turn looked at the empty serving plates with an expression of confusion.

"Which was the terrine?" he asked.

Kate's face flushed pink. She knew how much effort Brice had put into the dish. "The vegetable pâté," she explained to Michael.

Elliot, still picking up plates, circled around behind Michael. "With your head so clear you probably just call that 'thick dip,' huh," he said.

Kate winced. From behind Michael's back, Elliot held his nose and gave Kate a thumbs-down sign, almost dumping the plates he had gathered.

"Watch out for the Havilland!" Brice warned again.

"Elliot, you don't have to do that," Kate said, referring both to his comments and the clearing.

"Oh, but I do, I do," Elliot replied, grinning.

She gave him a look. Clearly they needed some private time in the kitchen. "I'll help you clear," she offered, noticing Michael didn't even attempt to help.

Brice began to protest and rise as well,

but Elliot shook his head and looked pointedly at Michael. Brice gave him a pleading look, but Elliot leaned close and whispered, "Somebody has to talk to him."

Brice gave Michael a weak smile. "So, what's new in anthropology?" he asked Michael in a bright voice. "Is the Sugerman grant a sure thing?"

"Sagerman," Michael corrected. "From the Sagerman Foundation for the Studies of Primitive Peoples."

Kate sighed, picked up some glasses, and followed Elliot into the kitchen. It was small but efficient, with black-and-white floor tiles, red walls and cabinets, and the latest stainless-steel appliances. Kate tried to prepare herself. Elliot was silent as he put the dishes in the sink. Then, as she knew he would, he turned to face Kate, his hands on his hips like an accusatory nun. "Where did you dig him up?" he demanded. "This guy's the worst of the lot."

"Oh, Elliot! He is not," Kate protested. "And keep your voice down."

"Come on, Kate. Wake up and smell the primitive peoples. He's dull, he lacks humor, and aside from his haircut, I don't see anything superior about him," Elliot said.

You *would* like that haircut, Kate thought.

"*You* come on, Elliot," she whispered. "You never like any of my boyfriends."

"Neither do you," Elliot retorted. "Not since Steven. And this one is not only boring, he's also self-involved, pompous, *and* a homophobe."

"He is not!" Kate exclaimed. "You blame everything on that."

"Kate, the guy didn't address a single word to either of us through the whole meal."

"That doesn't make him a homophobe. Maybe he's just shy. Or doesn't like you personally," she added. "It could happen." She put the wine goblets — one of them clean — on the counter.

"Doubtful. And he's probably an alcoholic. That's why he doesn't drink. Anyway, coming here to dinner is like meeting your family," Elliot explained as he rinsed a plate. "He should at least pretend to like us, since we're in loco parentis."

"Well, loco, anyway," Kate agreed. Elliot made a face. She opened the dishwasher and started to put in the china.

"Oh, no." Elliot sighed. "Not the Havilland. It's a hand-wash job. Brice wants gold leaf, Brice washes it." He rinsed his hands. "We better get back in there. At least the coffee ought to help get things moving. Would you fill the creamer?"

Kate nodded and opened the refrigerator. "Hey, Elliot, I've told you before. It isn't easy to find a good, interesting, educated stable man who doesn't want to date a supermodel."

"You may be right," Elliot agreed. "I certainly don't think you'll find him in the Sub-Zero. But you could take out the profiteroles."

"Very funny." Kate pulled out a quart of milk and a pint of half-and-half and placed them on the counter. "I admit you didn't see him at his best. Trust me. Michael is much better one-on-one."

"I bet." Elliot smirked.

Kate ignored his innuendo. "No. Honestly. Evidence. He can be funny. And he's really smart. He got his doctorate at twenty-one, was teaching at Barnard when he was twenty-four, and is considering his postdoc. I think he's going to get tenure at Columbia."

"I didn't ask for his curriculum vitae," Elliot snapped as he popped the chocolate sauce for the profiteroles into the microwave to heat. "He's just dull. Your father was an alcoholic and you never knew what to expect when he came home. Your mother died before you hit puberty. I know

86

you want a responsible male, someone you can depend on. But this guy isn't just stable, he's inert. Where's the magic between you? And he's not nearly good enough for you. Don't let your snobbishness over academic achievement blind you."

"I won't," she assured him, but a nagging voice at the back of her mind wondered about that. Despite all her professional training and the analysis she herself had been required to undergo, she still sometimes felt that much of what she did was a reaction to the desperate childhood she'd had.

Elliot shrugged, turned around quickly in order to pick up the tray of coffee cups, and knocked over Kate's purse, which had been sitting on the counter.

"There goes my cell phone," Kate said.

"Is it the Havilland?" Brice called from the living room.

"No. It's the Melmac," Elliot yelled. "He's obsessed with the damn stuff," he told her.

Then he knelt to pick up Kate's handbag and all the objects that had scattered over the floor. "I'm so sorry. I think I broke your makeup mirror."

"Uh-oh. It was a magnifying one. So do

I have fourteen years of bad luck, or just seven years of more intense bad luck?"

"Stop it, Kate. I'm a statistician, a mathematician, not a superstitious bumpkin."

"But you talk about magic . . ."

"Not Harry Potter magic. Not superstitious nonsense. I'm talking about magic between two people."

"Need any help?" Brice called. "We're waiting out here."

"No, dear," Elliot responded. He handed Kate her purse. Kate, kneeling beside him, picked up the rest of her items and threw them in. "Hey, what's this?" Elliot asked. Kate looked up. He was waving an envelope in the air.

"It's an invite to Bunny's wedding." Kate sighed.

"Bunny of the Bitches of Bushwick is getting married?" Elliot asked. "When did this happen? You never tell me anything."

"Hey, I got it today. And you're on a need-to-know basis." Kate stood up. "Can you believe it? She was just dumped by a guy a month ago. I don't know where this came from."

"Brooklyn. And on the rebound," Elliot said. "Can I go? Please, can I go?"

"No," Kate replied. "See, this is another valid reason why I shouldn't break up with

Michael. With Bina getting engaged and now this, I have to go with someone viable."

"But Michael is so —"

Elliot didn't get a chance to finish his critique. Suddenly there was a loud and frantic pounding at the front door of the apartment. "What in the world . . . ?"

The two of them hurried into the living room just as Brice was striding to the door. He turned back to look at Elliot, who shrugged. Brice opened the door. A woman, her hair wild, her face covered by her hands, threw herself into the room, sobbing uncontrollably. Everyone stood in silent amazement, and Brice actually took two steps back. It was only after a moment or two that Kate saw the woman's fingernails and realized, with a horrible shudder, that she had a French manicure.

"Bina!" she gasped. "Oh, Bina! What's happened to you?"

Chapter Seven

Bina looked around her wildly. "Katie! Omigod. Oh, Katie!" Then she threw herself onto the sofa and heaved with sobs. Kate stepped forward and put her hand gently on Bina's shoulder. Could she have been raped? Had someone mugged her? Her clothes were such a mess and her hair was so disheveled that for a moment, Kate thought only of physical calamities.

Elliot stood looking down at the weeping woman on his couch. "It's Bina?" he whispered. "This is the famous Bina?"

Kate ignored him. "Bina? Bina dear, what's happened?"

Bina shook her head violently. Kate sat and put her arms around her sobbing friend. "Shhh," she crooned, stroking Bina's hair. All the times Kate had witnessed Bina's hysterical outbursts over the years, at sleepovers and parties, flashed through her mind. It was a familiar sensation, kneeling with her arms around Bina. Then she looked up and remembered that they had an audience — and that this drama was playing out in Manhattan on a borrowed sofa. She hoped the whole thing wasn't as bad as it seemed. Then a new thought occurred to her. "Bina, how did you find me here?"

"Max," Bina said, struggling with her tears. "He heard me crying in the hall and told me where you were." She took a gulping breath and burst into tears again. Elliot and Brice drew closer to the couch, like rubberneckers, while Michael had withdrawn to a spot behind the dining table. Kate couldn't help but think that she was watching them all react in predictably typical fashion for men: Michael, the straight male, retreated in the face of emotional turmoil, while Elliot and Brice jumped right in.

She looked back at her friend. "Bina, what's happened?" she asked again.

"Choked," Bina wailed as fresh tears streamed from her eyes.

"Are you choking?" Kate asked, confused.

"I can do the Heimlich. Does she need the Heimlich?" Brice asked a bit too hopefully.

Bina, still sobbing, violently shook her head no.

Kate took Bina's hands in her own and spoke to her firmly but gently. "Who choked? Who's choking, Bina?" She turned to Elliot. "Would you please get her a glass of water?"

Elliot, turning to Brice, repeated the request. "Brice, get her a glass of water. This is better than *One Life to Live.*"

Brice didn't budge. "*One Life to Live?* This is better than *The Young and the Restless.*" He turned to Michael, still in the corner behind the table. "Put down the linen," Brice told him. "You get the water."

Michael seemed all too happy to leave the scene, and he disappeared into the kitchen. Bina gave another wail.

"Bina, you have to calm down," Kate said. "And you have to tell us what's wrong." Bina took some trembling breaths and got the sobbing under control. It occurred to Kate that she might have had an accident; maybe she was ill. "Does something hurt?" she asked.

Bina nodded.

"Do you need a doctor?" Kate continued.

Bina nodded more vigorously. "Yes. Jewish and unmarried. The kind who likes my type and who's looking for a serious commitment." She broke out into sobs again.

Elliot and Brice moved even closer to the circle. "Uh-oh," Elliot said. "Kate, check out her hand." He and Brice exchanged meaningful looks.

Kate, not quite understanding, thought of their manicure that afternoon. "Bina, have you hurt your hands?" She looked down at Bina's hands but didn't see anything more alarming than the French manicure.

"Not her right hand, Kate," said Brice. "Her *left* hand. Second finger from the pinkie."

Kate finally understood. She wrapped her arms around Bina and said, "Oh, my God. Jack . . ."

"Jack choked," Bina told her. "He had the ring in his breast pocket. I could see the bulge the box made." She began to cry again. "Oh, Katie! Instead of asking me to marry him, he asked if we could spend this time apart . . . exploring our singleness."

"That son of a bitch!" Kate, who thought that she understood enough about people and their motivations to be surprised at nothing, was shocked. While Jack had finished school and moved into corporate life, Bina had waited, worked, and collected every issue of *Bride*. She'd watched as all her other friends became engaged, she'd relentlessly thrown shower after bridal shower, a virtual preconnubial fountain. And now, when it was her turn at last, Jack had choked? "That goddamn son of a bitch!" Kate was ready to spit.

She looked up to see that Michael had returned from the kitchen just in time to hear her undeleted expletives and recoil at the outburst. Lucky she hadn't called Jack a motherfucker, she thought as she watched him approach the sofa and gingerly offer Bina the glass of water. Bina ignored the offer.

"I can't believe it!" Bina said, wiping ineffectually at her face and only making the raccoon eyes worse. "He got the ring from Barbie's father. Mr. Leventhal gave him a break. It was princess cut, Barbie said — just under a carat and a half." She paused for breath while Michael gaped and Elliot and Brice shook their heads in sympathy — and almost in unison.

"Everyone will know," Bina said, and began sobbing again. "I can't believe he'd do this to me. Just drop me. And shame me in front of everyone."

Kate took a napkin from the table, dipped it into the water, and held up her friend's face to mop up. "Bina, honey," she said with all the assurance she could muster, "you've been going out with Jack for six years. You grew up together! He loves you." She wiped mascara from under Bina's eyes. "Blow your nose," she said, and Bina did. "Look, this is just a temporary thing. Sometimes it happens. Picking a life mate is a serious decision. It isn't that Jack doesn't want to marry you. It's a lot more probable that he just got frightened. I'm sure he'll call you tomorrow."

"Tomorrow he'll be in Hong Kong. With my ring! I'll be dumped in Bensonhurst and he'll be the Christopher Columbus of singleness," cried Bina, who had a penchant for wildly inappropriate metaphor when under pressure.

"Maybe you should drink the water," Michael said awkwardly, and pressed the glass into her hand.

Bina looked down at the glass. "Is there strychnine in it?" she asked without lifting her eyes.

"Uh . . . no," Michael replied.

In a single smooth motion Bina dumped the water out over her shoulder and down the back of the sofa. "Then what good is it to me?" she said to no one in particular. She fell back onto the sofa and burst into a fresh batch of tears.

"That was a gesture," Elliot said, grabbing a napkin.

"On Fortuny fabric," Brice added. "This is *so* Brooklyn."

"I knew I'd love Brooklyn," Elliot said.

Kate looked up over Bina's head and gave the two of them a warning squint, her blue eyes narrowed to lizard slits. She wondered if she could get her friend home to her own apartment, but either getting a cab or walking back with Michael seemed impossible. Better to deal with it here and then go home. But first she needed to free the frightened Michael and stare off the spectating twosome — though, to be fair, it was their own home. "I'm sorry, guys," Kate said, looking up at the three men. "It looks like we might have to put off dessert."

"Don't be ridiculous," Brice said. "In times of pain, nothing works better than drowning your problems in profiteroles."

Elliot nodded, but Michael began backing toward the door. "I think you're right, Kate," he agreed, relief shining from every pore. "I'll just see myself out." He picked up his briefcase and headed out the door into the foyer. "Have a nice evening," he said, and closed the door behind him.

Kate jumped up. "Just a minute, Bina,"

she said, giving another narrow-eyed glance at the guys as a deterrent, and ran to the hallway. She was just in time to see Michael step into the elevator. "Hold it!" she called, got to the button, and pressed it. Michael stood in the fake mahogany cab like an insect suspended in amber. "You're leaving like that?" she demanded.

"Like what?" he asked, looking down at himself as if she were commenting on an unzipped fly.

"My friend just had her life shattered and you go out the door saying, 'Have a nice evening'?" Kate had learned not to expect too much of a date in the early stages of their mating dance, but Michael was *way* out of tempo. "Have a nice evening?" she repeated, mirroring him.

"Kate," Michael began, "Bina is your friend, not mine. I don't really think it's my place —"

"To be what? Nice, kind, caring? Can't you just pretend to be sensitive?"

Kate realized she was holding him hostage and took her finger off the button. The door closed slowly across his miserable face. She turned away, hoping he would press the open button and return, at least to give her a kiss and a moment of sympathy, but the elevator door remained as smoothly closed as Michael's emotions. She shook her head to clear it. She had to return to Bina.

She entered the apartment and found, to her surprise, that Bina had stopped crying. She was sitting up on the sofa beside Elliot, who was holding her hand and sharing his own heartbreaks. ". . . and then he said, 'I'm going back to my place to get my things and move in.' I was thrilled, just thrilled, so I said, 'Can I come and help?' And he kissed me and said, 'No, sweetie. It won't take but a few hours.' And I never saw or heard from him again."

Bina shook her head in mute sympathy.

"Just as well," Brice said. "Street trash. It's all worked out for the best." He kissed the top of Elliot's head. Kate saw Bina blink.

"Well, let me bring out the profiteroles," Brice said, and headed for the kitchen.

"Meanwhile I'll get a blanket," Elliot offered, and disappeared into the bedroom. Bina nodded gratefully to Kate.

Kate, with nothing else left to do, sat beside her. "I'm sorry," she said, comforting her friend now that they were alone. "You must be devastated."

"Oh, Katie, how could he do this? Who does he think he is? The Magellan of certified public accountants?" Bina asked. "How could he?"

Kate looked into her imploring eyes, but she had no easy answers. "Even if he leaves for Hong Kong, he'll have that long flight alone, he'll miss you, he'll remember the good times and how much he loves you. . . ." She paused, hoping that all she conjectured was true. She wanted to comfort Bina, but not lie to her. If an eight-year-old like Brian had to face the death of his mother, Kate believed it would be best for Bina to face the death of her relationship with Jack, if that's what it was. But it couldn't have suffered a mortal wound. Bina was lovable, and Jack, slow moving as he was, had always seemed to adore her. "I'm sure he'll call. Even if he leaves for Hong Kong, I bet he sends you a ticket to join him and proposes there," Kate ventured hopefully.

"Men are just funny. . . ."

"Not homosexual ones," Elliot said as he walked back into the room carrying a knitted afghan throw. "We're fucking hysterical." He knelt beside Bina and wrapped her up in it. Brice came out of the kitchen carrying a full tray, which he put down gracefully on the coffee table. Arrayed before them were four dessert plates, the plate of profiteroles, a silver server of piping hot dark chocolate sauce, lace-trimmed napkins, a crystal shot glass, and a frosted bottle of Finlandia. "All for you," Brice said.

Bina looked at the tray. "I'd love some dessert, but I don't drink," she told him.

"You do tonight, honey," Brice said, and poured her a shot. "Chocolate and alcohol together beat the shit out of Prozac."

Bina looked at him, at the brimming shot glass, and to Kate's utter surprise she took it from him and knocked it back.

"Good girl!" Elliot said. "And here's your chaser," Brice added, and handed Bina the pastries. "You know what they say: Just a spoonful of sugar . . ."

Bina picked up the plate to dig in.

"Wait just a minute," Brice said. "The doctor is in." He took hold of the silver pitcher, raised it theatrically, and poured the bitter chocolate over the ice-cream pastry.

Kate looked at the three of them, entranced, not sure if she was experiencing pleasure or discomfort. Her two worlds had merged here on the Fortuny upholstered sofa, and all one could have said was that it seemed quiet on the western front. Then Brice filled the shot glass again and handed it to Bina, who, docile as a kosher lamb, drank it down. That broke Kate's trance. "Guys, this is more serious than something a drink and an overdose of carbohydrates will cure," she told them.

"Honey, there's nothing that will cure this. But alcohol and sugar will temporarily dull the pain," Brice replied. "Trust me. I know."

Bina, fully involved with her dessert, looked up from it with a dazed expression on her face. Elliot wiped the chocolate from around her mouth with the lace napkin.

"Who are these guys, Katie?" Bina asked, looking at Elliot and Brice with some confusion. "Are they therapists, too? They're very good."

"No, dear. This is my friend Elliot, who works with me at school, and his partner, Brice," Kate told her. Bina smiled, but it was obvious that Kate's words were merely washing over her. She realized just how drunk Bina was.

"Why am I here?" Bina asked. "And why are they roomoots?"

She slurred her words, and only God knew how slurred her mind was. Again Kate wished that she hadn't mixed Brooklyn with Manhattan. They were parallel universes and, like parallel lines, should never touch.

Despite her concern, however, Kate was slightly amused watching Bina's expression — surprise mixed with curiosity and a soupçon of horror — as she looked from Elliot to Brice and back. At Bina's next words, however, her amusement dissolved, and she cringed in anticipation.

"Oh, so *you're* the —"

"Mathematical one," Elliot finished for her.

"And I'm the emotional one," Brice said with an exaggerated sigh. "Somebody's got to do it."

Kate had to get Bina home and onto her own couch before it became necessary to carry her. She knew once Bina was forced to stay here, Brice and Elliot would dig themselves in deeper. They were kind, but they couldn't help Bina now, and Kate knew she had a big job to do.

"You're coming to my apartment," she said. "It isn't far, and you could use the fresh air."

"She's welcome to stay here," Elliot offered, and Kate knew his kindness was mixed with equal parts of curiosity.

"Show's over," she said. "Say good night,

Gracie." She pulled the dazed Bina up from the couch and began to walk her to the door.

"Good night, Gracie," Elliot and Brice chorused.

Chapter Eight

Later, Kate could not remember much about the nightmare of getting Bina back to her apartment that night. It was called "selective memory" in her textbooks — some things were just too gruesome to keep in your consciousness. In the four long blocks from Elliot's apartment to Kate's, Bina alternately wept, sang, tripped, wailed, and sat down at one point on the sidewalk, refusing to move. Kate didn't think Bina had tried to throw herself in front of a bus or wet herself, but she couldn't be absolutely sure of either. It was lucky that Max had been home and heard her trying to get Bina up the stairs. Asking no questions, he took over. Kate didn't remember if he carried Bina up the stairs in his arms or over his shoulder. She did remember holding Bina's head as she vomited violently and washing her up. Max left her to that thankless task. Kate made an executive decision not to put Bina in her bedroom but instead to tuck her up on the sofa. Made in haste, it was a decision that Kate would not regret.

The next morning Kate was up early, brewing coffee, laying out the Tylenol, and waiting to call in sick to work. One look at the bedraggled, unconscious Bina gave Kate a pretty good idea of how she was going to spend her next twenty-four hours. She took down her favorite coffee mug. It was the only gift she could remember her father giving her. A ceramic one, the handle shaped like Cinderella. When she was little Kate used to imagine that Cinderella was bending over the top of the mug and looking into whatever liquid would be put there, as if it were a wishing well. She thought of calling Mrs. Horowitz or even trying Jack before he left, then thought better of it. Kate didn't mind being involved, but she didn't want to become the puppeteer pulling strings. Bina — despite many childlike qualities — would have to decide on her own what actions to take, and Kate would support her as best she could.

When the phone rang, Kate glanced at the caller ID, picked up the receiver, and without preamble said, "Yes, she's still sleeping. No, I'm not going into school today, and no, you can't come over."

"Good morning to you, too," Elliot's

voice said briskly. "Can I at least drop off a couple of bagels on my way up to Andrew?"

"Forget it. I don't think Bina is going to want to eat anything, and if she does, I have plenty of saltines." Kate poured the hot coffee into her Cinderella mug. She was careful, as always, to avoid the little blond head peeking over the rim.

"God, Brice and I feel so bad for her."

"At least you're not feeling as bad as her . . . I mean, she is. Bina doesn't have the genetics to handle a hangover," Kate told him. "You shouldn't have let Brice pour that booze down her throat."

"Well, he's not apologizing for getting her drunk, and I think it was the best thing for her," Elliot began.

"Well, it wasn't the best thing for me," Kate retorted, peeking at Bina. It wasn't a pretty picture. "I've had quite a mess — literally and figuratively — to clean up."

"Oh, the poor girl," Elliot said, his sympathy real. "How can I help?"

"Short of teaching Michael to deal with human feelings and finding Jack and slapping some sense into him, I don't think there's much you can do," Kate told him.

"Yeah, I told you Michael was a dud. What went on between you two in the hall?

I'll bet he got a pounding."

Kate thought of Michael's face before the elevator door closed and chose to change the subject. She spilled some coffee as she moved her mug to the counter beside the refrigerator. "I don't think there's much anyone can do, but I'm taking a sick day."

"Maybe you should call it a mental health day," Elliot said. "Except for once this one isn't about you. Do you want me to take the day off, too? The kids have standardized testing most of the day. I can keep you company and help with Bina."

"Forget it. I know you're just afraid you're going to get my cafeteria duty," she joked. "Anyway, you had your first and last dose of the Bitches of Bushwick. It ought to be enough Brooklyn to last a lifetime." Before he could protest, she added, "I have to go. She's waking up."

"I'll call you later," she heard him say as she put the phone down.

She quickly poured a glass of club soda — her favorite remedy for the dehydration of a hangover — and walked from her kitchenette into the living room with her mug in one hand and the drinking glass in the other. Bina groaned, put a hand to her forehead, and then opened her eyes, which

107

she closed again quickly. "Oh, my God," she said, and Kate wasn't sure if it was a reaction to the light or a remembrance of things past. She groaned again.

"It's okay, Bina, drink this." Kate held the glass in front of her friend, and Bina squinted at it.

"What is it?" she croaked.

"Well, it's not vodka," Kate told her. "Come on, sit up and take your medicine."

Bina did as she was told, took the glass, drank three or four big gulps, and then began to choke. She put the glass on Kate's coffee table, and Kate moved it onto a coaster before she went to Bina's side. "Omigod," Bina repeated. And Kate knew that this time she had remembered Jack and the night before. Bina looked up at her. "Oh, Kate. What am I going to do?"

Kate sat in the wicker chair and reached for her friend's hand. "Bina," she said, "what happened last night?"

"You were right about the French manicure," Bina said. She shook her head, and Kate could see the physical pain register on her face. She went back to the kitchen and brought her three Tylenols and a couple of vitamin Cs.

"Here," she said, thrusting them into Bina's hand. "Take these. You'll feel better." She left Bina again and went back into the kitchen, where she took out her emergency stash of saltines. Bina had just downed the last pill when Kate returned. She didn't want them all to lie there on an empty stomach, so she handed Bina a saltine. "Eat it," she said.

"Oh, please," Bina responded in a world-weary voice.

"Eat it," Kate commanded, "and now tell me what happened last night." She watched as Bina made an entire meal of the saltine, taking many tiny bites and washing them down with the club soda. The moment she was finished, Kate handed her another saltine and refilled her glass. "Good girl," she said. "So what happened?"

Bina lay back among the cushions and put a hand across her forehead. This time the tears were silent. Kate rose, went to her bedroom, and came back with a box of tissues. Wordlessly, she handed one to Bina, who mopped at her eyes and began to talk in an unsteady voice. "You know that I was meeting him at Nobu, and I was excited because it's one of the kinds of places you go to."

Kate almost smiled. Nobu was one of the most expensive, stylish Asian restaurants in the city, and she couldn't afford to eat there even on her birthday.

"Anyway, the place was beautiful, and when I walked past the bar I could see that all the women looked better than I did. I don't know why, because their clothes weren't as good as mine — at least they didn't look as good, but somehow they looked better, if you know what I mean." Kate just nodded. "Anyway, when I got to the dining room, the hostess wasn't there. I looked around, kind of self-conscious, then I thought I saw her. She had her back to me and was talking to some guy at a table and she was holding his hand up and laughing. When he laughed back, I realized it was Jack. I nearly plotzed."

Kate had a vision of Bina going into hysterics and throwing a scene in the middle of the Zen of Nobu. God, she thought, that would end a romantic evening quickly. Bina did tend to overreact. "So did you . . . ?"

"For a minute I didn't do anything," Bina said. "I couldn't believe it. Then I walked over to the table and —"

The phone rang, and Kate looked at the caller ID. "It's your mom," she said.

"Don't pick up!" Bina nearly screeched.

Kate let the phone ring until the answering machine kicked in. Mrs. Horowitz's concerned voice came on, and Kate turned the volume down. "You will have to tell her what happened. After you tell me, of course," Kate said. "And she must be concerned. Where does she think you are? Did she know about your plans last night?"

Bina covered her eyes again. "I can't talk to her now," she said. "And I didn't tell her anything because she would have nudged me to death. But I'm sure she knew about the ring, and I'm sure she knows Jack is leaving." She stopped for a moment and began to wail. It was a high-pitched keen of misery. "He's leaving tonight. Omigod, he's leaving tonight."

Kate crouched at the edge of the sofa and took Bina in her arms. She felt her friend tremble against her, shaking with every sobbing breath. "Bina, you have to calm down and tell me what happened. We can probably fix this."

Bina shook her head silently but lowered the volume of her crying. Just then the phone rang again. Reluctantly, Kate left Bina and went over to it. It was Michael. Kate looked over at Bina, who had turned on her side and was sobbing quietly into a bunch of tissues. She picked up the receiver.

"Kate, you're home?" Michael asked.

111

"Yes." She didn't need to tell him anything more. He knew that she was usually in her office by this time, and as a postdoc he might have had the brains to figure out that based on what he had reluctantly witnessed the night before, she might not show up at school.

"Hey, Kate, I . . . I just wanted to apologize."

Kate softened. She sighed but covered the mouthpiece to be sure that Michael didn't hear it. She had learned that there were two kinds of men: those who apologized and continued their behavior and those who apologized and stopped it. She hadn't known Michael long enough to know which type he was. The way she looked at things at this point in her life, most relationships were compromises, and all men had to be looked at as fixer-uppers. "Okay," she said to Michael with a voice as neutral as she could manage.

"I'm sure I looked like an unfeeling jerk last night. You know, it's just that . . . well, your friend was *very* dramatic."

That pissed Kate off. "I suppose a little drama is warranted when your entire life is ruined." She purposely kept her voice low and looked over at Bina to make sure she went unheard. What good was an apology, she thought, if it was followed by a further injury?

"I've done it again, haven't I?" Michael asked. He might not be empathetic, but he wasn't stupid, Kate reflected. "Look, let me take you out to dinner one night this week," he said. "Let's talk about it. I know I can do better."

Fair enough, Kate thought. But it couldn't be in a restaurant. There should be a lot of talking, a lot of negotiating, and maybe some conciliatory sex. "Why don't you come over for dinner," she proposed. "But not tonight." She looked over at the sofa again. Bina was just raising her head. "Gotta go," she said. "Let's talk later."

"I'll call you this evening," Michael promised, and Kate hung up. She returned to Bina's side. Bina, her eyes red, but not as red as her nose, looked up at her.

"How can we fix it?" she asked.

Kate sat down and the wicker creaked. "Well, to know that, first I have to know exactly what happened."

"Well, I went over to the table, and Jack was laughing, and the Chinese woman — who was smaller than a size two and taller than I am — looks at me like I'm the busboy. But Jack, he jumps and pulls his hand away. 'Hey, Sy Lin was just teaching

113

me how to say hello in Mandarin. Nee-how-ma!' So I look at him and say, 'Me-how-ma, right back atcha.' Then I turn to Sy Lin and said, 'How do you say good-bye?' So she just gives me this smile, does one of those look-overs — you know, the way Barbie does when someone is dressed really badly — and then looks at Jack and says, 'Enjoy your dinner.' Oh, and just to make it a really bad omen, she was wearing the color nail polish you picked out. I should always listen to you."

"Bina, don't be silly. This isn't about manicures. So what happened next? Did you pitch a fit?"

Bina began to cry again. "That's the worst part," she said, gulping back her tears. "I didn't do anything. It was Jack, Jack who —"

The phone rang again. Kate stepped over and looked at the handset and saw that it was Elliot's cell. "Wait a minute," she told Bina, who ignored her anyway. Kate picked up the phone.

"Okay. Don't worry about a thing," came Elliot's voice. "We've got the situation under control. Brice and I are on our way with bagels, cream cheese, and lox. We also have two pints of hand-packed Häagen-Dazs," he added. "Rocky Road and Concession Obsession. And that's not all. I have a couple of ten-milligram Valium that Brice 'borrowed' from his mother's medicine cabinet. We're the rescue squad. Don't try to get in our way. Besides, we're practically at your door."

"Elliot, this is serious," Kate admonished.

"That's why Brice and I took half a day off from work. Well, that and intense curiosity."

"The two of you are gossipmongers," Kate said.

"You betcha. Don't let Bina say another word until we get there, because even though I'm a social idiot, Brice knows how to fix up anything that's interpersonal. I hang the shelves."

Kate found herself holding a dead phone and looking at her almost dead friend. Maybe some food, ice cream, muscle relaxants, and diversions were just what she needed. But first she had to get the rest of the story.

"Was that Jack?" Bina asked.

"No," Kate admitted. She sat down again. "Tell me what happened next." And then the doorbell rang.

Chapter Nine

"It's Jack!" Bina shouted, and virtually levitated off the sofa. "Oh, my God! It's Jack and look what I look like!"

"It isn't Jack," Kate told her, and watched Bina struggle with both relief and disappointment simultaneously. "It's Elliot. He's the only one who can get into the building without my having to buzz. He has a key to the downstairs door."

Kate went to the tiny foyer and looked through the safety peephole. There was Elliot, smiling and gesturing to Brice, who was beside him and holding up the promised goodie bag. Reluctantly, Kate turned the knob and opened the door. If she didn't do it, the guys would come in anyway — Elliot had a spare set of keys for emergency purposes (like the time Kate locked her purse in the office and got halfway home before she noticed), and he wouldn't hesitate to use it.

Kate opened the door, and Elliot and Brice almost tumbled in. "Is she okay?" Elliot whispered.

"No," Kate told him.

"Well, is she better?" Brice asked.

"No," Kate repeated.

"Then it's a good thing we came," Elliot said.

"I told you," Brice responded, and then the three of them stepped into the living room, like all those clowns emerging from a tiny car at the circus. At least it felt like a circus to Kate.

"Oh, Bina! You poor girl," Elliot said, and flew across the living room to sit beside her in Kate's one good chair.

"Don't worry about a thing," Brice said, and began unpacking the shopping bag onto Kate's coffee table. "What's the last thing you ate? And when was it?"

Bina, a bit dazed, tried to answer him. "Well, I thought I was going to eat last night with Jack, but then I never finished the meal. I was too upset. Then I couldn't find Kate. I remember having some vodka. . . ."

"Well, you need one of these," Elliot said, and took out a waxed-paper parcel and handed it to her.

She opened it up. Kate winced at the poppy seeds that went rolling off the bagel, and onto the sofa, the floor, the rug, and places that wouldn't be found for months to come. "Oh, I can't eat," Bina said.

"You have to keep up your strength," Elliot told her.

Kate nodded. "It would be good for you to have some breakfast," she coaxed. "Just take a bite."

Brice nodded, moved to the foot of the sofa, sat down, and rearranged Bina's feet so they were on his lap and covered with the quilt. "Now, just tell Uncle Brice all about it," he said, his voice a combination of mockery and sincerity.

"I can't believe yesterday was supposed to be your big night and nothing happened," Elliot said. "You must be so distraught." At that point Kate realized she was fairly distraught herself; she took a throw pillow from the sofa and sank to the floor on it beside the coffee table.

"Tell me about it! I thought Jack was nervous. Like he was making sure the ring was still safe. Jack Weintraub was finally going to propose to me, and he was nervous. You know, he's such a perfectionist — Barbie said he insisted on a perfect stone: flawless D color."

"Flawless D!" Brice said approvingly.

"Right. See? I love him for a reason. He knows things. He wants things right. And I thought he wanted me to be happy. So I

118

was happy, and I decided to forget about Tokyo Rose."

"Oh, forget the hostess," Kate pressed. "Unless he asked *her* to marry him. You didn't fight over her, did you?"

"We didn't fight at all," Bina protested. "I was a little upset about the dragon lady — it just isn't like Jack to flirt with strange women — but I couldn't have loved him more. Anyway, he raised his glass of champagne, and I think he was about to make a toast when he realized I didn't have a glass. So he tried to get a waiter or a waitress, and they were nowhere to be seen. So Jack says he has to go to the men's room and on the way he'll order me a drink. But I think he might have been looking for the hostess. . . ."

"Her and many like her, the man-whore," said a heated Brice. "I just hate it when a man —"

"Hey. Don't make this personal," Elliot said, cutting him off with a meaningful look.

"Focus, darling," Kate said, touching Bina's face. Kate was quickly losing hope that a simple phone call before Jack got on the plane might put things right.

"Okay. So he excused himself and headed for the men's room. I watched him walk away from the table. I couldn't help thinking he was so handsome."

"I know. Men are so cute from behind," said Brice.

Bina nodded solemnly. "I mean, people are like 'Jack is just ordinary,' but that's what I like about him," she continued, either ignoring or oblivious to the sexual connotation of Brice's comment. It seemed to Kate as though Bina were bonding with Brice the way she did with her girlfriends. "Jack reminds me of the Goldilocks story," Bina went on. "He's not too tall or too short, he isn't too skinny or too fat, he isn't too handsome or too ugly. He's just right," she said. "At least just right for me." Then she realized anew where she was and what had happened. "He *was* just right, but I wasn't just right for him. Maybe it's me that's ordinary."

"Oh, Bina," Kate said, and put her arm around her friend, squeezing tightly. "You're not ordinary." That might not have been totally true, but that she was at the very least Jack's equal was a sure thing. Kate had never met anyone more ordinary than Jack. "What happened then?"

"Jack was gone for a little while. So finally that stupid hostess came back and asked me if I wanted a drink. I told her that my boyfriend was getting me something, and she said, 'Your boyfriend? He said this was a business meeting. Otherwise I would have given him a more private table.' "

"The bitch!" Elliot and Brice said simultaneously.

"Yeah. The beautiful, thin, exotic bitch," Bina agreed bitterly.

"This is not productive," Kate said. No matter what the story was, she was going to be sure they didn't criticize Jack too much, because when he and Bina patched things up — and they would — Bina would forever remember any criticism. Kate had learned that lesson the hard way with Bev, before she married Johnny. "Bina, you are so beautiful. Any guy in the world would be lucky to share the same air as you," she told her friend, and meant it. Every bit of Bina's soul was generous and giving. Her heart was loyal and loving. And she had an adorable, round little face and a curvy figure. Kate stroked Bina's dark, shiny hair. What the hell was wrong with Jack? It must have been a panic attack. Commitment was a very frightening prospect. "Didn't you tell me just last week that Jack said he found you beautiful in so many ways?"

"Honey," Brice said with a tilt of his

head, "greeting cards can tell you that."

"No, he said I was too beautiful and too good for him," Bina corrected.

"Uh-oh," Brice and Elliot said again in unison, and exchanged a look.

Kate gestured to them behind Bina's head. "Well, anyway, Bina, you *are* beautiful, and I am sure Jack still feels the same way."

"Yeah? You haven't heard the end of the story," Bina said.

"We're trying to," Kate told her, attempting not to snap.

"Go on. Get it all out," Elliot advised.

"Well, of course I was hating this . . . woman." Bina paused, and Kate was pleased that she didn't stoop to any slur. "So I told her to go away. Jack finally came back with my drink and said — and you won't believe this." Bina mimicked Jack's deep Brooklyn baritone voice: " 'I looked at you from across the room. You looked good from over there.' Was that a compliment or a diss?"

Kate pursed her lips but refrained from speaking. It seemed clear that her theory was right — Jack needed distance in both senses to see Bina. But up close and intimate, his anxiety paralyzed him. If only he could have stayed at the bar and proposed

122

by cell phone, Kate thought ruefully.

"I just gave him a look," Bina continued.

"And what did he do?"

"Well, I think he saw my reaction. He asked if something was wrong. He sounded so sincere, so concerned, that I felt bad, and I figured I had to let up on the poor guy. I thought he was a nervous wreck about proposing. Also, to tell the truth, Jack has never been . . . well, let's just say he's careful with his money."

"Oh, hell," Brice said. "Let's say he's cheap." Bina opened her eyes wide, and for a moment Kate thought her friend was going to giggle.

"Go on," Kate said.

"Well, I just shook my head and suggested that we make a toast. And all he said was, 'To us.' I waited for more, you know, like 'And to our future as Mr. and Mrs. Jack Weintraub, the perfect married couple,' but there was nothing more." A tear slid down her cheek, and Brice took her hand.

"So?" Kate prompted. She wondered what time Jack's plane was actually taking off, whether he planned to be on it, whether he had called the Horowitz household, whether he had called his cousin Max across the hall.

"Then he said he really wished he didn't have to take this trip, but said some of that stuff about markets misbehaving. So I suggested that in the future maybe we'd make the trips together."

"What did he say to that?" Kate asked.

"Well, of course then the waitress shows up before he can answer. Just my luck. And you know it takes Jack a long time to order. And then he has to make sure none of the things on his plate are going to touch any of the others."

Kate had forgotten about that phobia. She nodded to Bina.

"So we had our drink, and it seemed that the dinner was going fine until I told him how much I was going to miss him. I mean, that's okay to say, right? The guy is going away for months and it's halfway around the world. Jack and I haven't been separated by more than ten miles since we first started dating."

"Really?" Brice asked. "That's so romantic!"

"It's true, right, Kate? She was there the night Max — you know, Kate's neighbor who now lives across the hall — had the party where I met Jack."

Kate rolled her eyes. Bina had a habit of playing what her friends called "Jewish geography." Kate had gotten her apartment because Bina's brother knew Jason, the building owner's son, from summer camp and he had told Bina, who had told Kate about it. Kate got the place. Later she and Bina had been invited to a Manhattan party by Bina's brother, which had been thrown by Max at his old apartment. And Bina — on one of her infrequent trips across the East River — met Jack, Max's cousin, there. . . . Well, it could go on endlessly, between Hebrew schools, summer camps, bar mitzvahs, weddings, cousins, and on and on and on.

"The weird thing is we had grown up together in Brooklyn just six blocks from each other, but we were introduced for the first time that night, and we haven't been apart since. I mean, he took me out for a drink after the party and asked me out for the next night. And that weekend he came over for dinner with my parents and brother and . . . well, there we were, saying good-bye to each other for a very long time. So I thought it was appropriate to say I would miss him. And I thought it would be good to kind of, you know, get him started. I mean, we were finished with our appetizers and entrées. Did I have to wait until he popped the question?"

"Men spook easily," Brice offered. "I remember the time when Ethan Housholder told me —"

"Not now, Brice," Kate interjected.

"Right, sorry. Continue, honey."

Kate had to admit that Bina couldn't have two more sympathetic listeners than Brice and Elliot. And sometimes simply talking was the best therapy. But then, just when she thought they had gotten safely out of the water, Bina began to cry again. Elliot's soft pats and Brice's coos of sympathy only made it worse.

"Well, it was like all the color drained out of his face. And then he said, 'Bina, you know I have to be in Hong Kong for almost five months, and that's not going to be easy.' He kept touching his breast pocket, and the tension was almost overwhelming. I couldn't help but think, Here it comes. Then he just sat there. I wanted to scream, *Why don't you just take the damn thing out of there and ask me to marry you?* But, nothing. The man just sat there and then looked down and finished eating his fucking chicken Rangoon."

Chapter Ten

"What did you do?" Elliot asked.

Kate was afraid that she would hear that Bina had become hysterical, attacked Jack physically, made a huge scene, or something even more dramatic. But Bina surprised her.

"I went to the ladies' room, of course."

"Of course," Brice agreed. "I can't tell you how many times I wished I could go there myself."

"So, anyway . . . ," Bina continued. She opened her eyes wide and they glazed over, as if she could see the scene replaying itself.

Kate, Elliot, and Brice all held their breath. Then the phone rang. "Shit!" Kate said, and grabbed for the receiver, peering at the number. "It's your mother again," she said. "I think you'd better talk to her."

"Kill me first!" Bina pleaded. Kate froze for a moment. She couldn't bear to explain the situation to Myra Horowitz, and she didn't have the heart to give the phone to

Bina. But she couldn't refuse the call again. . . .

"I'll take it," Elliot said.

"Don't be ridiculous," Kate told him, realizing he was getting deeper and deeper into her Brooklyn life. She pressed the answer button.

"Katie! Thank God! Listen, do you know where Bina is?"

"She's fine. She's right here with me," Kate told Mrs. Horowitz, telling only one lie, not two.

"Well, put her on."

Bina was shaking her head wildly, putting her hands in front of her face as if to ward off a blow.

Kate was grateful for every moment she had spent at the Horowitz house, because even with her training it took more than therapeutic skills to talk Mrs. Horowitz down. Kate said soothing words, then distracted her with questions, then reassured her, then sent her love to Dr. Horowitz. All the while Elliot circled his hand, telling her to move it along, while Brice pulled his index finger across his throat, giving her the sign to cut it short. As if she wanted to be the middleman! Finally she hung up.

"At last," said Brice.

"So you were in the ladies' room," Elliot prompted.

"Yeah. You know, I just wanted to be by myself for a minute, just long enough to get it all together again," Bina said. "So I fixed my makeup — and I still had to give the woman there a dollar, even though I hadn't used the toilet — but I just looked at myself in the mirror and said, 'Bina Horowitz, this is the night that's going to change your life. Be nice and be happy.' "

"Good for you," Kate said.

"So I get back to the table and Jack stands up. He always does it when we're in a fancy restaurant. So he leans over to help me into my chair, and . . ." She gulped. "The ring box slipped out of his pocket. It was like a car accident in one of those movies. I saw it all happening in slow motion. The ring box fell over and over and over. The moment the box hits the floor, Jack lets go of my chair. The ring flies out of the box and he scrambles to retrieve it. I'm as frozen as a Swanson TV dinner, and I see the ring skid across the floor, and that stupid bitch hostess bends *all* the way over and picks it up."

"Wow," was all Kate could say.

"Wow indeed," Brice added.

"What did you do?" asked Elliot.

"I just sat there, like the turkey dinner that I am, and I realize that Jack, on the floor, can see up the woman's skirt — well, it was *so* short, and she bent right over. And not from the knees like you're supposed to, but from the waist. And she isn't wearing any underwear."

"What?" all three said in collective amazement.

"None. And Jack is on the floor, looking straight up her — well, up her —"

"We get the visual," Kate said.

"So did Jack. Everyone was looking. I think that was when he lost his mind. It must have been then. So Jack manages to get off the floor and tear his eyes off that woman's naked crotch, and she turns around and hands him the ring. He stands up and puts it in his right pocket. Then he scoops up the box and puts it in his left pocket." Bina stopped for a moment and shook her head. "He walked back to the table." She turned to Kate. "I couldn't stay happy anymore, Katie. I told Jack that if he was trying to make it a memorable evening, he was succeeding. I mean, I could have smacked him, I was so mad. And you know what the asshole said?"

"What now?" Kate asked.

Bina, using her Jack voice again, said,

" 'This isn't how I want to remember you, Bina.' "

"Uh-oh. Here it comes," Brice said.

"Wait for it," Elliot warned him.

"Please, you two — it's like Tweedledee and Tweedle Very Dumb," Kate admonished. "Let the woman finish her story, which, I pray, is almost over."

"Almost," Bina said. "So, I was wondering which pocket my ring was in now. It made me think of that game, Katie, that my father would play with us when we were little girls. You know, when he would have surprises for us and we would have to guess which pocket they were in."

Kate nodded, almost smiling in remembrance. Dr. Horowitz had been so kind to her. He used to give his daughter her allowance every Sunday morning, and since her father was usually sleeping one off on Sunday and rarely gave her money, Dr. Horowitz always gave Kate the same allowance as well: A big Sunday event was going to the candy store and agonizing over Junior Mints or Bit-O-Honey. Not to mention the Betty and Veronica comics. Bina and her family were good people, and she hated hearing how she'd been subjected to this hurtful slapstick. But maybe the situation could be salvaged. After all, Bina and

Jack had years of history and were made for each other. "So then what?" she asked.

"Well," Bina continued, "Jack then looked me in the eyes and said, 'Bina, I have something I want to say to you.' And I'm thinking at least someday we'll tell our grandchildren about all this and laugh! But then Jack says, 'I have to be honest; Hong Kong is far away from here. Very far away.' Like I didn't take geography, right? So I think maybe he's going to want to elope. It would break my mother's heart, and I want the dress and all, but I was like dying by now. I kept waiting for Jack to reach for the ring, but his hands are staying folded together on top of the table. He takes a deep breath, looks up to the ceiling, and says, 'I think it would be unfair of me to leave and ask you to just wait for me.' I told him I agreed, and I looked down at my hand to get my finger ready. But then he said, 'I think this time apart might be a good chance for us to . . . well, for us to . . . I think this might be a good chance for us to explore our singleness.' "

"I could kill him, Bina," Kate said.

"Oh, me first," Brice added.

There was silence in the room. Kate, Elliot, and Brice sat there with their mouths opened wide, until Bina started sobbing again. All three snapped back into action. Kate moved closer on the sofa and held Bina. "Oh, honey," she said. Brice got up, took a cushion, and put it under her feet as if she had internal bleeding. Elliot got up, went into the bathroom, and returned with a wet towel, a glass of water, and a blue pill. Ever neat — except in his clothes — he looked for a coaster. Before Kate could hand him one, he found a piece of cardboard.

"Take this and drink all the water," he told her. Bina did as she was told without question.

"What was that?" Kate asked.

"Oh, I just felt she needed a visit from cousin Valerie," Elliot told her. It was his code word for Valium, and Kate knew a blue one was ten milligrams.

"She'll sleep for a week," Kate said.

"What a good time for that," Elliot told her.

"Okay, Bina. Tell us what happened next."

"I just ran out," she said. "Well, ran as best I could in my heels. I went straight to your apartment, Katie, and when I couldn't find you, Max helped me. You can't believe how hysterical I was." Kate silently disagreed with her on that. Bina blew her nose and continued. "Max was home. And he told me he thought you were out to dinner and where Elliot lived, and I went straight there in the pouring rain, and . . . Omigod!"

"What! What is it, Bina?" Kate cried.

Bina reached over to the coffee table and picked up the coaster for the water. It was Bunny's wedding invitation. "Bunny? Bunny is getting married?" she asked.

"Is that a bad thing?" Elliot wanted to know.

Bina ignored him. "Why didn't you tell me, Katie?"

"I just found out. I got the invitation yesterday."

"Oh, this is it! I'm glad I didn't see my mail. But this proves I'm a loser," Bina wailed. "Bunny! She just broke up with a guy. That one I showed you on the way to getting a pedicure."

"The guy was getting a pedicure?" Elliot asked. Kate gave him a look.

"Bunny is going to be a bride, and Jack is off to become the Marco Polo of singleness. Why don't I just open my veins?"

"Well, it's very messy, for one thing," Brice told her. "And it's almost impossible to get blood out of clothes. Very cold water and hydrogen peroxide —"

Bina put the pillow over her face and wailed into it. It wasn't that she was competitive with Bunny, Kate knew. It was just that Bunny had been the last to join their group, hadn't had a date to the prom, had never been pinned. Bunny didn't do well with men, picking a string of bad boys and scoundrels. One she had lived with had stolen everything — even her sofa and kitchen table — when she went away for the weekend. "How can Bunny be getting married? She just got dumped by that guy we saw in SoHo. She's only just met Barney or whatever." Bina squinted at the card. "And how did they get invitations so quickly? They must be Xerox copies."

How had Bunny met someone? Kate wondered why it was so much more complicated for her than for Barbie and Bev and Bunny. When Kate found a warm man, he was often devoted to her, but just a little . . . dull. Or second-rate. And when she found a man with a first-rate mind and an engrossing career, a man like Michael, he lacked emotional heat. Of course, she reflected, Bina's father, a successful chiropractor, had doted on her. So in spite of her current troubles, it seemed only natural that she would eventually find a successful accountant who doted on her. Kate sighed. It didn't bode well for her. "Bina, everything is going to be okay," Kate promised.

"Fine for you to say. You've got that doctor Michael to go with. What am I going to do? Go with my brother?"

"Oh, I don't think Katie will want to bring Michael all the way across the Brooklyn Bridge," Elliot began. He turned to Kate and gave her a little smirk. "Unless you want to prep him for his journey to Austin, you know, a little bit at a time."

Kate grimaced at him. Elliot turned back to Bina.

"Anyway, if my calculations are correct — and they always are — we have here two women who need dates," he announced, "and two men with an insatiable curiosity for the customs and rituals of deepest, darkest Brooklyn."

"Really?" asked Bina.

"Not only that, but I have fabulous formal wear. I'll definitely be better dressed than the bride," Brice said.

"In a dress?" Bina asked, her voice about to rise into hysteria again.

"No. A great tux. Armani. And I'll do your makeup. You'll look absofuckinglutely great, and all your friends will want to know who the great-looking guy you're with is. You can tell them whatever you like. I once passed as the prince of Norway." Brice turned to Elliot, gave him a loving but exasperated look, and then stared at Kate. "I know what he looks like in a rented tux," Brice told her. "You're on your own."

"Thanks," Elliot said. "No offense meant, I'm sure, and none taken. So it's set. Brice and I will take you two girls, and we will all have a wonderful time."

"Maybe that's a good idea," Bina said. "But right now I think I have to take a little nap."

Kate watched as Bina's eyes fluttered shut. "You guys must be joking," she said. "No way."

Chapter Eleven

Kate and Bina, both carrying presents, were waiting for Elliot and Brice three blocks south of St. Veronica's Roman Catholic Church, the place where Kate had made her First Communion in the dress Mrs. Horowitz had sewed for her. Kate, all grown up now, was unaware that in the simple calf-length navy blue dress that set off her fiery hair, she looked stunning. She didn't think of her Communion dress; she was just grateful that she didn't have to wear one of the loopy bridesmaids' gowns she was usually stuck in.

Bina, at Kate's side, looked totally Brooklyn and smelled like fear. She wore a pink dress that poofed at the skirt. Her dark brown hair was done up in lacquered swirls of French twist curls as if she were going to their senior prom. Sal, the hairdresser who had "done" both of them for the prom, had probably done Bina this time, too.

"Is it going to be a high mass?" Kate

asked, remembering her boredom at the standing, the kneeling, and the standing again in the interminable services of her youth.

"Mass, shmass," Bina said dismissively. She craned her neck, looking for the guys. "I'm safe during the ceremony. It's afterward that I'm dead meat."

"Bina, this isn't a firing squad. These women are your friends," Kate tried to assure her. "You've known them forever. They're not going to judge you."

Bina turned back to stare at Kate. "Are you kidding?" she asked in amazement. "That's exactly what they're going to do. That's what friends are for."

"Hey, look: We got a great strategy," Kate reminded her. "Everyone may assume that Elliot is Michael; it will take a while to straighten that out, which will distract them. If Bev opens her big mouth and calls him Michael, I can do half an hour of material to make it look like I'm embarrassed. And everyone knows Jack left. So showing up with Brice will just daze and confuse them, or maybe even blow them away. I mean, he *is* gorgeous."

"Yeah," Bina agreed dispiritedly, "but he's no Jack." Jack had gone to Hong Kong without calling, and Bina had heard nothing from him since. Now, she looked up and down the street again. "Where are they?" she whined.

"They'll be here," Kate reassured her, looking down the all too familiar Woodbine Avenue. She felt slightly dizzy, and she wasn't sure if it was the heat or the location. Returning to Brooklyn and the old neighborhood gave her a kind of vertigo.

"But what if they don't show up? I'll have to go in alone. I can hide in the back during the ceremony, but if at the reception I have to go Jackless and ringless, they'll all want to know the reason he broke up with me, and —"

"Bina, calm down," Kate said with more than a bit of concern in her voice. For the past two weeks, Bina had been spending every day and almost every night alternating between Max's and Kate's. After a few days, Kate had remonstrated, but Bina refused to cross the bridge. "I can't go home. Everything reminds me of him," was Bina's first excuse. Kate had been happy, at first, to provide Bina with a safe haven, but after four days she'd insisted that Bina call her father and mother herself and break the news. Dr. Horowitz had threatened to fly to Hong Kong right then and there to "knock that *pisher's* block off," but

Bina had implored her father to stay in Brooklyn and had thereby kept Jack's block safe. Mrs. Horowitz, in the face of all the evidence to the contrary, remained convinced that her daughter was engaged.

"I can't take this," Bina said. "I'm melting from nervous perspiration. I'll never wear this dress again." Kate thought that was probably a good thing. Just then, a black Lincoln Town Car pulled up and Elliot and Brice emerged.

"You're late," she said in place of a greeting, but she was happy to see the two of them.

"Well, hello to you, too." Elliot smiled, his usual cheerfulness intact. "Who's late?" He looked at his watch. "You said the ceremony was three o'clock. It's two fifty-seven."

Kate sighed. "Being on time is late in a situation like this."

"Haven't they heard of fashionably late?" Brice asked.

"This is Brooklyn," Kate reminded him. But as she looked both men over, she couldn't be angry.

"Wow," Bina said. "I love your outfits."

Kate smiled. "You two do clean up well."

"Of course," Brice said. "We're gay." With that he grabbed Bina's arm. "But not

141

for this afternoon." He lowered his voice to a baritone. "This afternoon I'm devoted to you. Can't keep my hands off you." Bina actually smiled.

"Shall we, honey?" Brice asked. Bina nodded. "Hmm. Who did your hair?" Kate heard him ask Bina, that "anything she can do I can do better" tone in his voice.

"Sal Anthony. He has a little shop at the corner of Court and —"

"Burn it down," Brice ordered. "And we'll see if we can't soften it up a bit."

"He's so bossy," Kate said softly to Elliot.

"Yeah. Isn't it great?" Elliot asked.

They got to St. Veronica's and walked up the formidable stairs to the entrance of the church. Once inside, Kate indicated the way to the ladies' room downstairs.

"Follow me, princess," Brice told Bina, and led her off to the basement.

Coming in at the very last minute wasn't a bad strategy, Kate thought. There was no time to meet and greet — and to be interrogated. Kate and Elliot left the foyer and took a place in the next-to-last pew. Soon Brice and Bina joined them. They tried to be unobtrusive, but by now everyone was waiting for the ceremony to begin, and with their entrance, heads turned. Then, to

Kate's relief, in only a moment the organ began to play the "Wedding March."

Bunny, a meringue of tulle and taffeta, began to make her way down the aisle on her father's arm. There was the usual "oooh" from the guests. Oddly, Kate felt tears well up in her eyes. She'd never been very close to Bunny — she couldn't honestly say she even liked her. But the tears were there nevertheless. She wondered if she was simply being empathetic for Bina, who must be finding this almost unbearable, but it felt far deeper than that.

Kate blinked away the moistness, then took a chance and looked around at the other guests. She wondered if they had as many doubts and fears as she did about picking a mate for life. Certainly Bina and her other friends had talked of little else for many of the years they were in school together. Boys, and then young men, who was going steady, who was breaking up, marriages, and honeymoons were the fodder of many — maybe most — conversations. Yet despite all the talking and all the romantic notions, hopes, and dreams, Kate didn't see intelligent or realistic choices being made, and she also didn't see any marriages or relationships she envied.

She wondered sometimes if her view was darkened by her early home life or her professional training. But the truth was that she remembered very little of her parents' marriage and didn't believe that it was bad or violent. Her father's serious drinking had started after her mother's death. So why was she so frightened? Was everyone frightened and they just hid it better?

So what was Bunny doing now? She'd just met this guy. Was she simply on the rebound from whoever had dumped her? Or was she smitten, deep in that sex haze of infatuation that never seemed to last longer than several months? How could she be taking these steps so quickly down the aisle beside her father? Though a lapsed Catholic, Kate was still idealistic enough to believe marriage should be forever.

Here, standing in St. Veronica's watching Bunny meet the groom at the altar, she felt an uncomfortable combination of jealousy and fear: jealousy because she doubted she could give herself to Michael or any man without hesitation; fear because she wanted to and might lose her opportunity to do it. Though she had made up with Michael, his lack of compassion for Bina had made her look at him in a new way. Would he always dwell on his own issues and concerns and be insensitive to others? He had seemed sincere in his apology, but Kate felt it was important to watch him. Above all, she needed a partner with empathy for others.

She sighed. Beside her, Elliot gave her a smile, then returned his gaze to Bunny. Maybe it was Manhattan. Here in Brooklyn, love seemed so much easier, Kate reflected. Young women met young men. They dated for a while and either broke up or made a commitment to make a commitment. Women pressed for marriage, and the men, albeit sometimes reluctantly, seemed eventually to fall into line. It was expected. And families, ever present in the background, pushed for it.

Of course, there were the exceptions like Jack, but despite this glitch, Kate felt almost certain that he could get over the hump, have some fun in Hong Kong, and return to Bina, the woman he loved. But for how long, if they married, would they love each other? Looking at the older couples in the pews beside and ahead of her, Kate saw bored, middle-aged men and stoic or overly sentimental women. Many held handkerchiefs or tissues to their eyes. When Kate saw an older woman cry at a wedding — and she'd been to lots of weddings — she often thought they cried because unconsciously they remembered their own hopes and the subsequent disappointment that marriage had brought them.

Kate stood there, between her two best friends and between two worlds, and realized that she was not only envious, but also very, very sad. Even if Michael wound up being the right man for her, she simply couldn't imagine wearing the gown, she certainly wouldn't be in a church, her father couldn't walk her down any aisle, and it seemed impossible she'd feel the joy that she'd glimpsed on Bunny's veiled face. Worst of all, she'd probably want Elliot as her matron of honor, which would cause all kinds of difficulties and hurt feelings among her old crowd.

Kate had to smile at the thought. Of course, Elliot would love it. She looked over in his direction and saw that behind Bina, Elliot and Brice were discreetly holding hands. It was so sweet that Kate, without a tissue, again felt tears fill her eyes. She was so happy for Elliot, who had searched and searched for a wonderful partner. But it sometimes made her feel more lonely than she had felt in years.

"Having fun?" Elliot asked in a whisper

as he nudged her out of her reverie.

"Just thinking," Kate murmured.

"Bad idea at any time," Elliot advised. "*Particularly* bad during rituals." He flashed Kate another quick smile. "And did I tell you, you look extremely fetching in that dress?"

Kate smiled but put a finger over her curved lips. Religion was serious in Brooklyn. The ceremony was beginning. And so was the trouble.

Even though she was not Catholic, and was standing yards and yards from the altar, the moment the priest began to speak, Bina began to sob. At first they were silent, shoulder-shaking sobs. For a few moments Kate didn't notice them. But by the time Bunny and her groom had knelt and stood up and knelt again, Bina was audible halfway up the nave. Kate and Elliot eyed each other, then leaned forward and gave Brice a look. He already had one arm around Bina's shoulder and shrugged in the traditional "what else can I do?" gesture.

Kate looked toward the altar, desperate to think of options. A little crying at a wedding was acceptable, even mandatory, but this was getting out of hand. For no reason, her eyes focused on the incense-filled censer hanging from the hands of an altar boy. Really handy looking. For a moment she wished she could get hold of it and give a swing at Bina's head. Not to crack it hard, of course, merely to knock some sense into it. It was going to be difficult enough to get through the reception without Bina blowing her cover now by making a spectacle of herself.

Already a few heads had turned toward them. Kate smiled and nodded, wiping at her own eye as if acknowledging everyone's tears of joy. "So beautiful," she mouthed to someone's mother. Brice, in a moment of brilliance, turned Bina to him and planted a kiss on her lips. For a few moments, Bina's total surprise silenced her. Elliot, putting his arm around her neck from the other side, discreetly covered her mouth with his hand. Bina took the warning and they all watched as the couple stood up, knelt yet again, then stood up and faced each other.

"Is this a wedding or an aerobics class?" Elliot asked. Kate almost laughed out loud, but just then the couple got to "love, honor, and cherish," and Bina cut loose, crying louder than the baby somewhere up front.

Before everything got completely out of

control, Brice reached over, turned back Elliot's cuff, and removed a straight pin. Then, without a moment of hesitation, he stuck it into Bina's upper arm.

Kate, shocked, was not as shocked as Bina, who yipped, shut up, and looked from Elliot on one side to Brice on the other. Brice just leaned forward, whispered in her ear, and, magically, the crying stopped.

At last the service was over, the bride and groom kissed, and Brice and Elliot had to let go of each other's entwined hands to hold Bina's down so she didn't cover her face and begin to sob again. "Hey, look," Kate said, taking Bina by the shoulders. "Pull yourself together. This isn't the worst part. The worst part is about to begin."

"Oh, boy!" Elliot said. "Will there be a family feud?"

"With guns?" Brice added hopefully.

Kate ignored their remarks. "We have to get Bina out of here before the rest of the rabble," she told them.

"You aren't kidding. Just look at her." Elliot tilted his head toward Bina.

Kate had to agree. Bina's makeup was mostly smeared off her face, and mascara had run down her cheeks. Kate gestured, and Elliot tapped Brice on the leg.

"Time to go now," he told Brice.

"No fucking kidding," Brice responded. "The last thing Bina needs right now is to have rice land on her face. It would stick."

Elliot nodded, his face scrunched up at the thought. Then they all crept quietly out of the pew, out of the foyer, and out of the church.

They were lucky to snag a passing cab — not so easy in a borough dependent on car services. They piled out at Carl's of Carroll Gardens, where everyone in Brooklyn, it seemed, had their wedding reception.

"Well, here we go," Kate said as they stood before the entrance. She gave Elliot a nervous smile, and they linked their arms and went through the revolving doors together, followed by Brice and Bina. Fortunately the reception area was empty except for a few bustling waiters who had seen a lot worse than Bina's ruined face.

"Where's the bathroom?" Brice whispered in Kate's ear. "I'm going to take Little Miss Three Mile Island in for a makeup makeover. She's had a serious meltdown."

"It's down the hall to the left," said Kate. She had been to this banquet hall many times in the past. Maybe a dozen people she knew had gotten married here, but it would be a quiet day at Andrew Country Day School before *she* ever would. Assembly-line wedding, with the same music, the same guests, the same MC, the same cake. "Take her away," Kate said. "And Brice, darling, please be gentle."

"I'll do my best," he said, and started to push Bina from behind. "Come on, honey. Time for some surgery from Dr. Brice."

Kate heard Bina's nasal protesting voice trail off as she and Brice disappeared down the hall. "Well," she said, turning to Elliot. "Are you ready for your first Brooklyn reception?"

"Oh, Katie! This is going to be so much fun," Elliot said, grinning wickedly.

"Cut the 'Katie' before you get your tongue cut out," Kate warned him. "I've got a mission. Let's see where we are supposed to sit, change it if we can, and then avoid everyone until we've regrouped."

"Sure. I'm happy just to gape." Elliot craned his neck almost the way Linda Blair had in *The Exorcist*. "Where do they get these smoked mirrors? Are they left over from the sixties or can you still buy them?" he asked, his voice low. It was kind of like Halloween in Greenwich Village. Then he looked down at his watch. "Kate, I'm going to look around some, then maybe check on Brice and see what he's doing to Bina. I'll be back soon. You wait here for the resurrection." He sauntered down the hall.

Once alone, Kate walked over to the gift table and placed her box from Tiffany's right in the center. She knew it wouldn't be the only one there wrapped in distinctive robin's-egg blue, but she was fairly certain the beautiful cut-glass bowl would be the only gift that actually came from Tiffany's. Those blue boxes were often more highly prized than the contents they carried and were passed around over and over, filled with gifts from Bed Bath & Beyond or Pottery Barn.

The reception area was beginning to fill up. After about fifteen minutes, Kate began to wonder why Elliot hadn't come back with Brice and Bina. She could hear more cars pulling up outside. It wasn't only Bina who would be tortured at this event. Kate was definitely not in the mood to deal with all these people — well-meaning or not — asking her about her "love life" and whether "wedding bells" were in her future, too. People from the old neighborhood neither thought deeply personal questions were off-limits nor took notice of how she had managed to add a "Dr." before her name. All everyone here would talk about was when there would be a "Mrs." in front.

She put all this out of her mind because she had a goal to achieve. She had to get over to the table where the seating plans were and make sure her party of four was at the same table. Then she had to get into the closed banquet hall and move the place cards on that table so that Bina would be tightly cordoned off from attacking hyenas, the type that tried to take down a straggler or the weakest member in the herd.

She approached the assignment table with complete authority. If she didn't, she might get stopped by one of the staff. They were used to unmarried women putting themselves beside bachelors, bitter aunts removing themselves from tables with their relatives, even parents who moved their kids to other tables so they could eat dinner in peace. Kate quickly spotted her card: "Miss Katie Jameson and guest," table nine. She shook her head. Not only had the "Dr." been omitted, but she didn't even get her full name. And she hated being called Katie, but Bunny and her mother wouldn't care about such subtleties.

Two cards above her own was "Miss Bina Horowitz and Mr. Jack Weintraub." That was something Kate knew she couldn't afford to let Bina see. Bunny's mother obviously hadn't remembered about Jack's trip. Kate picked up the card, turned it over, and, using a black marker she had put in her purse for this very purpose, wrote, "Miss Bina Horowitz and guest" on the back of the card and replaced it. She hoped that Bina wouldn't turn the card over and that Brice would be smart enough to pocket it.

So far, so good, Kate thought. Next, and last, was getting to the actual table to manipulate the place cards. If Bina was seated next to Bev or Barbie, she wouldn't last five minutes. Of course, they might be seated in the traditional boy-girl-boy boring arrangement. Kate sighed, thinking of one more dinner beside Bobby, Barbie's excessively dull husband. She walked to the closed entrance of the banquet hall, and as luck would have it, a hassled-looking waiter came out. She grabbed at the door closing behind him as he departed with an armful of linens and stepped into the room.

A sign read "Tromboli-Beckmen Wedding Saturday." Under it was "Eisenberg

Bar Mitzvah Sunday." Kate surveyed the room. The interior of the hall was Bunny Tromboli's dream come true, amazingly close to Kate's nightmare. The decorations, the centerpieces, the candles — everything was a middle-class version of photographs Bunny had been clipping and saving from society pages since she was ten. All of the Bitches except Kate had done the same. Kate sighed deeply. Whenever she had allowed herself to envision the elements of a dream wedding, the major emphasis had been on the groom, not the flatware.

Yet despite the inconceivably garish tablecloths and place settings — hot pink and orange, a combination Kate saw no use for in either clothes or furnishings, along with black dinnerware and centerpieces that looked like patent leather with flourishes of net — there was something lovely, calm . . . even magical about a vacant room prepared for but empty of revelers. She allowed herself to pause for a moment to take it all in. Then the colors and her mission moved her forward. She found table nine, looked it over, and moved the cards so that the lineup on their side of the table was Elliot, then Kate, then Bina, and then Brice. She had to juggle Bobby and Johnny, Barbie's and Bev's husbands, to get it to work out, but in a few moments it was done. She pulled out the four chairs for her party and leaned the backs against the table — a very déclassé way to show the seats were taken and to ensure that nobody reedited her editing.

The noise of new arrivals outside the banquet hall had gotten much louder, and then, without warning, the doors swung open. The guests began to pour in. Kate, not wanting to be found alone in the room, a target worse than a lonely duck before the hunter's blind, decided to make her way out to the terrace that ran along the east wall of the room. She would wait outside, get a breath of air and a bit of privacy before the onslaught. Once her crew came back, there would be enough people and enough noise to allow her to slip back inside, find the Trouble Trio, and begin the minimum required mingling. She'd mingled at dozens of weddings before, and she could do it again, she told herself.

Out on the terrace, Kate had a moment to reflect. She was overwhelmingly glad that she had not invited Michael to the affair. She would have been self-conscious and, although she shouldn't be, rather ashamed. The clothes, the accents, the loudness, the . . . well, the vulgarity of it all, made her wince. She was used to it, and loved many of these people, but she did not want to have to translate them for Michael or anyone else. At the same time, she wasn't enjoying how much Elliot and Brice were enjoying their Brooklyn visit. It was too much like a visit to Great Adventure Safari Park. They were observing the wildlife with the detachment of another species.

Kate peeked into the room. It wouldn't take long for it to fill. And then Elliot and Brice would get to talk to the creatures they had been observing at church. Somehow, while it was all right for Kate to think of these people as strange, she didn't like the idea of outsiders observing them in that way, not even Elliot and Brice. Yes, she reflected again, it was the right thing to do to leave Michael out, and how on earth would she have managed Bina without the help of the guys?

She continued to watch as people entered, rearranged their own place cards, hugged or kissed one another, and went for the drinks. Even through the windows, she could hear them speculating about the estimated per plate cost of the upcoming meal, where the bride had bought the dress, whether there was a bun in the oven

. . . and then Kate saw Elliot, Brice, and Bina enter the room. She had to admit it: Bina did look a thousand times more sophisticated with the terrific makeup and more gentle upswept hairstyle Brice's lengthy ministrations had created. Kate reached for the handle of the French door to let herself in, only to find that it had locked itself behind her. She tried the second one, then the third. All locked.

Stranded. She knocked on the glass and tried desperately to get someone's attention, but the hall was abuzz with noise. She could make out older female guests loudly declaring the ceremony to be the most beautiful they'd ever seen, while the men called across the room to one another, inquiring about the outlook for the Mets.

In moments, the room had changed from tranquil to chaotic, from empty to full, and myriad poof skirts and dangerously high hairdos blocked her line of vision. She had lost sight of her friends. Kate thought she caught a glimpse of Brice and someone who might be Bina, now on the side of the room opposite their table, but she couldn't be sure. She ran back down to the remaining doors of the terrace to try to get in, but they were all locked. Well, she would just have to wait until someone —

Just then, a tall blond stepped out the door at the other end of the terrace. What a relief!

"Wait!" Kate yelled. "Wait! Hold the —"

But before she could finish her sentence or make a move, he had turned to the side and the door slammed behind him.

Chapter Twelve

"Damn it," Kate muttered. She walked over to the slammed door and tried the handle, but it was locked. Meanwhile, the guy had moved to the ivy-covered wall and was looking around casually. He was, she couldn't help but notice, one of the best-looking men she'd ever seen. His blond hair must have had a dozen shades in it — the kind of hair women paid hundreds of dollars to salons for but never achieved. He was probably only a little over six feet tall, but his wide shoulders and the way his jacket tapered from them, along with legs that didn't quit, made him incredibly well proportioned. Kate wondered whether his upper arms were muscled and cut in the way she found so attractive. She could barely see his profile, but even from here she could tell that he didn't have the usual pale coloring of a blond. There was a golden tone to his skin that . . . well, he was altogether a golden guy, the type who is all looks and no substance.

Then he saw Kate and turned to face

her. From a full frontal, he was — if it was possible — even more alluring. To her dismay, Kate felt a blush rise from her chest to her neck, but he didn't seem to notice. He just asked, "At the risk of sounding clichéd, what's a pretty girl like you doing in a place like this?" He took a few steps toward her. "And you look distressed. Um, in the damsel, not the furniture, sense." He smiled. The smile was the coup de grâce. It was marvelous the way his teeth lightened his face, how parenthetical dimples formed around it, and how his eyes, unlike most people's when they smiled, stayed wide open. He was what might be called *un canon,* a living embodiment of male beauty.

Kate took a step back. She was suspicious of men this good-looking and with charm as well, but she couldn't help staring. Something about him looked familiar, but she would never have forgotten him if they had met. Perhaps he was a newscaster or someone she had seen on television. She forced herself to take her eyes away from his.

"You could have helped by holding the door open," she said, trying to keep her embarrassment from showing. "Now we may have to wait until someone from the

Eisenberg bar mitzvah lets us in tomorrow afternoon." The words had come out more sharply than she'd meant them to. He cocked his head and observed her. She felt self-conscious at the way he looked at her. Not because it was a once-over, merely because it was so intent — as if he were memorizing every detail of her, from her exposed collarbone to her Jimmy Choo shoes. She turned and looked in at the party through the long window.

"Would that be such a bad thing?" he asked.

Still peering through the window, Kate could see Bina at the far side of the room, flanked by Brice and Elliot, who was looking around, presumably for Kate. Oh no, she couldn't let Bina sit down among their old crowd without her protection! There would be a feeding frenzy. She rattled the door handle. No luck. *"Merde!"* she said.

"Ah. Parlez-vous français?" he asked, almost too quickly.

She turned away from the party to look at him. This guy wasn't just an average hunk. He had the smile of a man who knew he was more than handsome and irresistible to women. It was a well-practiced smile that bathed Kate in warmth. She felt as if she were the first woman in the entire world to ever see such an expression of welcome. The guy was absolutely gorgeous, what French slang would describe as *"un bloc."*

"Oui." Kate blushed and cursed the paleness of her skin. She might as well have her feelings written in neon on her forehead. *"Je parle un petit peu, mais avec un accent très mauvais,"* she told him.

"Mais non. Pas mal. Vraiment."

Handsome as the guy was — and his accent was perfect — Kate was in no mood to test her skills in a foreign tongue right now, though the thought of his tongue provided a momentary distraction from her desperation. She turned and tried once again to open the doors, but they were clearly catch locks, openable only from the inside. "We're stuck out here," she said.

"What an unexpected bonus at an affair like this. Maybe it's an omen," Mr. Gorgeous continued. "Maybe we're not meant to participate in the Bunny Tromboli and Arnie Beckmen nuptials." He leaned back on the terrace railing, crossed one foot in front of the other, and gave Kate an appreciative once-over. "Personally, I would take that as a gift."

Kate was too uptight to flirt or respond

to compliments, especially from a guy as practiced at them as he obviously was.

"You don't look like you're from around these parts," he said, doing a passable Gary Cooper accent. He even looked a little like Cooper, and he probably knew it.

Kate had always preferred slightly nerdy boyfriends, no matter what Elliot said. They were more real, more sincere. Ever since a really handsome Oxford exchange student had asked her on their first date, "How can I possibly keep from falling in love with you," and subsequently dated her roommate a week later, she'd been wary of charm. *"Et vous?"* she asked, just as a test.

"Oui, je suis un fils de Broooklyn," he answered with a mischievous smile.

"Your accent is perfect," Kate observed admiringly.

"My French accent or the Brooklyn one?" he asked, and smiled again. Looks like his should be against the law, she thought, and despite herself, she couldn't resist glancing at his hand, checking for a wedding band. There was none. Not that it mattered to her, she told herself. She didn't know what this guy was about — the answer was probably *rien* — and she didn't have the time to find out.

Turning, she peered through the glass.

She could see that Elliot had found the table and their place cards. She couldn't see his face, but she could see Bev Clemenza and her husband, Johnny, headed directly toward him. Predictably, Barbie and Bobby Cohen were right behind them. "I have to get in there," Kate said in a panic. She grabbed the knob and shook the door frantically.

"Are you a friend of the groom or the bride?" he asked her.

She knocked again on the window. "Bride," she answered tersely, then realized how rude it sounded. "Bunny is one of my oldest friends," she added. Through glass she watched in a paralysis of horror as Elliot shook Bobby's hand and then Johnny's.

"A much older friend, right?" the charmer asked, and moved beside her.

Kate was not in the mood. "Bunny and I have been friends since grade school," she told him, waving wildly through the glass, hoping someone would notice the movement. "And yes, in fact, Bunny is older — by almost a month. But we didn't let that come between us."

"So what's the problem if you miss some of the earlier festivities?"

"I have to be there to support a friend from my posse."

"Your posse?" he asked, and smiled. "Anyone I know?"

"Bev Clemenza, Bina Horowitz, Barbie Cohen."

"You're kidding!" he began, and he stepped away to get a better look at Kate. She turned to him, just for a moment.

"C'est incroyable, mais vraiment." What was it, she wondered, with the friggin' French? She looked back in at the party. God, the DJ was starting to play! "You must be one of the infamous Bitches of Bushwick," he said. "I've heard about *you* girls."

"Excuse me?" Kate asked, turning to him in surprise.

"How come I've never met you?" he asked, oblivious to her hostility. Typical narcissist, Kate thought.

He looked over Kate's head into the room and pointed. "I already know Bev, Barbie, and, of course, Bunny. All the busy Bs. Who are you? Betty?"

"My name is Katherine Jameson," Kate told him.

"I'm Billy Nolan. Why haven't I met you before?"

"I left Brooklyn to go to college."

"I left Brooklyn to go to France. What did you do in college? And where have you gone since?"

"I got my doctorate. I live in Manhattan now." She paused. "Look, Billy, I have to get in there."

"I'm willing to cover my hand with my jacket and bust through the glass, but it . . ."

"It might be a bit much," Kate finished for him.

"They'll open the doors once it gets too hot in there," he said, sitting on the balustrade. "Have you noticed how no one from Brooklyn ever outgrows having their name end with an 'e' sound? Barbie. Bunny. Johnny. Eddie, Arnie." He chuckled. "Here in Brooklyn I'm never William or even Bill. I'm Billy."

He held out his hand, and Kate couldn't resist shaking it. She tried to appear casual, despite the thrill that ran up her back, causing hairs on her neck to rise. "Do you prefer Billy to Bill?" she asked.

"Hey. We're in Brooklyn," he answered. "Go with the flow. Here I'm Billy Nolan. And should I call you Dr. Katherine? Kate? Kathy or Katie?"

"Oh, please, Kate. Not Katie. I hate it," Kate confessed. "Oh, look, they must be playing their song."

To her complete surprise, Billy stood up, grabbed her hand, and started to dance. Before she could make a move, he stopped

167

abruptly. " 'Doo Wah Diddy' is their song?" He made a face, looking puzzled in a really exaggerated way, his head cocked to the side.

Kate laughed. "Well, maybe not."

"I hope not. If it is, I give the marriage three weeks. You have to at least *start* with some romance."

She bet he did — and that for him romance wore off fast. Kate looked him over. The sun glinted on his golden hair. He was one of those very few lucky Irish with the kind of skin that tanned and made their blue eyes bluer. "So you don't think you can keep romance going?" Kate asked him.

"If I thought that, I'd be married." Billy Nolan laughed, and from nowhere the phrase *coup de foudre,* a lightning bolt, entered Kate's mind. He was something — and he knew it, she reminded herself.

"Ah. The tyranny of commitment," Kate said, nodding.

Billy reacted with widened eyes. Then he clutched at his chest. "Now they're doing the hokey-pokey!" he said, as if that upset him.

"So unusual at a Brooklyn wedding," Kate agreed a bit sarcastically. They always played the hokey-pokey or the alley cat or both. She looked in the window, where dozens of old ladies were dancing, their backs to them. "We definitely won't be able to get their attention now."

"Uh-oh. I think I'm in trouble," Billy said, and began to shake. Kate wondered if he was still reacting to the word *commitment*. "Good thing you're a doctor," he said.

Kate looked at him suspiciously. "Why is that?"

"I may need treatment right now. I have a terrible phobia of the hokey-pokey."

"Really?" Kate said. She didn't need this kind of banter now, but as long as they were stuck outside . . . "As I say in my practice, 'Why do you feel that way?' "

"It seems obvious," Billy told her. "Did you ever think about it?"

"About what?"

"About the song? I mean, 'You put your left foot in, you take your left foot out.' Yadda, yadda. You do the hokey-pokey and you turn yourself around. And that's what it's all about." He did an exaggerated shiver.

"So?"

"Well, what if that *is* what it's all about? What if life is just putting one foot in front of the other and that's it? Doesn't the thought terrify you?"

Before Kate could decide how tongue in cheek he was being and come up with an answer, the doors at the other end of the terrace flew open and a big guy in a wrinkled blue suit stuck his head out. "Hey, Nolan!" he shouted. "Get your ass in here. Arnie wants to talk to you about the toast."

Before he vanished again, Billy shouted: "Larry! Hold that thought and that door!" He gracefully ran the length of the terrace, catching the handle just in time. Then he turned back to Kate, held the door ajar, and said, "After you, *chère mademoiselle*."

Kate felt her cheeks color again but wasted no time stepping through the doors and into the crowded room. She was about to thank Billy when she heard Bev Clemenza's high-pitched voice screech, "Katie! Katie! Over here," and didn't dare look back.

Chapter Thirteen

As Kate crossed the room toward her posse, she almost felt a gravitational pull back toward Billy Nolan. She was deeply embarrassed by the strength of her attraction and decided to put it out of her mind. He was just a superficial Brooklyn flirt. And she had an important job to do now.

"Katie!" Bev called again. Kate didn't want to see how terrified Bina was going to be. Though it wasn't her choice, she bitterly regretted that she hadn't been beside Bina during the first few critical minutes. As she moved through the crowd — now twisting again as they did last summer, or at the last wedding — she silently cursed Billy Nolan and the time on the terrace, diverting as it had been.

At last she managed to get across the dance floor and could clearly see table nine. Luckily, Bina was still somewhere in the crowd and Elliot had apparently abandoned the table for greater intrigues. There was Bev, her frosted hair slicked back and her visibly pregnant belly stretching her unsuitable Lycra dress. Barbie, with her big hair hanging halfway down her back, was already seated, too. Barbie's dad, in the jewelry trade, had been more successful than the other friends' fathers had been. She'd always had more clothes, trips to Florida, weekends in the Poconos, and things that seemed enviable at the time. But now she was a Brooklyn wife, a buyer for a women's clothing store on Nostrand Avenue. Her husband, Bobby, was in insurance. Kate could look at her now and feel no envy at all.

Barbie sat beside Bobby, her plunging neckline revealing the half of her breasts not covered by her push-up bra. Kate averted her eyes, but the husbands were, in their own way, more difficult to look at. If each of them hadn't been wearing a bow tie and cummerbund that matched his wife's dress, Kate wouldn't have been able to tell Bev's and Barbie's husbands apart. They were nice-looking Brooklyn boys, but neither of them was the kind of handsome that Billy Nolan was. And behind their eyes was none of the genuine intellect that Michael possessed. The thought of Michael trying to communicate at table nine raised goose bumps on her arms. "Hey,"

Bev yelled. "Look who's here."

For a moment Kate thought she was being greeted, but Bev was staring past her. Kate turned to see Billy Nolan join the wedding party at the head table, talking to the groom. Bunny looked down from the dais and gave Kate a quick wave and a big, proud smile, while taking Arnie's arm. Kate waved back, but her eyes strayed to Billy, talking earnestly to the groom, then laughing with him. Well, there would be no laughs at table nine, Kate reminded herself. She forced herself to turn back to her own companions.

"Wow, Kate, you look great!" Bev said. "Of course, you're a Scorpio and your ruling planet has come out this month, so no wonder."

"Yeah, there's that. And the sale at agnes b.," Kate said with a smile. Kate's simple dress, sleeveless and high collared, with a placket that covered the buttons, was the antithesis of all the overdone outfits of her old friends. If she but knew it, she easily looked the most elegant woman in the room. It was always curious to Kate that while her Brooklyn crew never missed an issue of *Vogue*, *Allure*, or *Cosmo*, they never seemed to dress any differently from the way they always had. Or if there had been

173

a change, it seemed merely to be that blouses had gotten tighter and patterns had gotten louder. Bev, despite her belly, was wearing a black-and-lemon tiger-striped Lycra thing. Barbie wore a tight, strapless dress in a Hawaiian floral print, all banana leaves and toucans wreathing (and writhing) around her torso. Kate could never quite decide if their taste was unbelievably bad or whether hers had been permanently repressed by the nuns at Catholic first school.

"You could use some accessorizing," Barbie opined by way of a hello. "A scarf, or maybe a pendant." Barbie herself was wearing an emerald — no doubt real — that was suspended just above her cleavage.

"I have to wait until I get the chest and the gem for it," Kate said smoothly.

"You are so cynical," Bev snorted. "Such a Scorpio." Since she had become pregnant, Bev, always a horoscope reader, had *really* gotten into astrology. Hormones or something, Kate thought. Or perhaps the feeling of being out of control and the comforting compensation of a system to predict the universe. Kate turned to face the wedding hall again, to try to spot Bina and the guys. She was getting nervous about them. At last she saw Elliot making his way across the room. He arrived carrying three drinks.

"For you, and you, and you," he said, and gave each of the women a cosmopolitan.

"Ooh. Thanks," Bev said, "but I can't."

"What a gentleman," Barbie said appreciatively, then dug Bobby in the ribs.

"This is my friend Elliot." Kate took Elliot's arm.

"We've already met," Elliot said. Kate raised her eyebrows. "Out in the reception area. Your friends are as unique as you are, Katie."

"Oh, we're very unique," Bev said.

"Where's Bina?" Kate asked Elliot out of the corner of her mouth. She scanned the room and saw Brice and Bina making their way toward the table.

Bev tugged on Kate's elbow. "Hey, that guy with Bina, is he her date or what?"

Barbie raised her highly waxed eyebrows. "I love the tuxedo," she cooed. "Armani."

Kate had to smile. If Judaism was a religion to Bina, fashion had always been Barbie's creed. And Kate remembered that Brice had predicted the impression he would make.

"But do you think Jack would approve?" Barbie asked. "I mean, he's gone only a couple of weeks and she's . . . Does he know?"

Kate shrugged. Let 'em guess. Keep 'em busy and distracted.

"His name is Brite or something," Bev said, rubbing her belly.

"Brice," Kate corrected.

"So, what's this guy Brice's sign, anyway?" Bev asked.

"I think he's a Taurus, you'll have to ask him," Elliot said, holding out a chair for Kate, who was grateful to sit down. It was going to be a bumpy ride.

"Oh, Katie, a Taurus! Not for Bina!" Bev complained. "Dangerous while her fiancé is gone."

"Oh, he's a dangerous man," Elliot agreed.

"Is he on the cusp?" Bev added, hopeful.

Kate didn't need or want to explain that Brice was way over the cusp as a mate for Bina. "I think they're just friends," she said.

"That's not what it looks like to me," Barbie said as she joined Kate on her other side. "And he's *gorgeous*. Like a *GQ* model. He'd be perfect for my cousin Judy. What does he do?"

"He's an attorney," Kate told Barbie.

"In a big firm or a solo practitioner?" Barbie asked.

176

"You'll have to ask him." Kate sighed. Same old Barbie. Putting everyone in boxes, fixing them up with one another. She turned to watch Brice and Bina, who were caught in the electric slide on the dance floor. She couldn't help but smile a little at Brice's artful moves as he side-stepped between the slides, dragging Bina behind.

"What happened to Michael?" Bev asked. "Is that all over?" Except Bev pronounced it "ohvah." They all dropped final r's and added inappropriate ones at the ends of words that didn't have them.

But Kate didn't have time to consider diction, because at that moment Bina and Brice arrived at the table. Bina said, "Hi there, everyone," and sat down immediately without making eye contact. In fact, the only contact she seemed interested in was grabbing what would have been Jack's waiting glass of wine with her right hand and pinning down Kate's hand with her left. To Kate's astonishment, she knocked back an entire glass.

"Hello," Barbie said, but not to Bina. She leaned over the table and extended her hand to Brice while exposing more breast than most foldouts did and a lot more than Brice needed or wanted to see. Well, maybe she was trying to scoop him for her cousin, Kate thought charitably.

Meanwhile, Bina picked up Kate's wineglass and drank off half of that. Before Kate could say something to slow her down, eagle-eyed Bev noticed. "Since when do you drink? Capricorns don't drink!" she cried.

"Plus ça change, plus c'est la même chose," Kate said, surprising herself. Obviously her encounter on the terrace had had an effect after all.

"What?" Barbie and Bev asked in unison. Kate just smiled and shrugged.

"Bobby, Johnny, this is my friend Elliot, and this is Bina's friend Brice," Kate said to the men, interrupting a deep conversation about the pros and cons of moving some football team to Dallas. "Elliot, Brice, meet Bobby and Johnny." The husbands nodded a greeting in unison.

"What do you boys think of them moving the Rangers to Dallas?" Bobby asked.

"I'm not really into spectator sports," Elliot said.

"Oh, I love football. Tight ends, wide receivers. *You* know," Brice said, smiling at them.

For a moment, the two husbands looked

confused. "You a Jets or a Giants fan?" Johnny asked, a little suspicion in his voice.

"Definitely a Giant. Love a 'Giant' —"

"Brice!" Elliot said, trying to interrupt.

"— game," Brice finished, and Kate let her breath out.

Bev and Barbie, now also totally confused, stared across the table and looked the two men over more carefully. Kate knew they were setting them up as potential husbands for their two poor, unmarried friends. Ha! When should she thwart them by breaking the news that Elliot and Brice were already married — to each other. But, as Kate hoped, they were at least temporarily distracted by their looks. Well, the delusion would do for now.

"What's your sign?" Bev asked Brice.

" 'Do Not Enter,' " Brice replied, raising his eyebrows and smiling innocently.

Elliot, always ready with a peacemaking lie, smiled at Bev. "Oh, he's a bull," he said, and gave Kate a nudge under the table, as if she wouldn't get the joke without it. On the other side, Bina was still clutching Kate's right hand with her own.

"Hmm. A Taurus," Bev murmured, reappraising him.

Meanwhile, Bina reached out and picked up the cosmopolitan Bev had refused. In another moment she'd gulped it down.

"Bina!" Barbie exclaimed. "What are you doing?"

"Yeah, you have to pace yourself," Bobby advised.

Brice nudged his chair closer to Bina and took away her empty glass. They had created a Bina sandwich, insulating her from her friends. Bina reached out for Brice's glass of wine. He paused for a moment, then shrugged and handed it to her. She downed it in a few breathless gulps. Bev and Barbie stared at Bina. Kate could see Barbie reevaluating Brice as a candidate for Judy.

There was a moment of complete silence. Then Barbie asked the dreaded question. "Bina, you have to tell us about Jack's proposal. Let's see the ring." Kate clenched Bina's hand and tried to change the subject.

"Look at the bracelet Michael gave me," she said hurriedly, holding up her wrist for them to see the sad little silver chain and the thin charm that hung from it.

They barely glanced at Kate's wrist. With her usual amount of discretion, Bev opened her mouth. "Yeah, what happened to Michael the doctor?" she wanted to know. "Bina told me about him."

"Why isn't he here? Is he gone already?" Barbie asked.

Kate shook her head. "He's away at a conference. Elliot is a nice change." Elliot and Kate exchanged looks of love. Barbie raised her eyebrows.

"What is Michael's sign, anyway?" Bev asked.

"Well, I'm not sure, but I think it might be —"

"Wait a minute," Barbie interrupted. "What's going on here?" Kate watched suspicion bloom on her face. "Bina, the ring!" she exclaimed. Then suddenly, without a moment's notice, Barbie reached across the table and grabbed Bina's wrist, yanking her hand from Kate's grip. There was a moment of total silence at table nine. Bina's naked hand, still French manicured, lay like a dying whitefish on the hot pink tablecloth.

Chapter Fourteen

"Where the hell is it?" Barbie demanded. "My father sold Jack a perfect stone." She looked down at the ringless finger and then back up at Bina, whose face was scrunched up as she tried to hold back tears. "Wait a minute!" Barbie said as the light began to dawn. To her credit, there was true concern in her high-pitched voice. "Bina, is everything okay with Jack?"

Two waiters arrived and began distributing plates of chicken and vegetables. Kate hoped it would give Bina a distraction, but she paid no attention to the bland food in front of her.

"Yes . . . in a way," Bina managed. Bev and Barbie exchanged looks, then frowned.

"Okay. How is it okay?" Barbie pressed.

"Well, after his trip we'll get . . . we'll probably get engaged then, after —"

"I knew it!" Bev exclaimed. "Mercury is in retrograde!"

"Very true," Brice said. "It's affected my whole law practice."

But the distraction didn't work. "You lost him, Bina!" Barbie said. "After six years on the hook, you still couldn't reel him in?"

"Barbie!" Kate remonstrated. Elliot put his arm protectively around Bina's little shoulder.

"Oh, God! Are you holding up okay?" Bev asked with genuine sympathy.

"Yes . . . and no," Bina said, and then began to cry outright.

"Well, is it yes or no?" Barbie asked.

"Looks like no to me," Johnny said, pushing away his plate and rising. He shot a look at Bobby, who nodded, wolfed down one last forkful of chicken, and pushed back his chair. "Uh, we'll get some drinks," he offered, and he and Bobby abandoned the table.

"Honey, is there anything we can do to help?" Barbie asked.

"Well, I've been staying with Kate, and Elliot, Max, and Brice have been a major support," Bina told her friends through her tears. "Look, I'm fine," she began. "I cried for a little while, but now I have found" — she looked fuzzily at Brice — "a new focus."

"Right!" Barbie chimed in. "Focus on the possibilities." She smiled at Brice. "You miss one bus, there's always another. A door closes and a window opens. You lose one house and you find one next door."

"Wrong street," Elliot muttered to Kate, who shushed him.

Kate couldn't let the charade go on. "Brice and Elliot are here together," she said.

"Well, we can see that," Bev said.

"No, I mean they're *really* together." Kate watched as the realization of what she said slowly dawned on all of the guests around the table. Despite *Queer Eye* and *Boy Meets Boy* — or maybe because of them — the old Brooklyn crowd felt that gay was a reality, but only on TV.

There was a pause. At last Bev spoke. "No wonder you guys are so well-dressed."

Barbie turned to Bina. "And just because you're desperate now, showing up with these guys doesn't mean there can't be a —" she cleared her throat — "a straight guy in your future. No offense meant."

"No offense taken," Elliot assured them.

"Yeah, look at Bunny," Bev said, waving her hand with its unbelievably long nails toward the bridal table. "Less than two months ago, she got dumped. Then she met her Arnie . . . and everything turned around."

"I don't want everything to turn around," Bina sniffed. Kate was actually grateful for the wine Bina had consumed, because without it there would be floods of tears. "I want Jack. . . ."

Eventually the waiters returned and removed the dishes, replacing them with a limp salad. A waltz began, and the seductive swell of Strauss drew their gazes toward the dance floor. At first, Kate was glad of any diversion, but then she realized the only two dancers were Billy and Bunny, whom he was twirling expertly around the floor. Kate, along with every other woman in the room, admired his moves, his mastery, and all the rest of him. His grace made Bunny look good. Spontaneous applause broke out, and then other couples started to join them on the dance floor. Kate was about to casually ask about him when Bobby and Johnny finally returned to the table, carrying a tray full of drinks. Kate was thankful for hers but had trouble swallowing at the sight of Bina guzzling down a Jack Daniel's with Coke.

"Oh, look at Bunny! Thank God she lost those last five pounds," Barbie said. "I told her not to buy a size six when you're an eight. It wasn't like she had eight months to lose the weight. She'd been on the

Häagen-Dazs diet after she got dumped the last time. Then bim bam boom, and she's getting married."

"It was in the stars," Bev said dreamily.

Kate was distracted from the conversation as the waiter stepped in to pour coffee. "She bought the dress three weeks ago," Barbie told them. "And they only got this date at all because another couple eloped. It's too bad. If she had done some Pilates, she could have worn a bias cut. They're big now."

"Stop!" Kate interjected. "She looks beautiful because she's happy."

Brice looked out at the couples on the dance floor. "I'm not sure I like her dress, but I like her taste in grooms," he said, snapping a Polaroid of Bunny and Billy as they passed by. There was greater interest and enthusiasm in Brice's voice than Kate would've preferred, but it didn't seem as if anyone else noticed.

"Oh, that is *not* her husband!" Barbie sneered. "That's Billy." Apparently a raw spot had been touched. "He's the guy who dumped her, but he introduced her to Arnie."

Kate leaned back to see around the waiter who was carrying the tray of dessert. Then, as clear as a movie flashback, Kate remembered the glimpse she had gotten of the man in SoHo, the one Bina had pointed out. Of course. She *had* seen him before.

"See, Bina? It could happen to you," Bev said, her voice warm with encouragement. "I'll do your chart and see what's up. It could be a Taurus," she added archly to Brice.

"And what a lucky Taurus he would be," Brice said gallantly. He sat back in his chair and picked up the developed picture of Billy. "Ooh, pretty," he said to himself, and slipped the photo into his pocket.

"Sure," Bina slurred.

"One day dumped and the next engaged," Barbie told her.

"I have not been dumped!" Bina exclaimed.

"Can you believe Billy's actually the best man?" Barbie asked the table at large, apparently still stuck on the subject.

"Didn't you date him right before you met me?" Johnny asked his wife. Bev blushed as she nodded that she had indeed dated the man in question. "I went out with him for a few weeks, right before we met, but it didn't work out." She leaned over and kissed her husband. "Anyway, he's an Aries," she offered by way of explanation.

"He's an asshole," Barbie clarified. "He's the asshole who dumped Bunny."

For once Kate was forced to agree with Barbie. Her assessment of the guy had been right: too good-looking, too facile, too smooth.

"Good old Billy," Bina said, clearly close to drunk. "Let's drink to 'Dumping Billy.'"

"Dumping Billy?" Elliot asked with interest. "Why do you call him that?"

"Because he's turned dumping women into a major lifestyle," Barbie told him.

"He's not really a bad guy," Bev said. "It's hard for an Aries to commit."

Johnny snorted. "I can't believe you actually dated him."

"Well, I wasn't the only one," Bev replied, on the defensive, "was I, Barbie?"

"No," Barbie said bravely, "Billy was the last guy I dated before I got married to Bobby. But he didn't mean a thing to me. When I broke up with him —"

"Excuse me?" Bev asked. "Reality check. He broke up with you."

"Whatever. He's not really so terrible. He's fun, and he's got a great sense of style. It's just that the word *commitment* isn't in his vocabulary."

Brice leaned across the table to whisper

to Kate, "Elliot was so right. This is so much better than *The Young and the Restless*. But a lot less realistic."

"That's because soap operas are art, and this is not real life," Kate told him. She didn't even want to imagine the feedback she'd get from these two after this nightmare was over.

She looked over at Elliot, who had taken out a pencil and paper. "Let me see if I have all the facts right," he said to himself. She wondered what in the world he could be up to. But before she got a chance to ask, Bina stood up unsteadily and decided that this was the moment to announce to the assembly just how unhappy she was.

"Ladies and gentlemen," she said, "you are looking at Bina Horowitz, loser and future spinsper."

"Spinster," Brice corrected.

"Whatever," Bina said, and tried to climb up on her chair. Elliot caught her before she fell, but he couldn't stop her from raising her voice. "Single women can have children, you know. Not just Rosie O'Donnell. Michael Jackson did it, and he wasn't even a woman. I'm a woman, goddammit!"

Despite the incredible din in the room, people were beginning to stare. Luckily, at that moment, the sound system crackled and Billy Nolan's voice covered Bina's.

"*Excusez moi,*" Billy tried once, and then tapped the microphone and said more loudly, this time in English, "Excuse me. Everyone?" The chattering continued until finally he tapped the microphone so firmly that the high-pitched squeal of feedback quieted the crowd. "Stop talking!" Billy nearly shouted at them all. It was a perfect opportunity to get Bina calmed down. Kate and Brice tried to take her by the hand as she resisted. Meanwhile, over the speakers Billy Nolan seemed to be having trouble of his own. "Jeez, I know it's imp-possible for B-Brooklyn women to b-be quiet, b-but if you could just g-give a guy a b-break here."

Kate cringed as he struggled to overcome his stammer. Kate looked down at the bracelet Michael had given her and sighed. Then she turned to see what Elliot thought of Billy, but he didn't seem to be paying attention. In fact, he looked as if he were trying to solve a math problem. As the best man started to lift his glass in a toast, Elliot was scribbling frantically on his napkin with a pen.

"I raise *my* glass to Arnie and Bunny," Billy began. "*À vous, mes amis. Toujours l'amour.*"

"Oh, Jesus," Barbie spat, rolling her eyes, "he's pretending to be French again."

"Who in the hell does that guy think he is?" Bobby wanted to know. "Speak English!" he shouted from the table.

"Sorry" — Billy blushed — "English it is." He took a deep breath and continued. "I, uh — I introduced Arnie to B-Bunny," he said quickly. "I've known Arnie for years, and B-Bunny . . . well, I've known her, too!"

Kate frowned at the chorus of salacious hoots and catcalls that caused Bunny to blush and Arnie to hang his head. Kate wondered about Billy's stammer. If he was putting it on, he was an even bigger asshole than she suspected. Fortunately he made the rest of his toast French free and brief.

"Congratulations to Arnie and Bunny!" he said. "They're good p-p-people. And marriage is a beautiful thing . . . to witness from afar. To Arnie and Bunny." He lifted his glass to signal that he was finished.

The crowd cheered and clinked their glasses with their silverware, and Arnie and Bunny obligingly kissed. When the cheering and jeering stopped, Kate turned to the others at the table and asked, "Did you two really date him?" Bev and Barbie nodded ruefully and shrugged.

At that moment the band started playing again, and people drifted back onto the dance floor. This should have been all right, since it would make slipping out unnoticed easier. Except Elliot stood up and excused himself from the table. "Where do you think you're going?" Kate asked. "We ought to get Bina out of here."

"I'll be right back," he said, and hurried into the crowd.

Kate kept hold of Bina and watched as couples did the twist and slow-danced to "Every Breath You Take." Finally, Elliot returned. He had a self-congratulatory look on his face.

"Where have you been?" Kate demanded. "We must take Bina home. She's all ready to start doing the hora all by herself."

"I was just doing a little probability research," Elliot replied.

"Great!" Kate snapped. "Why? Going to set up a whole new group of word problems for third-grade math in a wedding hall? If X serves four cocktail wieners to three guests and Y serves two stuffed —"

"Look, statistics are involved," Elliot said, "but no word problems will be solved. Merely a romantic one. You'll see." He

192

turned to Brice. "Get her left arm," he said, pointing at Bina. "And I'll get her right."

Without a word, the two men surrounded Bina and coolly and unobtrusively led her away from the table, across the room, and out the exit. Kate followed, forbidding herself to turn and take one last look at Billy Nolan.

Chapter Fifteen

Some days later, as Kate finished her notes and was ready to lock them in her file cabinet for the night, the phone rang. She hadn't seen Michael for over a week. He'd been off on a seminar, and she'd been held hostage by Bina since the wedding. Tonight he was coming to dinner, and she expected his call. She lifted the receiver.

"Kate?" It wasn't Michael's voice, nor was it a voice she recognized. Male, youngish sounding, but deep.

"Yes, this is Kate Jameson."

"Hi. This is B-B-Billy Nolan." The stammer gave him away, even if he hadn't identified himself by name. Kate felt the color rush to her face.

"How did you get my number?" she asked. "My number here at work." What nerve! As if it wouldn't have been inappropriate enough to have him call her at home. Kate always worried about protocol. After all, this was her first professional job. Now this . . . this . . . jerk had her work number. She'd kill whichever one of the Bitches had given it out.

"Look, I hope this isn't a b-bad time."

She'd had a rough afternoon. Stevie Grossman, a fifth grader, was showing disturbing signs of schizophrenia, very unusual in a child his age. Kate knew he needed to see a psychiatrist — she had a friend at the Ackerman Institute for the Family who might help — but both his parents and Dr. McKay were trying to minimize the boy's troubles in the face of her professional advice. And now this bozo — albeit gorgeous bozo — was calling her at work? "I'm afraid it is," Kate said coldly. How many women had he scored with? Did he expect to add her name to the list?

"Would there be a better time?" Billy asked.

"I'm afraid there wouldn't be," Kate said. She should have hung up the phone at that moment, but something, she wasn't sure what, tugged at her. It was hard for her to be really rude. "I'm sorry. I have to go." She placed the phone back in its cradle as a twinge of guilt doused the tiny glow of pleasure she felt from the call. She was seeing Michael in just a little while. Who did Billy Nolan think he was?

She put the thought from her mind,

gathered her things, and locked her office. As she passed Elliot's third-grade classroom, she caught a glimpse of him teetering on a chair, sticking transparencies on the windows. "Math Is Fun!" they said. He was hanging them so they showed their faces to the outside world and read backward to the class.

"Well, that ought to convince them," she teased. She needed her dose of Elliot to cheer her up. "Good for the dyslexics, at least."

Elliot whirled, startled by her voice, and nearly fell off the chair. He grabbed at the window to steady himself, then looked down at her and smiled. "Nice to see you, too." He sighed. "Andrew Country Day. Home of learning for learning's sake."

Kate walked in and took a seat in Elliot's chair, putting her feet up on his desk. Maybe he could suggest something she could do to convince Stevie's parents to get him professional help. He could be pretty resourceful. But he beat her to the punch.

"How's Bina doing?" he asked, swiping at her feet to get them off the desk.

"As well as can be expected," Kate said, shrugging. After the wedding, Bina had agreed to go home to face the music and begin her "exploration of singleness." Somehow that had translated into coming over to Kate's constantly for sympathy and getting gossip about Jack from Max.

"Poor Bina," Elliot said. "I really like her."

"So do I," she agreed. "She's like a sister to me."

"I liked Bev and Barbie, too," Elliot said. "What a hoot."

"Well, I wasn't as close to them," she reminded Elliot. "But I'm glad you and Brice had fun."

"Fun? Brice hasn't talked about anything else since. He's dying for the next installment."

"There is no next installment. It's not a soap opera. It's life, sort of. Bina is back managing her father's office. Maybe she'll meet some guy who needs a spinal adjustment."

"I'd like to see Bina," Elliot said.

"Look, Brooklyn isn't a spectator sport." Kate stood up. She didn't want to hold her friends up to derision and criticism, even if she did so herself. "Bina is very low. She had a lot invested in Jack." She sighed. "I've gotta go. I have a date with Michael tonight."

"Sit down another minute," Elliot requested, for once without saying a word against Michael. Kate was surprised enough to do it, but only at the edge of the seat, ready for a quick exit if he got started. "Look," he said, "I think I have a way to help Bina."

"Oh, Elliot. Please," Kate began, rolling her eyes. "Unless you have a written proposal from Jack in your pocket, there's nothing you can —"

"Just listen," he told her. "This might be as good as a written proposal."

Kate looked at him skeptically, as if he were about to reveal the secrets of the mummy's tomb.

"Remember how at the wedding Barbie said she got dumped by that gorgeous guy?"

Kate couldn't believe it. Was she going to be hounded by mentions and visions of Billy Nolan? She would never tell Elliot about the call or he would become hysterical. "What gorgeous guy?" she asked.

"The best man. Billy," Elliot reminded her. "Remember? The one who looked like a much more handsome Matt Damon?"

"Oh, yeah. The toaster. What about him?" Kate said, trying to look bored.

"Well, Barbie dated him."

"Barbie dated everyone," Kate said.

"She'd just about run out of Brooklyn guys and had to start on Staten Island."

"Try to hold your focus," Elliot said. "As you may or may not remember, Bunny also dated and got dumped by Billy. Right before she married Arnie."

"Bunny had really bad luck with men," Kate said. "So?"

"Well, she had good luck, as you call it, after Billy . . . if you consider Arnie good luck."

Kate shrugged and tried to remember if she had picked up her white blouse from the dry cleaners or not. She wanted to wear it tonight. "And your point would be?"

"Well, Bev had dated Billy, been dumped, then got married, too. When I noted this odd probability, my brilliant mathematical mind went into high gear and I started to do some digging."

"And?" said Kate.

"And so," Elliot continued, sounding a little annoyed, "I went on a little fact-finding mission and found out six women at the wedding dated Billy and got dumped by him."

"So he's a slut," Kate said. She thought of the way Billy had charmed her on the terrace, his phone call, his incredible good looks. She was surprised there weren't thirty women there he'd disappointed. "Wow, Elliot. You're a regular Sherlock Holmes."

"You're not getting the picture here. You remember how I had to help you with statistics?"

"How could I forget? You remind me at every possible opportunity."

"Well, I'm a genius," Elliot told her. "Geniuses are always disrespected." He spoke primly, holding his nose a little higher. "Stay with me here, Kate. You'll see. All six of these women, after getting dumped by Billy, *married* the very next man they dated."

Kate shrugged. "Anyone would look good after that guy. He's just a player." Even to her, her voice sounded too bitter. A little flirt and a phone call. What was Billy Nolan to her?

"Kate. Kate! Don't you get it!" Elliot almost shouted, clearly exasperated. "It's not about him. It's about what happens *after* him. Do you know the statistical likelihood of this phenomenon?"

"Obviously not," replied Kate, who was getting pretty irritated herself by now. She stood up. She wouldn't have time to stop at the cleaners, and if her white shirt wasn't at home, she'd wear the green silk one. She picked up her purse. "Gotta go."

"Kate, I've worked it out, and the probability ranges from one in six million and three hundred and forty-seven to one in eighty-two million six hundred and forty-three. And that's *with* standard deviation."

"Talk about deviation," Kate said, "when do you have time to shampoo your hair?" She got to the door. Then she stopped for a moment. "Anyway, how does that help Bina?"

"Don't you get it?" Elliot yelled. "We *use* it in Bina's favor."

She stopped. Then she turned around. "Use it?" she asked.

At that moment, Dr. McKay showed up in front of Kate like a migraine on a sunny day. "Is there an altercation going on in here?" he asked.

"Certainly not," Elliot assured him. "We were testing the acoustics of this room. For some reason, the students in that corner near the door don't hear all of the class discussion. Kate thought it might be the corkboards."

Kate nodded. "Proust and all," she said.

Dr. McKay blinked, and Kate almost laughed out loud. He was so easily impressed by literary allusion. "Oh, I see.

Well, that will suffice for now," he said, and was gone as quickly as he had appeared.

"He thinks we're having a lover's quarrel," Elliot said.

"That, or he's going off to bake some madeleines." Dr. McKay brought his own baked goods to every cake sale. "So just tell me what the point of all that was before I run for the subway."

"The point," Elliot told her, "is that Bina is supposed to explore her singleness, right? So we get her to date Billy, get her dumped, get her to see Jack, and wham, bam, thank you, ma'am, he'll ask her to marry him."

Kate could hardly believe what she'd just heard. "And I thought Stevie Grossman needed therapy," she said. "Elliot, you're certifiable. Next you'll tell me to adopt Bev's black magic and that Bina needs to be a Pisces so she can swim to happiness."

"Kate," Elliot said, his voice deepening as he got more serious, "we're talking statistics and probability here, not astrology. I'm not Bev. I calculated it out, and it's as close to a sure thing as possible."

"Oh, come on, Elliot!" Kate exclaimed. "You've lost it. I don't even begin to have the time to tell you how flawed your plan is."

"Try," Elliot challenged her.

"Number one: Bina doesn't want to date anybody else. Number two: Billy is an asshole who has slept with every truly attractive girl in Brooklyn — and possibly lower Manhattan. Number three: Bina, as much as I love her, couldn't pick up a guy if he had a handle on him, much less get a date with Billy Nolan. Will that suffice for now?"

"Okay," Elliot conceded. "But give me one more good reason it won't work."

"You're insane." She began to walk down the hall.

"You won't be saying that when I am Bina's matron of honor," Elliot called after her.

Jesus, Kate thought, McKay would be on them in a private school minute. She turned around to face Elliot. "No, Elliot. Just no."

Elliot examined her face. "Who tutored you so you passed your GMATs?"

"You did." Kate sighed. She knew the litany.

"And who graduated top of his class from Columbia?" he asked her.

"You did, but —"

"And who was invited to accept an adjunct professorship and a grant at Princeton?"

"You, but that doesn't —"

"But that doesn't mean that you can still doubt my abilities?" He shook his head. "In the land of the blind . . . Kate, this is an absolutely fascinating finding, and a tremendous opportunity to exploit, and you are calling it hooey?"

"I don't think I ever actually used the word *hooey*," she said, and lowered her voice. "That sounds more like something McKay might say."

"But you know I'm *never* wrong when it comes to numbers," Elliot told her, grinning.

Kate looked down at her watch and then again turned to leave. Let him screech down the hallway if he wanted to. "Elliot," she said as she began to walk, "I don't believe in magic, I don't believe in superstition, or horoscopes, or coincidences that predict the future. Now I've got to go. I've got a date with Michael, and I haven't shaved my legs in a week."

"Ah, yes, Michael," Elliot said, walking past the lockers. "I thought —"

"I would rather not go into your thoughts right now." She got to the entrance. "Bye, bye."

Elliot put his hand on her shoulder. "Look, Kate, this doesn't involve just you, it involves Bina and *her* future. At least let me present the facts to her. It ought to be her decision."

Kate looked back at her friend, shook her head, and shrugged. Then she hurried down the steps on the way to her date.

Chapter Sixteen

Kate strolled along Eighth Avenue with the pleasant anticipation of the weekend before her. She decided that after the Bina siege, Bunny's wedding, and Elliot's insane reaction, she wouldn't allow herself to think about any of it. She wouldn't even think about her little clients at school. She had done a bit of what she thought of as indulgent grocery shopping: stopping at some of the superb food specialty stores in her neighborhood and buying prepared curry chicken salad, a bunch of perfect red grapes, and poached sole with lemon-zest garnish.

Friday afternoon was a special pleasure to Kate. She had finally reached the point in her adulthood where she had hired a cleaning lady. Teresa came for only half a day each Friday, but the $50 was well worth it, because at the end of a hard week, Kate could look forward to walking into a vacuumed, dust-free living room and a bed freshly made up with clean sheets. When she remembered her teenage years, she thought of the reluctance she had felt in going home to the four dirty rooms that she shared with her father and the misery of shopping for the cheapest basics — sardines, canned soup, and cold cereal. She would open the door fearfully, never knowing what she would find inside. All this had given her an enormous appreciation now for the security of knowing what to expect when she opened her own door, as well as a pride in the order and cleanliness of her apartment.

She passed by a Korean market, and her eyes were drawn to roses of an unusual apricot color. It would be nice if Michael brought her flowers, but if he didn't, it would be lovely to have some of these roses in a bowl in the living room and a vase beside her bed. She stopped, and when the old merchant offered her "special discount two bunches for ten dollars only for pretty lady," she smiled at him, took out a $10 bill, and walked away with the paper-wrapped roses tucked under her arm.

Kate turned the corner to her block. Many of the windows were open, and as she walked by the brownstones, she could see people in basement kitchens preparing dinner, others in living rooms with books or a glass of wine, and even a few children playing on the stoops and tiny yards in front of the buildings. When she got to her stoop, she strode up the steps quickly, had her key ready, entered the vestibule, and managed to pick up her mail and get up the flight of stairs to her apartment without dropping the delicacies, her purse, the flowers, or the mail.

She entered her small but orderly space and sighed, kicking off her shoes and leaving them at the door. It was past five, and she needed enough time to put away the food, arrange the flowers, take a shower, and change her clothes. She would have to rush. She was just putting the last rose into the vase for her bedroom when the phone rang. She picked it up while she carried the flowers to her bedside table. She checked her caller ID. She simply didn't have time for another call from Bina. Cruel as it might be, they were starting to annoy her.

"Look, I don't want you to be angry," Elliot's voice said.

"I'm not angry, I'm just in a rush."

"Of course you're not angry yet," Elliot said. "I don't want you to be angry after I tell you what I'm going to tell you."

"Is it that I look fat in the skirt?" she asked. "It's too late for me to take it back now. You told me it looked good." She put the flowers down and stood back to get the full effect. The room looked charming.

"I know you're just joking, but I'm serious. Don't be mad. I'm inviting Bina to brunch on Sunday."

Kate, in the act of slipping out of the new skirt while she cradled the receiver between her shoulder and her neck, nearly dropped the phone. "Why would you do that?" she asked. "Why in the world would you do that?"

"I knew you would be mad," Elliot said. "But I've done a little more sleuthing, and —"

"Who are you? Nancy fucking Drew?" Kate asked. "No one does sleuthing, no one drives a roadster, and no one is inviting my Brooklyn girlfriend to their Chelsea apartment for brunch except me — and I'm not even sure *I'll* do it." She hung up her skirt and was delighted to see that she *had* brought home her white sleeveless blouse from the cleaners. She would wear it with the top two buttons undone and the gray pants from Banana Republic. But first she'd get rid of Elliot and stop this stupid plan.

"Kate, it isn't just Barbie and Bunny. There are six women who have dated Billy, and right afterward — right after he dumped them — they got married to other men."

"Are you still on that?"

"The statistical probability is almost unheard of. You owe it to Bina to —"

"Elliot, I don't know why you've gotten this bee in your bonnet, but kill it right now." Kate, truly annoyed, put her clothes on the bed and held the phone so that she was speaking right into the mouthpiece. "You only want to have Bina over so that you and Brice can watch her up close and personal and then make fun of her later."

"That is so unfair! This is just a way to help Bina."

Kate looked at the alarm clock on her dresser. "Michael is coming over. I have to go. Bye." As she replaced the phone on the receiver, she could hear Elliot whining.

"But Kate —"

She rushed into the bathroom, showered but kept her hair dry, got dressed, and primped for a few minutes in front of the steamy bathroom mirror. Then she picked up her hairbrush, went into the kitchen, and began brushing out her hair while she poured herself some peach iced tea.

Since their reconciliation after the night of Jack's failed proposal, she and Michael had begun to slip into that comfortable stage where both of them assumed that they would spend most of the weekend together and called each other just about every day. Although it was a hot day, Kate kept the window open and she sat at it, sipping the tea and waiting for Michael's arrival. She had only to toss a few greens and take out the rest of the food and they would be ready for a pleasant dinner. She had a bottle of Frascati chilling in the refrigerator, and the table was set. Michael, as usual, was just a little bit late, but Kate didn't mind. It gave her more time to enjoy the peace of her apartment and the pleasant view of brownstones.

Last winter, after she had broken up with Steven, when the trees were bare, the view had seemed gray and empty, just like her life. Elliot had nursed her through, and time . . . well, time had passed and done what it does.

She smiled for a moment, grateful that she had put those days behind her. It was funny; someone should write a book about the new, twenty-first-century stages of commitment and separation in relationships. Perhaps she would suggest it to Michael. Each action represented either a step in growth or a diminishment in love and trust. First a couple only had each other's home numbers. Then they exchanged phone numbers at work. Then there was the important moment when you programmed both numbers into your home and cell phones, followed by the ceremonial leaving of the toothbrush, followed quickly by the leaving of personal hygiene products — deodorant, moisturizer, a razor. Then, most symbolically, came the critical exchange of keys. Eventually, of course, each of these actions was reversed. Kate didn't know when Steven had wiped her name from his cell phone, but she remembered clearly the day she had deleted his.

While she and Michael had not yet exchanged keys, Kate felt that they were moving nicely from the dating phase into what she would call "a relationship" if the word didn't make her wince. And that was a relief. When she was in her twenties, it had seemed that dates had either been more casual or guys had played games, and when they parted after a time together, Kate never knew if they would call her the next day or the next week or even ever. Maybe it was because she was in school and there was a big pool of people to date, so it was easy to meet someone to replace the someone of the previous month. Now, however, since Steven, she felt some kind of shift. Dates always seemed to be an assessment on her part of the chance for a long-term hookup, and if she didn't feel a strong level of interest from a man, she found herself losing interest in him.

As she looked down at the street, thinking of him, Michael appeared around the corner. From her vantage point, she could observe him and remain unobserved. There was something about his walk that, seen from above, looked a bit prissy, but Kate put the unworthy thought out of her mind.

"Yo, Michael!"

Down below, he stopped, looked up to the trees for a moment, and then caught her waving from the window. "Hey," he yelled up. "Sorry I'm late."

She hadn't meant to make him feel guilty. She just shrugged, smiled, and gestured for him to come up. She left the windowsill and buzzed to unlock the downstairs door, then opened the door to her apartment and waited for him.

She heard his steps on the stairs before she saw him, ignored his second apology, and kissed him instead. He held her for a moment, and it felt so good that she was disappointed when he let go. But dinner was pleasant, and Michael was appropriately grateful. She talked about the progress she was making with Brian Conroy, the motherless little boy, and about some trouble they were having with two brothers — twins — who kept trading places and confusing not only the staff, but their classmates. Michael told her about his week. All of his news lately had been about the mutual courtship between him and the Sagerman Foundation. He was still hoping for an offer to chair a department at the University of Texas. Kate wasn't sure whether or not she was included in his Austin plans. He didn't speak about it, and she didn't ask. Did he plan for her to go? Or would he bring it up at some point in time? Maybe he only wanted to be offered it and then wouldn't accept. Austin . . . Kate tried to put it out of her mind. Texas was not for her.

When dinner was over, Michael helped her clear the table and produced a white paper box containing a poppy seed pound cake for dessert. "I have some vanilla ice cream that might go well on top of that," she told him.

"I can think of something that might go well on top of something else before dessert," Michael said. He took her hand. "Did I tell you how pretty you look?"

She shook her head. "Are you telling me now?" she asked, hoping for more.

Instead he looked down at her. "You have a problem with the buttons on your blouse." From his height he could see her modest cleavage. She smiled up at him. "You've made a mistake." He put his hands on the next button. For a moment, she thought he was about to button her up, but then she realized what he was doing. "You silly girl. You've neglected to leave them all open," Michael said. And in a moment, he had undone them.

In a few moments more they were on her bed, and she was — in the Victorian sense — being completely undone. After Steven, with whom she'd shared such an intensely passionate relationship, Kate had been afraid that anyone she slept with would be a second best; but what Michael lacked in humor, he more than made up for in bed.

Kate was so engrossed in her own thoughts that when she felt his hands move deftly over her body, she had to rouse herself to put her arms around him and do more than simply lie back and enjoy it. Together they kissed, fondled, and held each other. When Michael pressed his hands against her shoulders and rolled onto her, she was more than ready.

Chapter Seventeen

When Kate awoke on Saturday morning, she was smiling. She stretched out, arching her back in the delicious relaxation of postsexual languor. Her smile widened as she thought of the weekend of leisure ahead of her. She wanted to snuggle up and whisper a thank-you to Michael, perhaps even entice him into an encore, but when she turned on her side, she realized he was gone. It took her a moment to remember that he always ran for an hour between six and seven. "No matter what," he'd told her when they'd first met, and she'd admired his self-discipline. Now she was just disappointed. He'd come back wide awake, he'd shower, and he'd want coffee, which she'd have to serve him.

Kate sighed, lifted herself up, saw that it was a quarter to seven, and lay down again. She considered her options: She could get up, shower, and begin to make breakfast, or she could go back to sleep and wait for his return. Despite wanting some snuggle time, she knew if she waited for Michael, he would go straight to the shower, thoughtfully leaving her alone to sleep. He'd probably read the *Times* quietly until she got out of bed. She decided to replay last night's sex in her mind and was just closing her eyes when the phone rang. No one would be calling her this early on a weekend morning except . . .

"Hello, Elliot," she said. "Do you know that it is ten minutes to seven on a Saturday morning?"

"Am I interrupting something?" Elliot asked coyly. "I can call right back. Or does he take longer than a few minutes?"

"Elliot! You are interrupting my sleep," Kate said. "What's the emergency?"

"Look, Kate, I don't want you to be mad."

"Mad? What have you done?"

"Look, I know how you are. And I didn't mean for it to be more than Bina, but she told Barbie, and you know how *she* is . . ."

Yes, Kate reflected, she did know how Barbie was, but she didn't need to hear about it, and certainly not from Elliot before seven a.m. on a weekend.

"I had to do it. The mathematics and the potential for happiness here were just too big to be ignored."

"Elliot, what are you going on about?"

"About the brunch. I had already told Bina about the findings, and she wanted to hear more, and Brice suggested a brunch, but then I was going to cancel after I spoke to you. Now, though, she's invited Bev and Barbie. And Bunny is back from her honeymoon, so Bev told her, and now —"

"Oh, God," Kate cried. "Don't tell me you bothered Bina with this geeky idea of yours. Stop it, Elliot! And what does it have to do with the others? Or a brunch?" She had hoped for a Bina-free weekend, a time to relax with Michael and refuel. She tried to focus on what Elliot was saying, but she wanted to be unfocused, soft and fuzzy and feminine and pampered. "Elliot, don't get Bina crazy with your nonsense."

"You don't understand the clarity and magnitude of the numbers, Kate," Elliot told her. "Since Bina talked to the girls, they found two other cases where a woman married *immediately* after Billy broke up with them."

"So what?" Kate heard the door to her apartment squeak open. Maybe, if she got up right now, she could negotiate a little more time in bed. She liked Michael sweaty, but he was too fastidious to comply with her wishes. Still, there was a chance. . . .

"I have to go," she told Elliot.

"I understand," Elliot said meaningfully. "Have fun. Just close your eyes and think of England. And be here tomorrow at eleven-thirty."

"I hate you," Kate said.

"But doesn't it feel good, in a strange and exciting way?" Elliot asked. "Eleven-thirty tomorrow. Be there or be . . . talked about."

On Sunday morning, Kate knocked on Elliot's door at a quarter to eleven. She wanted to arrive before the Bitches, lay some ground rules, vent a little anger, and limit the way Elliot and Brice would toy with them.

"Kate!" Brice shouted in false surprise when he opened the door. "You're early! Whatever could be the reason?"

"I thought perhaps I could help you get ready by putting some ground glass in the chicken salad," she said with an insincere smile.

"My, my. Little Miss Hospitality," Brice said.

She stepped past him and walked into the apartment. She had a bone — well, more like a whole skeleton — to pick with Elliot.

Her quarry was standing at the sofa, barely visible, behind an armload of charts and graphs. When he saw her he dropped everything onto the coffee table. Brice, never dumb, disappeared into the kitchen, from which delicious smells were emanating. "What's all this?" she asked Elliot, who had begun to sort out the charts, placing them on an easel.

"This is the evidence," Elliot replied. "I thought putting the facts right in front of Bina's eyes would convince her."

"Elliot, I absolutely forbid this. You are not allowed to interfere in people's lives in this way."

Elliot gave an exaggerated blink, lowered his chin, and looked over his glasses at her. "This from a woman who is attempting to reshape two dozen kids at Andrew Country Day."

Kate bristled. "My work is very different. I'm professionally trained to assess and assist children, some of them in crisis, while they are developing their personalities. I am trying to prevent future problems. You're dealing with adults, you have no training, and you're going to *create* future problems."

"I beg your pardon, Dr. Jameson," Elliot said, "but you forget that I am a professional in my field, and this data is astonishing." He touched the charts for emphasis. "And I'm dealing with adults who have free will. Bina doesn't have to listen to me. She is not a captive audience."

Kate did not like the implication; her kids were not captive, but maybe she was being a little unfair to Elliot. Maybe he was only trying to be helpful, even if it ended in heartbreak.

"Just take a look, Kate," Elliot coaxed.

Kate picked up the first chart. She had no idea if what she saw there was true or not, but if it was accurate, it was fascinating. She looked at the other carefully constructed models, then sighed. Elliot had put in a lot of work, and it was impressive, but she was not going to budge from her veto. Elliot was smart. He knew Bina and the others would be gaping and amazed by the brightly colored charts and graphs, just the way tourists in Times Square were stunned by the lights and ads. But tourists didn't change their lives based on a huge Pepsi ad.

"Kate, it really can't hurt. At the very least, it's a distraction for Bina, and that's what she needs right now. She can't keep herself in her father's office and wait for something to change."

Kate thought of the three or four long messages from Bina on her answering machine each night when she got home. "Okay," she said, "but I want you to play this down, not up. It may be Fun with Math for you, but it's Bina's life. Anyway, even if all of this crazy nonsense is true, a troublemaker like Billy Nolan would never be interested in dating someone as ordinary as Bina Horowitz. So don't get her hopes up."

Elliot nodded vehemently. "No hopes up," he said.

Brice came back out of the kitchen carrying two bottles of white wine. He put one down and popped the cork on the other. "Bottoms up," he said, pouring a glass and handing it to Kate. Just then the buzzer rang. "I'll get it," Brice sang as he strode over to the door and opened it. "Hello, ladies!" he greeted the group.

And there they were, in all their splendor, the Bitches of Bushwick. Barbie came first, wearing a bright pink halter top with a leather jacket over it. She was followed by a nervous but hopeful-looking Bina. Next came Bev and her belly, and then in walked Bunny, who had returned from her honeymoon and had the tan to prove it.

"Hi. You're Bunny the bride," Brice said. "I'm Brice, and that stud muffin over there is Elliot." The girls giggled, except for Bunny, who actually blushed. Without the "breaking in" that had happened at table nine, Kate could see that the adventure wasn't comfortable for her. She had grown up in a strict Italian Catholic home where, Kate was sure, homosexuality was synonymous with sin, perversion, and the molestation of little boys. Brice, sensing her hesitancy but never one for subtleties, threw his arm around Bunny's shoulders. "We didn't have a chance to talk at your wedding. But it was beautiful. Absolutely beautiful!"

He couldn't have said anything better. "Wait till you see the video!" Bunny exclaimed, suddenly ready to bond.

Kate winced. The ordeal of watching that video might be worse than going to the event itself, but Brice was all enthusiasm. "Oh, you *have* to show us. And what a dress!"

"Size six," Bunny said proudly. "Priscilla of Boston."

"I knew it!"

"She got lucky," Barbie told him. "It was a special order, but the bride was pregnant and didn't tell. By the time the dress arrived, well, you can imagine."

"I got it at cost," Bunny told Brice.

The attention seemed to relax her. Soon they were all standing around the buffet, filling their plates and — with the exception of Bev — drinking wine. Kate looked around at them covertly. Bev's belly looked as if it had doubled in size since the wedding. Kate tried to avoid staring at it in horror, although she couldn't escape a twinge of jealousy as she felt her own flat stomach.

Elliot, too, was caught by Bev's very apparent expansion. "Wow," he said to her. "Are you going to go into labor right here, or are you carrying twins?"

"I know, I'm huge and I've got months to go." Bev looked down at her belly and shrugged.

"Remember after graduation how you dieted all summer and were a size four by September?" Bunny asked. She was the group's weight historian and could tell any one of them what they had weighed at any event or moment since they'd met.

"I'm trying to cut back on eating so much," Bev explained to Elliot. "I think I've gained about forty pounds." Despite the confession, she piled her plate with Nova, cream cheese, a poppy *and* a sesame bagel, and, with a final guilty flourish, some herring in cream sauce. "Unless I give birth to a thirty-five-pound baby, I'm gonna be in big trouble," she said, and laughed.

"Do you want a girl or a boy?" Elliot asked her.

"Doesn't matter," Bev said, waddling to the sofa from the buffet, Bina and Bunny right behind her. "Johnny says he just wants it healthy."

"He'll get healthy when he sees your ass after the baby is born," Barbie said, snickering.

Kate never stopped being astonished by the way the women passed over cruel taunts without a ruffled hair. She watched as they sat down and checked out the apartment around them as if they'd just stepped into a den of unimaginable iniquity. It was a big adventure for four girls from Bushwick to finally see the inside of a homosexual couple's apartment — even Bina hadn't really had a chance to look around the last time she was there. Kate could only imagine what they thought they were going to find. And she wasn't going to point out that Bunny's uncle Tony and Barbie's youngest brother were most certainly gay but hadn't come out. Anyway, it must have been reassuring to see that there was nothing terrifying or exotic about Elliot's home — thanks to Brice, it was all done in stylish taste (though the Beanie Babies were a little camp). The situation made Kate smile. She knew how frightening good taste could be to someone from Bushwick.

They all sat on various perches like colorful birds with big mouths. Toucans, maybe, Kate thought. Despite their provincialism (and some morbid curiosity), it was really moving to see that all the girls had shown up for Bina. Kate loved them for that.

Barbie, of course, was the most brazen. She looked around as if she were assessing everything. "How much does a place like this cost in Manhattan?" she needed to know.

"It's a steal," Brice obliged willingly. "It's stabilized. We're still paying only eighteen a month."

"Eighteen dollars a month for rent?" Bina asked in utter amazement. "My grandmother's apartment on Ocean Parkway is rent-controlled, but she pays sixty-six bucks a month."

The better-informed Bunny was not as confused. "Jeez," she spat in disgust, "for eighteen hundred dollars a month, you'd get three bedrooms and a balcony in Brooklyn."

"Honey," Brice replied, "call me crazy, but I'd rather have a closet in Manhattan than a palazzo in Prospect Park."

"I thought you guys were all out of the closet," Barbie said, grinning and obviously pleased with herself.

"Sweetie, some of us were never in it," Brice said. There was silence for a moment.

Almost desperately, Kate spoke first. "Well, isn't this nice?" she chirped, turning to Elliot as if to say "I told you so." "Finally, all of my girlfriends together in one room."

Bina let out a rather nervous giggle in response, but Bev just agreed. "You have a lot of girlfriends, Kate. But then you're a Scorpio. Scorpio women always have lots of girlfriends."

"And lots of boyfriends," Elliot added sotto voce.

"So you have some plan to kill Jack the scumbag?" Barbie asked.

"Not exactly," Elliot told her. He put down his fork, stood up, and self-consciously stepped next to the easel. He looked first to Bina and then back to Kate. He placed one hand on the first chart, turned it over so they could all see it, and said, "As Bina knows, I made an incredible mathematical discovery while we were at Bunny's wedding."

"Like what?" asked Bev.

"Probability," Elliot said. "Some events can be predicted because of constancy and reliability of past data."

"Huh!" Bina said. Kate suppressed a giggle. Poor Elliot.

"This helps us take down Jack the scumbag?" Barbie asked.

"Hey, what good would that do anyone?" Elliot asked. "What if I told you that instead of revenge, I've found a surefire way to get Jack to propose to Bina?" he asked the room. "And marry her."

Bina dropped her coffee spoon, Bev choked on a mouthful of bagel, and Barbie and Bunny began to murmur together appreciatively. Only Kate let out a snort of derision. "Elliot!" she warned. Then she turned to Bina. "Remember, this is just a theory, a suggestion, Bina. It may not be correct. You don't have to pay any attention to it. Personally, I think it's a lot of hocus-pocus."

Elliot looked down at her from his full height. "Kate," he said, "I think we all know your views on magic. So it's a good thing this has nothing to do with it. This is mathematical theory put into practice."

"What's wrong with you, Katie?" Bev asked. "Such a spoilsport."

"What are you actually talking about?" Barbie asked.

Elliot nodded and pointed to the chart and said, "These statistics are . . . well, they are just incredible. But they are absolutely accurate. I've done a bit of research and worked out the probability, and you'll see that even with a differential for the —"

"Is he a college teacher or something?" Bina whispered to Kate.

Kate snorted. "He's an obsessive neurotic gone compulsive."

"I know. Isn't he wonderful?" said Brice, placing his hand over his heart.

Elliot was in his teaching mode and ignored them both. "Remember how Bev and Barbie both said that they had once dated that Billy guy who had just dumped Bunny?" He turned to her. "No offense."

"None taken," Bunny said. "When I dated him I was a size four — and weighed one hundred and sixteen pounds. My personal best."

"Well, we both got dumped by him, too," Bev added.

"Which was just fine with me," Barbie assured everyone. "The guy's a jerk."

"That's right," Elliot said, nodding to Barbie, "and right after that you met Bobby and got married."

"Well, it wasn't right after. It was at least three weeks." Barbie paused, then added, "And Bev got married to Johnny right after she got dumped."

"My Johnny and I had our moons in Venus. It was fated," Bev observed. No one paid any attention to her.

"So at the wedding, Elliot . . . well, began to snoop," Brice explained.

"I collected data," Elliot corrected Brice with dignity.

"Did I tell you about Gina Morelli and Nancy Limbacher, Elliot?" Bev asked, already eager to be part of the plan. "Billy dated and dumped them, too."

"I found that out on my own. Both of them married right after Billy Nolan. They were at Bunny's wedding."

"Sure. I worked with Gina, and Nancy is best friends with my cousin Marie," Bunny said.

"Marie Genetti?" Elliot asked. "Billy dated her, too."

"He dated Marie? You're kidding. She never told me!" Bunny exclaimed.

"So now we know that Billy Nolan has dated and dumped every woman from here to Albany. Who cares?" Kate spat out angrily. She thought of him charming her on the terrace. And to think that she'd been attracted to an idiot like him.

"Bina should, and as her friend, so should you," Elliot told her. "I did some digging, and I made some calls. Everyone this guy drops gets married."

"How did you find that out?" Barbie asked. Kate smiled. As the professional gossip of the group, she must be feeling a bit defensive.

"He pretended he was doing an article for *Jane* magazine," Brice told her proudly.

"You're a regular Columbo," Bev said admiringly.

Elliot laughed and acknowledged Bev's compliment with a slight bow. Then he turned back to his first chart. "Look at this," he said, pointing. "All five of these women dated William Nolan." On the chart were the names of each woman and the date, time, and place of their first encounter with Billy Nolan. "Now here," he said, flying to the next chart, "is a time line that follows the period of each relationship. Please note that where Billy drops out there is a segment of between three point

231

two weeks and four point seven months before each woman marries." The room was silent. Even Kate was momentarily impressed.

"Was the bastard going out with Gina Morelli the same time he was dating me?" Bunny asked.

"From the data I've collected, he only goes out with one woman at a time. Anyway, that doesn't matter," Elliot said. "The point is" — he indicated the first chart — "soon after each woman got dumped by Mr. Nolan, each met or returned to another man — and sometimes, as in Bunny's case, she was introduced to that man by Billy himself. In all cases, that very next man was the one they married." He stopped and looked at Kate and the Bitches with a broad smile, as if his message were perfectly clear.

"Wow, congratulations, Elliot — it's quite an achievement," Bev said, more serious than was necessary.

"Right. Now you qualify as the biggest gossip in all five boroughs," Kate said coldly.

"Yeah. What's the big deal?" Bunny asked. "We all know that Billy Nolan is the biggest player that has ever lived."

"But you didn't know this," Elliot said,

and flipped over a third chart. On it was a row of fourteen names with a column listing the time each had dated Billy and another column with wedding dates beside each name — except two. "It isn't *most* of the women Billy Nolan dates. It's *all* of the women Billy Nolan dates."

The women examined the list.

"Don't you get it?" Elliot asked. "Do you know the statistical likelihood of this phenomenon?" He flipped to his next chart. "I've worked it out with and without the standard deviation, the probability ranges from one in six million three hundred and forty-seven to one in eighty-two million six hundred and forty-three."

Kate wondered about the two out of the fourteen but figured she'd get her chance to debunk all this later.

"I don't get it," Bunny admitted. "I don't think even Billy Nolan could date and dump eighty-two million women. It's just not humanly possible. Are there even that many women in New York?"

"He doesn't have to date eighty-two million women," Barbie told Bunny dismissively, "he just has to date Bina. Right, Elliot?"

"Really? Really, Elliot?" Bina asked, her voice filled with more hope and animation than it had since the afternoon of the manicure.

"Oh, Jesus H. Christ," Kate said, no longer able to control her disgust. She stood up and started to pace around the room. "Elliot, you know I don't approve of this whole scheme. It's just ridiculous."

"Be quiet, Kate," Bev said, "I'm trying to understand this." She narrowed her eyes and looked at Elliot. "You're saying that anyone who dates Billy gets married right afterwards?" she asked.

"Everyone?" Bina asked.

Kate felt she couldn't let this go on. Instead of spending the morning in bed with Michael, then reading the *Times* together and having a nice meal before they parted, she was stuck with this bunch of maniacs and a berserk plan. She never thought any of them would buy it. "It's a bunch of superstitious crap," she told Bina and the rest of them.

"This isn't about superstition," Elliot insisted, sounding hurt. "These are the facts."

Bunny kept staring at the charts and now tried to sound smart. She used to do it in sixth grade to about the same effect. "Are you saying that the odds against Bina ever getting married are about eighty-two million to one unless she dates Billy Nolan?" she asked Elliot.

"Well," Elliot said, pretending to give the ridiculous question some thought, "that's not *exactly* what I'm saying. I can't compute the odds of Bina getting married. I don't have enough data. But the odds are eighty-two million to one in her *favor* if she does date Billy."

Kate saw Bina pale and felt her own face grow warm with anger and agitation. She was about to speak when Barbie stood up and brushed off her skirt.

"Then it's settled," Barbie said. "Bina has to go out with Dumping Billy. That's all there is to it. After all, what has she got to lose?"

Bina stood up, too, but she hesitated before she spoke. "Elliot, I appreciate all the time you must have put in this, but I'm not interested in dating anyone except Jack." Kate watched as tears filled her eyes. "I just want Jack back."

"This is a way to *get* Jack, Bina," Elliot said. "You date Billy, then get dumped, then see Jack and . . . voilà!"

Kate turned to Bina. "This is all ridiculous. I didn't know it was quite *this* insane, but I promised him I'd let him show you —"

"Why is it insane?" Bev asked.

"Well, it's a long shot that we could get Billy to go out with Bina in her current state," Barbie said, then narrowed her eyes speculatively. "But if we did some work on her . . ."

"Just look at the numbers, sweetheart. The numbers don't lie," Brice said to Bina. He took her hand in his, but he was watching Elliot with the look of a proud mother on his face.

Kate was sure that Bina, monogamous for so long, wouldn't consider this nonsense.

"They *all* got married?" Bina asked Elliot in disbelief.

"Yes. Well, to be totally accurate, one joined a convent, and one came out as a lesbian," Elliot confessed, "but both are hooked up, one to God and one to her girlfriend. So that makes fourteen for fourteen."

"Isn't he wonderful?" Brice asked no one in particular.

"He's absolutely nuts," Kate snapped. "Bina, don't even consider it."

"We'd have to time it so that Jack was back at the strategic moment — just after the breakup," Bev said.

"And to be safe, we have to make sure he drops her," Elliot cautioned. "I have no in-

236

dication of what happens to his partner after she dumps him."

Bev and Barbie laughed. "No one dumps him," Barbie said.

"Of course, he's gorgeous," Bev said (it sounded like "Ov cous, he's gowjus"). "But that doesn't explain it. That only explains why he gets women."

"And probably why he dumps them," Elliot said.

"No," Bunny told him. "To be fair, he is always nice, and he seems . . . well, I don't know." She thought for a minute. "Like really disappointed when things don't work out."

Elliot took a deep breath. "I don't really care about his psychology," he told them. "The key question is why women marry right after he leaves them."

Kate wondered, too.

But Bina wasn't listening; she was staring at the charts before her. Kate knew how desperate she was. Elliot, seeing that he had Bina hooked, asked, "Do you want a detailed cross section?"

Kate could see Bina's love for Jack and the longing for him written all over her face. "I don't need one. I'll do it!" Bina exclaimed.

"Bina!" Kate cried, shocked.

"Then it's all settled," Bunny said, and stood up. "I gotta go back to Arnie."

"Well, we're not exactly finished," Barbie said in the tone that had driven fear into many preteen girls in their junior high days. "He doesn't go out with just anyone. He looks for a certain . . . style." She preened for a moment. "Do you think Billy would go out with *Bina?*"

"Barbie!" Kate turned from Bina to Barbie, shocked yet again. Despite the usual cruelty of the girls to one another, this went too far.

"The boy is certainly hot," Brice said to himself, pulling out the Polaroid from the wedding. He put it on the table.

"Very hot," Bev said, also looking at the photo while pretending to fan herself.

"Good point," Bunny agreed. "Maybe Bina would be out of her league."

Before Kate could jump to Bina's defense, her friend took control. "I'm still in the room!" Bina suddenly exploded. "Why are you talking about me like I'm not here?"

"We're sorry, Bina," Kate said, apologizing for the group. She could feel her friend's mortification at having been reduced to a statistic. And for what? All she really wanted was to be with Jack.

"We didn't mean to hurt your feelings, honey," Bev said, and put her arms around her friend as best she could manage.

"Look, no one said you couldn't become Billy's type," Barbie said by way of an apology.

"Right. We only wanted to help, not to hurt," Elliot added.

"And to make it up to you . . ." Brice began to mime a drumroll. "A makeover!"

Once the magic word had been spoken, Kate knew there was no going back.

Chapter Eighteen

Kate sat in her office and tried to put the problems of Bina, Jack, Billy, and what for a moment she was thinking of as "the rest of that nonsense" out of her mind. Bina's makeover and the idiocy of getting Billy to date her was not as important as the problem facing her at the moment. Jennifer Whalen, a pretty and neatly dressed nine-year-old, was sitting in front of her doing what she seemed to do best.

"So my father opens the door to the limousine and Britney Spears steps out. And she came into our building and right up to our apartment. She even had dinner with us. We had meat loaf. And if you don't believe me, she gave me this bracelet." Jennifer pulled the elastic of the bead bracelet she had around her wrist. "See? I have proof."

Kate withheld a sigh. She knew there was no point in discussing this particular lie or any of the other whoppers that Jennifer had told not only her classmates, but also her teachers. The question was why Jennifer needed to lie. Did she crave attention? She was a middle child, with an older sister at Andrew Country Day and a year-old brother at home. Had the baby usurped her position in the family constellation?

Or was it feelings of inferiority? Kate knew that both Jennifer and her sister were receiving financial aid because their family, though well-off by Kate's childhood standards, were only middle-class and could not afford full tuition for both girls. Maybe Jennifer felt inferior to her friends simply because their homes were bigger, their school vacations were often spent in Aspen, the Hamptons, or even Europe, and Jennifer couldn't compete.

The worst-case scenario, of course, was that Jennifer might be showing early signs of a delusional problem. However, as Kate looked at her, she felt that she was studying a healthy, outgoing little girl who doubtless knew the difference between fantasy and reality.

Kate didn't want Jennifer's lies to continue, but neither did she want to argue with her. She had listened quietly without showing much reaction. She could, of course, recommend a therapist for the child, but she and Jennifer had a good rapport. This business was always tricky, but Kate thought of a quote from A. S. Neil: "Sometimes you simply have to trust your instinct with children. Analysis with them is an art, not a science." She decided to take a chance.

"Want to know a secret?" she asked. Jennifer nodded. "I'm going to get married. And I'm going to have a really big wedding. It's going to be in a castle, and Justin Timberlake is coming." Jennifer's eyes opened wide. "He's going to bring *NSYNC, but my sister is really angry because *she* invited the Backstreet Boys, and you can just imagine what would happen if they came, too."

Jennifer's eyes were popping, and she nodded. "I bet they hate each other," she said.

"They do. And they all hate my husband-to-be. Do you know who I'm marrying?"

Jennifer shook her head back and forth, her mouth opened slightly.

"Dr. McKay," Kate said.

Jennifer's face froze. Then Kate watched as doubt, then disbelief, then relief, and even, perhaps, understanding bloomed on it like one of those flowers opening in time-lapse photography. "No way!" Jennifer said.

"Way," Kate insisted, and nodded. "Know what else? We're both going to ride white horses down the aisle of the church."

"No way!" Jennifer repeated more vehemently. Then she started to giggle. "Dr. McKay on a horse!"

Kate laughed, too. Then she paused. "I really like you, Jennifer. You know why?" Jennifer shook her head. "Because you are smart and cute and funny. And you have a great imagination. You have a gift for fiction."

Jennifer frowned. "What does that mean?"

"It means that I think you could write really good stories. Or maybe books. Or maybe movies."

"I could write down a movie?"

"Sure." Kate nodded. "Movies all start from someone writing down a story." She didn't want to start another round of lying. "Not every story is good enough to be a movie, but once you write one down you never know what could happen." She paused, letting the compliments and the idea sink in. "Of course, it isn't easy. Do you think you would like to have some special time with Mrs. Reese?" Joyce Reese was the creative writing teacher for the sixth grade and a friend of Kate's.

"I'm only in fourth," Jennifer said, but

that, of course, added to her enthusiasm.

"That's true," Kate agreed, "but I would say that you could probably write sixth-grade stories. Maybe even eighth-grade stories. If one was in the school magazine, everyone would read it."

Jennifer stared at her. The two of them sat like that for a few moments in silence. Kate could see the child's mind working behind her gray eyes. "Britney Spears didn't come to my house," Jennifer said.

"But it was a good story," Kate told her, keeping her tone neutral. "If you tell it like a story or write it down like one, people would want to hear the next part. They'll think you're special because you can make up really good stories."

"But then they get mad," Jennifer said. "They get mad when it isn't true."

"Did you feel angry at me when I told you about my wedding?"

Jennifer sat for a moment, looking down at her nails. "First I liked it. I thought it was a secret. But then when I knew you were . . . lying . . . I got a little mad," she admitted.

Kate nodded. "That happens when you fool people. They get mad."

Out in the hall, the bell rang. In a moment, they could hear the sound of doors being thrown open and the noise of classes getting out.

"Why don't you come in and visit with me next week? And in the meantime I'll talk to Mrs. Reese."

Jennifer nodded.

"But now, I'm sorry, but you'll have to go or you'll be late for the bus."

Reluctantly Jennifer stood up. "You told a lie," she said.

"Don't tell anyone," Kate whispered. "And especially don't tell Dr. McKay."

Jennifer laughed. "*Nobody* would want to marry him," she said, and marched out of Kate's office.

Kate had just gotten home, thrown her purse onto the sofa, and kicked off her shoes. She hadn't even had a chance to sit down before there was a knock at the door. God, she wasn't in the mood for a visitor! She turned around and opened it. Max stood there, still dressed in his suit and tie, clearly just back from work, though he was not usually home until after dark. He was leaning against her doorway, one arm raised, his head resting on his inner elbow. He must have been away during the last weekend because he had a bit of a tan. It made his blue eyes bluer. "Hi," she said.

"Hi," he returned. "Is Bina here?" he asked, his voice low.

Kate felt a stab of irritation. Since Jack had flown the coop, she'd felt like Bina Central. "No," she snapped. "You can call her at home."

"No, that's a good thing," Max told her in a normal tone. "See, I want to show you something, and . . . well, I don't know if she should see it or not." Kate rolled her eyes, but she let Max take her hand to lead her up the stairs.

His apartment door was open. Inside was the usual requisite bachelor setup: black leather couch, workout equipment, an expensive stereo, and the pile of newspapers that seemed a requirement for all male apartments. Max also, of course, had the latest titanium laptop, and it was that toward which he led her.

"I want you to look at this and tell me what to do," he said. He loosened his tie before he hit a few keys. For one crazy moment, Kate thought he might be asking her opinion about some stock meltdown, but she had never had a share of anything in her life except a dorm room. But instead of charts, graphs, or analysis, the screen filled with a photo. It was Jack, bare-chested, standing on a balcony with a view of a beautiful harbor behind him and an equally beautiful woman next to him.

"Oh, my God," Kate said. "Where did you get this?"

"He e-mailed it to me today," Max said. "Do you think I should show it to Bina?"

"Do you think I should set fire to your hair gel?" Kate asked. The thought of Bina seeing this grinning ass literally made her sick to her stomach. When she'd found out Steven had been cheating on her, she'd been so distraught that she couldn't get out of bed for three days. Bina would just collapse.

Unconsciously, Max smoothed down his wavy hair. "I didn't think so, either," he said. "But, you know, I feel responsible for this. I introduced them and all. . . ."

Kate felt her irritation melt away. She had always thought of him as a stereotype, a kind of Wall Street/jock/yuppie clone. When he'd had girlfriends for any length of time, he hadn't seemed particularly committed or passionate. Now, however, his concern seemed genuine and moving. She began to feel a new warmth toward him and a little guilt over how she may have misjudged him.

"I know Jack, and he is a one-woman guy." He shook his head. "I saw Bina. I know what this has done to her, and I told her that he was just talk. I mean, who would think Jack . . ." Max stared at the picture displayed on the screen. Kate could feel him getting lost in it for a moment. "She is very pretty," he murmured.

"Well, I hope they're very happy together," Kate said tartly. "I'm sure they share common goals and interests."

"Hey, he isn't married!" Max protested. "Even Jack isn't that stupid."

"How do you know?" Kate asked.

"Read the e-mail," Max said, and displayed the message from Jack.

What a place! The views are incredible, electronics are cheap, and the women are incredible and cheap. You gotta come! Money is king here, and the dollar rules.

Kate didn't bother to read any more. "He is disgusting," she said. She turned away and started to walk out of the apartment.

"So you don't think I should show this to Bina? Right?"

"Right, Einstein," Kate said, and ran down the stairs to her own place. As she walked in her door, the phone began to ring. She grabbed it and saw Elliot's number on the caller ID. "Shoot me in the head," she said into the receiver.

"And a good evening to you, too," Elliot said. "I didn't catch you during dinner, I hope, but Brice and I are getting together with Bina on Saturday morning for the big renovation. Are you in?"

Kate hesitated for a moment, torn between the news from upstairs and her disapproval of the whole scheme. Wasn't a makeover a kind of lie not much different from little Jennifer's stories? It was a visual way of saying you were someone different. But Jack's e-mail had shocked her. "I'm in," she said.

It was only after she hung up that she realized her commitment would mean canceling Michael. They spent every Friday night together and each Saturday. After Steven's unreliability, Kate appreciated the fact that Michael saw her every Wednesday, Friday, and Saturday night. During the week, they usually went to a movie and stayed at her house afterward. They alternated places on the weekends.

Perhaps Michael was a little too routinized, because he always seemed upset when she had to change their schedule and apologetic when he — rare though it was

— had to do the same. Well, Kate would regret the pleasant, leisurely Saturday they would lose, but perhaps she could persuade him to work while she was off with her friends instead of on his usual Sunday night. She picked up the phone again and, feeling uneasy, dialed Michael's number.

Chapter Nineteen

Two days later, the Bitches, accompanied by Brice and Elliot, were walking down Fifth Avenue. They had all insisted on being a part of Bina's makeover.

"All I can say is it's about time," Barbie said. "You're starting to look like an Orthodox Jew."

"It's the hair," Brice agreed. "It looks like a bad wig."

"Brice!" Elliot warned before Kate could.

"The truth hurts," Bev said, patting Bina's arm and then her own tummy.

"I think I need to, uh, go to the bathroom," Bina said. "I'm so nervous. Jack liked my hair."

"Not enough," Barbie said.

"Don't worry. They have a ladies' room at Louis," Brice told her, and took her into a marble lobby. Kate shook her head. The whole crew knew she disapproved, but they ignored her except Brice, who turned to her and said, "You know, while we're here

Pierre can cut your hair, too."

"I don't think so," Kate snapped. She loved her hair long. So had Steven, and so did Michael. It was sexy and easy to put up if she had to. Now, completely offended, she joined the party as they got onto the elevator to go up to the fourteenth-floor salon overlooking St. Patrick's Cathedral.

"Wow!" Bina said as she stared out at the skyline. "It looks almost as good as Epcot." Kate rolled her eyes.

Brice didn't bother with the view. "Pierre, please," he told the woman at the desk. "Tell him it's Brice and we have a cut with him and a consultation with Louis." Bev, Barbie, and Bunny looked at one another, obviously impressed. All those years of reading *Allure* magazine had familiarized them with Louis Licari, the god of hair color. And Brice had just called him by his first name. "Now c'mon. I think we can do everything your head needs here," he instructed Bina as he clutched her hand and escorted her to the stylist's chair.

"Except get it examined," Kate muttered. She looked over to Elliot, but he just shrugged. Barbie, Bunny, and Bev were right behind them. Kate was delighted that Bina was getting so much help and attention. It was just what she needed at a time like this. But, oddly, she also felt a bit of envy. She had never asked for help when her crisis with Steven had taken place, not that the Bitches would have been much help.

Bina spent four hours at the salon. While they were there, Barbie got a good cut, Bev had a facial, and Bunny got a massage — as a belated wedding present from Brice and Elliot. Kate merely had a manicure and didn't even care for the color she'd selected. But it was Bina who was transformed. Her hair had been lightened a bit around her face, and then streaks of ash blond made the dark brown of her natural color glow. Kate was stunned by the subtle artistry of it. The style, a chin-length, undercut masterpiece, made it seem as if Bina had a head of moving light, a kind of nimbus of hair. Even Kate had to admit the transformation was remarkable.

"Holy haircut, Batman," was all Elliot said as he looked up from the papers he was marking. Bina giggled and shook her head from side to side. The nimbus moved like a saintly glow in a chapel. The receptionist and two cashiers oohed and aahed, as they were paid to do. Barbie, Bev, and Bunny kept cooing like demented pigeons. For an insane moment, Kate wondered if she should get her own head shorn. Maybe a haircut, a few highlights, and a makeup makeover would . . . She took a deep breath. Then she got a grip.

"Okay," Brice said. "We did the drapes. Now on to the upholstery." He looked at Bina's outfit, an old Gap blouse and a charity skirt. "First stop, Prada!" he called, and the entire group headed outside and into two taxis.

Before Bina even had a chance to take note of the ambience or the price tags, she was standing in front of a three-way mirror while a saleslady pinned up the hemline on a skirt that, in Kate's opinion, was already far too short and far too tight. It draped to one side, exposing a thigh. "Do you really think this is *me?*" Bina asked the admiring group.

Barbie backed away from Bina and gave her an approving once-over. Kate remembered squirming under those looks back in tenth grade. Barbie liked what she saw. "Isn't it nice to wear something red? It's the new beige, you know," she confided.

Kate didn't have a clue as to what that meant, but she thought that Bina looked ridiculous. But that didn't stop them from buying the skirt and moving on to

Victoria's Secret. Brice picked up a Wonderbra and then handed it to Bina.

"Here you go, honey," he said. "Every girl needs a little support."

"Don't forget this." Bunny handed her a lacy black thong.

Bina looked down at the bra and dental floss in her hand. "I'm not wearing these." She lifted up the thong and held it two ways. "I . . . I don't even know how to wear this," she admitted. "Besides, I'm not sleeping with him. My underwear isn't relevant." She looked at Elliot. "The charts didn't say I had to have sex with him, did they? Because I'm not doing that."

"Honey, it's not about having sex, it's about feeling sexy," Brice said. "And if you feel sexy, you'll look sexy to others. Right, Elliot?"

"I plead the Fifth," Elliot responded.

"Bina, you're a Capricorn," said Bev, "and trust me, they need all the help they can get when it comes to attracting men. See what it does for you."

Bina disappeared into the dressing room and came out with her eyes and breasts bulging. She'd put her blouse on to step out of the dressing room, but she hadn't buttoned the top two buttons. Barbie leaned forward and unbuttoned the third.

"Now, that's a nice rack," she said.

Bina stared at herself in the mirror. Then she turned to Kate. "I wish Jack could see me now," she said. Kate's breasts, unexposed, felt a stab of sympathy for her friend. Cheerful little Bina, a cupcake of a girl, now looked more like a Pop-Tarts pastry and still she thought only of Jack. She was doing all of this because of him, and Kate honestly couldn't decide if it was an act of self-mutilation or love. She doubted that any of this would make a man like Billy Nolan want Bina. After all, she was still "Bina, the good girl from Ocean Avenue." At least, she decided, it gave Bina something else to concentrate on, and who knew? Looking like a hot tamale, she might meet someone else. One thing Kate did know was that while she could go on without Michael and even without marriage to anyone, Bina always had only one goal: marriage and children, preferably to and by Jack.

"Hey. Turn around," Bev said. "Let's see if there's a panty line."

"How can there be?" Bina asked. "There's hardly any panty." She turned as directed. "This is so uncomfortable," she said.

"Beauty has to hurt," Bunny told her.

At Tootsie Plohound, Bina once again followed Barbie's directives and bought her first pair of serious "fuck me" sandals.

"You need a low-cut top," Bev said, taking inventory of their progress to date. "I mean, you've got 'em, and you've lifted 'em, might as well show 'em. And you've always had a small waist, so we should find something tight." She looked down at her own stomach. The Lycra she was wearing couldn't be any tighter without crushing the fetus, Kate thought.

"Yes, that would complete the outfit," Brice agreed.

As the seven of them walked down the busy West Broadway sidewalk, Kate had to marvel at how seamlessly Elliot and Brice seemed to join in with her Brooklyn friends. She'd avoided this for years and never introduced Bina and the others to Rita, her friend from graduate school, or Maggie, a choreographer she'd met in her exercise class. Somehow she hadn't thought a mix like that would work as smoothly, and she suspected it was because Brice and Elliot were observing all this as they participated.

But while everyone else seemed to be enjoying themselves, Kate was feeling distinctly uncomfortable. She had worked diligently for as long as she could remember to change her style, her look, her vocabulary . . . well, almost everything that she had believed didn't reflect who she was or wanted to be. She thought she had succeeded in creating a unique persona. Hers, she felt was valid. Now, watching Bina's instant transformation, she wondered if it wasn't valid as well, even if it had been overseen by others. After all, Kate had made all of the changes to herself based, in part, on what others — even if they were people in magazines or strangers she'd observed in Manhattan — had shown her.

As Elliot led the way to hail yet another pair of cabs, Brice took stock. "Give me half an hour in Make Up For Ever and I'll have you looking like a queen," he promised.

A look of horror came over Bina's face. "I'm not changing my makeup," she protested as the cab pulled out into the traffic.

"You have to *wear* makeup if you want to *change* makeup," Bunny said sharply. She reached into her purse and pulled out a lipstick tube. "Just try a little of this."

"Oh, leave her alone!" Kate begged. She wondered what all the criticism and change was doing to Bina's self-esteem. But Bina took the tube and applied it. It was awful — it made her look like Mrs. Horowitz at a funeral.

"I don't think red is her color," Kate objected, and then realized she had now added to the critique.

"I agree with you there," Brice said from the front seat beside the driver. He handed Bina a tissue. "I see you more in a sizzling salmon."

By the time they were ready to head home, Bina had charged more on her credit cards in one day than she ordinarily spent in three months. Kate was exhausted but happy to see that Bina finally seemed to be enjoying herself, even if it was over silly things and a harebrained scheme. It was the first day she had paid more attention to herself than Jack since he'd left. Elliot helped Bev waddle up the steps of Kate's building.

"A fashion show!" Brice demanded once they were inside. Barbie, Bunny, and Bev added their chorus, and so did Kate, a little reluctantly. Having all of them in her living room felt not just crowded but claustrophobic. It was a clash of cultures and sexual orientation in the tiny space that was, in a way, sacred to her. But Kate was the only one who seemed disoriented. Bev had her feet up, her hands over her belly, Barbie sat primly in the rocker, Bunny stood in front of the fireplace, glancing every so often at her honeymoon tan in the mirror that hung over the mantel, and Brice was busy going through the bags, while Elliot just sat back on the sofa, smiling to himself.

Bina took the shopping bags into Kate's bedroom and, a few minutes later, returned completely transformed. There was a moment of silence. Kate was shocked. In a single day, Bina had changed literally from head to toe, and she could barely recognize the hot little number pirouetting in front of them. She thought of Billy Nolan and the look he had given her out on the terrace. Would a man who had approved of her style and looks want a woman arrayed the way Bina was?

"Wow! You look great!" Bev said, breaking the silence.

Then Elliot gave an excellent wolf whistle, and Barbie, Brice, and Bunny began to applaud. Kate joined in. "Okay, so now all we have to do is bring you over to Billy and serve you up on a platter," Elliot said.

"How?" Bina asked, as if playing the

trussed fowl on a plate came naturally.

"We go to his place of business," Elliot said, "the Barber Bar in Williamsburg. Then we —"

"Is that where he works?" Kate interrupted. Elliot ignored her and laid out the time, the rendezvous spots, the assault on the watering hole, and all the rest as if he were the Iron Duke planning an invasion.

"Now, not that you can't do it, but let me come over and do a touch-up to your hair and makeup next weekend," Brice said. "And I'll have a surprise for you."

"I'll hafta be surprised later," Bev said. "I need to get home for my Johnny."

"Sure, Bev," Barbie said. "Bunny, are you in?"

"Sure," Bunny said.

Kate looked at her and wondered if Bunny had enjoyed her honeymoon, especially after . . . after Billy. Then she wondered if she'd like to go on a "honeymoon" with Michael. They had spent one weekend at the Jersey shore, which had been pleasant. Two weeks, though . . .

Kate brought her focus back to the party that was breaking up. "We'll see you all later," Barbie told them. "Oh, Bina, I'm so excited for you. Good clothes open all doors." Kate tried not to laugh. How had

Barbie's mother known in advance how to name her so accurately?

There were many kisses and hugs, and then the three women disappeared out the front door.

Bina was left with Brice and Elliot, who were walking her to the subway. At last Kate was left alone. She wondered what Dr. and Mrs. Horowitz would say when Bina walked in the door. Mrs. Horowitz had a mild heart condition; maybe she should call ahead to prepare her.

It wasn't until Kate was in bed, just at the edge of sleep, that she wondered again what she would look like after a makeover. Then she closed her eyes and slept — poorly — for the rest of the night.

Chapter Twenty

Kate sat in her office across from two identical twin boys wearing identical green corduroys and white T-shirts, each with the same picture of a *Tyrannosaurus rex* clawing across his chest. Each had a name tag stuck to his shirt — one reading "James" and the other "Joseph." Kate was perched on the front of her desk purposely, to appear to tower over the two small third graders. The three of them had been talking for a while already, and Kate thought she'd cleared up the situation.

"Now, I am going to take you back to Mrs. Gupta's class, James," she said, pointing at one of the boys — the one who was wearing the "Joseph" name tag. "And you, Joseph, are to go back to Mrs. Johnson's," she said sternly to the other boy. "Where each of you belongs," she added.

The Reilly twins were good boys, well behaved and intelligent. But they had been assigned separate classes this year with the consent of their parents, and since the separation, they had developed a bad habit of fooling not only their classmates but their teachers and even Dr. McKay about their identities. They switched at will, but when Kate suggested to their parents that the third graders might be better off if they dressed individually instead of in matching clothing, they had insisted that it was up to the boys. And the boys still wanted to dress alike.

Lately, the mischief had escalated, but Kate felt her talk about trust and fooling people had penetrated into the strange and interesting world of twinship. "So we're agreed?" she asked.

Just then the phone rang. Kate turned her back to the twins and reached for the receiver. "Dr. Jameson," she answered.

"Dr. Jameson? This is Dr. Bina Horowitz. I'll be at your office ready for our conference tomorrow at six. I've been told we have to consult with Dr. Brice first," Bina said.

"No one is listening in, Bina," she told her friend. Years of eavesdropping by her mother on the extension had made Bina paranoid. "Come on over for Operation Ridiculous. I'll be there at five. Gotta go. I'm working."

Kate hung up and turned back to the

twins. "I want the two of you to exchange your name tags now," she said. They nodded, peeled off the sticky-backed strips, and handed them to each other contritely. Her phone rang again. She sighed and turned her back on the twins, who quickly retraded name tags and seats.

"A Dr. Michael Atwood is here to see you," Louise, the secretary from the front office, informed Kate in her nasal voice.

"Thanks, I'll be right out," she said, and cradled the receiver. This was unexpected. Michael was nothing if not a creature of habit. Kate wondered what had prompted such a spontaneous visit.

Kate's mind was so preoccupied with these thoughts that she didn't notice the twins' subterfuge. "Remember," she said to them absently, "it isn't just a trick to switch places. It's unkind to fool people. And after you fool them, they won't trust you when you want them to. Understand?" Normally, she wouldn't have repeated herself, but she was a little thrown by this surprise and was anxious to hear what Michael had to say.

The twins nodded innocently. She hopped off her desk and took each boy by the hand. She led them out the door and down the hall. Michael was standing at the far end. He gave her a big, if somewhat sheepish, smile, which Kate did not acknowledge. Instead she stopped in front of a classroom door and nodded for "James" to go in. "Joseph" let go of her other hand, gave her a triumphant smile, and raced to another door on the opposite side of the hall.

Only then did Kate smile back and walk up to Michael. "Nice surprise," she said to reinforce his spontaneous behavior. "What are you doing here?"

"I thought I'd see you in action. Very stern." He smiled. "You're such a natural with kids."

"Thanks," Kate replied. She wondered — just for a moment — if he ever thought of her as the mother of his children, but then she stopped herself. It was too early for that.

"You almost ready to go?" he asked. "Do you mind that I dropped by?"

"Not at all," Kate said. "I like it." And she did.

"I have something else I wanted to show you before tonight," Michael said, reaching into his briefcase. He pulled out an academic journal with a bit of a flourish.

"Oh, Michael! Your article!" He had been working on this piece for months. He had even gone into the field for research. It meant a lot to him and to his career. Kate was delighted for him.

"Hot off the press from the University of Michigan's *Journal of Applied Sciences*," he said proudly.

Kate gave him a big hug. "I'm so pleased for you," she said. "What a great surprise!" She took the journal and opened it to the article. He had already marked the page with a bright red sticker. She smiled at that. There were things about him that were . . . surprisingly childlike. It was endearing.

They walked back to her office. "That's the very first copy," he told her. "I thought as soon as you were done here we could go out for a drink and then maybe dinner." She smiled at him and nodded. "I'm looking forward to our weekend," he said, and he put his arm around her and nuzzled her neck. She felt his stubble tickle her and giggled, just as Dr. McKay appeared at the door.

"Excuse me," he said.

Michael pulled away, and Kate did her best not to look like a guilty schoolgirl. In fact, she found herself having to suppress a smile, since Dr. McKay's face clearly showed his confusion as well as his disapproval. She could imagine him trying to decide whether she was two-timing Elliot or had moved on, slutlike, to a new man. Since it wasn't his business, she smiled at him. "Yes, Dr. McKay?"

"There seems to be a problem with the Reilly twins," Dr. McKay told her. Kate could see him trying to keep his eyes off of Michael.

"I know," she told him. "I had them in my office and we had a talk about it. Dr. McKay, I would like to introduce Dr. Michael Atwood."

Dr. McKay nodded curtly in Michael's general direction, then turned back to Kate. "I know you saw them," he told her, "but apparently they pulled a switcheroo again."

"Oops," Kate said. "I guess I'll have to do some more in-depth work with them," she told him.

"I guess you will." Dr. McKay turned and disappeared.

Michael looked at Kate. " 'Oops'?" he asked. "Is that a Freudian or a Jungian term?"

Kate had to laugh, though she felt some embarrassment and concern. Well, she would deal with it on Monday. Now she had to deal with her changed plans for the weekend.

As they walked out of the school and passed the playground, Kate took Michael's hand. "I'm so glad you came to the school," she said. "It gives us some extra time together." Michael nodded and smiled. So much for the setup, Kate thought. "The thing is, Michael, I have to go out tomorrow night."

"Tomorrow night? But it's Saturday."

"I know. But it's Bina . . ."

"Oh. Bina."

"It will just be for a few hours," Kate told him.

"A few hours on Saturday night," Michael said, and Kate could hear the reproach in his voice.

"I'm sorry," she said. "It's not going to be fun. I just have to." As she voiced the words, she felt annoyed with herself and him. She didn't have to apologize. Why did she feel so guilty? It was a small change, and it wouldn't hurt him to learn to be a little more flexible.

Michael nodded, then looked down at his shoes for a moment. Kate watched him adjust, and then he put his hand in his pocket, pulled it out, and opened his fist. There, nestled in the palm of his hand, were two shiny keys on a new key ring. "Well," he said, "I'm glad I got these for you. It'll make Saturday more convenient. You can let yourself in to my place."

Kate took the keys as if they were a piece of jewelry. Indeed, exchanging keys was the equivalent of what getting pinned had been decades ago. It was a sign of trust and commitment. "Oh, Michael," she said, taking the keys. She kissed him, then realized that she would now have to give her keys to him. She also realized that she didn't really like the idea.

The next evening, a guilty Kate and a new, hot, trendy Bina met Elliot and Brice at Kate's apartment to do a hair and makeup touchup and begin their trek into Brooklyn. Kate looked down at her own simple blue knit dress — short, but with a turtleneck — and felt distinctly under-dressed, though she knew it was flattering. Steven had liked it. Then she reminded herself that this was about Bina, not her. Billy meant nothing to her.

"This is even better than that trip to Nevis last fall," Brice said. "The cultures of indigenous people have always fascinated me."

Kate cleared her throat to catch Brice's attention and gave Bina a sideways glance. Bina, however, was too absorbed in trying to learn to walk in the "fuck me" sandals to notice Brice's comment. Brice, taking pity on Bina's poor soul, not to mention poor soles, cocked his head and said, "Think up, dear. Lift! Lift!"

Bina jerked her shoulders up higher, and in just a moment the look of total concentration on her face passed into a smile. She took a few tentative steps, then walked around Kate's small living room almost confidently. "Hey! Wow!" she exclaimed. "Thanks, Brice. That really works."

Kate couldn't resist. "Brice," she asked, "where did you learn about walking in stilettos?"

"Hey, is there a party going on?"

The voice, muffled by the door but clearly Max's, stopped the conversation. Elliot, closest to the entrance, reached out and turned the knob. Max, with his dry cleaning hooked over his shoulder and a bag of takeout in his other hand, was staring across Kate's living room at Bina. His eyes moved up and down, and Kate watched as both hands opened in surprise and the takeout and plastic-wrapped dry cleaning fell to the floor. For a moment, despite the spills, Max couldn't pull his eyes away. "Bina?" he asked. "Is that you?" Then, as if waking from a spell, he looked down, flushing with embarrassment. He crouched to pick up the hangers while Elliot went for the plastic containers of what looked like Chinese food. Fortunately, they hadn't spilled their contents.

"Hi, Max," Bina said. Kate had to turn away from the wreckage in the hallway because she could hardly believe it was Bina who had managed to pack so much flirtatiousness into the two syllables simply with her tone. In all the years she had known her, Kate had never heard a coy sentiment escape Bina's lips. But there was definitely something new, some come-hither timbre, packed into her words. Suddenly Kate felt that perhaps Bina could manage to nail a date with Billy Nolan.

"Here's your dinner," Elliot said cheerfully to Max, handing the bag back to him. "Gotta go."

Kate grabbed her purse and ushered Bina out the door behind Brice's broad back. Unfortunately, she had to stop to lock the door, and in the moment it took her to do so, Max, still immobilized, asked Bina, "What happened to you?"

Bina opened her mouth, but before she could put her sandaled foot in it, Brice intervened. "Only I and her hairdresser know for sure. Toodles." He took Bina's hand and led her to the stairs.

As Kate followed them, she turned and saw Max, still frozen, above her. "Don't worry. It wasn't Bina," she told him. "It's Bina's evil twin."

The taxi had sped across the bridge and now seemed lost in Brooklyn. "Do you know where this Barber Bar is?" Kate asked.

"Sure," Elliot said. "We'll stop right here. It's just a block or two, and we're meeting the others on the corner. I need some time to coach Bina." Turning to her, he said, "Now remember, if you want this to work, you have to remember LAID."

Kate sighed. "If that's a requirement, we may as well go home now. Bina already made it clear that she's not going to sleep with that man."

"I thought I didn't have to go to bed for this to work," Bina whined. "I love Jack and don't —"

"Oh, calm down, both of you," Elliot interrupted. "Not *laid*, LAID. L-A-I-D," he spelled. "God, I hate acronyms. They're so military and butch. Anyway, it stands for lick, arouse, ignore, and disturb."

"What am I supposed to lick, Elliot?" Bina asked him, her voice tentative.

"Your lips," Elliot answered.

"And that's all you lick, missy!" Kate added.

"And that will arouse him?" Bina frowned. "And what do I ignore?"

"Him!" Elliot answered, as if to say, "Uh, duh!"

"And why?" Kate demanded, not liking this acronym at all. She was only afraid that Billy would ignore Bina and the entire plan would fall apart.

"Because he obviously has intimacy issues," Elliot explained, turning to Kate with exasperation. "God! You're the shrink, not me."

"I don't get it," Bina admitted.

"If you ignore him, he won't be afraid of you," Elliot said. "And if he's not afraid, he'll ask you out again. We just have to get past the two-point-seven-month requirement."

"Fine," Bina said good-naturedly. "Then what?"

"Disturb," Elliot answered.

"That should be easy," Kate told them. "Just tell him why we're doing this. I think Billy Nolan would find this whole idea very disturbing."

Elliot ignored Kate. "Try to be just disturbing enough to be a challenge, but not

274

challenging enough to be a turnoff. You get it?" he asked.

"I — I think so," Bina stammered.

"Well, come on, kids," Brice said as the cab pulled over to the curb. "The Bitches and Billy are waiting!" He looked at them and started to laugh. "This is a little like the Osbournes visiting Sesame Street."

The cab had pulled up to the subway stop at Bedford Street, where they had all agreed to meet. Bev and Barbie were already there. Bev was looking *very* pregnant, while Barbie appeared to have raided the closet of a fifteen-year-old girl.

"I haven't had a night out with the girls in I don't know how long!" Bev squealed.

"Me either. Biological girls, at least," Elliot said, looking lovingly at Brice, who had immediately gotten into a "deep" conversation with Barbie about hemlines.

"We're going to meet Bunny at the bar," Bev told them.

"Isn't she newly married?" Kate asked in disbelief. "They're barely back from their honeymoon. Doesn't she want to spend her weekend with Arnie?" Once the words were out of her mouth, she realized how her new culture was colliding with her old.

"Hey, she just got married to him and finished their honeymoon. How much do you expect?" Bev asked.

Kate had to smile. The gang had a very split but pragmatic view of marriage: that it was necessary to have but easy to ignore. The girls hung with the girls, and the guys hung with the guys.

Now, however, as she looked at her motley crew, she began once again to have serious doubts about the whole expedition. Quietly she pulled Bina away from the rest of the group. "You don't have to do this, you know," she said in a near whisper.

"Kate," Bina began, "after I've dedicated years of my life to him, he wants to explore his singleness. Who does he think he is? Ponce de León?" She looked over at Bev — more specifically, Bev's swelling belly. "Neither of us has found the fountain of youth. Don't you worry about your biological clock?"

Elliot, having overheard the entire conversation, chose this moment to break in. "Like every modern girl," he said, putting his arm around Kate, "Kate has had her eggs frozen for future reference."

"You have?" Bina said in awe.

"Really?" Barbie joined in.

"Don't listen to him. He's crazy," Kate

told them as if his nonsense didn't embarrass her, although a telltale blush was tingeing her cheeks. "Anyway, where the hell is this place?" she asked, refocusing attention on the task at hand.

"I think we turn down at the next corner." Bev indicated a side street. "Bunny gave me these directions. I know it's here somewhere." They turned the corner. "There should be a barber's pole —"

"There it is!" Brice pointed down the block to a barely visible red-, blue-, and white-striped pole, and they all walked toward it.

Chapter Twenty-one

"Since I'm supposed to meet Billy here, I'm buying." Bina's voice cut through Kate's thoughts. "What's everybody drinking? Beers?"

"I'll help," Kate offered. "The rest of you see if you can find us a table. And if we're not back in ten minutes, send a search party."

Kate led Bina through the crowd to the bar. "Try to get Billy's attention," she said. She could see him down at the end of the bar. His white shirt emphasized both his wide shoulders and his tan. Kate wondered briefly if he was so vain that he went to a tanning parlor, but there wasn't time for much reflection. "Call him," she told Bina.

"Call him what?" Bina asked.

Unfortunately, at that moment a different bartender, older, balding, and with a beer belly, approached them from the other end of the bar. "What'll it be, ladies?"

"Omigod!" Bina whispered to Kate. "That's not him."

"Great pickup line," Kate told Bina. Turning to the bartender, she said, "Thanks anyway, we're just looking."

Kate did a quick scan of the crowd at the bar. It was clear that it was far busier at Billy's end and that a gaggle of girls had monopolized the stools. A younger man had crouched under the bar top and began taking drink orders. She grabbed Bina and pulled her through the crowd to the other end of the room, and then, mostly by pushing and a couple of shoulder moves, she got the two of them right up to the bar again, this time at the right place.

Waiting to be served, Kate sighed. She felt way too old for the bar scene. Did that mean she was getting old at thirty-one? At least this place was a little more imaginative than most, she had to admit, looking around. The old barber chairs, obviously restored, were still screwed into the black-and-white marble floor, and the bar, a dark mahogany, was backed by what must have been the original mirror and shelves of the barbershop. Among the vodkas and malt Scotches lined up, there were also antique shaving cups and old bottles of hair tonic, aftershave, and the like.

The place had obviously been expanded from the original barbershop. Aside from the bar and the row of chairs where people clustered, there were banquettes along the far wall and tables and booths in the back. The noise was deafening, like screams of laughter in a subway tunnel, and Kate thanked God that she had chosen not to bring Michael. The scene was so . . . outer boroughs.

Bina looked behind Kate. "Omigod! It's really him."

Kate kept her back to the bar, facing away from Billy and toward Bina. "Yep. Elvis has not left the building. Get on my left and get his attention," she commanded, hoping it would work.

"What comes first?" Bina asked desperately. "The lick or the annoy?"

"Just call his name and order our beer," Kate told her, turning toward the bar to help her. Billy, his teeth as white as his shirt, his hair more golden than Kate remembered, finished pouring a drink for another customer. She gave Bina an elbow poke. "Say something."

"Billy! Here," Bina gasped. Perhaps he heard the urgency in her voice, because he came right over.

"What'll it be, ladies?" he asked, flashing his perfect Crest commercial smile. Kate turned away, but it was too late. Billy looked straight into her face, and she didn't think it was her imagination that she saw his eyes widen in recognition. She elbowed Bina again.

"Two pitchers of Shirley Temples and a beer," Bina sputtered, and then flushed bright red.

"Better line, but not effective," Kate said softly to Bina, who had apparently frozen with an exaggerated smile, her eyes bulging.

Billy narrowed his eyes for a moment and searched Kate's face, but Kate was careful to keep hers perfectly blank. "Is this for a whole table of designated drivers and one drunk?" he asked, grinning. He ignored Bina's embarrassed giggle and looked directly at Kate.

"It's two pitchers of beer and one Shirley Temple," Kate replied, not as amused.

Billy wouldn't take his eyes off Kate. "At the risk of sounding like a cliché," he began, "haven't we met before?"

"I think you met my friend Bina. At Bunny and Arnie's wedding," Kate said. "Bina, this is Billy." She noticed how Billy did not even look in Bina's direction, but rather kept his gaze on her. Her face felt hot beneath his stare.

"Nice to meet you," Billy said to Bina

without so much as a nod in her direction. "But you and I," he said, still looking intently at Kate, "we met —"

"Bina lives here in Brooklyn, too," Kate interrupted, pulling her eyes away from him and focusing on her friend.

"Oh, yeah? Nearby?" Billy asked, glancing over at Bina for the first time.

"Well, kind of. In Park Slope," Bina replied much too anxiously.

Billy began to pour the two pitchers of beer. "Hey, there's a big difference between Park Slope and Williamsburg, Reina."

"Bina, her name is Bina," Kate snapped.

Billy shrugged and handed over the tray with the drinks on it. Kate took the tray and hustled Bina to the table where the rest of the group was sitting.

"That was him!" Bina exclaimed.

"Who?" Elliot said slyly.

"*Him!*" Bina squealed.

"Mel Gibson?" Bev asked, playing along.

"Bill Clinton?" Barbie joined in.

"It was Billy," Kate said in an aside to Elliot, "but he didn't have the ightest-slay interest-ay." Elliot grimaced. It was becoming clear that Bina was going to need all the help she could get. "Well, here are your pitchers, ladies," Kate said, handing over the tray. "I'm going to run to the bathroom."

She made her way through the crowd to the tiny one-stall bathroom. It was surprisingly clean. She had just entered when she heard two voices just outside the door.

"Hey, did you see the way that redhead looked at me?" said the first. It was a thick voice, raspy and guttural: the older bartender, the one Kate heard customers call Pete. "Man, she's hot! Did you see the eyes on that girl? And she had two other beautiful things." He snickered suggestively.

"What redhead?" This voice Kate recognized immediately: Billy Nolan.

"The one who carried off those two pitchers of beer."

"She wasn't looking at you," Billy said with thinly veiled contempt.

"You know," Pete grunted. "You do all right for yourself, but sometimes you miss the subtleties. She wants me."

Kate heard Billy groan, and then the two were quiet for a moment. Billy's voice broke the silence. "Susie was in earlier."

"Shit!" cried Pete. "And I missed her. She was so fucking hot. Why'd you dump her?"

"I dunno," Billy answered. "Anyway, she comes in and tells me that —"

"Don't tell me," Pete interrupted, "she's engaged, right?"

"How did you know?" Billy asked.

"Billy — buddy, look. I don't know what it is that you do to these women, but once you date them they become like marriage roach motels. Other guys check in, but they don't check out."

Kate was finished, and she really didn't want to hear any more. But even as she flushed, washed her hands, and hit the dryer button, she could hear the men still talking.

"Usually it wouldn't bother me," Billy said, "but I was at Arnie's wedding a few weeks ago and I realized that I'm like the last single guy out of all my friends."

"You're a bartender," said Pete. "Bartenders are supposed to be single. You're not the marrying type. Besides, what's happening with Tina?"

Kate had heard enough. She opened the door quickly, hoping to get back to the table before Billy and his friend were finished with their break, but she was moving too late. Just as she stepped into the passage beyond the rest room door, she found herself face-to-face with Billy Nolan.

"Whoa! Slow down, Red," he said as Kate tried to continue on her way without speaking. She ignored him. The hallway was narrow, and a guy pushed past them and nudged her up against Billy. He steadied her with a hand on each shoulder and looked at the passing customer. "Hey, watch it!" he shouted. He looked again at Kate. "*Je pense . . .*," he stopped. "*Je n'oubliez pas*," he said, slipping into French.

What was it with this guy and French? Kate wondered. "I haven't forgotten you, either," she admitted, but as a throwaway line.

"Right. We discussed existential issues. I always like to combine Sartre and weddings," he added, and Kate couldn't resist smiling, though she tried. This guy was impossibly self-assured. How could she entice him to date Bina? "So what are you doing on this side of the river?" Billy asked.

"Having a drink with my friends in that corner," Kate said, pointing to their table. Just then Pete tapped Billy on the shoulder from behind.

"Yo, Bill," he said. "Forget the conquest. There're customers waiting."

Kate blushed against her will, angry at the thought of being considered "a conquest." "See ya," she said, and forced herself to give him an enticing smile.

She returned to their table, hoping the

hook had worked. Sure enough, just moments after their glasses were empty and Barbie had refreshed Bina's lip gloss, Billy appeared at their table, a pitcher of beer in each hand. "Welcome to the Barber Bar," he said, and put down the pitchers. He smiled at Kate. "So, you weren't lying about your posse at the wedding."

All eyes at the table focused on Kate. She hadn't mentioned their little pas de deux on the terrace to anyone. Now, she regretted that. Across the table, Kate saw Bev dig an elbow into Bina's side.

"Hey, Billy," Bunny said, "business looks real good."

"You gotta pretty full crowd," Bev said approvingly. "And dancing."

"Yeah," Billy said, and then looked back at Kate. "We do a little hokey-pokey."

"Don't you get a night off?" Bev asked.

"Usually Saturdays. But one of the guys called in sick. Lucky I was here and got to see all you beauties," Billy said.

Above the general noise, Pete, the older bartender, bellowed, "Yo, Billy! This ain't a one-man band. Where's Joey?"

Billy didn't turn around. Bunny, clearly desperate, grabbed his hand. "This is my friend Bina," she said. "You two ought to get together."

286

Billy looked at Bina blankly for a moment. "Yeah. Nice to meet you." He turned back to Kate, who felt desperate herself.

"How about bowling with Bina and me next Wednesday?" she asked.

He blinked, then smiled. "I wouldn't have guessed you for the bowling type," he said.

Barbie, always prepared, pushed Bina's phone number scribbled on a piece of paper into Billy's hand. "Here," she said, "give Bina a call to set it up. She's in charge of all the bowling events with Kate." There was another yell from the bar, and this time Billy turned.

"Coming," he said, and gave the group a dazzling smile before he disappeared into the crowd.

"My God," Brice said. "He's gorgeous. Can I come, too?"

Elliot gave Brice a look, then turned back to Kate and gave her a more searching one. Before he could say anything, Bev began to high-five everyone at the table. Next, Kate thought, they'd do the Wave. "Nice work," said Barbie, slapping Kate's palm.

"Good save," Bunny agreed.

"I think he believes he's going out with you, Kate," Brice said.

"Well," she told the table, "he'll find out differently when he meets Michael. Anyway, he has Bina's number."

"Thanks, Katie," Bina said, and looked totally exhausted. Kate smiled at her but wondered how she would talk Michael into a Wednesday night of bowling.

Chapter Twenty-two

Kate felt guilty as she pressed the buzzer, then she remembered she had Michael's keys. Silently she cursed herself. She checked her watch and was even more concerned when she realized it was a quarter to one. She was sure he was sleeping and equally sure she had more beer on her breath than she would like him to smell. Somehow it was all right to go out with friends because of obligation but not to have a good time.

When Michael came to the door, still dressed but obviously rubbing the sleep out of his eyes, she greeted him with a quick hug and passed him in the narrow foyer.

"You shouldn't have waited up," she said. What she meant was, she should have gone home to her own apartment or, better yet, not gone to Brooklyn at all.

But Michael just yawned and stretched. "Time to go to bed," he said. Kate agreed with a nod but headed to the bathroom.

"I have to pee," she said.

Once she had the door closed, she washed her face, brushed her teeth, gargled, and then brushed her teeth again. She caught a glimpse of herself in the mirror as she reached for the face towel. She looked so . . . furtive. For a moment, Kate saw — in her jaw, the set of her eyes, and her hairline — a frightening similarity to her father. It sent a shiver through her. Then she realized that more than the physical resemblance, it was the guilty, skulking body language and expression that had conjured up his image. She stood immobile under the light of the bare bulb in Michael's bachelor bathroom and looked herself in the eye. You have nothing to feel guilty about, she told herself. If Michael is rigid with his schedule, there is no reason for you to feel guilty. Having drinks with your girlfriends is nothing to feel guilty about.

But Kate knew it wasn't just that. Her thoughts about Billy Nolan were unsettling. She didn't want those thoughts; she didn't want the feeling she had had as she'd flirted with him. And even if she had done it for Bina, and even if she was only tricking Billy, the fact was she had acted as if she were making a date with another man and the other man had believed it. Wasn't that kind of cheating on Michael? Raised as a Catholic while her mother was alive, Kate had never quite gotten over the concept of sins of commission and omission. Was she guilty of the latter?

Now she was returning to sleep with her lover, and she felt uncomfortably like a slut. It wasn't the beer on her breath or the smell of cigarette smoke on her clothes that embarrassed her. It was her own feelings.

Kate washed quickly and emerged from the bathroom in her panties and bra. As she walked into Michael's bedroom, she was dismayed to see that he was completely undressed under the sheet and had lit the candle on his nightstand. Michael usually slept in pajama bottoms and a T-shirt. The lack of them and the lighted candle sent a clear signal.

"May I borrow a shirt?" Kate asked meekly.

Michael nodded and gestured to the bureau. She took out a plain white Fruit of the Loom and slipped into it, then slid into bed beside him.

"Was it fun?" Michael asked, putting his arm around her.

"Not really," Kate said. "And I'm so exhausted." She paused. Michael was good with this kind of sexual nuance. She waited a minute. "Can we just spoon?" she asked, and turned her back to him, feeling his chest against her shoulder blades.

"Sure," Michael said, and Kate was relieved not to hear disappointment in his voice. He shifted for a moment, blew out the candle, and pressed his body up to hers. Kate sighed, and out of either shame, exhaustion, or too much beer, she closed her eyes and was asleep in moments.

Sunday morning, she and Michael fell into their comforting ritual. He had bought *The New York Times* and bagels, and they spent two hours reading bits of the paper to each other and nibbling on cream cheese and pumpernickel. Kate opened the "Styles" section to read a continuation of a story about beauty parlors in Afghanistan and accidentally ran into the Weddings/Celebration page. It was something she tried to avoid, something unsettling, like stepping around a dead pigeon on the sidewalk.

She then went on to read the rest of the section, as she always had to when she forgot to avoid it. It was a bad mistake. Column after column describing happy unions, listing the groom's parents, the bride's family, with quotes from their siblings and descriptions of the celebrations that always left her feeling depressed and different from everybody else. If she married Michael, what would the *Times* possibly run about her wedding? "The bride, close to her 32nd birthday and an orphan, elected to have a small wedding. 'I couldn't really afford a big party, and I don't have enough family and friends to attend one,' Katherine Jameson-Atwood said. 'In fact, I'm not sure I'm doing the right thing, but then, who is?'" Covertly, she peered over the top of the paper at Michael and wondered how he would look in one of the grainy gray photos, his head leaned toward hers. She closed the paper and put it aside.

Restless, she got up and went to the window. Michael's building, a large white brick postwar complex, consisted of several hundred boring apartments, but the views from the upper floors were spectacular. She looked out the window down at Turtle Bay. She could even see a glimmer of the East River. "It looks like it's clouding over," she said.

Michael came up behind her and wrapped one arm around her chest and shoulder, like a high collar on a coat. "Well," he said, "we could either go out and skateboard competitively or we could lie down in the bedroom. The choice is yours."

Kate laughed and let him take her hand, leading her to the bed, though she wasn't certain she was in the mood. But when they were lying down and he had undressed her, she relaxed into his kisses. When he bit her, gently, on the back of her neck, it sent a pleasant shiver down her spine. She began to forget herself in the trance of sexual pleasure that began to rise slowly like a tide at full moon. She felt his hands slide over her, deft and knowing, if a little predictable. When he rolled from his side on top of her, she wanted him. Swept away by the rhythm of his movements and her hungry response, Kate felt good for the first time that weekend. She closed her eyes and felt the rise of an orgasm about to take place. At the edge she whispered, "Yes." She squeezed her eyes shut, and then Billy Nolan's face flashed before her, as clear as it had been the night before. She caught her breath and groaned, but it was not with pleasure.

When Michael came, Kate realized to her dismay that she was relieved.

As they lay there together, she thought about the bowling plan. She couldn't imagine Michael running down the lane, but she had to go with him or Billy would continue to believe that she was his date. She couldn't take Elliot, because any man could tell there were no vibes between them — at least not the sexual kind. And her guilt compelled her to end the charade as quickly as possible. "Michael," she whispered, "are you asleep?"

"Not quite," he murmured.

"I want to ask you something."

He turned to her with that deer-in-the-headlights look men got when they thought you were going to talk about "the relationship."

"How do you feel about bowling?" Kate asked.

Chapter Twenty-three

"Pee-yeuw!" Bina said as she, Kate, and Michael struggled to get their rented bowling shoes on.

"Strike!"

"You lucky son of a bitch!" Behind them, a bunch of blue-collar bowlers were in some sort of fierce competition, either bowling or drinking — or perhaps both.

They were at Bowl-a-Rama. The noise was thunderous as pins fell and madmen screamed. "The thrill of victory, the agony of defeat!" Kate chirped.

"The agony of de feet is only starting," Michael quipped, looking down at the smelly shoes. It seemed that Bina had qualms, too, but they were more fashion-related.

"Do you think this red goes with my outfit?" she asked Kate nervously.

"Sure," Kate told her, though the shoes were hideous, as was Bina's new outfit. Kate could see that Barbie had "helped" dress Bina for the big occasion.

Thinking of that, Kate scanned the crowd, looking for Billy Nolan. All was chaos. In the lanes next to them, a league was just finishing up, and the clash of orange-and-brown shirts was almost nauseating to look at. Kate herself was wearing a simple white shirt and jeans, while Michael was wearing a sports coat, perhaps the only sports coat in a ten-block radius.

Bina stood up. Kate reassessed her outfit and realized that the short black miniskirt would reveal all when she bent over to release the ball. Her clingy green top was set off by a fuchsia scarf, Barbie's trademark color. Unfortunately for Bina, the scarf gave her face a mauve cast that clashed with the blouse. Oh well, Kate thought, nothing would make this double date from hell work anyway.

They were assigned an alley, and as they slipped into the molded plastic seats, Michael, ever the gentleman, asked if they would like something to drink. Bina asked for a cola, and before she thought about it, Kate ordered a beer. She imagined that Michael raised his brows before he went off to the bar.

The moment he was gone, Bina turned to her. "Where is he, Katie?" she asked, eyeing the entrance. "He said he'd be here on time. Maybe he's going to stand me up. Oh, I'm so nervous."

"Calm down, honey," Kate said. "He'll be here." In truth, she was nervous herself. She knew she had deceived Billy, though Bina hadn't a clue. And if she couldn't make the transition gracefully and make it look as if any confusion were a natural mistake on Billy's part, she was afraid of the fallout. Billy Nolan wasn't going to be thrilled when he realized that he'd been tricked into an evening with Bina.

"God, I'm sweating through my blouse," Bina said. "I'm going to run to the ladies' room and check my makeup one more time." She stood up and wound her way through the bobbing heads and fat bellies in the crowd.

Michael returned with the beverages, and Kate saw he had also bought some snacks.

"Bina's looking . . . um, different since the last time I saw her," he stammered.

"Well, I think you only saw her when she was having a case of the hysterical fantods," Kate reminded him.

"No, that's not what I mean," Michael said. "She looks . . . jazzier."

"Please! She looks like she belongs in the

cast of *Forty-second Street,*" Kate told him. She realized she sounded as tense as she felt. She put her arm out and took Michael's hand. "It was sweet of you to come," she said. "Launching Bina in her new life is really important after what she's been through."

"Well, it didn't seem to take her long to recover," Michael said. He sat down and picked up a paper cup of soda. For a moment Kate felt irritated. Because of her background, she had always looked for a man who avoided drinking to excess, but perhaps never drinking at all was a bad thing. It occurred to her for the first time that Michael might be terribly afraid of losing control.

He squeezed her hand. "It was sweet to see you at work last week," he told her. "I suppose that you could do that anywhere. Or even have a private practice."

"I like working in the school setting," she said, her mind elsewhere. "You get more feedback about behavior and change."

He didn't respond, and she craned her neck, looking first to the ladies' room and then to the door, hoping that this mad scheme with Billy would work out. At that moment, Billy walked into the bowling alley. He spotted Kate before she could even raise her hand and walked over to their lane. Damn Bina, Kate thought. It was going to be difficult enough to subtly show him who his date was; now it would be virtually impossible. What the hell was she doing in the ladies' room for so long, taking a shower?

Kate introduced Billy to Michael. They shook hands. Kate couldn't help but notice how incredibly attractive Billy looked. He was wearing very old black jeans and a slightly clingy T-shirt of the same color that revealed the body of a natural athlete. She could see his arms and figured the guy didn't have 2 percent body fat. Typical narcissist, she thought. He must be a gym rat to have that kind of bicep definition. And she was amused to see that he had his own equipment. She hadn't known anybody who owned their own bowling ball in fifteen years.

Billy dropped his bowling bag on the seat next to Kate. "Let's rock and bowl!" he said, looking down at her a little too intensely.

Kate stood up quickly, scanning the bowling alley. "Bina will be back in a moment," she told him.

"Fine," Billy said, clearly not at all interested in Bina's whereabouts. To her alarm, he put his arm around Kate's shoulder. "Hey, you look great," he said, his voice way too personal.

Kate quickly stepped out of his embrace and moved closer to Michael, who was still seated. She put her hand on Michael's shoulder. Billy paused for a moment, then sat down and began to put on his own shoes. Kate, feeling both guilty and awkward, sat beside Michael. Michael, as if in response to Billy's overly warm greeting, put his arm across the back of the seats and rested it on her shoulder.

Billy looked up from his laces and eyed the two of them. "You two just meet?" he asked. "Or are you related?"

"No. We've been going out for a while now," Michael replied innocently. Kate thought she saw Billy's face color up, but he looked down again at his shoes.

Just then, to Kate's enormous relief, Bina returned to the lane. She looked as if the entire research staff of Max Factor had worked her face over. A great look for bowling. But when she smiled, her natural warmth showed. "Well, hey," she said to Billy as she sat beside him.

Billy looked from Kate to Bina. And then he looked back across at Kate, leaning against Michael's proprietary arm. "I was afraid you weren't going to make it," Bina told him. Kate tried to avert her eyes, but not soon enough. From the look on Billy's face, she knew that he now understood what was going on and was clearly unhappy with the territory as it was currently staked. She decided to hope for the best.

"Okay," Kate said, sliding into the double seat behind the scorekeeping board. She quickly entered their information into the keypad, and their names lit up on the overhead screens — hers with Michael's and Bina's with Billy's. "Now we can get started."

"Yeah," Billy said, looking at the screen, "but what are we starting?"

Kate thought she heard some anger or maybe bitterness in his voice but felt it was best to just ignore it.

"We can't start," Bina whined. "I haven't found a ball." She looked at Billy and did everything except bat her eyes. "Would you help me?" she asked. Then she licked her lips. Kate wondered if she had confused Elliot's ridiculous instructions and was trying to annoy instead of arouse.

Billy shot Kate a look, and it said everything. Then he grabbed Bina's hand and, without taking his eyes off Kate, stood up. "Sure," he said. "I'm no expert with balls, except my own, but I'll try. Though it often seems to me that other people have a lot of balls."

Kate blushed. She knew this type of behavior; she had seen it with her child patients. He was going to act out and make sure she paid for her little deception by being as horrible as possible. Billy and Bina left the pit, and Michael waited until they were out of earshot.

"Charming," he said. "Will he discuss other parts of his anatomy as the night progresses?" He sat beside Kate in the scoring seat. "How long have you known him?" he asked, echoing Billy, consciously or not.

Kate was surprised to feel a slight surge of pleasure at his possessiveness. "Oh, he picked up Bina at that wedding I went to," she replied.

"A friendly guy. And well equipped," was all Michael deigned to say.

Then Bina and Billy returned from the rack. Bina was carrying a hideous-looking bowling ball, blue with patches of fuchsia. "We finally found a ball that matches my scarf!" Bina said with excessive enthusiasm. "Billy helped me." Kate restrained herself from shaking her head. Bina was acting as if the selection of a piece of sporting equipment were akin to slaying a dragon. She held up the hideous ball, then nearly dropped it. Kate remembered, all at once, just how klutzy Bina was. "Klutzy, smutzy," Mrs. Horowitz used to say. "As long as you get good grades." Bina then attempted to stick her plump fingers into the tiny holes.

Billy, meanwhile, unzipped his bag and took out a much larger black ball. "And look," he exclaimed, laying on the sarcasm, "I found a ball that matches my outfit, too!"

Kate, concerned about hurting Bina's feelings, decided to comment. "Well, *you're* wearing all black and you coordinated by bringing your own ball."

Billy served Kate an insincere smile. "That did make it less of a challenge." He looked over at Michael. "Hey, Mike, how big is your ball?"

"Ten pounds," Michael answered. "And I prefer to be called Michael," he added flatly.

Kate saw him narrow his eyes. It was clear that he wasn't enjoying himself. But it seemed as if he also sensed or observed that something was going on between her and Billy.

Bina reached over for her cola. "I haven't been bowling since Annie Jackson's sixth-grade birthday party. Remember, Katie?"

"How could I forget?" Kate said, smiling at the memory. "I threw up Pop Rocks all over myself."

"Oh, yeah!" Bina squealed. "Gross." She looked over at Billy, licking her lips again.

Billy joined the two of them at the scoreboard. "Oh, I don't know," he said, and put his foot down right beside Kate's and on her shoelace. Kate moved her foot away, pulling out the bow. "I think some women look cute in their own vomit." Kate, totally nonplussed, pulled her foot up to the seat and quickly retied her shoe.

"Well, I'm sure you've had plenty of opportunity to see it," she said, and turned to Michael. "Billy works in a bar."

"Lots of chances with drunken women," Billy said. "Right, Mike?"

"Michael," Michael corrected. "Not in my experience."

"Well, owning my own bar, I'm sure I have more experience," Billy said coolly.

Kate was surprised to hear that Billy owned the Barber Bar, if that was, in fact, the truth.

Billy stared her down for a moment and then wrapped his arm around Bina. "I'm sure I have a lot more experience in quite a few things," he said.

Chapter Twenty-four

"Ouch!" Bina yelled. "Ow. Ow." She shook her hand as if it were a limp fish at the end of a pole, then put her index finger into her mouth. Kate hadn't been looking, but as Bina had tried to retrieve her ball from the ball return, her finger had been crunched by another ball spewed from the maw of the machine.

Billy bent over her hand, taking it in his. "Are you okay?" he asked.

Kate turned away from the two of them and looked at Michael, who was sitting beside her. When she had put together this ridiculous scheme, she had thought of Billy and how he might be angry and difficult. She had thought of Bina and how she might be disappointed. But she hadn't thought of Michael and the effect that a night of Brooklyn bowling might have on him. She put her arm around him. He was a lot quieter than usual and obviously disturbed by his poor performance. While he was not a jock, Michael was fit and played squash regularly, where, she knew, he was a tough competitor. He didn't like to lose.

Kate looked down at the board, then put her head on Michael's shoulder. "The score doesn't matter," she cooed, realizing at once that her tone was the one she used when she was talking to her young patients. "Are you having fun?"

Michael ignored the question, as he so obviously was not. "I can't believe I'm coming in third," he said, and shook his head. Kate wondered if she should try to do poorly, just so Michael would have a shot at second place, but she knew that her score and Bina's didn't matter. Michael was pissed because Billy was beating him, and doing it by so wide a margin.

Just then Billy approached them. He picked up his drink from the holder, then shook his head as he took a look at the scoreboard. "Well, we're all having a pretty dismal night," he commented, but Kate thought she saw him smirk as he went up to help Bina prepare for what would almost certainly be yet another gutter ball.

Kate ignored them and turned back to Michael. She felt responsible for this and didn't like to see him upset. If she was completely truthful with herself, she'd have to admit she also didn't like to see him bested by Billy. It was foolish, she told herself, to feel that way or to allow Michael to have that view. It was some vestige of the *Homo sapiens* fight for alpha male position. "People often confuse athletic scores with personal identity," she said.

"Sure. When the Cubs lose my world falls apart," Michael said, almost sneering.

Michael was from Chicago, and the fact was that he did root for the pathetic Cubs. But this wasn't the Cubs pitted against another, superior baseball team. This was Michael pitted against Billy Nolan. And Michael, in a word from her youth, was getting *shmeisted*.

"This isn't that hard. I can't believe I haven't rolled a strike."

"Oh, it's just for fun," she tried to remind him. "Bowling was never your game. Anyway," she said, waving toward Bina, who was still at the line, dithering, "no one does worse than Bina."

Billy, sipping his soft drink, overheard her, grinned, and laughed. "Eye on the head pin, Bina," he encouraged. Then he put back his cup. "Hey, wait!" he called. He left the pit and stepped behind her, put his arms around her, and changed her stance.

Kate, watching them, felt a twinge of

what she wouldn't admit was jealousy. Then Bina, guided by Billy, released the ball down the lane — this time with her eyes closed. The group watched as the ball rolled directly down the middle of the lane and almost miraculously knocked over all the pins. Kate's mouth dropped, but not as much as Michael's pride.

"Omigod! Omigod! I hit them! I hit them all!" Bina shouted. She did a victory dance that involved reaching both arms up to the ceiling and incidentally exposing a significant part of the fuchsia underpants beneath her tiny skirt. Kate watched as bowlers from other lanes smiled, pointed, and gave her a thumbs-up sign.

"Touchdown!" Bina yelled. She gave Billy a big hug, then ran over to Kate. "Katie, I can't believe it," she said, her arms under Kate's while she jumped back and forth. "I knocked them over!" Then, flinging her arms wide, she accidentally knocked the beer out of Kate's hand and all over the front of Michael's shirt.

"Bina, you seem to be on a roll at knocking things over," Kate said as Michael jumped up.

"I'm so sorry," Bina said to Michael, flushing bright red. She grabbed for the already damp Bowl-a-Rama cocktail napkin that was lying on the scoreboard top. Michael was holding his shirt away from his body, his elbows extended like a man impersonating a rooster. Kate could see the beer had soaked not only his shirt, but also his pants. When Bina began to dab ineffectually at his chest and crotch, Michael took a step backward.

"No. Let me help," she begged. "I can get it right out. Club soda on the shirt. Club soda and salt on your pants."

Kate almost smiled, despite Michael's discomfort. The Horowitz family were experts at removing every stain from every possible material: wine on linen, ballpoint on silk, tar on leather. The list was endless and often discussed. Kate took Michael's arm. He looked at her helplessly.

"Hurry up," Bina insisted, taking his other arm. "We have to do it before the stain sets. Trust me, I know."

"She does," Kate said, nodding at him.

"Maybe it's all right," Michael volunteered, but then he looked down at himself.

"Go with her," Kate said.

"Yeah. Let's get you cleaned up," Bina told him as she led him away from the lane.

Kate watched him go and felt deeply

sorry for having invited him. He disappeared into the crowd like a damaged ship being pulled by a determined little tugboat. Kate sighed.

"Not Mike's day."

Kate turned around to face Billy, who was leaning on the side of their banquette, his legs crossed and his eyebrows raised. "Not much of a player."

"Just because he's in third place . . . ," Kate began.

"Last," Billy corrected her.

"Excuse me?" Kate asked. Billy pointed at the electronic scoreboard. He took a step closer to her. She felt his arm against her shoulder. She also felt heat rise up from her chest to her neck and hoped he wouldn't notice the blush on her face.

"Last," he said again, and leaned forward to tap the score. "Since Bina's strike, he's in last place." Kate felt a little light-headed. Billy Nolan was so close to her, she could smell his soap and the heat of his body. For an insane moment she had an impulse to close her eyes and fall into his arms. Instead she took a step away and picked up a bowling ball.

"You're just jealous," she said without thinking, not quite sure what she meant.

He turned to face her instead of the

score. "You're right, I am," he said in a steady voice.

"You are?" Kate asked, but she couldn't match his steadiness. She was surprised at this admission.

"Yeah," Billy said. And then he continued, a lot less casually. He lowered his voice, but it rose in intensity. "I thought I was going on this date with you. And you knew that. I can't believe I fell for the old bait and switch, or that you played me that way."

Kate dropped the ball back into the ball return. Despite the truth of what he said, she felt indignant. She'd done it for the best of reasons, and who was he to claim a higher moral ground? "You're on a date with my best friend," she said defensively.

"Really?" Billy asked, his voice heavy with sarcasm. "Is that what you thought?"

"Yes," Kate lied. "And then you insult my boyfriend and come on to me. What is wrong with you?"

"Well, for one thing, I like to pick my own women," Billy said. And he looked her over from head to toe. He paused, took a couple of steps away from her, and sat on the banquette, crossing an ankle over his knee. "For another, I certainly wouldn't pick Bina," he said bluntly.

Kate felt a surge of anger on behalf of her friend. She had feared something like this would happen, and now her main concern was that Billy would humiliate Bina. She silently cursed Elliot, Barbie, and the whole bunch of them. Playing with people's lives was always dangerous, and right now she was the one about to face retribution for their stupidity. "That is just plain rude," she told him.

"Rude to be angry when I'm tricked? I'm just calling it as I see it," Billy said.

"I guess that's why everyone calls you like they see you," Kate snapped.

"What's that supposed to mean?" Billy said, sitting upright and putting both feet on the ground.

Kate controlled herself, but with difficulty. She didn't want to see Bina hurt, and she had to try to get out of this somehow. She turned away from him. "It means every woman in Brooklyn, perhaps with the exception of Brooklyn Heights, knows your reputation," she said, and went to pick up her purse.

"What reputation?" Billy asked. He stood up and followed her. When she didn't answer him or turn around, he put a hand on her shoulder and turned her to him. "What reputation?" he asked again.

"Oh, come on. Don't you know everyone calls you 'Dumping Billy'?" Kate answered, exasperated.

" 'Dumping Billy'? Why?"

Kate looked up at him. He was tall, at least seven or eight inches taller than she was, but she could see his eyes cloud. He seemed to have been completely unaware of his nickname.

"Why the hell would they call me that?" he asked.

"Because you dump every woman you date." Kate looked toward the bar and the rest rooms beyond. When would Michael and Bina return? She was tired of this conversation and wanted only to salvage the rest of the evening.

"I don't dump women," Billy said. For the first time, he seemed defensive. "I mean, I've broken up relationships, but I don't dump people."

"Oh, come on," Kate said. "My friends know a dozen women you've dumped. I didn't make up the nickname. Anyway, your behavior is pathological."

"What?" Billy demanded. He'd clearly gone from defensive to angry.

Kate knew she'd gone too far and spoiled what was left of the evening, but she couldn't resist taking a deep, annoyed breath. "Path-o-log-i-cal," she said slowly, as if for a child. "It means —"

"Any abnormal variation from a sound condition," Billy finished for her.

Kate blinked, taken aback. Billy pushed past her, grabbed his bag, and turned back.

"It also means I'm out of here. The bad news is, I did just dump Bina, but I wish I could've dumped you. The good news is that now your friend Michael has a chance of coming in third."

He was gone in a minute, and Kate stood beside their almost deserted lane, wondering what she could possibly say when Bina and Michael returned.

Chapter Twenty-five

The next morning, Kate sat in her office face-to-face with a young girl. Tina, a high-spirited third grader, was sitting in one of the tiny chairs with a big bandage on her arm. Tina had injured herself over and over, but Kate didn't think clumsiness or a need for self-mutilation were behind the injuries. She thought Tina probably had a repetition compulsion: For some reason she had to keep acting out the trauma of being challenged and frightened and forced to respond. While many professionals in her field dismissed the idea, Kate had always found the concept valid.

She had been talking with the child for over an hour and she felt some progress had been made. "So you won't do that again?" she asked Tina.

Tina looked up at her and smiled. "No," she said, then added, "Not unless Jason dares me."

"If he dares you to jump off the roof . . ." Kate stopped herself. Where had that come from? It was the kind of line her father might have used. Instead, she smiled, almost closed her eyes, and leaned forward toward Tina, the girl who couldn't refuse a dare. "I dare you not to," she said. "I bet that you have to do anything Jason dares you to."

"Do not," Tina said.

"Dare you not to," Kate said.

She wasn't sure the counterdare would work. Tina really might jump off the roof. Just then the bell rang and interrupted her thoughts. "We'll talk about your friendship with Jason next time, okay, Tina?" Kate said.

Tina nodded again, slid off the chair, and bounded from the room.

"I told you, it just won't work." Kate said each word slowly and distinctly so Elliot might possibly get it through his mathematical head. "Zero, null set, no way. *Impossible*. Finished. Kaput."

"But are you sure?" Elliot asked.

She gave him a look. They were going to their gym, Crunch — a place that ran cool ads on television and that had as its motto "No judgements." But Kate was ready to make a few judgments now. Even for him, Elliot looked awful. They were walking up

Eighth Avenue, and he was wearing baggy shorts, a torn T-shirt, and a madras fishing hat that must have come from some thrift shop, while his feet displayed two mismatched socks. "You know," Kate said, trying to change the subject, "you look like a recently released mental patient."

"Thank you," Elliot said. "It was the look I was going for. Brice helped me."

Against her will, Kate smiled. How a guy as fashion impaired as Elliot could couple up with stylish Brice was inconceivable to her. But they were a solid and happy couple with enough things in common to make their lives congenial and enough respect for their differences to make life interesting. It was hard to imagine Brice letting Elliot out of the house dressed like this, but she knew that he'd probably just shrugged, laughed, and hugged Elliot. Then the image of Michael and his sports jacket the night before came unbidden to her mind. Just because Michael dressed inappropriately was no reason for her to judge him, but somehow she did.

"I want to find out exactly what happened, sentence by sentence, word by word, act by act." They turned west on 18th Street, and Kate looked at Elliot with hostile amazement.

"If you think I'm going to go through last night one more time, you can think again." They reached the door to the gym. "And you can warm up by yourself."

They had both gotten memberships at Crunch so that they could work out together and force each other to go. It usually worked pretty well, but Kate was in no mood to dissect the previous evening. The fact was she was a little bit ashamed, both of her ruse and of her behavior. But that didn't mean she had to tell Elliot that. At the door to the women's locker room, she turned to him and said, "Spot yourself. I'm going to find a straight guy to work out with."

After she had changed into her workout pants and loose top, twisted her hair into a scrunchie and stuck it on top of her head with hairpins, then stowed her stuff in the locker, she came out to find Elliot standing there, just where she'd left him.

"Oh, come on," he pleaded as if she hadn't just been gone for ten minutes. "You never tell me anything anymore."

"Oh, for heaven's sake." Kate laughed, exasperated. But she couldn't refuse him. So she went into detail about the whole awful night — how Barbie had dressed Bina up like a Las Vegas showgirl, how

Billy had showed up thinking he was her date and not at all happy to find out he was Bina's, and how they'd finally gotten into an argument at the end of the evening.

By then they had reached the mats, and Kate grabbed a big blue plastic ball to begin their warmup. She leaned backward over it to stretch the front of her body. The stretch felt good, and she took a deep, soothing breath. Stretching was the only part of working out that she actually enjoyed, and she needed it after last night and today. While Brian Conroy had improved and was able to cry over the loss of his mother, a new child, Lisa Allen, had been sent to her because she seemed "withdrawn." And Tina Foster had been sent to her for the second time because she had taken a ridiculous dare and jumped off the top of the playground wall. Kate sighed.

She and Elliot now clasped hands and bent away from each other in order to stretch out their backs. They had been coming to the gym together for seven months now and had their routine down pat. They continued to pull each other — first arms, then legs — around the big blue ball. "Well, you know," Elliot said, "I got a partial report from Bev last night, who got it from Bina."

"Bev called you?"

"Oh, yeah. She and I are bonding. I want to be godfather to the baby."

"God forbid," Kate said. She really felt irritated that Elliot was so . . . integrated with her Brooklyn friends and pissed that Bev would stick her two cents in. "Look, I didn't think Billy Nolan would like Bina. It turns out that he resented the way I manipulated him and — shock, shock — he doesn't want to go out with Bina despite Barbie's outfits, Brice's haircut, and your plan. Not only that, *I* don't like him. He isn't a nice person."

"*You* don't have to like him," Elliot began. "*I* don't have to like him. Even *Bina* doesn't have to like him. She only has to date him for an average of two point four months. That's roughly ten weeks, or seventy days — give or take."

"But he has to like Bina," Kate pointed out. "And he doesn't. Case closed."

"Technically we don't know that," Elliot gurgled with his head tilted backward. He was arching himself in a back bend.

"What do you mean?" Kate asked, standing upright again.

"I mean, from your retelling it sounds

like he had the argument with you," Elliot said.

"Yes. So?"

"So his problem is with you, *not* Bina." Elliot looked at her sternly.

"Elliot, trust me. There was no chemistry between them."

"Kate, from what you told me and what Bev said Bina said, I think last night was an opener. The fact is, you did trick the guy and he was angry at you and he doesn't like you, but he might, given the chance, like Bina — at least long enough to date her for seventy-three days."

"Oh, Elliot, don't be ridiculous," Kate snapped. She let go of his hands, and he went sprawling, his butt hitting the mat with a splat. "Are you trying to tell me the fiasco was my fault?"

Elliot rose slowly from the mat, his hands rubbing his backside. "That's exactly what I'm telling you. That and the fact that you owe him an apology."

Kate stared at him in amazement. "That is the most outrageous thing I ever heard," she told him. "I would never apologize to that insufferable, arrogant . . ." She turned and began to walk away.

"You like him, don't you?" Elliot asked.

Kate stopped where she was, swung

around, and stared at him. "I do not!" she said.

Elliot shrugged. "Just asking," he told her. "It's just that I've never seen you this excited about Michael." He threw his towel over his neck and sauntered toward the treadmills.

"Leave Michael out of this," Kate snapped. She took a deep breath. Elliot, who probably knew her better than anyone, was pressing all her buttons. But she wouldn't let him. As she watched him set the program on his treadmill, his back turned to her, she made herself slowly and carefully go over the facts and feelings from the previous night. Maybe she *had* been both a catalyst and a stumbling block. Maybe if she hadn't been in the way, Billy would be interested in Bina. He seemed to have dated every other woman east of Court Street. However, even if she had gone about it badly, she knew her intentions had been good. She got onto the treadmill beside Elliot and punched in her own stats and program.

As she started walking, she said, "If you believe in this and Bina believes in this, I'll do what I can to make it work. But I can't make him date her." And not for two point four months, she thought. I don't believe he can rise to the challenge. The image stopped her in her tracks, and she almost flew off the back of the treadmill.

"Have you just thought of something, or are you just being klutzy?" Elliot asked as she regained her position and matched her stride to his.

"Maybe I have," Kate admitted. "But I hate the idea of apologizing to him. Do I have to?"

"Kate," Elliot said, ignoring her tone, "I don't see that you have much of a choice. It doesn't matter that you don't believe in the 'silly' plan. Bina does, you are her best friend, and you alienated Billy. You have to apologize."

God, Kate thought. I hate how Elliot is always right.

Chapter Twenty-six

On Tuesday morning, Kate stood in her bedroom before a full-length mirror, holding a hip but dignified blouse up to herself. Deciding against it, she threw it onto the pile of rejected clothes that had already formed on her bed. "What am I going to wear?" she asked her reflection. She turned away and paused for a moment. Why did she even care? Billy meant nothing to her, despite his obvious attractions. She went to her tiny closet and began to look for the green crewneck top that looked so good on her. As she pulled it off the hanger, she stopped dead. Billy Nolan was taking up more space in her mind than he ought to. And he had seen her before. It wasn't as if she were going to make a different impression on him this time.

She took a deep breath and looked back steadily at herself. "Hello," she said as if talking to someone else. "Billy, I wanted to apologize for my behavior the other night. . . ."

She gritted her teeth. This was more difficult than she had imagined. She thought of all the children she had asked to engage in role-play: children who were supposed to talk to the fathers who had left the family, children who were tired of being scolded, children who had to practice asking for what they wanted. Now it was her turn, and the experience was humbling. It was leaving her with a deeper sense of compassion for her little clients.

The phone rang and she was relieved for the distraction, until she saw the phone number. Somehow, she didn't feel like speaking to Michael right now, and it was odd for him to be calling her on a school morning. Reluctantly, she picked up the phone.

"Hi," he said cheerfully. "Did I wake you up?" Kate assured him that he hadn't. "Look, I just thought that we might get together tonight."

For a moment, Kate was confused. They never got together on Tuesdays. It was always Wednesdays. "Is something wrong?" she asked.

"Yeah. I miss you," Michael said.

"I miss you too," she replied automatically. Then she paused, surprised to realize it wasn't true. But why not? she wondered. Would she perhaps be missing Michael right now if she weren't so focused on Billy? She felt a stab of irritation. No, of course not! It was ridiculous. "I'm sorry, but I . . . I have errands I have to run tonight."

"Oh. Okay. No problem. See you tomorrow, I guess."

"Yes," Kate said. "I'll see you tomorrow." She hung up the phone, sighed, and went back to the task at hand.

Later that day, after school, Kate arrived at the Barber Bar, her hair perfectly coiffed, looking as if she were about to take over a Fortune 500 company. She'd taken the subway from school to the closest stop. All was quiet in the area, and the bar itself looked closed, but she knocked on the door anyway. A woman's voice called out.

"We ain't open until —" The door jerked open and a tall, skinny woman in her late thirties in old jeans and a cut-off top stood before her. She was polishing a glass with the apron she had on and looked at Kate suspiciously. "Hey, listen. If you're lost, I'm dyslexic, so I don't give directions. And unless you're a customer you don't get to use this toilet." She was about to slam the door when Kate put up her hand and held it open. Then the woman paused. "The redhead," she said as if she already knew everything about her.

"Excuse me?" Kate asked. Had her reputation preceded her? "Actually, I'm looking for someone who works here . . . Billy Nolan." She blushed, thinking of all the women who must have turned up on this doorstep and said the very same thing.

"Of course you are," the woman said tiredly. "But he ain't on tonight until six."

Kate looked at her watch. She had almost two hours to wait. She sighed, more aggravated than ever. "Well, thank you anyway," she said, and turned to leave. She'd find somewhere in this ruin of a neighborhood to have a cup of coffee.

But before she'd taken more than three steps, the barmaid called after her. "Hey! You the one who told him his nickname?"

Kate turned around and nodded. "Dumping Billy," she said. "Isn't that what everyone calls him?"

"Yeah. He just didn't know it." She laughed. "Put him in quite a spin." She looked Kate over again.

"Well, I'll come back later," Kate said. At least she'd had some impact on the arrogant bastard. That might help her on this errand.

"Look, if you gotta see him now, he lives

above the bar." She pointed to a buzzer on the other side of the doorway.

"That's okay. I'll come back another —"

Before Kate could get the words out, the woman rang the buzzer and shouted into the intercom. "Hey, Billy! You got company and — surprise, surprise — it's a woman."

"Thanks, Mary," Billy's voice said through the speaker. "I'll buzz."

Kate gave Mary a small half smile. "Thanks," she said, although she wasn't sure she meant it.

"Don't mention it, Red," the barmaid replied.

"I'm Kate," Kate told her.

A smile spread across Mary's face. "Oh. Kate . . . ," she said knowingly, and she went back into the bar.

The door buzzed open. Kate smoothed her hair once and put her hand on the doorknob. She ascended the steps to the landing of the first floor, where a door stood open. She peered in at the room before her. It was not at all what she would have predicted. Instead of being a "bachelor pad" filled with empty pizza boxes and furniture that looked as if it had fallen off a truck, the room had a polished wooden floor, a shabby but attractive Persian rug, a big worn brown leather Chesterfield sofa, and two walls of bookshelves filled to the ceiling with hundreds of books. A window seat was built into one bookshelf wall, and the window was open. Through it there was the view of a tree and a bit of the sky, though the blowing white curtains kept obscuring the small vista. Altogether it was charming and far more homey and sophisticated than Kate would ever have given Billy Nolan credit for.

Billy sat at a mahogany desk with his back to her, transfixed by the laptop screen in front of him. Kate entered the room and looked around. Her surprise continued to grow. Almost half the books on the shelves were in French, and she now could see two nicely framed Daumier prints. A woman must have furnished this place, she thought. "Hello," she said.

Billy did not take his eyes off the monitor. "Hold on. Hold on. I'm just catching up on my e-mail," was all he offered as a greeting.

"This won't take long," Kate began. Billy pulled his hands off the keyboard and spun around. There was an awkward silence.

"I d-d-didn't realize it was you," he stammered. "I thought I had to interview a n-n-new barmaid."

"I don't think I'm qualified for the job," Kate said, and was then ready to bite her tongue. She sounded snotty, and she really hadn't meant to.

Billy stood up. "So did you just come over here to turn down a job offer, or is there more to this unexpected visit?" he asked.

The two of them stood across the room from each other, the sofa and plenty of tension between them. Kate tried to decide whether it would be best to just blurt out her apology and throw out her dare or first try to bridge the gap between them. Everything she had practiced seemed inappropriate. "I wanted to . . . ," she began.

"Yes?" Billy raised his eyebrows. It was annoying to see how attractive he was, even with his hair in disarray and his shirt untucked and open to the third button. She tore her eyes away from him.

"I wanted to apologize for . . ." It was coming out wrong. "I wanted to apologize for not telling you the truth the other night."

Billy laughed. "That doesn't sound like much of an apology to me."

"I realize after what happened I may not be your favorite person, but that's not what

331

counts," she explained. She put her purse on the desk.

"It isn't?" Billy asked.

"No. What counts is that Bina really likes you," Kate said. This was going badly. She was being either too direct or too indirect and was annoyed at her inability to really express herself to this guy. "And I think you might like her."

"Oh, really?" Billy smirked. "And what would give you insight into my feelings?"

"Look, it's none of my business, but —"

"Well, you finally got something right," he said, and sat on the Chesterfield. "What is your business, anyway?"

"I'm a psychologist," she said.

He shook his head. "I should have known," he muttered. "Nothing worse than a psychologist except a psychiatrist."

"How would you know?" she asked. "Have you dated both?"

"No. I consulted both. A long time ago. And they were ineffectual intellectuals."

She wondered what a mook like him had gone into therapy for but knew better than to ask. She just walked over to the little window seat and tried again.

"I don't like this 'Dumping Billy' stuff," he said.

"I'm sorry. I shouldn't have said anything, but I'm not responsible for the name. Apparently, everybody uses it."

"Apparently," he said dryly. "As if my personal life is anyone else's business."

Here was her chance to put in one more plug for Bina. She pushed forward. "Well, that's why I dropped by. Of course, it's none of my business, but I think you two would be very . . . you know . . . good for each other . . . which would be quite . . . something . . . so what I'm saying is basically what I have already said . . . you know?" What the hell had she just said? she thought. She'd never been less articulate in her whole life.

"Actually, no," Billy said, smiling gently at her obvious unease.

"Oh, I just knew you would make this difficult!" Kate stood up and walked to the door in frustration. It was never so hard to speak with children. Or to Elliot. Or Bina, the girls, or even Michael. Why was she having such a hard time talking to Billy Nolan?

"Why should I go out with Bina? I pick my own women. And she looks like a husband hunter," Billy said. "Not my type."

Kate could take his slight mocking of her, but how dare he insult her friend! "That is totally out of line. You're the loser!" she almost shouted at him.

"Me?!" Billy asked. He got up from the couch and faced her. "Hey, I own this place. I built it up from nothing. I've got bigger plans, too! I'll be opening a restaurant next year."

"Yes. But can you manage one decent relationship?" she asked.

"And I can date anyone I want!"

"*Not anyone. You can't date me!*" Kate flared. "You are still just a Mick who never even got out of Brooklyn. The trick with you is you are slightly better looking on the outside than you are on the inside, and the inner and outer you are in constant conflict. That's why you don't know you're a loser." Kate was out of breath, and her face was hot. This was not going well. She looked at Billy, who was surprisingly cool.

"Are you speaking as a doctor or as a bitch?" he asked with a coldness that cut right through her.

Kate opened her mouth, then checked herself, remembering her mission. She crossed to the desk, picked up her purse and muttered loudly enough for Billy to hear: "You couldn't do it anyway."

"Do what?" he demanded.

Kate turned around to face him, eyes blazing. They stared each other down as they had in the bowling alley the other night. "Nothing," she spat. "Absolutely nothing."

"Tell me," he said through clenched teeth, leaning across the back of the sofa toward her.

Kate almost smiled, because she knew that she'd be victorious. He was no more difficult than Tina Foster. "It's just that when I came here I knew you couldn't date Bina for more than a week or two," she said, self-assured. "You obviously have a repetition compulsion."

"A what?" Billy asked, indignant.

"A repetition compulsion," Kate replied impatiently.

"What's that? Some jargon from the *DSM-Four*?"

Kate was surprised he knew about the *Diagnostic and Statistical Manual of Mental Disorders*. The *DSM* was the bible of mental dysfunctions that was compiled regularly for mental health professionals. Still, she didn't let him see her reaction. "It's not a *DSM-Four* construct. It's an older Freudian theoretical position."

"I thought Freud was unpopular these days. Oedipus complex, penis envy. Isn't that all pretty much out-of-date? After all, he was a guy who didn't know what women wanted."

Once again, Kate was surprised by his casual familiarity with things she figured he had never heard of. "I think it's still valid," she said. "Especially in your case. It's roughly defined as compulsive neurotic behavior in which a person repeats an altered version of traumatic events from his past. Once it starts, the compulsion requires the person to keep doing the maladaptive behavior."

"Oh, really?" Billy asked. As she hoped, he was becoming belligerent. "And what maladaptive behavior would I be repeating?"

"An attempt at intimacy that has to be followed by abandonment. And each time you pick an inappropriate partner to ensure the eventual split."

"And how do you know all of this about me?" he asked.

"Well, I am a doctor," she said, "and I do know several of the inappropriate women you've played the pattern out with. I just thought Bina might be a real person, someone you could actually bond with. She isn't one of your typical Brooklyn big-haired bimbos. And she's quite sad at the moment. Anyway, it didn't work, and it doesn't matter to me or to Bina. I'm just sorry I gave you an easy excuse not to conquer it."

"You didn't give me anything but a headache," he shot back.

"Well, we're not really talking about me, are we? We're talking about you. And you find it impossible to date a nice girl with whom any kind of commitment might be possible."

"That isn't true," he told her.

"I guess that isn't why you have the nickname, then," she said.

"I'd have no problem dating Bina. She's a nice enough girl, and she knows how to have a good time. Unlike some uptight, word-dropping psychologists I've met. And I don't have a . . . petition . . . whatever."

"Sure you don't," she said.

"I don't," he insisted.

"Great. Then prove it," she said. "Date her for a couple of months without dumping her, and I will be proven totally and utterly wrong. Well, if you can manage a real relationship, you might also lose the nickname. But I don't think you can do it."

"Done," he declared. "And only because I want to. And because she's a nice girl. Not my type, but nice. And I'll see her as long as I want to. I don't need a shrink to manage it, or to psychoanalyze me later."

"I wouldn't dream of it." Kate smiled and headed to the door. She put her hand on the knob, but before she turned it, she looked back at Billy.

"I can give you Bina's number," she said.

"Thanks, but I already have it. And it's memorized: Bina Horowitz, on Ocean Parkway." He looked at her with a glint of triumph in his eye. And Kate, for some reason she didn't quite understand, was annoyed.

Well, her feelings didn't matter in this ridiculous escapade. She'd accomplished what she'd set out to do. So she simply opened the door, exited, and slammed it behind her.

Chapter Twenty-seven

Kate was almost a quarter of an hour early at LaMarca on Wednesday evening because she didn't want to be late. The restaurant, an unpretentious bistro in Chelsea, was not the kind of snotty place where you had to "wait at the bar until your party has joined you." Kate was seated at a window table and had a chance to freshen her lipstick and twist her hair up into a knot. Then she waited, trying hard not to think. Nestled next to her lipstick in the makeup bag she carried in her purse was a pretty blue box that contained a pair of new keys on a silver Tiffany key ring. The ring was actually more like a U than a circle, with sterling silver balls at each end that unscrewed so that keys could be added and subtracted easily. It also had a small silver dogtag on it. The number engraved on the sterling was registered at Tiffany's, and if the keys were ever lost and dropped in a mailbox, Tiffany's would return them. Kate felt that perhaps she had gone overboard, that she might be compensating with the gift for a diminution in her passion for Michael.

She'd tried over and over to analyze why she seemed to have cooled toward Michael. Certainly their sex was fulfilling and their relationship sound and based on shared interests, though she had never felt truly passionate about Michael as she once had for Steven. That, however, she had considered a good thing. After Steven, Kate had promised herself she would never allow an obsession with a man to take over her life. And until now she had been more than happy with Michael. Despite Elliot's prejudice against him, Michael was a grown-up — perhaps the first male grown-up in her life — and he respected and liked her. Unlike a lot of guys, Michael wasn't intimidated by her work, her looks, or her independence. And he was not the kind of man to run from intimacy. So why, she wondered, did she find herself resisting? Was she afraid of the next step in their relationship? She didn't think so. But as Anna Freud had pointed out, resistance was an unconscious thing.

"Would you like something to drink while you're waiting?" the waiter asked, startling her.

"A glass of Chardonnay, please," she said, and then felt a bit guilty, which in

340

turn made her feel annoyed.

As she was taking her first sip of the wine, Michael strode in, an unusually wide smile on his face. He was, she reminded herself, very nice looking. Not dramatically gorgeous like that idiot in Brooklyn, but handsome in an understated way. His hair was thick, and a little silver was mixed prematurely with the brown. The steel-rimmed glasses he wore went well with his hair, and Kate had sometimes wondered if he knew that. If his shoulders were a little narrow, he made up for that with his height. Now, he bent over her, took her chin in his hand, and turned her head so he could kiss her on the mouth. She smiled at him, and he slipped into the banquette opposite her.

"Very nice choice," he said, looking around. They alternated in choosing restaurants, Michael most often referring to *Zagat* on-line, while Kate depended on Elliot, her own personal restaurant rating service.

"You seem in a good mood," she said.

"Better than good!" Michael told her. "I've gotten the offer from Austin." He beamed. "It's almost too good to be true."

"It's official?" Kate asked. She felt her stomach tighten.

"Well, as good as. I got a call from Charles Hopkins at the Sagerman Foundation, and he told me, in complete confidence, of course, that they had selected me and that I'd hear from Austin soon."

"Wow. So you'll chair a department?" Kate was impressed and delighted for Michael, but her feelings were mixed and she felt a kind of tension in her chest, as if her bra had suddenly become two sizes too small. Austin, Texas, was supposed to be a lovely place, with a great university and very pretty countryside. And for someone as young as Michael to get the chairmanship of a department was almost unheard of. But Kate didn't want to think of the ramifications: If Michael chose to go, would he ask her to go as well? And if he did, what would she say? She loved her job and her friends and . . .

The waiter approached again. "Something to drink, sir?" he asked.

Michael nodded. "A bottle of champagne, please."

Kate was startled, but she merely smiled. Michael was obviously very excited.

When the champagne came, Kate toasted him. "To the smartest, most deserving man I know," she said, and she thought she saw Michael blush. The moment seemed appropriate, so she reached into her purse and took out the little blue Tiffany box. "I'm not sure these will be useful in Austin," she said, and placed the box between them on the table. "I would have picked something else, if I had known."

Then Michael did flush, either with pleasure or embarrassment — some men were awkward with gifts — and Kate felt that he would surely be disappointed. But he opened the box, held up the key chain, and grinned. "How nice," he said. "How very nice."

They ordered dinner, and Michael actually took a sip or two of champagne. He spent most of the time chatting about the Sagerman Foundation and the University of Texas. She was surprised to discover how unprepared she was for this eventuality, something that a part of her had been expecting for months. Why was that?

She had been waiting for a moment when he would ask her her opinion about what he should do or, at least, tell her his plans and ask if she might consider joining him. But it didn't seem to happen. He continued talking and it was hard for her to tell whether he had no intention of asking her to come or if he was simply taking her for granted.

After dinner they walked to her apartment. It was a balmy night, and Michael, swinging his briefcase with one hand, held her hand with the other. When they got to her door he reached into his pocket and took out the keys. "Allow me," he said, and opened the door for her. As they walked up the steps, Kate reached into her bag. For some reason she wanted to open her own apartment door, and she managed to beat him to it.

When they entered the living room, Michael threw his briefcase onto the sofa and immediately pulled off his tie. Kate thought he might be a little bit high from the bit of champagne that he had drunk. She, on the other hand, was as sober as a judge. In fact, she felt like a judge, busy weighing the pros and cons of the situation before her. When Michael took her hand and led her to her bedroom, she simply followed.

He began unbuttoning his shirt, sitting on the side of her bed. He took off his shoes, unsheathed his feet from their socks, and tucked the socks carefully into his shoes. When he stood up and undid his belt buckle, his chest bare, he looked over at her and smiled. "Do I have to undress you?" he asked.

Kate smiled back and hoped the smile didn't reveal her uneasiness. She wasn't uneasy because Michael would leave her. His great good humor was certainly inappropriate, and Michael was not an insensitive man.

Yet, like most men, he didn't feel her mood as he began to make love to her. She felt his hands on her waist, then lower, and he slipped her panties off. Then he moved his hands upward to cover her breasts. He kissed her, long and deeply, but Kate felt unmoved. When he began to touch her, she realized there was no way she could possibly have an orgasm. Ashamed to reveal herself, she simply eased herself into position over him and worked to make sure he achieved pleasure. But later, when they were finished, Michael sighed and dropped his head deep into the pillow. "You'll like Austin," he said.

Kate wasn't sure she'd heard the words. "What?" she asked.

"You'll like Austin," he said. "It's really great." Then he turned on his side and after a few deep breaths she knew he was sleeping.

She lay there silently but a storm of feelings swept through her. Had she just been proposed to? Clearly, Michael assumed not only that she was coming with him but that he didn't need to ask her to do it. He had talked plenty about the Sagerman chair and what it meant to him but never about what it might mean to her. She supposed that was because he knew it meant nothing. To him she meant nothing. She was someone who would go where he wanted. She couldn't believe his presumption or how little he knew her. Suddenly she felt deep shame, though she wasn't sure if it was for him or for her. How could she be sleeping with a man — how could he be intimate with her — when they didn't know each other at all?

Kate looked over his head at the dresser and the statue of the Virgin on it and wondered what was wrong with her.

Chapter Twenty-eight

It had been a few days since Kate had heard from Bina. When Bina did call, she just chattered on, not leaving a moment's opening for Kate's news. Apparently, she had been kept pretty busy by Billy. Kate supposed that was a good thing, since she needed time to figure out her own emotional landscape.

Still, after a few moments, Kate found herself feeling oddly resentful of Bina's harmless blather. She went on and on about Billy: how funny he was, what a good time they'd had over dinner, how sophisticated he seemed to be, and, last, what a gentleman he was. This, Kate knew, was Bina talk for him not jumping her bones when he said good night. "I can see why he gets all the girls," Bina said. "He just seems to really listen when you talk. You know how guys are so busy talking or else they kind of glaze over when you start talking?" Kate, thinking of Michael, reluctantly had to admit she knew. "Well, he doesn't do that."

"How refreshing," Kate said dryly. "So all is going well." Not that she was coming to believe in Elliot's ridiculous plan, but Billy's attentions must at the very least be a welcome break from the recent drama of Bina's life.

"Oh, we had the best time," Bina was saying. "He's just so much fun. When we went to this club that he knew, he . . ."

Kate found it hard to listen. Besides, she had her own tribulations. She hated to admit it, but she was beginning to believe that Elliot's assessment of Michael had been right. Although sweet and caring in some ways, Michael was self-involved, and lately she had found him . . . dull. In the past week, he had called her daily, giving her updates in what Kate was beginning to think of as the "Sagerman Situation." Since their dinner, he had spent most of their time together talking about nothing else.

". . . So then he goes, 'I would if I was crazy,' and I go, 'You are crazy. . . .'"

Kate had spent only a half day at Andrew Country Day today as the school year was winding down, and she had another half day tomorrow. She'd asked Michael over, but he had to attend a business lecture. Suddenly it came to her that tonight

348

would be the perfect evening to take a break from her own relationship and catch up with Bina's. And as a psychologist, she was interested in seeing how well Billy was handling himself with Bina. So far all seemed well, but she would find out this evening, if Bina had the time and inclination to see her.

"Hey," she said, breaking into Bina's monologue, "you wanna walk the bridge?"

Since they were teenagers, Kate and Bina had found pleasure in walking from one side of the Brooklyn Bridge to the other. Now, since Kate had moved across it, they occasionally met in the middle and then walked to one side or the other.

"You kidding?" Bina said. "God, we haven't done that in ages."

"Why not?" Kate asked. "I'll buy you dinner in Brooklyn Heights. At Isobel's." They both loved the restaurant, and Kate knew it would be great bait.

"Same old Kate," Bina said. "Let's go Dutch."

"Same old Bina." Kate laughed, and they agreed to meet in the middle of the bridge.

The walk was good for Kate. It felt as if it blew some of the cotton out of her clogged head. She thought about some of the children and how they might get through the summer; she thought about Michael and his "proposal"; but mostly she thought about herself. She had to be prepared to talk to Michael. She felt as if she should be happy. After all, wasn't this possibility what she had been hoping for? Even if it was, though, something nagged her about the way Michael was going about it. It wasn't that he was cold, exactly. It was more self-centered — but then weren't all men? If she was brutally honest with herself, she also had to admit that she didn't like the idea that he might be assuming she would just drop everything and go with him. Still, she had no one to blame but herself for that. And why shouldn't he assume (if he was assuming) that she would be willing to go to Texas with him? Unfortunately, there were plenty of dysfunctional families and a need for child psychologists everywhere. She could set up her own practice. She would be the first member of her family not only to become a doctor, but also to marry one. The Horowitzes would be so proud! And if there was something, well, something missing in her relationship with Michael, wasn't everything imperfect in some way or other? Relationships were built over time, with both people willing to listen and try to understand each other. Michael would certainly listen.

Kate, her thoughts tumbling about in her head, walked faster than she expected. When she hit the midpoint of the bridge, she was alone and couldn't even see Bina in the distance. She stopped for a moment, turned north, and looked up the East River. The water looked almost blue, and the Williamsburg and Triboro Bridges sandwiching Manhattan created a magical illusion. When she looked to the right, Brooklyn seemed flat and dull in comparison. Kate felt a little tug on her heart. She looked back at Manhattan. There, small as it was, she had a place of her own, a place she had created and lived in. Could she leave it? Why should she? She was so deep in thought that she didn't hear Bina until her friend was beside her and put her hand on Kate's shoulder.

"A nickel for your thoughts," Bina said.

"A nickel? I thought it was a penny."

"Inflation. Plus your thoughts are better than other people's."

Bina took her hand and led her away from Manhattan, just the way they used to do.

"So how's it going?" Kate asked. "Have you been proposed to?"

Bina laughed. With the wind catching her hair and the sunlight glancing off the blond streaks, she looked almost as good as a shampoo ad.

"That guy is crazy," she said. "We went to this club where they know him. Well, they know him everywhere. So everyone was saying hello. We didn't even have to wait to get in." She began to ramble on with details that Kate found tedious. ". . . and then they start playing 'Flavor of the Week' . . . you know the song?" she asked Kate.

"Yeah. I know it," Kate said.

"Well, it must be like his theme song. And everyone in the bar starts shouting: 'Billy! Billy!' And at first he's like brushing it off, you know what I mean?" Bina asked.

"Yeah. I know," Kate replied. She was feeling odd, as if Bina's simple story were upsetting her on some high school level.

"Anyway, they won't stop. So he gets on the bar and starts singing at the top of his lungs. It was such a riot." Bina laughed at the memory.

"Sounds like one," Kate said dryly.

"He's so not like Jack!" Bina said. "Can you imagine Jack . . ." A look came over her face, as if she had just heard her own words.

Kate knew her friend well enough to recognize conflict. Could Bina be falling for Billy? "Thank God he's not," she said, looking at Bina. "Right?" Bina nodded, but she looked slightly dejected.

Max had dropped by several times to inform Kate of Jack's latest bulletins. It was hard to tell if he did it because he was trying to be helpful, was horrified, or was just gossiping. Certainly he seemed outraged as he told her about Jack's barhopping and his delight in the beauty and apparent availability of Hong Kong women, both Asian and Caucasian. She wondered whether Bina had heard anything, but she guessed that Bina still hadn't heard from Jack, who had been gone for so many weeks now.

They had come to the end of the bridge. "Do you want to walk on the promenade before we eat?" Kate asked.

"Sure," Bina said, and they made a right, crossed Cadman Plaza, passed Isobel's, and walked up Cranberry Street. This was the charming part of Brooklyn, which looked virtually unchanged since the late 1800s. Brownstones lined the blocks, complete with little gardens in the front, and the trees arched overhead. "So how are things with the fruits and nuts?" Bina asked.

Kate raised her eyebrows, taking Bina's remark as a comment on Elliot as well as her little clients. Then she realized that Bina probably didn't know the connotation that "fruit" had. "They're not nuts," she said. "Although their parents sometimes are."

"Sorry," Bina said. "Didn't mean to hurt your feelers."

Kate had to smile. She and Bina had replaced the word *feelings* with *feelers* when they were ten years old, and Bina still used the joke. Kate decided to change the subject. "What have you bought Bev for the shower?" she asked.

"Omigod! Omigod!" Bina exclaimed, a new level of animation lighting up her face. "I went with my mother to the Macy's on Flatbush. We got the most adorable outfit you've ever seen. Tiny little booties, a matching sweater, and a bonnet. You should see the stitches, they're tiny. You know, everyone's knitting now. You think Bev would believe me if I told her I knit it myself?" Kate shook her head. "I showed them to Billy and you should've seen the look on his face. I don't think he believed a real person could be that small."

"Why in the world would you show baby clothes to Billy?" Kate asked, and was surprised by the irritation in her voice.

They reached the promenade, and Kate looked around appreciatively. Bina didn't pay much attention. She chatted on about the shower and then suggested they walk back to Isobel's to eat.

Brooklyn Heights was not really part of Brooklyn, Kate had always thought. It was Manhattan once removed, and the view of the island from the promenade was breathtaking. They were quiet for a little while, and then Bina broke the silence. "All I've been doing is talking about myself. So," she said with contrived casualness, "where did you and Michael go last night?"

"We went to a movie," Kate informed her friend, and realized she had said it with about as much enthusiasm as if they had gone to a funeral.

"The new George Clooney?" Bina asked, her eyes lighting up. To Bina, George Clooney was a walking god.

"Not exactly," Kate began. How could she explain their visit to the Film Forum? "We went to see a documentary."

"Oh," Bina said. "About what?"

"Afghan women and their struggle for

literacy," Kate said flatly.

Bina looked confused by the very thought. Kate figured that the last documentary Bina had seen was something they'd had to watch in grade school.

"That sounds . . . serious," Bina stammered, apparently unsure how to respond. She paused and looked across the bay at the Empire State Building, whose red, white, and blue lights had just been lit. "So, are you two getting serious?"

Kate could hear Mrs. Horowitz's voice channeled through Bina's lips. "I'm not sure," she said.

"There's not a serious bone in Billy's body . . . and what a body," Bina added.

"Bina!" Kate exclaimed. She looked over at her friend, whose change since Jack's departure seemed to be a lot more than physical. "You didn't . . . I mean, you wouldn't . . ." The thought of Bina with Billy disturbed her deeply. She tried to decide whether it was fear for Bina or envy.

"Of course not. I still love Jack," Bina said. Kate breathed a sigh of relief. "But I've got eyes. And he's got hands." Bina raised her brows playfully.

Kate was not sure this talk was as lighthearted as Bina was making it out to be. She herself had felt Billy's devastating, if

356

shallow, charm, and Bina was nothing if not inexperienced. "Bina, remember you are not supposed to be getting attached to this guy. He's only a means to an end — at least according to you and Elliot."

"I know. Believe me, I know. This whole plan is going to work. I just have a feeling." Bina paused. "And there's something else. Billy makes me feel . . . well, it's like I feel prettier when I'm with him." She looked away for a minute, and her face reddened. "I mean, I know people are probably looking at him, not me. But it makes me feel special, too." She smiled as if remembering something. "He always tells me how nice I look, and he notices things, like if I wear a barrette." She paused again. Then she lowered her voice, as if what she had to say were fragile and could be broken easily. "You know how much I love Jack." Kate nodded. "Well, I saw Max — you know, he's so nice. I don't understand why he isn't hooked up with someone. Anyway, he told me that Jack was sending him e-mails."

Kate managed not to gasp or show any emotion. A single one of those pictures would break Bina's heart.

"Anyway, I'm certain he misses me. And when he comes back, I'm sure he'll ask me to marry him."

The two of them walked down Henry Street. Kate was afraid to say a word to her friend. She didn't want to encourage her about Jack, and though she did want to discourage her about any attachment to Billy Nolan, she was not sure of her motives. They came to Henry's End restaurant, which was already bustling even though it was early for dinner. Well, Kate reminded herself, people ate earlier on this side of the river. "Are you hungry?" she asked. "Shall we eat here instead of Isobel's?"

"Sure," Bina told her. "Just don't make me eat a Bambi — and don't you eat Thumper." Henry's End was famous for wild game, though Kate would settle for steak.

"You can trust me on that," she told Bina.

Her friend took her arm. "I'll always trust you, Katie." They paused for a moment. "Hey, maybe you and Michael will get married and we could have a double wedding. My parents would love that."

Kate had a flash of an overdone ceremony, with the two of them walking down the aisle on Dr. Horowitz's arm. After that it would be a life full of documentaries, talks of anthropological discoveries, and Texas cocktail parties.

"Please, Bina," Kate said. "Not when we are near a very high bridge with a lot of cold water underneath it."

Chapter Twenty-nine

"There's a possibility you're actually going to get engaged?" Elliot asked Kate, his face pruning up with disapproval. They were sitting in the Starbucks located exactly halfway between his apartment and hers.

"You better stop disliking him," Kate told Elliot. "If I *do* marry him, and you stay snotty, I won't be able to see you anymore."

"Wedding bells are breaking up that old gang of mine," Elliot warbled. Kate shook her head. "Like I'm really threatened that you'd give up our friendship," he continued. "Who else do you have to talk about every detail of your emotional seismograph and Barbara Pym, too?"

Kate smiled. It was true she described every tremor to Elliot, and like a geophysicist, he had predicted when the earthquakes were coming to rock her world. And Barbara Pym, a British author she and Elliot both reread frequently, was one of her secret addictions. Kate found her novels soothing because almost nothing happened in them; no one's feelings were hurt, and very little changed. A big event was a visit from the vicar, and most chapters ended with someone having a hot, milky drink. Which reminded Kate about Elliot's beverage.

"Did you know that there are more calories in that coconut frappuccino than three Big Macs?" Kate asked.

"Speaking of Max," Elliot said, ignoring her concern, "is he still sniffing around? And is he sniffing around you or Bina?"

Kate made a dismissive gesture. Like a good mom, Elliot always thought every man was in love with Kate, and if they weren't, he was offended. "He seems to be busy carrying news about Jack to anyone who'll listen. I think he still feels guilty because he introduced Bina to him. Anyway, he's harmless." Kate grimaced as Elliot used his straw to suck up every last molecule of liquid at the very bottom of his cup. "That is truly disgusting," she said.

"Well, I promise not to do it in front of your friends at the shower."

"Bev's shower?" Kate asked, her voice rising. "You're invited to Bev's shower?"

"You sound surprised," Elliot said. Then, in a mocking tone, he added, "You

361

know, Bev and Brice and I are *very* close." Kate merely rolled her eyes.

"Hey, I saw Brian Conroy at lunch today, and he was actually laughing with two other little bandits," he continued. "I think they were slinging tunafish salad at the girls' table, but I didn't catch them at it. You might actually be doing some good work," he said.

They looked at each other for a long moment, Elliot smiling at her, his brown eyes warm and affectionate, and Kate basked in his approval. Then, as was their custom, they simultaneously shook their heads and bleated, "Nah!!"

"So what is it with you and Michael?" Kate asked, returning to the subject. "He's the kind of stable, nice guy you've wanted for me. And he likes me." As she looked down at the bracelet hanging from her wrist, her cell phone rang. She was expecting a call from Rita about drinks after Rita got out of work, which wasn't usually until six or seven o'clock. She pulled out her cell phone and, without even glancing at the caller ID, hit the green button.

"Hi," she said cheerfully, fully expecting Rita's nasal voice.

"Hi back atchya," said Steven's voice.

Kate felt her stomach contract and drop.

Suddenly there wasn't enough air in her lungs. "Oh. Steven. Hello." She opened her eyes wide, but not as wide as Elliot's.

"Steven? *The* Steven?" he mouthed.

Kate, already rattled, looked away. She could feel her throat tighten.

"Am I getting you at a bad time?" Steven asked.

She wanted to say, "No. The bad time was the six months after you stopped calling," but needless to say, she didn't. Any time was a bad time to talk to Steven, as far as she was concerned. "No," she said. "I'm just having coffee with Elliot." She could have bitten her tongue. Why couldn't she have said she was with a date?

"Good old Elliot," Steven said, which made Kate even more annoyed with herself. "I miss him." His voice dropped a half register. "I miss *you,* too," he said.

Kate felt a flush spreading to her neck and chest. Meanwhile, Elliot was crouching in front of her, pulling his index finger across his throat to get her to cut off the conversation. She turned her head to the right.

Kate didn't need to be reminded of how dangerous Steven was. She had really loved him, and he had encouraged her attachment. Long ago, Kate had made a rule never to care for any man more than he cared for her. But Steven had cared for her — at least as long as the early lust stage had lasted. Then, after eighteen months his ardor and his commitment had dropped off. Kate hadn't felt it at first, and by the time she had realized that he was not still focused on her, she had run into him walking with the woman to whom his focus had shifted. When Kate, humiliated, had confronted him, he had been reluctant to admit the truth and had reassured her that nothing had happened between him and Sabrina, but after Kate broke up with him, a miserable six weeks later, he and Sabrina had hooked up. Now, the question Kate longed to ask was, "What's happened to Sabrina?" But she wouldn't let her curiosity overwhelm her common sense and pride.

"Look, I thought we might meet for a coffee or something," Steven said.

"I don't think so," Kate said. "I'm having coffee right now."

"You're not making this easy," Steven said, and the depth of feeling in his voice gave Kate a little thrill. All at once she realized what she had felt was missing in Michael — access to deeper feelings or the ability to express them.

But Steven's feelings, deep or not, had not been dependable. He was either an excellent actor (Elliot's opinion) or a man afraid of his own emotions, longing for connection and then backing away from it (Kate's theory). Kate still believed that Steven had loved her but had been afraid.

"Was it my job to make it easy?" Kate asked. Elliot rolled his eyes and put a hand over his own mouth to indicate that she should shut up — as if she didn't know that already. She swatted at him.

"Kate, you have every right to be pissed at me. But I swear that a day hasn't gone by that I haven't thought of you, or missed you, or even tried to get up the courage to phone you."

"It must have been a tough year," Kate said.

"Don't tell me you haven't thought of me," Steven said, and all of it — the miserable nights, the lonely weekends, the mornings she woke up alone and missing him — came rushing back.

"I've been pretty busy," she said. "And I'm about to get engaged. . . ."

Elliot bolted upright, gave her a thumbs-up with both hands, and then sank back into his chair as if exhausted.

There was silence at the other end of the

phone, and Kate was torn between two emotions: She wanted Steven to give up and feel just a little bit of pain on her account. She also wanted him to try harder, and she was ashamed and embarrassed by that.

"Would that stop you from just having a drink with me?" Steven asked. "I really feel as if I need to tell you what happened. I mean, I'm in therapy now and . . . I just understand a few things that I didn't know before."

Kate wasn't sure she wanted to know what Steven had learned about himself. And she knew it wasn't a good idea to see him. But she felt an irresistible pull toward him. "How about next Monday," she said. "About four o'clock."

"That would be great," Steven said. "Onieal's?" It was a restaurant on Grand Street, a cool but lush bar and dining room. It had been a place they often went to, not far from his loft.

"No," she said. She didn't want to be seduced into drinks followed by dinner followed by anything else. It was out of the question. She thought as quickly as she could about a more neutral site. "How about Starbucks?" And after he agreed she hung up and threw her phone into her purse.

"You are not going!" Elliot said. "You know why you're not going? Because I cannot hear one more word about that stupid fucking ass-fuck. Do you know how much Steven I had to live with last year? How many times can a man — even a gay man — sing 'I Will Survive' with you?"

Kate didn't know if she wanted to laugh or cry. They did actually sing Gloria Gaynor's song a few times, but only at Elliot's demand and because it always made her laugh.

"We wore out three CDs, and speaking of wearing out, you might be self-destructive, but I have a life and I can't go through another Steven bout. Maybe you don't remember what it did to you, but I do. And I just can't take it. Neither can you."

"I'm not going to go through another Steven 'bout,' " Kate snapped. "But he's in therapy and he probably needs some closure."

"What he probably needs is some pussy," Elliot said. "And that's fine with me as long as it isn't yours."

"Elliot!"

"I can't believe he calls you for the first time in a year in the middle of the afternoon on your cell phone and you make a date with him. Have you no pride?" Elliot asked, then continued without waiting for an answer: "You're a disgrace to your sex. It's because of you that women need to read *The Rules* and those other stupid self-help books." He moved his arms in a spasm of disgust and completely upset Kate's drink. "Oh, shit," he said, and Kate wasn't sure if he was referring to the spill or her mistake.

Because it was a mistake. Wasn't it?

Chapter Thirty

It was crowded in Bunny and Arnie's new apartment; everyone sat or stood in perfect silence in the dark. Which was quite a trick when Kate considered the compulsive talkers she was there with. Bunny, Barbie, Mrs. Horowitz, Bina, two of Bev's cousins, Bev's mom and two aunts, assorted friends from work, and Bev's astrologist, not to mention Elliot and Brice, were all there and quiet. But only for a moment.

"Surprise!" the entire crowd shouted as the door opened. The lights went on and pink and blue balloons — big, but not as big as Bev's third-trimester belly — cascaded from the ceiling. Flashbulbs went off all around the room, capturing forever Bev's rictus of fear as she screamed and jumped. Guests screamed and jumped as well. After the explosions were over, Kate watched as a palpitating Bev leaned on her mother's arm.

She took a seat, from where she surveyed the scene of laughing friends and relatives.

She clutched her face and screamed, "Aah, you guys," as soon as she could speak. "I swear my water almost broke! You shouldn't have." She'd been told to "drop over at Bunny's new apartment for a look-see."

Kate agreed with that. There was something sadistic about surprise parties, but, "Yes, we should have and we did," Barbie told Bev, joining her on the sofa, a hideous blue three seater.

In fact, virtually all of Bunny's new apartment was in blue, and most of it was hideous. Kate had forgotten that nobody in Brooklyn south of Prospect Park believed in antiques — things were either new or junk. Kate considered the royal blue rayon-damask upholstered furniture in the living room new *and* junk, but everyone else had oohed and aahed over Bunny's new marital home on the obligatory tour before Bev's arrival. Even Elliot, not only color-blind but largely tasteless, had raised his eyebrows at the smoked mirror framed with golden cherubs and the Museum Shop lamps with fake busts of antiquity mounted under the shades. Brice, however, was in ecstasy. "Just like Picasso," he had murmured to Kate and Elliot. "She's having her blue period."

The wall-to-wall carpet was a peacock blue in the living room, a Madonna blue in the master bedroom, and a royal blue in the second bedroom. The bathrooms, one full and one half, were also, needless to say, blue. One was papered in periwinkle with green vines and matching green towels, "the essential accent" (as Bunny had explained). The other was done in navy foil. "I wanted something masculine for Arnie," she'd told them, though why shiny dark walls were manly was something Kate couldn't fathom.

"I didn't know they still made foil," Brice had said, marveling.

"I know. I had to go on-line to find it," Bunny had confided.

But Kate wasn't looking around only at the apartment, she was also looking at her friends. Each one was committed to a life that would almost inevitably include children, PTA meetings, family holidays, trips to Disney World, and all the trimmings that came not only on the Christmas tree (or Hanukkah bush), but also with the comfy order of family life. She wondered if she would ever leave the little nest she had carved out for herself in Manhattan and, if she did, what she would trade it for. Somehow the prospect of doing it in

Austin without either her Manhattan or her Brooklyn friends to support or encourage her seemed grim. At least when she had been with Steven she knew that her future — if there was one — would be in New York.

Once Bev got over her surprise, all of the guests felt free to tear into the platters of food. Set out on the dining table and credenza (both covered with sky blue cloths, with napkins to match) was a truly impressive spread. Everything from bagels with four varieties of cream cheese to pasta salads, Thai sate, canapés, and cannolis was arrayed in overwhelming profusion. Elliot picked up a plate and heaved a big sigh of happiness. "I love it here," he said.

"Oops. He's up another waist size," Brice said, and patted Elliot lovingly.

Everyone seemed to be enjoying themselves enormously, except Bina. Kate didn't want another recitation of Billy Nolan's charms, so she had avoided Bina just a little. But it didn't seem necessary: Kate realized that Bina was avoiding her. She was sitting, her plate heaped high, next to one of Bev's cousins, but she wasn't talking or eating. Only Bev's nephew, a four-year-old who sat on the floor dutifully chewing whatever his grandma or mother put in his mouth, seemed capable of bringing a smile to her lips.

"Okay. Let's get down to business," Barbie told everyone once the food frenzy had subsided. "Open the presents! Open the presents!"

Everyone cheered and agreed except Bina. Kate kept an eye on her as box after box was unwrapped.

All the gifts had been opened, and Bev's mother was wrestling in the wrapping paper as if it were a pile of leaves that had been raked up in the fall. Bev was holding up a tiny sweater and examining the knitted bonnet that went with it.

Kate touched the tiny piece of hand-knit material, and all at once, she was almost overcome by a wave of feeling so unexpected and so strong that she had to sit down. Up till now, for some inexplicable reason, Bev's pregnancy had been just that — a swelling stomach, a few inappropriate outfits, and some complaints. Holding the tiny sweater, Kate realized that very soon, Bev — and Johnny, of course — would have a new person as tiny as the little bit of wool, to hold and love and care about for the rest of their lives. Kate felt so very far from that reality that tears of envy and despair filmed her eyes. She had to turn her head away so no one would notice her sudden rush of emotion.

I want a baby of my own, she thought, and realized at the same time that she was further away from that possibility than she had been for a long time. Because she suddenly knew, absolutely knew, as she held the little sweater, that she wouldn't want to be putting it on Michael's child. The very idea was . . . well, it just wasn't possible.

"Have some rugelach, Katie," Mrs. Horowitz offered, and Kate looked up. She must have appeared as dazed as she felt, because Mrs. Horowitz exclaimed, "You're so pale. Are you all right, darling?"

The answer, of course, was no, but how could she explain that to kind, concerned, simple Myra Horowitz?

Now that all the gifts had been opened, the women went back to the food. Soon, overfilled paper plates were being balanced precariously next to plastic cups of juice, margaritas, or New York State champagne. The Bitches, Brice, and Elliot gathered in a small group in the corner near the easy chair that Bev had settled into.

"So, is it a girl or a boy?" Barbie asked, taking a bite of her bagel.

Bev looked at her mother, then

shrugged. "Johnny and I want a surprise," she said, but Kate saw the look that passed between them and knew better.

"I think you should name him William," Elliot said.

"After the prince?" Bev asked.

"No. After Billy Nolan. The man who made all this possible," Elliot told her.

"See, Elliot's theory works. Just think. You're next," Brice told Bina with frightening assurance.

"That's right, Bina," Bunny agreed.

"Jack'll come around," Bev's mother told Bina in a comforting tone. "Remember how hard it was to get her Johnny to propose? I'm glad you stayed local, Bina, and didn't go into Manhattan like Katie."

"Yeah," Barbie echoed. "It's even harder to get them to commit."

"That's not true," Kate began to protest, "I don't think that location has —"

"Kate's doing okay," Elliot cut in defensively.

"Yeah," Brice echoed. "She's getting a proposal from this doctor guy."

Kate felt the blood leave her face.

"Get outta town!" Barbie cried.

"You sneak! You didn't say a word," Bunny squawked.

"What's his sign?" Bev demanded.

Kate was kissed and pummeled for a few minutes, until she could get a word in. "I'm not 'getting a proposal,'" she told them all, then gave Brice a dirty look. He shrugged an apology. Kate tried to find words to describe her situation with Michael and put out the blazing fire of curiosity around her. "We're talking about options."

"Options, schmopshins," said Mrs. Horowitz. "So what kind of doctor? Not a surgeon," she warned. "Surgeons are cold, Katie."

"He's not a medical doctor," Kate said, then heard all the sighs of disappointment that moved through the room like a summer breeze.

"It doesn't matter if he's not a *real* doctor," she said to Kate, her voice low. "As long as you love him." Kate managed a smile and took a pastry.

Then she shot Elliot and Brice a murderous look. "They don't know what they're saying. Anyway, we were talking about Bina."

"Maybe we shouldn't," Bina said quietly.

"Oh, everything is going to work out fine," Bunny said, and she put her arm around Elliot. It seemed to Kate that the group had adopted Elliot and Brice as girlfriends in drag.

"She's got Dumping Billy on her side," Barbie said.

"He hasn't dumped you yet, though, has he?" Bev asked Bina.

"No. Not yet. But I'm really looking forward to it," Bina said, obviously uncomfortable.

"Well, it's been a long time," Barbie pointed out.

"According to Elliot's theory, that makes sense," Barbie said.

"No. Actually, it doesn't. This whole thing doesn't make sense, and it's making me crazy," Kate told the women irritably. Somehow everything seemed wrong: her with Michael, Bina with Billy, Jack with a bevy of foreign beauties, Steven calling her from out of the blue. It was like a French farce. Looking at Bina and suddenly feeling sorry for herself, Kate blinked back tears and took a piece of the shower cake to comfort herself.

"Oh, well, it has to be at least two months or else it doesn't work. And I'm a little uncomfortable," Bina admitted.

Bev put her hand on the back of the chair to help herself up. "Honey, you don't have any idea what uncomfortable is. You *cannot* give up now," she said matter-of-factly.

"Stay the course," Barbie advised Bina. "Billy can't last much longer. You're not his type."

"Oh, no? He's asked me to the Hamptons this weekend," Bina said without enthusiasm.

The Bitches squealed with delight, wisecracked, elbowed, and laughed to one another.

"What's so funny?" Bina asked them.

"What you don't know about men could fill a library," Bev said.

"A big one. A Manhattan one," Bunny added.

"What don't I know?" Bina demanded.

"Bina, honey, this will be the end. Men like Billy freak out after a weekend alone with a woman," Barbie said. "He's sure to drop you after that."

"But then why would he ask me?" Bina did look really upset. Kate wondered again if her friend was falling for that self-centered idiot. "It wasn't my idea."

"That's the point," Bunny told her.

"They like the idea of intimacy . . . ," Bev began.

"But the reality is they freak out because of all the one-on-one time," Barbie continued.

"Really, Bina. Go to the Hamptons and

you are as good as dumped," Bunny assured Bina.

"I don't know. It seems like false pretense," Bina told them.

"Maybe it is, but you can't turn back now," Bev said as she walked to the refreshments table.

Bina had been juggling her plate of food on her lap and suddenly lost control of it. The entire thing fell down her dress and onto the floor. The Bitches fell silent and stared at her.

Kate had felt something was wrong with Bina's behavior since they'd arrived, and now, as if to confirm that, instead of cleaning up the mess, Bina took Kate's hand and began to pull her down the hall. "I have to talk to you," she whispered.

"Wait a minute," Kate said, and put down her glass of red wine as they passed a side table, afraid that a spill would turn the carpet an irrevocable purple. Bina pulled her into the guest bedroom and sat her down on the sofa bed.

"I can't believe it, Katie," she said, and her voice caught on a sob. "I'm so ashamed. I never thought . . . I could never believe that I . . . Omigod, Jack."

Kate had no idea what Bina was going on about, but she was upset to hear her so upset. And in a different way from her usual innocent hysteria. "What *is* it, Bina?" she asked gently.

"If my mother knew . . . Oh, Katie! I cheated on Jack."

"Bina, a few dates doesn't mean —"

"No. I mean I really did. I had sex. I mean the whole thing. And it was . . . wonderful."

As Bina burst into tears, Kate felt the room and the noise of the party receding. And this new information, this sexual misadventure of Bina's, was exactly what she had been afraid of. She felt herself becoming angry but wasn't sure whom she was angry at or with. Elliot should never have proposed this, she should never have allowed it, Bina shouldn't have fallen for Billy's empty charm, and she was most angry that Billy, in true Lothario fashion, had taken advantage of Bina's inexperience.

What had she done? She and Elliot and the Bitches had interfered in Bina's life, and the results were this: a girl awash in guilt and tears and confusion. Hadn't they all succeeded in ruining Bina's loyalty and single-minded devotion? Perhaps it was a bad thing, to count on one man to come through for you and to believe there was nobody else. Still, Bina should have been left to make her own choices. Setting her up with a man like Billy Nolan was sure to be her undoing. And now, what if she decided she loved him? What if after the heartbreak of Jack's desertion she was dumped again, as was inevitable? It would destroy her self-confidence. Kate didn't even want to imagine what Bina might do.

She took her friend by the shoulders and stared into her eyes. "Listen to me, Bina. Whatever you did is all right. Jack has been off sleeping around, and if you had a slip, so —"

"But I don't feel like it was a slip," Bina said, and began crying anew. "I feel as if he appreciates me. He says that since he saw me he's felt that not grabbing me up was a mistake."

Kate recalled how she'd had to challenge Billy even to consider Bina as date material. She was furious at everyone — at Jack, at Elliot, at the Bitches . . . even at herself. But beneath all of that, there was another feeling. "Bina, you can't believe everything men say," she began cautiously.

"Katie, I never doubted my love for Jack. I mean, I do love Jack. It's just that now that I've had some more experience . . . well, I just can't explain it. He's so understanding. And it's like we never run out of things to talk about." She paused.

"Look, Bina, you have not been disloyal. Just don't confuse this, this little adventure with real love."

Bina looked at Kate solemnly. "You're right," she said, and nodded. "I won't let it happen again. Because I really, really do love Jack."

"Good girl," Kate told her. "Now, just don't think about it anymore. You don't have to do what you don't want to do."

Bina nodded, then wiped her eyes. "But he was so very, very good in bed." She blushed, and Kate felt her own face color because she realized what the other feeling was.

She was envious.

Kate left the shower before Brice and Elliot. She was too despondent to take the subway, so as an indulgence, she looked for a taxi. It wasn't easy in Brooklyn — another reason to stay in Manhattan, she reflected sourly. But at last she flagged down an off-duty taxi who was merely avoiding a fare that would take him deeper into Brooklyn.

Kate sat in the backseat, grateful for the time alone. Though she loved both Brice and Elliot, she simply wasn't up for their chatter. She had a lot of thinking to do, and though she had put off dealing with her reality until now, she would have to come to terms with it. What was it that she really wanted? Of course, that was easy to answer: a perfect life with a rewarding job, a loving, dependable, and passionate husband, healthy children, and good friends. Good fucking luck, she told herself. She couldn't see any indications in her future that would promise it all. If you got one part, you wouldn't get the other. Yet Kate had promised herself for all these years that she wouldn't compromise.

As they crossed the Brooklyn Bridge, she stared at the city. The skyline, as always, moved her deeply. But now she had to admit that she was even more deeply moved by Bina's revelation. How could she go on with Michael when she felt drawn to someone as useless as Billy Nolan? His behavior with Bina had only further convinced her of his heartlessness, and the fact that a part of her — not the good part — still desired him was shameful. One thing she was certain of: She wouldn't become confused and reassess Steven's actions in light of Billy's. What did it matter which of them was worse?

Kate looked out the taxi window and wished that she could stay forever suspended on the bridge between the two boroughs in her life.

Chapter Thirty-one

Kate sat at a window table in the Chelsea
Kitchen and played with her fork, laying it
down, picking it up, tapping the bottom, and
then touching the tines to her water glass,
her plate, and even the folded napkin. She
was uncomfortable in the restaurant, but she
had decided that she would do this in a
public place. That's what men do, she
thought, and remembered Steven. Probably
it was because they were afraid of scenes.
Kate knew that wasn't a realistic threat with
Michael, but she couldn't imagine having
this talk and then moving through his apartment on her way to the door or, worse,
asking him to leave her place. Since yesterday at the shower, Kate had known with
blinding clarity that Michael was not for her.
And today she'd asked Michael to meet her
here, to avoid having to engage in senseless
chatter as they walked along.

Beside her on the floor was a Big Brown
Bag from Bloomingdale's. When she
forced herself to put down the fork, she

used the same hand to check again that the bag was there — as if anyone would want to steal folded shorts and athletic socks, a razor, half-used-up toiletries, and an old tie Michael had left at her house. She wiped her palms on the napkin, surprised to find how sweaty they were. The truth was that she had little experience in being the initiator of a breakup.

When the waiter came over, she asked for vodka on the rocks. She didn't usually drink hard liquor, and when she did it was generally a cosmopolitan, a drink that had come in and gone out of fashion but that she still liked. Today, however, she needed a jolt of something. She remembered a phrase her father used to use — "Dutch courage" — and for the first time she really appreciated its meaning. She needed courage, Dutch or otherwise.

When the waiter returned with her order, she downed it in two long gulps with barely a breath between them. Only then did she realize that she didn't want Michael to see her drinking, and she also didn't want him to smell alcohol on her breath. Why? That had always been a strained part of their relationship. Though he had never tried to intimidate her or force her to change, Kate realized she had often walked on eggshells with Michael. She wondered now if she had ever really been herself with him. She wasn't sure if it was his personality that had imposed restraints on her. Perhaps that wasn't fair. Perhaps his academic credentials and his comfortable suburban background had created a sense of inferiority in her. Maybe they both had a classic fear of intimacy. But whatever it was, Kate knew something was not right, something not fixable, about their relationship.

She waved to the waiter and handed him the evidence. "Can I get you another?" he asked, no doubt taking her for a heavy drinker, but she shook her head. Then she picked up a piece of the garlic bread from the basket on the table. Better to smell of garlic than vodka. People mistakenly thought you couldn't detect it on a person's breath, but Kate always could — maybe because of her father.

She munched on the bread and looked out the window. In the late afternoon, there weren't many people on West 18th Street. She wondered where the man with the red tips at the ends of his black hair was going and whether the woman who looked like a real estate broker in her fake Chanel suit actually was one. Kate sighed.

She'd probably never be able to afford to buy an apartment or own her own home. Here in Manhattan, it was difficult enough as a couple. As a single person, it was impossible.

She had no home of her own, no summer plans, and soon she'd have no man in her life.

Kate took a sip of her water and looked out at the traffic. It was a wet day, and though the drizzle had stopped for the moment, it had put a sheen on the macadam, the trucks and taxis, and even the sidewalks and buildings across the way. She loved Manhattan, and this simple silvery scene outside the restaurant window calmed her. Could she leave this for Austin, or anywhere?

On the other hand, she could be completely crazy. Aside from the Arnies, Johnnys, Eddies, and the rest of the Brooklyn world, it seemed there were no marriageable men. Rita and every other one of her Manhattan girlfriends complained about how the men here were players or neurotics or commitment phobes. She thought back to Steven and the pain she had gone through after he left her. She wasn't having this talk with Michael just because of her upcoming meeting with Steven. Steven was out of her life, although she couldn't help feeling a bit of excitement, the old buzz, when she thought of seeing him. It would be nice to look at him, talk with him, and feel nothing. She hoped she could manage it. She looked down and saw that the fork in her hand was actually trembling. Could she hurt Michael like this? Could she bear to be alone, start dating again, and risk being hurt again?

The waiter returned with a pitcher of water. Her glass was half-empty, or half-full. She supposed, as he poured out the water, that it was all in the eye of the beholder. If she discussed what she was about to do with Barbie, Bev, or even Mrs. Horowitz, they would tell her she was crazy. Her glass was half-full. Still, while she knew that Steven was dangerous and not for her, simply hearing from him had reminded her of how much she had felt for him when they were together. The disparity between that feeling and the pale echo of it that she felt for Michael frightened her. She just didn't think that she could bear to go through life without stronger feelings for her companion.

Kate couldn't suppress the surge of feeling she was experiencing not only from

Steven's call, but also from the overwhelming envy she'd felt when Bina told her about her actual affair with Billy. Kate knew she couldn't stay with Michael. Michael was a safe, dependable partner, and yes, he'd make a responsible father. But for someone else's children, not hers.

Even if she was ruining her last chance of settling down, Kate couldn't settle for him. She placed the fork she'd been holding back in its proper place. A young woman, obviously an au pair, walked by with a little girl who looked about four. Both were wearing yellow raincoats. Kate smiled and thought of the children she was working with at Andrew Country Day. Everything about her job, from her little office, to Elliot down the hall, to the easy commute from home, to the children she worked with, seemed precious to her. Now, at the thought of losing it, she could feel just how precious it was. Even Dr. McKay seemed lovable in his ridiculous way. And Michael believed it was nothing to her? Did he know her at all?

When Michael walked in, Kate was still staring out the window. She jumped when he put his hand on her shoulder. "I got caught in the rain," he said as he shook his umbrella and took the seat across from her.

Kate looked at him. His jaw was still strong, his nose still regular, his eyes a warm brown. But as if a spell had been broken, Kate no longer found him the slightest bit attractive. As he set his brief-case on the empty chair, she wondered whether this kind of reversal had happened to Steven: whether one day he had just looked at her and felt nothing but . . . a mild distaste. The idea made her skin crawl. The combination of the drink and what she was about to do made her stomach feel queasy.

"Would you like something to drink?" Michael asked her.

She managed a weak smile. "No, thank you," she told him as soberly as she could manage.

The solicitous waiter appeared un-bidden, and Kate hoped he wouldn't blow her cover by asking if she wanted *another* vodka on the rocks.

"A cup of tea," Michael requested. "Earl Grey, if you have it."

"Nothing for me," Kate said.

After the waiter moved off, Michael looked out the window, as Kate had been doing. "Well, we won't have to put up with this kind of weather in Austin."

"Why?" Kate asked. "Doesn't it rain

there?" But she didn't pursue it. Why be unpleasant? She didn't know how to begin, so she just launched into her prepared speech. "Michael, I can't go to Austin. First because I don't want to; I like it here. Secondly, because you didn't ask me. You *assumed* I could come with you. We had no discussion. It was as if you were granting me some kind of favor. You just thought I would jump at the chance."

Michael blinked and put down the cup that was halfway to his lips. Kate saw some of the tea splash over the lip and onto the tablecloth, but Michael didn't seem to notice. "Kate. Kate, I just felt —"

"I'm not sure what you felt," Kate said. "But it isn't what *I* felt. And you didn't know it."

Michael sat absolutely still, and the table — no more than twenty-six inches wide — seemed to Kate to be expanding to tundra proportions. She could almost see Michael receding into the distance, his face bluish in the reflected light from the white cloth that stretched between them. "Kate, I never meant to be presumptuous. I just thought, well, I thought you wanted what I wanted."

"That may be true, but since we never actually spoke about what we wanted, how was I to know?"

Michael sat still and looked at her as if he were seeing her for the first time. Had she been guilty of trying too hard to please? Had she kept her feelings and fears from him? Somehow it didn't seem to matter anymore. Even if Michael now told her he was willing to give up the Austin job and make a home with her here, Kate was no longer interested. Am I fickle? she thought. She couldn't answer the question, but she knew that a single life, alone and with no children, would be better than a half-life with Michael. He simply wasn't the man for her.

"Kate, I can't tell you how floored I am by this. I mean, it's coming out of nowhere. I've been busy making plans, assuming —"

"Never assume, Michael," Kate said. "Never presume. My life is just as important to me as yours is to you. I'm not sure you ever recognized that."

"Of course I did," Michael said. "But you could make new friends and set up a practice in Austin. You could visit back here whenever you wanted. And it's not as if you have family here."

"Oh yes, I do," Kate said. She thought of Elliot and Brice and Bina and the Horowitzes. Even the Bitches meant a lot to her. "They might not be DNA related, but I have family all the same." She paused. "I don't know whose fault it is, Michael; let's not talk about fault, and let's not blame each other. It isn't as if I've felt this way for months and withheld the knowledge from you. It's just that once you told me about Austin and made your decision unilaterally, I guess I made mine. I'm very sorry." She reached across the tablecloth to touch his hand, but he pulled away, spilling the tea in the process. It spread, like a brown blot, across the pure white space between them. For a moment Kate was reminded of the bowling alley and her spilled beer. "I'm sorry," she repeated, "because there's nothing else to say." She stood up, holding the shopping bag. "Here are your things," she said. "If I've forgotten some of them, let me know."

Oddly, she didn't feel sad, and she didn't feel free. She felt nothing. Michael was still looking at her, his face torn between disbelief and anger.

"Good luck in Austin," she said, and walked out of the restaurant.

Kate walked in the drizzle, which had started up again and now perfectly reflected her frame of mind. She felt she'd be miserable for the rest of her life, but she couldn't imagine Michael feeling too bad for too long. It wasn't his style. That was the reason she'd left him: He didn't feel things.

After about half an hour, she found herself in front of the gym. She walked in in time to see Elliot just finishing up his cardio on the StairMaster. Once he caught sight of her, he became instantly concerned.

"What have you done? You're supposed to take your clothes off before you shower." He led her over to one of the leather banquettes and helped her out of her sodden raincoat. "You're wet right through," he said, and fussed for a few minutes with towels. When Kate's wet hair had been wrapped in a turban and the towel hugged her neck, Elliot was ready for conversation.

"I broke up with Michael," Kate said.

"Good." Elliot nodded, then put his arm around her. "It was only a matter of time. And this saves you a ticket to Austin, which you can spend on a share in our house this summer."

Kate, who had expected more surprise and a lot more sympathy, shook her head. "I don't think being the only woman in a house full of gay men in Cherry Grove would be the thing for me right now."

"Oh, come on. You'd have more fun than you would with any of your straight boyfriends. When did Michael ever make you laugh the way Brice does? When did Steven *ever* make you laugh?" Elliot stopped and stared at her so intently that she knew she was in trouble. He leaned forward, his elbows on his knees, his nose an inch away from hers. "You're not still going to meet up with Steven, are you?"

And, of course, Kate was.

Chapter Thirty-two

Kate expected nothing from the meeting with Steven the next afternoon, but her pride made her primp. She was vain enough to want to look her best, and she put on extra mascara and French-braided her hair. Steven had always liked it like that.

As she was leaving her apartment and pulling the door shut behind her, she stopped, gazing out into space, remembering too vividly the last time she'd seen Steven and the way they had parted at this door.

"Forget something?" Max asked from behind her.

Startled, she spun around. "Oh, no, just thinking is all. What's up with you lately?"

"Not much. How about you?" He lounged against the wall.

Now was not the time to explain what she was doing or going to do, and Max certainly wasn't the person she should confide in. "I'm actually going to be late for a meeting," she said, and tried to step by him. Max wasn't exactly a nuisance: He was a nice guy, but she didn't have time for him.

But he wouldn't let her go. He reached out and touched her arm. Again, she was startled. "I've heard from Jack again," he said, and shifted from foot to foot. "Or should I say, I've gotten e-mails. He sent me more pictures."

Kate sighed. It was bad news that didn't have to be shared.

As if he could read her mind, Max looked away and said, "I still don't think I should show them to Bina."

"Absolutely not," Kate told him. "You know she's pretty tight with Billy now, and I don't want her to get upset about Jack again."

"Billy? Who's Billy?" Max asked, his forehead wrinkled.

"Oh, that's a long story you don't have the time to —"

"I'll listen. Try me. I've got the time." He sounded more anxious than casual.

God, he was such a gossip! "Unfortunately, I don't," Kate told him. "I'm going to be late." She made her way to the stairs at the end of the hall, then looked back to see Max sliding down the wall to sit on the floor. Since when was Max so compassionate about her friends? Sure, Jack was his cousin and he might feel some responsibility for Bina, but not to this extent.

"You know, I worry about Bina," Max said. "I need to talk to Jack."

"No, you don't," Kate called to him as she ran down the stairs. "Leave well enough alone."

Steven looked terrific. Well, Kate reflected, Steven had always looked terrific to her. As he stood up, his length unfolded, reminding Kate of one of those hinged yardsticks. He smiled, and his smile broke the parentheses, the lines on each side of his mouth that looked so attractive on men.

"Hi," he said. "What can I get you?"

Kate was glad she hadn't committed to dinner. Though he lived in the East Village, Kate had selected the Starbucks near her apartment. It was safe: Steven wouldn't expect her to have a meal with him, and Elliot never frequented that place. Steven had what looked like a very large caffè latte in front of him, half of it gone. He must have arrived early. "An iced tea," she said in answer to his question, and took the seat across from him at his tiny table in the corner. He nodded and was at the counter in a moment. It gave Kate a chance to smooth her hair and look at him from behind.

He was still long and lean — at six feet three it was easy to be long, but perhaps he wasn't quite as thin as he had been. His hair, however, was still as beautiful: a thick black waterfall that gleamed like a crow's wing. Kate remembered too vividly how she had loved to stroke his hair. He turned and came back to her, the iced tea and a paper plate of biscotti in his hands. They were the anise ones that she liked. She was touched and surprised that he remembered, but when he picked one up himself, she thought that perhaps he'd gotten them for himself.

It was the time of day when few people dropped in for coffee: after the rush that followed lunch, but before the rush that followed dinner. No clients lingered except for the inevitable madman writing in something that looked like a journal and an older gentleman — obviously — who sat in a plush chair near the window, reading a rumpled copy of *The New York Times* in the waning afternoon light.

She took a sip of her tea and they sat for a moment in silence. Kate had promised herself that she wasn't going to do much talking. She felt him looking at her and returned his gaze passively.

"You look terrific," he said.

Kate smiled and hoped the smile was what art historians and novelists called "enigmatic." "I'm glad you could meet me," he added. He paused, but Kate maintained her silence. "Well, enough about you," Steven said, "how do I look?"

"I think you've grown," Kate said, tongue-in-cheek. "Do men have growth spurts?"

"Sure, but only emotional ones. And it's pretty rare." He stopped smiling, and his face took on the lean and hungry look that Kate remembered from their lovemaking and his talk about his ambitions. He wore it, she knew, when he wanted things. But she remained silent, waiting to hear what it was that he wanted now.

"Kate, do you ever think about how it was . . . I mean, how it was between us?"

She was grateful that Elliot wasn't there to smack his forehead and whine about the months she had relived every detail of her time with Steven. "I've been busy," she said.

Steven nodded. "I deserved that," he said. "But I've been thinking about you. Actually, I can't stop thinking about you. I do it all the time."

"That isn't good," Kate said in exactly the same tone of voice Elliot would have used.

Steven didn't seem to notice. "I'm here to tell you I was an asshole. I would say cad, but it's too archaic. Asshole covers a lot of territory, but you know what I mean."

Kate nodded and took another sip of her tea. "I think lying asshole would be more accurate," she said. She turned her head toward the window so that she wouldn't display any visible emotion to him. To her horror, out of the corner of her eye she thought she saw Max walking by. Was he with a woman? She couldn't see them as they turned the corner, but she prayed they wouldn't step into the shop. Max had met Steven more than once and would definitely agree with Steven's current self-assessment.

"I don't know what to say, exactly," Steven told her. "Except that I've been reading Piaget and I think I'm a case of arrested development. I was emotionally somewhere between seven and nine years old when we were going out." Kate raised her eyebrows. She'd expected an apology, but not such a complete and accurate one.

"Kate, I don't regret anything in my life

as much as I regret letting you go."

Kate tried not to let his words sink in. There had been so many weeks, months, that she had hoped to hear them. Now she told herself to stay cool and calm.

Steven looked around. "God, this place is murder," he told her. "Please, Kate, let me take you out for a drink and dinner. Just give me a chance to explain everything."

Kate meant to say no. She meant to shake her head. She had gotten the satisfaction and closure that she craved, and now she only had to be cold and polite and negative. Just one shake of the head. "My job is very demanding right now," she told him.

"When will it let up?"

"With term-end reports, maybe a month."

"So if I call you, could we see each other?"

When she found herself nodding, she was as surprised as Steven appeared to be.

Chapter Thirty-three

Kate barely had time to shower and get into bed, totally exhausted from her meeting with Steven, when the phone rang. She looked at the caller ID, wondering, and when she saw that it was Bina's number she heaved a sigh of relief and answered.

"I can't believe it!" Bina almost yelled. "It's working! It's working almost too good! And he hasn't even broken up with me yet."

Kate was totally confused. "What are you talking about?" she asked.

"He called! He's going to ask me to marry him!"

Kate felt a jolt of jealousy mixed with complete surprise. "Billy is proposing?" she asked, incredulous.

"Not Billy! Jack! Jack called from Hong Kong." Bina was almost shouting. "He said he's flying home the day after tomorrow and he's doing it to see me. Kate, don't you get it? Elliot's plan worked. Jack is coming back to me."

Tired as she was, Kate had trouble digesting this news. Her head was a jumble of Max's e-mails, Elliot's numbers and graphs, Bina's gossip about her dates, the recent shocking news from the baby shower. All of it seemed to converge, making her dizzy. "Jack called and proposed?" she asked.

"Well, yes and no," Bina said, sounding slightly less joyous now to admit the truth.

"Okay. Tell me exactly what happened," Kate said, and wished that she hadn't given up smoking years ago. This was going to be the kind of long, involved description that only a cigarette could help get you through. "And tell me it in order from beginning to end."

She heard Bina take a deep breath. "Well, first the phone rang."

Kate realized it was just as well she'd given up cigarettes: She'd probably need a whole carton for this. "Yeah. Then what?"

"Then I picked it up. No, actually my mother picked it up. Then she handed it to me and said, 'It's for you.' "

"Did she know it was Jack?"

"Not then. Not until I screamed. Well, maybe she did, do you want me to ask her?"

"No." Kate pushed an extra throw pillow

behind her head and wished she had a glass of beer. "Just tell me what he said and what you said, Bina."

"Okay, so he said, 'Bina, is that you?' So I said, 'Who wants to know?' But I knew it was him because I knew his voice right away. You know, it sounded like he was calling from Coney Island or something, not from the other side of the world."

Kate sighed. "Then what did he say?"

"He says, 'Bina, I got to talk to you,' and I say, 'I'm listening,' and he goes, 'I've made a big mistake, Bina.' And I go, 'Well, how is that my business?' So he says, 'This is Jack.' And I say — you're gonna like this, Katie. I say, 'Jack who?' Wasn't that good?"

"Great," Kate said.

"So he says, 'Jack Weintraub.' And I go, 'Oh, I was confused. I thought it was Jack Marco Polo.' And he's like, 'What?' And I'm like, 'You know, the single guy that discovered a whole new world in the Orient.' "

Kate thought for a moment of hurrying Bina along, but now was no time for lessons in geography and political correctness.

"So he says, 'Bina, don't mock me. Have you been going out with someone else?' And I say, 'What's it to you?' And he says,

'Now I know you are.' And I say, 'Think what you want, but I know the truth.' And then he's like, 'Bina, I really have to talk to you.' And I say, 'Whatever.' And he says, 'I know you're probably angry at me and everything —' And I interrupt him and I say, 'Think again, because I hardly remember you.' Hey, Katie, do you think he heard gossip all the way in Japan?"

"He's in Hong Kong, Bina."

"Isn't that a part of Japan?"

Kate just shook her head. "So what happened then?" she asked.

"Now it gets really good. He goes, 'I have to talk to you.' And I say, 'Isn't that what you're doing now?' And he says, 'I've got to talk to you face-to-face.' So I go, 'That will probably be difficult since you're so two-faced.' And he says, 'Meet me at the airport on Thursday, Bina. I'm flying into JFK just to see you. Please don't say no.'"

Kate waited. There was silence at the other end of the phone. "So what did you say?" she asked, hesitating.

"I said yes!" Bina almost yodeled into the phone. "And he says, 'I have something I want to ask you and something I want to give you.' Isn't that great? So do you think it's too late to call Elliot and

Brice and tell them, or should I wait until tomorrow morning? I mean, if it wasn't for Elliot's statistics, I never . . ." She paused. "Omigod, Katie! Omigod! I have to get Billy to dump me for this to work, right?"

"Come on, Bina, that's all nonsense. Jack called you because he loves you and misses you."

"Forget that. This is because of Elliot. If I didn't go out with Billy . . ."

Kate flung off the blankets and stood up. "Don't be ridiculous," she said. "You don't have to do anything now but show up at the airport."

"I'm calling Elliot," Bina said. "I have to find out how long I have to date Billy, and then you and Elliot have to figure out how we break up."

"Oh, come on," Kate said. "You can just tell him it's over."

"Nahuh," Bina said while Kate stomped into the hall and across to her tiny kitchen, phone in hand. She prayed there was just one beer left somewhere in the back of the refrigerator. "He has to break up with me, remember?" Kate opened the refrigerator door. It shone that lonely light that illuminates single women at one a.m. after they've had some horrible disappointment.

"I have to figure out a way for him to

dump me, Katie," Bina continued. "And I have to do it by Thursday. Otherwise . . ."

Behind the mayonnaise jar, Kate glimpsed the brown neck of a Samuel Adams. She uttered a silent prayer to the god of alcohol and grabbed it. "Look, Bina, you don't have to believe me," she told her friend as she poured the beer into a glass. She never drank from a bottle; it reminded her too much of her father. "Jack has just about proposed. I don't know if you should accept him, but if that's what you want, that's what you're going to do when you see him."

"I'm calling Elliot," Bina said. "I'm calling him and then I'm calling Barbie and then —"

"Fine," said Kate. "Call them all, but leave me out of it." After the baby shower, she didn't think she could do one more function with the Bitches. She hung up the phone and chugged all the beer. Then she put down the glass and left it on the counter while she went, alone, to her bed.

Chapter Thirty-four

The morning dawned beautifully. Kate knew because she was awake — as she had been, on and off, for most of the night. The window in her bedroom faced east, and she saw the murky brown that passed as darkness turn first beige, then pink, and then, last, salmon as the sun rose. The light would last till past eight that evening, but there was no light in Kate's heart. Though this was Kate's favorite time of year, she woke with a heaviness in her chest and a gray despair that no dawn could affect. For the past few days she had been working and eating — though without an appetite — and walking to and from school, but she felt barely conscious of any of it. Although she didn't regret breaking up with Michael and she didn't expect anything from Steven, she felt lonely and hopeless. Like so many women in Manhattan, she would go without a partner because either she wasn't good enough or they weren't. Her Brooklyn friends had exhausted her, and like a sore spot on her gums that she couldn't keep her tongue away from, there was something annoying and painful about Billy Nolan and Bina's affair with him that she preferred not to think about but kept going back to over and over. Perhaps worst of all, she couldn't talk to Rita or her other Manhattan friends about it because they would never understand, and she couldn't talk to Elliot about it because he was the instigator, and the truth was she didn't want him, like a dentist with a fine instrument, picking at this sensitive spot.

She drifted into a light sleep. It was a quarter after six when the phone rang. She couldn't imagine who it would be. She picked up the phone to hear Bina's imploring voice at the other end. "Please, Kate, help me! I couldn't do it right, and now I have to go to the airport. I went out with Billy last night and I acted as snotty as I could, but he just laughed. I flirted with another guy, but he didn't seem to mind —"

"Whoa. Bina, slow down."

"Kate, I tried everything everyone suggested. You have to help me. Billy hasn't dumped me, and Jack lands in an hour and a half, and . . ."

Bina began to cry. And while Kate had heard Bina cry through almost every phase of their lives, there was an element to this that was new. Kate made shushing noises while she tried to wake up enough to figure out what was different. And then it came to her. For the first time, Bina was crying like an adult. Gone was the hysteria that allowed Bina to be so infuriating and yet sweet. Instead, Kate heard overlays of guilt, and shame, and anxiety.

"I made a mistake, Kate. But I don't want to have to tell Jack, and if Billy doesn't dump me, Jack won't propose and I've ruined my life."

"It's all going to be all right," Kate assured her. "I'll get a limo and pick you up this afternoon. I'll drop you at the airport. Just look good. I'll take care of everything. I promise you, it's all going to be all right."

"Cross your heart and hope to die?" Bina asked. Kate smiled. Same old Bina, she thought, and reassured her friend.

Dressed, made-up, coiffed, and scented, Bina sat beside Kate in the limo. Kate had done some deep thinking, called the car service, picked up Bina in Brooklyn, and swept her into the backseat. Although she was impressed with the car, Bina was still nervous.

"But what are you going to do?" she asked.

"That's for me to know, and for you to never find out," Kate said, and leaned forward. "Take the BQE," she told the driver, who seemed to be taking the scenic route — as if there were one — to JFK.

"Do you know which terminal he's coming into?" the driver asked.

"International arrivals," Kate said. "Follow the signs." She leaned back into the leather of the seats and turned to her friend, looking into her eyes. "Listen to me," she said.

"I am," Bina told her.

"Okay, really listen to me. You have nothing to tell Jack. You have nothing to confess." Kate paused. The idea of Bina and Billy together, the idea of him, of her . . . She repressed both the thought and her jealousy. "It only happened that once."

"Well, no. Last week I saw him and we got caught in the rain, and he took me to his apartment to towel me off, and . . ."

Kate imagined the scene too vividly. The image of Billy gently drying her hair and other body parts was disturbing and arousing. She could see why Bina would fall from grace again. "It doesn't matter. You and Jack broke up. He's been a free agent, and so have you. Remember the army had that policy: 'Don't ask. Don't

413

tell'?" Bina nodded. "Well, follow it. And if you're asked anything by Jack, remind him that you love him. Ask him if he loves you."

"But I slept with —"

"There are no buts."

"But even if I don't tell him about the sex . . . Okay, I won't tell Jack anything."

"You promise?"

"I promise. But to make this work, I have to get Billy to dump me."

"I'm going to take care of that," Kate said. "Now, fix your makeup." Obediently, Bina rooted around in her huge purse and pulled out a cosmetics case. Kate helped her with her primping and then turned the mirror on herself. She looked a little pale, and there was bruised-looking skin under her eyes because of her lack of sleep, but she would take care of all that later.

"Okay," she said as they pulled up to the sidewalk at the airport. "You look great, you should feel great, and Jack is coming here just for you. Because he loves you."

Bina hesitated. "But I'm not sure —"

"I'm sure," Kate said. "Now go to the arrivals waiting area, where passengers get out of customs. He'll probably be out of there in less than thirty minutes or so."

"Aren't you going to wait with me?"

Bina asked, her eyes opening wide.

"No. I have something else to do," Kate said, and gave Bina a hug. "Keep your cell phone on and your powder dry. Call me the moment anything happens."

Bina got out of the car and walked through the sliding glass door entrance, then she turned and waved and gave Kate the thumbs-up sign. As soon as she disappeared, merging with the crowd inside the terminal, Kate leaned forward to speak to the driver. "Take me back to Brooklyn," she told him.

Chapter Thirty-five

Kate rang Billy Nolan's bell. It took several minutes before he responded. Kate put her hands over the intercom and murmured something, pitching her voice higher than normal. Surely this wasn't the first time that he'd had an unexpected visit from a woman at an inopportune time. The more realistic worry was that some other woman was there. But, as she'd hoped, the door buzzed and Kate pushed into the hallway. I'm only doing this for Bina, she told herself, but she knew it was a lie.

Since Bina's confession at the shower, Kate had felt herself possessed by her desire for Billy Nolan. No matter how hard she had tried to deny it, she had been jealous and intrigued by Bina's flirtation with Billy. To be brutally honest, from the first moment she had met him on the terrace, she had felt an almost irresistible pull toward him. She had tried to resist it, knowing that he, like Steven, was not "relationship material." However, she reasoned, if she did this for Bina, maybe she would also be able to get Billy Nolan — his smile, his charm, and his easy physical grace — out of her system once and for all. She wasn't going to waste time in a meaningless relationship, but if this would precipitate a breakup with Bina and give her confidence, then . . .

Kate stopped to look in the mirror at the stair landing. She wasn't wild about what she saw. Her face was pale, and there were still dark circles under her eyes. Well, it would have to do. She pulled out a brush from her purse and puffed up her hair. Her lipstick was still holding up, but she did a full-face smile to see if there was any on her teeth. Walking up the stairs, Kate caught herself licking her lips. Then she remembered Elliot's absolutely ridiculous acronym and regretted it. Well, she told herself, I'll regret more than that after this day is over. She got to Billy's door, took a deep breath, and knocked.

Billy, his hair tousled and a loose cotton robe drawn around him, obviously just out of the shower, opened the door. "What . . . ?"

His physical presence was almost a blow to her. She could smell shampoo on him. It was better than any cologne.

Kate pushed in past him. She walked

across the room, put down her purse, sat at the edge of his bed, and crossed her legs.

"Sit down. Make yourself at home," Billy said with as much sarcasm as he could muster. He closed the door behind him. "To what do I owe . . ." He gave up trying to be urbane. "You want a cup of coffee?" he asked, and, scratching his head, began to move toward the kitchen.

"No, thank you," Kate said, trying not to lick her lips. "I didn't come here for coffee."

Billy stopped at the sink, his hand midway between the coffeemaker and the faucet. She had not gotten an opportunity to look at his hands since the dreadful bowling evening. Kate had always been interested in men's hands. She considered herself a sort of connoisseur, disliking short, stubby, or hairy-backed hands, yet equally turned off by overly slender, almost feminine hands. Now she was transfixed by Billy's. They were perfect, strong yet sensitive, the hands of competence and sensual knowledge. She blushed. He walked toward her slowly, pulled a chair opposite her, and sat down. "What did you come here for, doctor?" he asked. "Is this another consultation?"

Okay. She deserved that. And probably

418

more. If he was going to make her eat humble pie, she would. But couldn't he feel her almost ridiculous longing? She was grateful that it wasn't palpable to him, since it suffused her being. "Look, I was wrong," she admitted, then paused. She'd rehearsed this coming from the airport, but all that she had prepared seemed to have evaporated. "The thing with Bina isn't working, is it," she blurted.

Billy looked at her. "Have I missed something? Are we still in high school?" he asked.

Shit! Jack should be walking with Bina at this very moment. "Just tell me the truth," she said. "Bina means nothing to you, does she."

"Bina is a very nice girl," Billy told her.

"I know that, but that isn't the question I asked you." She looked down at her exposed toes, and the Pre-Raphaelite painting titled *King Cophetua and the Beggar Maid* appeared before her eyes. She'd always found it erotically charged. "Look," she said, "I came over here to admit that I made a terrible mistake. Bina is beginning to be really attached to you, and it isn't fair. She's going to get hurt, and it's going to be my fault as much as it is yours."

For the first time since she had arrived,

Billy actually looked alert. He looked down at the floor for a long moment, then back at her. "Look, I never meant to hurt her. I go out with women who know how to take care of themselves."

"Well, Bina isn't a woman like that."

"I know. That's why I never slept with her. Not that it's any of your business."

Kate looked away from his beautiful face. So he was a liar as well as a flirt and a serial dater.

"Don't waste my time with lies," she told him.

"Hey!" He stood up. "I don't lie. I've never dated more than one woman at a time, and I break up with one before I start in with anyone else. I never promise what I don't deliver. I own a bar, for God's sake. They know I'm . . . well, not serious right now. And if that's a repetition compulsion, well, that's my problem. Meanwhile, I make them feel good about themselves."

"It's time to break up with Bina," Kate said firmly. The fact was she felt anything but firm. She was more frightened than she could ever remember being. What if he was disinterested or, worse, if he laughed at her and threw her out? At that moment she felt it would be unbearable. Yet she couldn't show her fear. She looked at him, his hair still messy from the shower but as adorable as ever, his brow wrinkled in incredulity. "It's time," she repeated.

"What are you? Her social secretary or her mother? And how do you know how I feel?"

Kate stood up, leaned forward, and looked into his eyes. She felt the heat from his chest, and she could have melted. There was a place beyond words where honesty and intention are felt. Kate did more than apologize. She bared herself and let him in through her eyes. Silently, she kept her eyes on his and let him feel her intentions. All of the sexual heat, all of the longing that she had repressed, was there, visible to him if he would look. Billy actually pulled back for a moment, then leaned forward.

"Doctor, are you . . . ?" His expression changed from confusion to incredulity to . . . well, it looked like delight.

Kate stood up, took the sweater off her shoulders, and tossed it onto the chair behind her. Then she sat back down on the bed and unbuttoned the top button of her blouse. "I think you should call Bina," she said. "She won't be home now, but you can leave a message."

"That seems pretty cold," Billy ventured.

"Her old boyfriend is in town. She won't mind if you break up with her right now."

"B-b-but over the phone?" he stammered.

Kate looked him full in the face. She felt surprised at his sense of honor and guilt at her own manipulativeness. But she put both emotions out of her mind. "I promise this way is best. I wouldn't hurt her for the world."

And, as if hypnotized, Billy did just that. He picked up the phone, and Kate had the delicacy to leave the room while he left the message that Bina felt was so crucial. In the bathroom, she called in sick — only the third time she'd missed a day of work. Then she had a moment to look at herself in the mirror. What are you doing? she silently asked her reflection. She couldn't convince herself that she was giving her body to this man simply to ensure the ending to a crack-brain scheme that she certainly had never believed in. She wanted to sleep with Billy, but she was already afraid that she wanted more. And she knew his record with women. Could she afford to spend more of her time in a relationship that would lead to nothing in the end?

She looked away from her own pale blue

eyes. She knew she didn't really have a choice. She wanted Billy Nolan more than she had ever wanted anyone. But this has to mean nothing, she told herself. There is no future, only the present. I won't make the mistakes I made with Steven and Michael. This isn't a relationship, she told herself firmly. This is what other people call "fun."

Fun was not exactly the word Kate would use for coupling with Billy.

"I've wanted you since the first time I saw you on the terrace," he said.

Kate felt something within her tighten. They were the words she wanted to hear but didn't dare believe. They were true for her, though she had not admitted it to herself and she certainly wouldn't admit it to Billy. That way lay madness. She just smiled enigmatically and tried to put all thought out of her mind. That was easy to do, because no one had ever made love to her the way Billy did. She wasn't surprised by his strength or his skill, but his tenderness took her aback. He cradled her head with both hands and held her face to his as he kissed her. He stroked her hair. "It's so beautiful," he murmured. "I love your hair." He buried his face in it, just beside her ear. "I love how it smells and how it feels. I wanted to touch it, but I didn't think I'd get the chance."

Kate turned to him, and he put his mouth on hers. She couldn't decide what she liked better, when he used his mouth to kiss her or when he used it to speak to her. His hands spoke to her as well. They moved miraculously from her breasts to her thighs and up again to her mouth, each time going further, becoming more probing, more intimate, and even more responsive to her.

Kate had always found the first few times she made love with someone to be a little awkward and unsatisfying. But with Billy it was different. He heard and registered every intake of her breath, the slightest movement of her hips or shifting of her body. She felt she could ask him for anything without speaking a word. But she didn't have to ask. He was slow and practiced and skillful, but she also felt such a flood of feeling, such an exchange of emotion, that she lost herself. As they made love, Billy kept his mouth on hers, and it seemed as if he had a hundred variations of kissing, all of which were in sync with his movements and her own. He took his mouth off hers only when he paused to look at her or when he moved his mouth to her nipples and then lower.

He brought her to the brink with his hand and with his mouth and then moving against her and then again with his hand, until Kate was trembling all over. She almost couldn't catch her breath, but the feeling was wonderful, not frightening. And when she put her hand on him, his gasp was so deep that she felt an almost greater pleasure in touching him than she felt when he moved on her body. She had no idea what time it was when he finally slipped inside her for the last time, and when both of them fell asleep, exhausted and satisfied, he kept his arms wrapped around her waist, holding her to him even as they slept.

Chapter Thirty-six

Kate opened her eyes. She had one of those moments of waking dislocation. Where was she? It wasn't her ceiling or Michael's. Then she turned her head and saw Billy, still sleeping. The events of the previous day flooded back. Kate smiled and felt her cheeks flushing, but, uncharacteristically, she didn't mind.

While they had slept her hair had fanned out, and now a red tendril was curled around Billy's upper arm. Simply looking at his arm lying on the sheet, bathed in the sunshine that spread from the window across the upper part of the bed, made her feel . . . extremely happy. It was a feeling she wasn't used to.

Kate stretched and luxuriated in the feeling. Happiness this deep was something you could not hold on to, and she was wise enough not to try. She only drank in the sunlight, the clean white sheets rumpled around them, and cherished the moment. She wasn't thinking about the sex, though it had been exquisite. It was simply looking at Billy and experiencing the feeling of warmth, comfort, and protectiveness that staring at the hairs so perfectly aligned on his forearm seemed to give her. It was a moment of pure joy.

Slowly, so as not to wake him, she lifted her head to look at his sleeping face. Even without animation, his features had a beauty and liveliness that made her wonder. From their conversation the previous night, she felt Billy Nolan was not just another pretty face. After all, in his own way, Steven had been very handsome. But Billy seemed to have a depth of feeling, a sense of compassion and understanding, that had been blocked in Steven by his narcissism.

As if feeling himself observed, Billy opened his eyes. "Hello," he said, his voice dipping somehow in the middle of the word, making it sound like a self-assured and very happy greeting. Kate felt herself blush again, and this time it did embarrass her. She fell back on her pillow. Billy raised himself on one elbow, bent over her, and kissed her. His kisses were so sensitive, so searching and gentle. That reminded her of the way they had made love, his lips almost never leaving her own — except when he was kissing some other part of her. He lifted his head.

"Good morning," Kate said, and tucked the sheet in on either side of her.

"Now you're my prisoner. Stuck in my bed for life."

Kate thought that that sounded like a delicious idea, but she only smiled.

"What time is it?" Billy asked, then fell back and yawned.

Kate hadn't a clue. At the moment, she couldn't even remember what day it was, and that also felt delicious. Lying in his bed, she felt suspended in time. If she could have asked for one place and feeling to have for all eternity, this moment would be a good choice. Then she forced herself to turn and look at the clock on the bedside table. "Oh, God," she gasped. "It's Friday! And almost nine. I have to call the school," she told him, and fell back onto the bedclothes in horror. She couldn't go running out of his apartment, scuttling like a bug to gather up her belongings, because she was way too late to get to school. She *never* missed work two days in a row; even when she'd had the stomach virus that had torn through the school, she'd still managed to come in after one day off. The children had to be able to count on her.

But it was the end of the term, a half-day, and she had her reports to write up and the summaries that would go to the administration and the children's parents. She ought to be at school, going through her notes, but for once she was tempted to think of herself first. Dr. McKay, on the other hand, would have to be told, and he wouldn't like it. She knew her contract was being considered for renewal right now, and it was not a time to screw up. Still, she couldn't leave. Billy was looking at her, his eyebrows raised in question.

"My job," she said. "I have to make a call."

He picked up his phone and handed it to her. "Feel free," he said. "As long as you don't call another man, my minutes are yours."

"He isn't exactly a man, he's a principal," Kate told him.

"Well, I'm glad you've got at least one principle," he said, and kissed her again as she was punching in the Andrew number. "When you arrived I wasn't sure." She made a face and pushed him away. He lay down, holding a curl of her hair between his fingers and playing with it.

When Vera, Dr. McKay's secretary, answered the phone, Kate was relieved. She asked for Dr. McKay but hoped he might not be available so that she could just leave a message.

Unfortunately, Vera put her right through. Kate heard the principal's nasal voice at the other end of the phone. "McKay," he said. "Yes?"

"This is Kate Jameson. I'm very sorry, but I won't be able to come in again today." There was a pause at the other end. It was amazing how powerful silence could be. She wanted to fill it, to blurt out excuses, but didn't let herself.

"Are you still ill?" Dr. McKay finally asked.

"No," she said, "but I have a personal emergency." She looked over at Billy, under the sheet and clearly aroused. "Something's just come up." Billy gave her a look. Kate would have smiled, but she felt McKay's silent curiosity move like a snake through the telephone lines. Stalwart, she kept silent on her end. She watched Billy, who picked up the ends of her hair and held them to his mouth in a kiss.

"I'm sorry to hear that," Dr. McKay intoned, and Kate thought he sounded sorry about it, although she wasn't sure why.

"Because it's half a day, I'll be able to

catch up easily. Most of my reports on the children are done."

They discussed scheduling for a few moments, and then Kate was able to hang up. She gave a sigh of relief, and Billy grinned at her. "Playing hookey?" he asked. She nodded. "I'd like to play something else as well," he said. "And if you don't agree, I'm afraid I'll have to call the truant officer and report you."

Kate giggled. "I'm not in school anymore," she said.

"Oh, we'll see about that," Billy told her.

She supposed if she thought about it, she'd get crazy. After all, here was a man who had slept with half the women in Brooklyn, including her best friend. The idea did make her a bit queasy, so, like some of her young patients, she compartmentalized. She simply put that thought in a mental box, which she closed tightly and put aside. It wasn't possible that Billy Nolan could fake all of these feelings, or could he? His vast experience showed in the skill he displayed when they made love. Every touch, every movement, felt wonderful, perfect almost. If it got any better, it would be frightening. As it was, it was spooky. He seemed to know almost before she did where to put his hands, how hard to press, where to put his mouth, when to be playful, and when to be intense. If she compared his lovemaking to Michael's, which she was trying with little success not to do, she felt as if Michael were only a sandwich while Billy was a Thanksgiving feast.

The two of them spent the morning making love. Then Billy made breakfast. He was a good cook, and Kate was hungry. She looked around the sunny living room. "This is a really nice place," she said as she finished the last of her bacon.

Billy laughed. "You sound surprised," he said.

Kate blushed. "Have you lived here long?" she asked.

"My dad moved in when he got sick. Emphysema. He didn't like being alone in our old house after my mom died. He couldn't work as a fireman anymore, so he began working full-time in the bar, and I helped him turn this into an apartment."

"So you can cook and do carpentry?" Kate asked as she brought the dirty dishes to the sink.

"Yeah," he said. He paused and looked away from her. "It was fun to work with my dad, but we barely got the place finished before he died."

"Was it from the emphysema?" Kate asked.

Billy nodded and grimaced. "Well, complications thereof. It's a terrible way to die. Terrible to watch."

"I'm sorry," Kate said.

Billy shrugged and began to scrape a plate. "You shouldn't be a fireman and smoke," he said.

"My father was a policeman who drank, and you shouldn't do that, either," Kate said.

Billy nodded, filled the sink with hot water, and put the dishes in to soak. He looked around. "Anyway, I liked this apartment, and when I took over the bar, it seemed handy to live here. This place still reminds me of him." He turned back to the sink and added some dish detergent. Then he wiped his hands on a paper towel and turned back to her. "Funny thing," he said. "We just had breakfast, but I'm hungry again." He raised his brows suggestively, put his arms around her waist, and nuzzled her neck. Kate felt herself responding to the pressure behind her, and with his arms still around her waist, they went back to bed.

It was after their encore, when Billy had gone off to shower, that Kate's cell phone began to ring. She saw that it was Bina and picked it up.

"Katie? Katie?"

"Yes, of course it's me," Kate said.

"Omigod, Katie! He proposed. Just like Elliot said. I couldn't believe it, but Jack proposed."

Kate was flooded with a kind of horror as she remembered — for the first time since she had gotten to Billy's place — that she had originally come to facilitate Bina's long delayed engagement. Was she a selfish or selfless friend?

"That's great! That's really, really great!"

"And you won't believe this," Bina continued. "This is how I know Elliot was right. You won't believe it."

"Try me," Kate said dryly, knowing what was coming. Just then her phone starting beeping for a call waiting. She glanced at the caller ID and didn't recognize the number, so she let it go to voice mail.

"Well, I had a message from Billy breaking up with me — just in time! Jack asked me to marry him right after I checked my voice mail and got Billy's message!"

"Congratulations. Or best wishes. Or

mazel tov," Kate said. "Your mother must be thrilled, and your father. And me. I'm thrilled for you."

"I'm thrilled, too. And the best part is that he apologized for what happened, you know, about him not, well, you know. He said he just panicked. He got frightened and couldn't get the words out." She paused. "Do you think that's true?"

"I'm sure that was part of it," Kate said, remembering his request for exploration. It seemed Bina hadn't forgotten it, either.

"And he said he wanted just a little more time to, well, you know . . . we've been going out so long, and he's never cheated on me, and he just wanted to be sure. I don't blame him for that. Would you?"

"No."

"Yeah, but . . ." Bina paused, then lowered her voice. "But I can't forget what happened. You know, about . . . well, you can't imagine how fantastic it was with —"

"I think I can," Kate said as she glanced toward the bathroom. "Look, I gotta go. I'll talk to you tonight."

Kate had just stepped out of the shower herself when her cell phone rang again. She looked at the caller ID and knew she was in trouble. She thought for a moment that she would just ignore it, but she knew Elliot would never give up.

"Where are you?" he asked without any preamble. "You're not here at work and you're not at home. You're out, so you're not sick. Unless you're at the doctor's. Are you at the doctor's?"

"No," Kate said. "And I can't talk right now." She was self-conscious. She felt Billy listening, even though she wasn't sure that he was.

"Okay, so where are you?"

"I'll tell you later," Kate said, lowering her voice.

"What?"

"I'll tell you later."

"Oh, God. You're in bed with Steven."

"Not exactly," Kate said.

"What is that supposed to mean?" Elliot asked. "Oh, I knew it. This is really terrible. So you are with Steven."

"No."

Elliot paused, doing the math. "But you're in bed with someone."

"Yes, Einstein."

"I can't tell you how relieved I am," Elliot said. "At first I was going to call all the hospitals, then, when I thought of Steven, I was going to call all the mental hospitals. But instead of getting neurotic, you just got lucky."

"This may not qualify as luck," Kate said.

"Well, girlfriend, I want to hear all of the details the minute you get home."

Chapter Thirty-seven

"We're coming to a rise. You ready?" Kate nodded.

It was hot, and the heat was already radiating up from the macadam they were skimming over. Kate had been in-line skating once or twice before but had never felt really secure. Now, on this beautifully warm afternoon, everything seemed easy as the two of them skated in Prospect Park, their hands intertwined behind their backs. Billy was a surprisingly good and patient teacher, coaching her until she felt secure enough to lean into her strokes. But the fun was doing it with Billy. He held her with the gentlest pressure, but his support gave her confidence. He warned her of every hill and curve before it came up and tightened his grip when they swooped down an incline. It was exhilarating. Kate believed their skating was almost as sensual as their sex.

"You skate so well," she murmured as they glided into the tree-shaded part of the road.

"Six years on the hockey team and only one chipped tooth to show for it," Billy told her.

Kate looked up and smiled at him. She had wondered about the tooth. It was the imperfection that made the rest of his perfection bearable. She was reminded of the Brad Pitt film in which he had played a boxer. Special makeup had transformed his nose and given it a broken jauntiness. Kate had read somewhere that more women found him attractive in that movie than in any other.

"I like that chipped tooth," was all she said and then felt his arm push her slightly. She thought for a moment it was a reaction to her compliment, but, "Eyes forward," Billy said as he avoided a stumbling skater, and then moved Kate smoothly through a crowd of children crossing the road ahead of them. Out of the shaded alley, the sun beat down fiercely, but their gathering speed created a pleasant breeze. Once they were on the flat open stretch, they really began to move.

"I can see you've had a lot of practice," she noted while she kept her face forward as instructed.

"Hey," Billy said, "you're no virgin yourself."

"I wasn't any good," she told him truthfully. "It's because of you."

Everything was different because of him. It had been over a week since Jack's return and Kate's visit to Billy, and in that time she had spent every free moment with him. The first weekend had been spent being deliciously idle. Then, after work on Monday, he had made her dinner. She'd stayed at his place, but the following evening — traditionally a slow night at the bar — he had come to her house and they'd eaten takeout pizza and one of her great salads. And they'd been together ever since. She had seen Elliot at school but had ducked him, her friend Rita, and the entire Brooklyn cadre. Now they were spending their second weekend together.

Kate was amazed by how much she and Billy had in common. It wasn't only the French. He had also lost his mother early, although he never spoke about her death. He had spent his teenage years being raised by his father. They were both only children and both orphans.

Kate had to admit that she had been prejudiced about him; he wasn't a dunce, and he didn't get by just on his good looks. In fact, if she could put aside his appalling record of conquests, he was the most compatible male companion she had ever spent time with. Kate's work for the semester was ending, and with more time for shopping and cooking, she found that she enjoyed having Billy to her place for dinner.

Over the past week, when it was Billy's turn to close the bar, she'd gone to his apartment early and worked or read until he was through. He'd come up intermittently for quick kisses, usually bringing a treat or a drink. On nights he got off early, he'd made the trip to Manhattan, driving into what he referred to as "the city." Kate remembered when she used to call Manhattan that, and it made her smile every time he said it.

"Another hill," Billy told her now. "Let's put our backs into it."

Kate did. It wasn't just his skating that was impressive. There was almost nothing about Billy Nolan that did not impress her. He wasn't at all what she had thought; he didn't seem glib, or shallow, or arrogant. Not once you knew him. And his affection for her seemed so warm and real. Could he be acting? Kate hated to doubt him. He seemed so sensitive, not only to his own vulnerabilities, as Steven had been, but also to the feelings of others.

The only cloud over her happiness was

the nagging thought of the host of women he had previously conquered. In the time she spent away from him, Kate sometimes wondered if all the women he had known had felt like this and, more important, if he had felt just the same about them as he seemed to feel about her. It was hardly the kind of question she could ask, and even if she did, it was not the kind of question that would elicit an honest answer.

They crested the hill, and the long slide down actually made Kate scream, partly with pleasure and partly with fear. Not so different from the way she felt about this relationship. At the bottom of the hill, Billy released one of her hands and coasted over to a bench beside an ice-cream vendor. Just behind them was a field for roller hockey and beyond it a park exit. Kate was grateful for the sit-down. "I'm exhausted," she admitted.

"So am I," Billy told her, though she doubted that was true. There didn't seem to be an ounce of body fat on him, and Kate knew that under his clothes he was lean and powerful without any extra bulk. Thinking of his body gave her a momentary frisson of desire.

"Thirsty?" Billy asked, and she nodded. "Let's go." They took off their Rollerblades, put on their shoes, and bundled their gear into his backpack.

They were just leaving the park when her cell phone rang. She pulled it out and saw that it was Elliot. For the last week she had been ducking his calls when she could and had been equally evasive when she saw him at school. She had talked about Bina's engagement, the shower they were going to throw for her, Elliot and Brice's plans for the summer — everything but the identity of her new boyfriend. She hadn't wanted to lie to him, but she knew how strongly he would disapprove of the truth.

"Are you going to pick it up? Or is it another boyfriend?" Billy asked. Just then the phone stopped ringing.

"It's a he, and he's a friend, but he's gay," Kate told Billy. "Does that count?"

Kate and Billy made their way to Jo's Sweet Shop for some ice cream. Jo's was an institution, the old-time confectionary where parents brought their kids for hot chocolate after winter skating and for sundaes when the weather turned warm. Kate had always envied the kids who got taken to Jo's. A game broke, and behind them an after-the-skating/roller hockey crowd complete with blades, skates, and Prospect Park parents swarmed in to get drinks and ice cream to cool off. With the usual pattern of bullying, the bigger kids elbowed the smaller, some parents pushed ahead of other parents, and chaos reigned. Billy and Kate watched as a seven- or eight-year-old boy was virtually trampled. He began to cry.

"Oh, God!" Kate cried. She worked her way over to him, knelt, and put her arm around him. "Oh, sweetie. Are you hurt?"

"He stepped on me!" the boy sobbed, pointing upward. Kate looked up at a big hulk of a teen hockey guy still in his gear. From low vantage point, the guy looked like a giant. But Billy grabbed him by the back of his hockey shirt and tugged him.

"See? He's gone now." Kate comforted the child.

People began screaming their orders. "Two cookies 'n cream sugar cones with sprinkles!"

"A vanilla Coke!"

"Three large chocolate cones and an iced tea!"

The shouted orders were almost drowned out by the kids' excited yelling and by loud complaints about people pushing ahead and whose turn it was. The adolescent working behind the counter was clearly overwhelmed by the crowd. Kate reunited the little boy with his dad, while the poor soda jerk tried and failed to gain control. With more parkgoers pushing in from the back, those in the front got even rowdier. "Please form a line!" the teen shouted desperately. No one was listening.

Billy returned to Kate's side. He positioned her at the entrance to the work space behind the counter. "This is madness," he said. Then he leapt over the counter and moved to the center, facing out to the crowd.

"All right," he began in a voice loud enough to be heard all the way into the park. "All right now! Kids with hockey sticks on the left. Kids with skates on the right."

There was silence for a moment, and then pushing and shoving began as the crowd tried to part.

"Keep it down! I mean it!"

As if he were Moses and the crowd were the Red Sea, his will was done. Kate smiled as the two lines formed. Billy leaned toward the poor, overwhelmed kid in the apron. "You take the so-called adults and I'll do the Mighty Ducks."

The teen nodded and began taking orders from the line on the right. Billy looked at the children and gestured to the eight-year-old who had been crying. "Service first to the player who was body-checked."

His dad brought the little boy up to the counter. Kate couldn't help but glow. Billy leaned toward the little boy. "What position do you play?" he asked him.

"Goalie," he replied, and looked at his father as if he weren't completely sure.

"Your lucky day!" Billy exclaimed. "Goalies get free cones! Wanna double scoop?"

The teenager behind the counter gave him a look of "No way." Billy ignored him, took out his wallet, and placed it beside the ice-cream tubs. "What's it gonna be?" The little boy asked for a vanilla cone with sprinkles and hooted with joy when he saw the double dipping he received. Billy moved to the next in the line.

"What's it gonna be?" he asked.

"A cup of chocolate with nuts and whipped cream," the next kid said.

"You got it. And it's on me." Billy sprayed some of the aerosol cream on his shirt. "Get it? It's on me."

The portion of the crowd that was up front laughed. Kate watched Billy with a combination of astonishment, awe, and delight. When he took his next order, he smiled at the kid. "Position?" Billy asked him.

"Guard," the boy said proudly.

"Whoa!" Billy pretended to be taken aback. "Guards get free toppings."

"Wow!" the boy cried. "Hey, Mom! I get a free topping."

Billy leaned over to Kate and gave her a quick kiss right below the ear.

"What do I get?" she asked him coyly.

Billy was already busy making up a cone, but he looked up at her.

"Depends on what position you play," he said, and smiled.

The thing about him, Kate thought, was that he knew the way things worked. He wasn't a macho guy, but he was strong enough and confident enough to be willing to take chances. When the manager of the shop came from out back, leaving the booths and table behind, he took over for Billy. Thanking him, he insisted on giving Billy and Kate free cones.

As they finally made their way out of the sweet shop, Kate looked at Billy. "That was quite a scene, Mr. Nolan," she said. "You're a take-charge kinda guy."

"Hey, what would you expect from a

bartender who has dealt with bachelor parties?" Billy said.

"Well, you really managed that crowd."

Billy looked down at his cone, melting over his hand in the heat. "Yeah. If only I could manage my own ice cream."

"Okay. This I know how to do," Kate said, and moved him over to a trash bin. She knocked two scoops off his cone and into the bin, did the same with her own, pulled a Wet-Nap out of her pocket, wiped his hand, and then, with her finger, cleaned up the last trace of whipped cream from his neck.

"Hey, no fair," said Billy. "That was mine."

Kate just smiled and put her ice-cream-covered finger in her mouth. Billy took her hand and licked the remaining ice cream off her finger. Then he gently pinned her against the wall of the sweet shop and, keeping her left hand in his, lifted his arm and pushed his weight against her. Kate thought of Victorian heroines and how they "swooned." She was feeling pretty swoony.

"What do you call this position?" he asked her, his voice low.

At that moment the door of Jo's opened and a bunch of kids streamed out. When a couple of them saw Billy, they began hooting.

"Exhibitionist," Kate told him, and smiled.

On the subway, the unruly park crowd pushed as the train doors opened. Kate was about to be crushed against a pole until Billy corraled her, placing her in the corner of the car against the front window. He protected her with his body, but the crowd had the two of them pushed against each other. She was shocked when his hands disappeared under the back of the waistband of her jeans. He leaned forward to whisper in her ear, "What do you call this position?"

"Tight. Very tight," she said.

Back at Kate's apartment, Billy undressed her slowly. She was surprised and touched by his tenderness: He took off her sandals as if she were a very young child. But by the time he had worked his way up from her feet and unbuttoned her blouse, she knew he considered her grown-up. Then he was on top of her, kissing her neck and making his way to her breasts. She could barely manage to hold back a moan of pure pleasure. Then he stopped, took each of her hands in his, and held them beside her face on the pillow. He looked at her. "And what do you call this position?" he asked.

"Perfect," Kate whispered.

Chapter Thirty-eight

Despite his nose for news and Kate's constant exposure to Elliot at school, she had managed not to raise his suspicions or start him questioning her on why she seemed so happy. If he wrote it off to relief at her breakup with Michael, it was just as well. Although she and Elliot often fought and sometimes didn't speak for a day or two, they had never lied to each other, and Kate did not want to set a precedent now. A sin of omission, however, was less than a fib. But Elliot would be a veritable bloodhound if he got wind of a juicy tidbit like this, and Kate was afraid it was only a matter of time before he sniffed her out. Sooner or later, he would discover the reason for her sunny disposition, and when he did, thunderclouds would gather.

Kate stood in a patch of sunshine and watched the kids all around her. Andrew Country Day was one of the few city schools that had been able to maintain an almost campuslike setting. Old trees, including a giant willow, and a perfect border of manicured lawn gave the enclave the beauty and dignity of a New England college quad.

She felt her first year had been successful but wasn't quite certain that Dr. McKay and the board shared her view. When Michael had assumed she would leave Andrew Country Day, she had suddenly realized how much the job meant to her, the deep pleasure it gave her. The scene around her was so lovely and her work with the children so meaningful that she felt she couldn't part with them. A small but dark voice within her whispered that she would never be allowed so much personal happiness without suffering a professional loss of some sort. Of course, she recognized the fear as superstitious nonsense, something from her childhood that would probably always haunt her when things went well.

Kate brushed a wisp of hair from her face and drew it back into her barrette. A group of fifth-grade girls sat in the grass in the sun, as languid and colorful as the women in a Monet painting. "Hi, Dr. Jameson!" Brian Conroy yelled as he streaked across the lawn, and Kate winced. Dr. McKay was somewhat obsessive about "his" lawn, and running on it was strictly against the rules. But Kate didn't have the heart to scold him. He looked happy, at least for the moment.

The breeze died down and the sun grew warmer. Kate took off her sweater, tied it around her shoulders, and surveyed the schoolyard.

She thought of Billy and smiled. Of course, if she allowed herself to think too much, doubts and questions crept in. Was she deluding herself about Billy being the right sort of man for her? Brooklyn, alcohol, Irish men, dysfunctional families — how could she go back to everything she had run from?

To retain her happiness, Kate put Billy and the future out of her mind, simply watching over the children running and playing in front of her. She smiled. It was almost like watching seawater eddy in tidepools — the children's allegiances, posses, and games changed at different rates, making swirls of motion that were faster in one corner, slower in the middle, and stagnant at one side.

Again her hair escaped from its mooring and blew across her face. As she grabbed it, her fingers brushed her jawline in exactly the way Billy's had stroked it just hours ago. A little shiver ran down her spine, and she felt a flutter in her stomach. Sleeping with him had been so extraordinary, so passionate but tender, that thinking about it seemed dangerous — Kate was afraid she might discover that it was all a dream and have to awaken to a much colder reality.

She walked over to the willow but didn't take a seat on the bench beside it. It was well-known that Dr. McKay frowned on staff sitting when on playground duty. Instead she leaned one hand against the bench, picked up a tendril of the willow in the other, and again lifted her face to the sun. It amazed her how life could change in such sudden, profound ways. She felt, for once, like one of the lucky ones, one of the people in the world for whom things worked out, someone who could simply exist and breathe warm air without struggling. She felt as if everything she wanted would come to her.

Although she wasn't sure she wanted Dr. McKay, when Kate turned her head she saw him scuttling toward her on the flagstone path across the lawn. She straightened, and the bit of the willow wand still in her hand broke off. She hadn't talked to him since she'd called in her absence. The thought made her blush.

"Dr. Jameson," Dr. McKay began, "I've been wanting to talk to you."

Kate felt another flutter, but this one was not nearly so pleasant. Was he going to criticize her for daydreaming or for neglecting to scold the girls who were sitting on the lawn despite the interdict against it? Worse yet, was he about to reject her contract renewal? Was the small, dark voice the voice of truth?

But Dr. McKay looked at her with something approaching a smile, and to her relief he ignored his precious sod for once. "I'm glad I caught you here," he said, and for a moment his voice sounded almost cordial. "Your contract is up for renewal, and the board and I would like to extend it." He paused. "We feel that you are becoming an important part of the Andrew Country Day School tradition."

"Thank you," Kate said. "I'm very happy here, and I hope I'm making a contribution."

Dr. McKay nodded, his face once again poker straight, as if he had lost all his cordiality chips. "Good. Vera will have your renewal contract."

As he walked away, Kate watched his narrow back and managed to feel some affection for him, even when he waved the fifth-grade girls off the lawn.

The bell rang, the children began to line up, and Kate was free to go back to her office. But on the way down the hall, Elliot appeared at his classroom door.

"Are you trying to avoid me?" he asked.

She averted her eyes. "No, of course not."

"Look, I figured it out. I know who your mystery man is and why you're embarrassed to tell me."

"Shh," Kate said anxiously, and took hold of his sleeve. "Come into my office." She was filled with dread. Elliot knew, and he would tell everyone, and Brooklyn would be abuzz with the news.

Once in the office, Elliot closed the door and she turned to face him. "I figured it out," he repeated complacently. "It's Max. You're sleeping with Max and you're embarrassed. But there's nothing wrong with him. I've always thought he was kinda hot myself. It might be a little awkward after you end it, since he lives just upstairs, but any port in a storm."

For a moment Kate was tempted to let him think he'd found her out. But she simply couldn't lie to such a close friend.

"Okay. What is it, then?" Elliot demanded as she shook her head.

"Dr. McKay wants to renew my contract," Kate told him.

"That's not what I'm talking about." Elliot stopped and looked her over. "You're seeing *him*, aren't you?" he said accusingly.

Once again Kate felt her complexion betray her. As a blush suffused her cheeks, she turned her eyes away. "Yes," she said.

For a minute, Elliot was stunned into silence. Then he shook his head. "You little sneak. I should have known you were up to something," he said. "I thought, well, I suspected you might be thinking of that idiot Steven. But no, you have to sniff out worse trouble. And I didn't think there could be worse trouble than Steven Kaplan."

Kate, who thought she was prepared for Elliot's anger, was taken aback. "You don't even know Billy," she said. "To you he's some kind of magic charm, some statistical improbability."

"And what is he to you? A good bonk? Because that would be all he's good for."

Kate felt herself go livid, and the blood that drained from her face actually made her almost dizzy. "I appreciate your concern," she said, her voice cold. "But I don't think you know what you're talking about."

"Right! I haven't been around for the last ten years to witness and dissect every bump and curve in your so-called love life. You forget whom you're talking to, Kate." He pointed to the drawings on her walls, many of them new, farewell gifts from children who would not see her until the autumn. "You want to mess up your life?" Elliot asked, his voice lowered. "I've watched you grow in the last year. Michael might not be right for you, but he was stable and a professional and probably a good father-to-be." He moved closer to her, but Kate pulled away. If he touched her, she was afraid she might slap his hand away.

"You're being unfair and horrible," she said, and realized she sounded like a child. She took a deep breath. She owed a lot to Elliot: his loyalty, his friendship, his help in graduate school, and his assistance in getting her this job that she loved. But it didn't give him the right to judge her let alone Billy in this way. "You don't understand," she said.

"Oh, yes, I do. I know masochism when I see it. And I'm staring at it right now."

"Shut up," Kate told him, her voice lowered to a hiss.

Elliot shrugged and turned away. In the

midst of walking out, however, he turned back to her. "Out of the frying pan and into the furnace. This is going on your permanent record, missy."

Chapter Thirty-nine

Kate looked at the pan bubbling on Billy's burner. It certainly didn't look appetizing, but it smelled pretty good, though she couldn't honestly say she was hungry. Her argument with Elliot that afternoon had not only upset her (and her stomach), it had also made her nervous. What was she doing here? Elliot had told her this was only a get-over-Michael fling, but it didn't feel like one. It felt . . . well, she needed to hear that this feeling she had for Billy, who was poking at the contents of the pan with a fork, was mutual.

He was cooking dinner for the two of them. Kate was keeping out of his way while he worked over the shallow pan, in which he seemed to be simmering a lot of tomato sauce, meat, and capers. "What is it?" she had asked him, looking at it doubtfully.

"An old Nolan family recipe. Hey, don't judge it until you've tried it." He grinned at her expression, then reached around her for the bottle of red wine he was using in the sauce. "Listen, before I forget, would you like to go out for lunch on Saturday? I'll have to work Saturday night."

Kate shook her head. "I have a previous engagement," she said. "Bina's bridal shower. How about Friday?"

"That sounds good," he said. Then he shrugged. "We've got the bar booked for Bina's fiancé's bachelor party. Let me tell you, I'm not looking forward to that."

Kate looked down at the pan again and thought about Bina and how upset she seemed. Between the end of school and her time with Billy, Kate hadn't had much time for her friend and couldn't bear to hear all the ongoing wedding preparation details. Bina was obviously bewildered about her seeming indifference.

Seeing the look on her face, Billy patted her shoulder. "Don't you worry, everybody likes it. It's a guaranteed way to tenderize the toughest meat. My mom used to make it." He had never spoken of his mother before, except to say she was dead. For a moment Kate considered asking about her but decided against it.

She took the glass of red wine Billy had poured her in between doctoring the sauce and wandered over to the window. After her fight with Elliot, he had called to make up. He'd asked her to meet him for a drink, but she'd been forced to admit that she was spending the night with Billy. Elliot had made his disapproval obvious and vocal. Kate had tried to ignore all of the calmer, more logical things he had said to dissuade her: how Billy was a playboy and she was barking up the wrong tree, how Elliot loved her but didn't want to have to "pick up the pieces." Then he had stopped, as if at a sudden thought. "You're not doing this just to get a proposal, are you?" he'd asked. "After all, you turned Michael down and you don't know what the cat might drag in after Billy dumps you."

The words had chilled her. "I never believed that ridiculous theory," she had snapped.

"How can you say that?" he'd asked. "It got Bina engaged. Proof positive."

With a lot of effort and sidestepping, Kate had managed to convince him that she was not taking this affair seriously. Now, as she stared out the window at the rain, she admitted to herself that she had lied. She was taking Billy seriously, and she was beginning to hope that his feelings for her were totally sincere. Elliot's assured assumption that Billy would, of course, dump her had shaken her more than she liked to admit. Was it possible that she was nothing to him but another notch on his belt? She looked over at him, busily throwing far too much pepper into the pan. He wasn't even wearing a belt, for God's sake, and his Levi's rode his hips in the most provocative way. Kate turned away. She'd never looked at Michael with this kind of carnal longing.

She gazed around the room. Steven's West Side apartment had always looked like a student's place with its sprung sofa and the books he still had in cartons, while Michael's place, though it was neater and furnished with new Ikea pieces, looked in comparison temporary. But Billy's three big rooms indicated that he had put down deep roots. Beneath her feet, the Persian rug in blue and maroon looked faded and worn, as if his grandmother might have walked on it. The Chesterfield sofa didn't look as if it had been bought from a catalog — the oxblood leather didn't appear to have been professionally "distressed" at the factory before it was shipped. But there were new things, too: On one wall there was a big art piece — Kate couldn't call it a painting or a collage because it was something in between, a crazy-quilt consisting of torn bits of white paper glued to a white canvas. On the wall between the windows there was a small abstract of a woman lying under what looked like a very fluffy duvet. And over the sofa, hanging in a row, was a series of lithographs. Kate studied them.

"What do you think?" Billy asked her. He had come out of the kitchen. "Are they art, or did the artist who owed me a big tab rip me off?"

She smiled at him. "I like them," she said.

He took an appraising look. "I think I do," he said, and indicated the art on the walls with a flourish of the meat fork still in his hand. "Valuable art or bad debts. You be the judge." He smiled. "Dinner's almost ready."

Kate nodded, and Billy disappeared back into the kitchen. Watching him, she had to admit that Billy Nolan was the first man she had felt this kind of desire for. It was too comfortable to be infatuation, but too passionate to be completely comfortable. Most likely, it would end in tears. And the rain against the window seemed appropriate.

"Hey! How about a little help here?" Billy asked, coming out of the kitchen again, this time with plates and flatware. "You set the table." He went to the mantelpiece and took down two candlesticks, the candles in them stubby and of two different heights. "Spare no expense," he said. "Candlelight. Paper napkins. The works."

Kate smiled and set the table. She fetched a wineglass for him and put out the salt and pepper. A matchbook from the bar lay on the coffee table, and she used a match to light the two black wicks. As she did, it occurred to her that the last time Billy had used these candles it might have been to dine — and sleep — with Bina. She stood absolutely still until the match burned down, almost to her fingernail. Then she dropped it, just the way she dropped the idea of Billy with Bina or anyone else, and moved away from the table.

To distract herself, Kate looked around at all of the French volumes lined up neatly on Billy's bookshelves. She reminded herself not to be too inquisitive, not to bring up the past or the future, but she couldn't help being curious, and it seemed harmless enough to ask. "What's with the French?" she called to him in the kitchen.

Billy emerged with his mystery dish and

began to fill her plate. "Oh. I like it. It's not as rich a language as English, but it has subtleties that we lack."

Kate sat at the table and placed her napkin on her lap. "Did you learn it in school?" she asked, accepting her plate and eyeing its contents with uncertainty.

"A little," said Billy. He filled his own plate, then took a seat.

Gingerly, Kate tasted the stew. It was delicious, the meat so tender it fell off the bone. She looked across at him and smiled.

"Good?"

"Very. Really." She leaned back in her chair and smiled at him. "You must have been a terror growing up. A real class clown," she said.

He shook his head, his mouth full. He had to swallow before he could answer. "No. I didn't even talk in class. I had a stutter so bad that I was really self-conscious. I didn't want to talk to anyone."

Kate put down her fork and stared at him. She had almost forgotten his slight stammer. But stuttering, she knew, was almost impossible to cure completely, and many of the treatments had only a temporary effect. "How did you . . . when did you lose the . . ."

"Oh, I went all through high school with

it. But when I was a junior, I had a good French teacher, and I noticed that in French I didn't stutter. It was strange, to be able to say whatever I wanted to without worrying about certain words and letters I always got stuck on."

"It must have been amazing."

"Yeah. I felt like I was being let out of a prison. Man, I learned every word I possibly could in French. I wanted to know how to say 'dude' in French."

"What is 'dude' in French?"

"There's not really an equivalent. Believe me, I looked. Senior year I really didn't study anything else. And I didn't care about the grade. I just wanted to be able to speak whenever I felt like it."

Kate was fascinated. "What happened then?" she asked, like a child being told a bedtime story.

"My teacher introduced me to some of her French friends, and she helped me get into L'Ecole des Beaux-Arts in Paris. I was supposed to be studying French history, but what I was really doing was reinventing myself. I felt like I was reborn. I wasn't the kid who stuttered. I was the American who spoke French as well as any Parisian. Sometimes people I met wouldn't believe I was American."

"And what happened to your stutter? In English, I mean?" Kate asked.

Billy shrugged. "When I had to come back because of my father, it just seemed to be gone. Sometimes when I'm tired or under a lot of stress, I stammer a little bit."

Kate remembered his speech at the wedding. He had stammered a little then. "How do you control it?"

"I just relax and it goes away."

"You never had speech therapy? No one ever tried to help when you were younger?"

"Oh, there was some attempt in grammar school. You know, a speech therapist. She used to come and take me out of class. I was mortified."

"Didn't your parents try to help? I mean, was there any other —"

"Well, both of them were very concerned. Every time there was an article about stuttering with some new cure, they got excited. But it was expensive and nothing really worked for long, and by the time I got to junior high I just told them to forget it."

"And you found a way to cure it yourself," Kate said. His resourcefulness amazed her.

"Well, I kind of fell into it, didn't I? I

shouldn't get full credit. I just wasn't so stupid that I ignored the possibility of change."

"And what did you study in Paris?"

"Girls. I mean, for the first time I could talk to them. I also studied cheap train tickets. I got to Berlin and Bruges and Bologna for about a dime."

"Only places that began with Bs?" Kate asked with a smile.

Billy stared at her. "B was the letter I had the most trouble with," he said. "I wonder if that was just a coincidence."

Kate shrugged. "Jung would say no," she told him, "but I'm not sure."

"What did Jung say about repetition compulsions?" Billy teased, and Kate didn't know if she should laugh or cry. But she didn't have to do either, because he rose and cupped one hand around her neck, then combed his fingers through her hair. "I have ice cream," he told her, "but I can think of a much more delicious dessert." Kate smiled up at him.

Chapter Forty

The afternoon was lovely, warm in the sun but cool in the shade of the buildings, with a breeze that kept the slightly humid city air from being uncomfortable. "Let's take a walk," Billy suggested. "I'll show you some parts of Brooklyn you might not know."

Luckily, Kate had worn her Nikes and felt energetic. "I'm sorry that we can't spend the night together this Saturday," Billy told her as they left his apartment. "I'm always on watch during bachelor parties."

Kate nodded. Billy seemed completely accepting of Bina's nuptials. Had their relationship meant absolutely nothing to him? She shivered, though the weather was perfect. Surely what she felt for him was not unrequited.

Always sensitive to her movements, Billy put his arm around her. "Yeah," he said, "those bachelor parties make me shiver, too, but I just close my eyes and think of England."

Kate hadn't even considered the kind of raunchy goings-on that were typical. She didn't want to ask if Jack would have lap dancers or strippers or even worse. The sun and the cloudless sky were so lovely that she decided to put the whole idea out of her mind and do her best to live in the present. The present was perfect.

Billy took her hand, and although it was sentimental and wrong of her, Kate felt protected and loved just because he cradled her hand so safely in his own.

"This is Windsor Park," he said as they turned a corner and walked along a block of small houses, each with a garden in front of it. "Mostly Italian. Cops. Plumbers. A nice family neighborhood, but the yuppies are moving in from the north."

Kate enjoyed the gardens, some of which were planted with so many colorful flowers that they were almost in bad taste. In some front yards, as if the flowers weren't enough, stood garden statues of everything from Bambi to the Blessed Virgin. They walked past a big Catholic high school and crossed a walkway over the BQE.

"This is the edge of Park Slope," Billy told her. "You can't touch a house here for less than eight hundred thousand dollars anymore."

Kate looked from side to side at the brownstones and brick facades. Billy pointed to one where, unlike the others, the paint was peeling off the front door and the windows were old metal casements instead of the elegant flat expanses on the other houses. "You can always tell a holdout from the old days," he said. "The old lady who owns that place probably hasn't painted her kitchen in a decade."

They came to a corner where a tavern had set a few tables outside. "Not quite a café yet," Billy said with a smile. "Wanna drink?"

Kate nodded. They shared a beer and sat on a bench, watching women with strollers and kids with bikes and dads move past them. "So you drink?" Kate asked, though it was now obvious that he sometimes did. She had feared he might be a sober alcoholic and not drink at all. Or a control freak like Michael.

"My father told me there were two kinds of people not to trust: the ones who drank too much and the ones who didn't drink at all." He stood up. "You ready to continue?" he asked. Kate stood and took his hand.

They walked for another half hour until they reached a building that was neither as perfect as the gentrified ones nor as run-down as the one he had pointed out to her. He stopped and searched in his pocket for a moment. "Come over here," he said as he ran down the three steps and stood in the doorway. For a moment Kate thought he was only looking for a slightly private place to kiss her, but before she reached him he had inserted a key into the door. He took her hand and led her down the hallway of the brownstone, which had been divided into apartments. At the back he used another key to open another door. Inside there was an empty white room.

"Come through this way," he said, and led her across the gleaming wood floor to a back door.

Once through it, Kate felt as if she had entered another world. It was a backyard garden, but what a garden. A small lawn was perfectly tended. It made Dr. McKay's patch of grass look bald. Here and there, the lawn had bluestone placed in it, like islands in a green sea. They led in a lazy, curving path to a bower of trees that were in bloom. Behind them was a tiny pond surrounded by iris and fern. Kate could see goldfish darting under the lily pads and duckweed. Two chairs, their wood weathered to a silvery gray, sat beside the pool.

Behind them, ivy crawled up the brick wall that divided the yard from whatever lay on the other side.

But Kate didn't care what was on the other side or anywhere else. It was the most serene, most beautifully groomed city garden she had ever seen. She didn't want to be anywhere but here. She looked at Billy, who had stopped in the sunshine on the lawn and was watching her. She walked back to him. "How did you know about this place?" she asked.

"It's mine," he said.

"What do you mean?"

"Well, when I was a kid we lived here. It was my grandmother's house. She lived on the ground floor and we had the top. But my mother took care of the garden. She taught me, and then I started to like it." He took her hand and led her to one of the chairs. "Do you like it?" he asked.

"It's breathtaking," Kate told him. She thought of *The Secret Garden*, her favorite book when she was growing up. "You've kept it up? Do the people who own the house now —"

"I own the house now," Billy told her.

"But you live —"

"Yeah, I live over the bar because it's convenient and it's the right amount of space and it reminds me of my dad. I've been renting out this place, but I keep the bottom floor empty so that I get the garden. I renovated the house — I mean, not by myself, but with a carpenter friend and a plumber who used to work with my father. Anyway, it's apartments now, but easy to turn back into a family house, maybe someday."

Kate sat, trying not to show her amazement.

"*Ça te plaît?*" he asked.

Did she like it? "*Je l'adore,*" she told him. "*C'est un vrai paradis.*" She didn't want Billy to see just how impressed she was because it would embarrass her and possibly embarrass him. She was a psychologist and supposed to be aware of people's psychological depths, but she had misjudged Billy at every step. The idea of him tending the grass, planting flowers, and raking leaves had never occurred to her. Why should it? She wasn't yet sure about all that this garden revealed about Billy, but she could see how much it said to him. More important, she already knew what it meant to her. A man who could create and tend a garden like this was obviously very special. Why hadn't she been able to see? Was it because he acted so casual, so carefree? But a garden like this took care and . . .

diligence. It also took vision. She looked around again at the perfectly tended beauty. Kate caught her breath. A man with such tenderness as this could surely be a good father, husband, best friend.

She dared to look at him. He shrugged. "*Il faut cultiver notre jardin,*" he said, quoting Voltaire. "I used to work here with my mother."

Billy had told her about his father's death, but she hadn't yet asked him questions about his mother's. Now she did. "Pancreatic cancer," Billy told her, and Kate winced. She knew it was a particularly ugly and painful death.

"I'm so sorry," she said. "When?"

"Quite some time ago. The day before Thanksgiving. It still makes the holidays tough."

Kate nodded. Although she didn't miss her father, and she was always included at the Horowitz table, she felt like the orphan she was from Thanksgiving to New Year's. They sat for a while, both silent, but it wasn't an uncomfortable silence. Kate felt that by bringing her here, Billy had shown her more than his landscaping skills. She took his hand, and the two of them watched the fish move in golden darts under the surface of the water.

476

Chapter Forty-one

"My God! These girls and showers! They are the cleanest people in the city of New York. Not to mention the ones with the most gifts."

Despite his sharp tongue, Brice was smiling. He sat between Elliot and Kate in the cab, a big, beautifully wrapped gift sitting on his lap. Kate wasn't sure she could face everyone in Brooklyn, but Bina's bridal shower couldn't be missed.

Elliot was silent. She knew he was angry at her, but there was nothing she could do. She thought of the Pascal line *Le coeur a ses raisons que la raison ne connaît point*. The heart has its reasons that reason knows nothing of.

The story of Billy's French lingered in Kate's mind. She tried to imagine what a silent, humiliated young Billy Nolan had been like. She couldn't. It was either a failure of imagination or too sad to visualize. Somehow, his history changed her view of him in the present. Instead of cocky and too self-assured, she saw his outgoing personality as a celebration of his freedom. It made her feel far more tender toward him, as if he needed protection. This was ridiculous, of course, since the days when he was a vulnerable child and adolescent were long over. Billy Nolan could certainly take care of himself, but despite her intentions to keep a lid on her feelings, she found herself feeling more and more for him.

They were crowded in the back of the taxi, and Kate was relieved when the cab pulled up in front of the Horowitz house.

Before they even reached the front door, it was flung open by Mrs. Horowitz. "Come on," she called. "Hurry up or you'll spoil the surprise." Kate would never tell her that she had already "spoiled" the surprise by telling Bina in advance about the party. The two of them had made a pact long ago that they would never allow either one of them to show up badly dressed and be scared out of their wits by a "wonderful surprise."

Kate and the guys walked in and joined the others. There were kisses and hugs and introductions. Kate added her gift to the big, colorful pile already stacked on a card table. Then Mrs. Horowitz called out, "Sha! Sha! They're coming!" Kate sighed while everyone else in the room seemed to suck in their breath so they could shout more loudly. Dr. Horowitz flung open the door and made way for Bina. Kate thought Bina did a miserable imitation of a surprised person, but no one seemed to notice. When Bina gave her a special look, Kate smiled at her.

The party went through each of its traditional phases: the weren't-you-surprised-yes-I-was part; the no-you-shouldn't-have-this-wasn't-necessary section; and the oh-let's-eat-isn't-this-delicious portion (and they were big portions). The party culminated in the traditional oohing and aahing over gifts. Kate knew she was watching an important female rite of passage, but she just wasn't in the mood. She regretted giving up the day with Billy, she was annoyed by all of the Horowitz extended family and their questions about when it was her turn, and she was bored by the chatter and old jokes, not to mention resentful of the way Brice and Elliot seemed to relish it all.

Kate wondered why Bina kept throwing looks at her and hoped that Elliot hadn't told her about what he was now referring to as the "Billy thing." Several times Bina seemed to try to get next to Kate and talk to her, but Kate managed to slip away. Elliot wouldn't — couldn't — break the confidentiality of her private situation without her permission.

When the cake was cut and being passed around, Kate could take no more and went into the bathroom to revive herself. She looked about as lousy as she felt. She put on some lipstick and a little blush, but it didn't seem to do much. She decided it didn't matter. She had been so happy for the past few weeks that her discomfort seemed especially painful. Why was seeing her friends such an onerous task? She thought about it for a little while. Kate believed she wasn't like her friends. She had a career and loved her work. She hadn't been out looking for a husband from the time she was twenty. She didn't feel as if she needed a man to protect her or to support her. But somehow, because of breaking up with Michael or seeing Steven or because of this . . . thing with Billy Nolan, she felt as insecure and lonely as she used to feel back in high school.

Since her talk with Elliot, she had felt more and more doubt. Somehow, being here with Bina and all her married Brooklyn friends made it seem more unlikely that she would ever get to share their experience of this kind of group celebration. Billy wasn't "a safe bet." He was not the kind of man women got to marry or men threw bachelor parties for. Kate imagined his whole life had been a kind of bachelor party, and Elliot was right: There was no reason for her to think that would change. She began to feel extremely sorry for herself and realized it was best to leave the bathroom now before the tears set in.

As she walked into the hallway, Bina sidelined her. "I have to talk to you," she hissed. "Quick, before anyone notices." She took Kate's hand and drew her down the narrow hallway to her bedroom.

Nothing had changed. The same flowered pink curtains hung at the window, the same matching wallpaper covered the walls, and the print repeated itself on Bina's bedspread. The dressing table with the pink skirt that Kate had envied so when they were in seventh grade still sat between the two windows. Kate herself sat on the bench in front of it. "What is it?" she asked.

"Oh, Katie, I just can't keep this lie going," Bina said.

Kate took a deep breath. She loved her friend's simplicity, but sometimes it was just too much. "Oh, Bina. Nobody cares. If you just act normal now and carry on, everyone will be thrilled."

Bina's face registered horror. "I can't believe that you would tell me to do that," she cried.

"Bina, it's just a party. It's not a lifetime."

Bina's mouth dropped open. "I'm sorry," she said. "I beg to differ with you. I think a marriage is supposed to last a lifetime."

Kate stopped examining the pictures and mementos on the dressing table. "What are you talking about?" she said. "Just because you pretended to be surprised doesn't mean you're starting your marriage with a lie. For God's sake, have a sense of proportion."

Bina took a step backward, as if Kate had physically attacked her. Then her lips began to tremble. "Is it really you saying this?" she said. "Max thought you would understand, but even if you don't, I can't go through with it. I can't marry Jack. It's not like he really loves me. I know what he was up to in Hong Kong. Max showed me."

Kate sighed angrily. After all that Bina had gone through to finally get Jack, it seemed a little late in the day to find a misplaced sense of pride. "Well, that was very wrong of Max. Remember, you were dating, too."

"Yeah, but I didn't want to."

"Oh, come on, you had a lot of fun with Billy."

"But that was just fun."

Kate raised her brows. "And why are you feeling guilty about that little sexual escapade?"

"Because it wasn't an escapade," Bina said. "I keep comparing it to being with Jack, and . . ."

Kate certainly doubted that Jack could be anywhere near as erotic and imaginative and warm in bed. But she certainly couldn't tell Bina why she suspected that. And it was hopeless for Bina to think about Billy as an alternative to Jack. Kate truly believed Bina loved Jack, and with a little time she would get over this guilt and unhealthy comparison and settle down.

"Bina," she said, rising and taking her friend by her shoulders, "you have to get over this guilt. You have to move on. This is what you have wanted your whole life."

"But I was wrong," Bina wailed.

"No, you weren't," Kate told her. "You're wrong now. So just calm down. Enjoy all this."

Just then the door opened. "Oh, here they are," Mrs. Horowitz sang out. "The best friends are at it in here," she called, and lifted her camera to take what would develop into a hideously unflattering picture of both of them.

Chapter Forty-two

Kate fumbled with the lock to her door and pushed in. The lights were on, and she gasped and almost jumped when she realized that her living room was filled with people. For a moment she was terrified that Elliot, Barbie, Bina, and the rest would scream, "Surprise!" But no one yelled — in fact, no one said anything. She couldn't believe that Elliot — whom she had trusted with a key — would invade her nest, bringing a flock of raptors with him. She would get her keys back, and she would get him back some other way. Before she had a chance to ask what the hell was going on, Elliot, who was perched on a windowsill, spoke.

"Some of you might ask why we are gathered here today," he said in a pretty good imitation of Dr. McKay's pompous tone.

"What's going on?" Kate asked. Her stomach sank, as if she were in a plunging elevator. But at the same time, she felt her rage ready to choke her. She didn't even have a place to sit or put her bag down.

"We're worried about you," Bina said. She was the only one there who looked apologetic.

"Katie, look, you're allowed to go out with him, and you're even allowed to sleep with him, but you're not allowed to fall in love with him," Barbie added.

"What are you talking about?" Kate asked. But of course, she knew. Elliot must have told everyone, and now they were trying to do some kind of . . . intervention, or something, as if she were a drunk who needed to be confronted with her self-destructive behavior.

"Time to go now. Party's over," Kate told them, using the phrase Billy did when he was ready to close the bar. She turned into her little hallway to get to the bedroom and away from all of these so-called friends. Unfortunately, Brice was standing there, leaning against the wall.

"Sorry, girlfriend, you have to hear this," he said, and gently turned her around, marching her into the middle of her living room. Bina got out of the wicker chair, and Brice maneuvered Kate over to it. Bev leaned forward as far as she could given the state of her belly and took Kate's hand.

"I know how it is, Katie," she said. "You want a home of your own. You want a wedding and a husband and a baby."

Kate snatched her hand away. "I have a home," she said. "It's right here, and I would like you all to do me a favor and get out of it. Please," she added so that she didn't sound quite so rude. After all, they probably meant well.

Elliot came up from behind her and put his hands on her shoulders. His face was beside her own. "I wouldn't have done this if I didn't think it was really serious," he said.

"I want my keys back," Kate told him, and extended her hand. "I mean now." It was better to lock him out permanently, she thought, than ever to walk into a scene like this again.

"Look, you moved out of the old neighborhood. You might not remember what players in Brooklyn are like, but you've wasted enough of your time on jerks. You're not getting younger this week," Bunny said. "Or any other week."

"Yeah. A fling is okay, but once you're thirty your flings are flung," Barbie added. "Whaddya think? A blow job's a commitment?"

"Shut up, Barbie," Kate told her. "None

487

of this is your business." She turned and looked around at the room. She couldn't defend herself with logic. And a part of her knew they were probably right. But that was a part she didn't want to listen to.

Elliot sighed. "I told you this wouldn't be easy," he said to the assembled bunch of gossips, yentas, and morons that up till now Kate had considered her friends. He leaned toward her again. "Kate, I'm not saying you did the wrong thing in turning Michael down."

"I am," Bev interrupted. "He was a doctor and a Pisces. Perfect."

Brice silenced her with a look. "I think what Elliot is trying to say is that you can waste a lot of time with men like Steven and Billy, but you get propositions, not proposals, from them."

Kate could feel her face getting warm with anger and embarrassment. "We only want what's best for you," Elliot said.

"We're worried about you," Barbie added. Then she looked down at Kate's feet. "Where did you get those shoes?" she asked. "Are they Ferragamo?"

"Not now, Barbie," Brice admonished. "This isn't *Full Frontal Fashion.*"

"No. It's *Full Frontal Confrontation,* and it's over." Kate took a deep breath. She looked at Bina, who had been the quietest. "How was the bachelor party?" she asked.

"Didn't you hear?" Bev asked.

"There was a fistfight."

"You're kidding?" Brice said. "Why haven't I heard about this?"

"My Arnie said it was incredible. Max and Jack really went at each other."

"Yeah, my Johnny said Jack's black eye probably won't heal before the wedding. And if Billy hadn't of broken it up . . ."

Once again Kate felt her stomach lurch, this time over the scene in a Brooklyn bar during a bachelor party. She knew Billy kept a baseball bat beside the cash register, but she wondered if he had been hurt. This, however, was not the time to ask.

"So what happened?" Elliot wanted to know.

"Oh, Max called Jack names and he got mad and took a swing at Max, but then Max got wild and jumped him. Whaddaya expect? They were all drunk."

Kate stood up. She wanted to call Billy and find out if he was okay. She also needed all of these so-called friends of hers to leave her in peace. But Elliot had other plans. "Kate, you have to promise us all that you'll break off this thing with Billy," he said. "I mean, what's the point? After he dumps you, you don't want to get proposed to by a stranger."

"Will you stop that!" Kate told him. "What makes you so sure he'll dump me? And if you believe that garbage about proposals . . ."

The room filled with half a dozen hushed oohs. "Jesus," Barbie said. "Do you actually think he's serious about you?"

"Kate, this is a guy who has made fear of commitment a permanent lifestyle," Bev said. She stood up with difficulty. She opened her mouth, but before she could continue her rant, a strange look came over her face. "I feel a little twinge." She put a hand on her belly, and as she did her water broke.

Chapter Forty-three

It was the last day of school, and Kate was straightening out her files, packing her two plants, and saying good-bye for the summer to the children who dropped in. Once she was finished, she knew she should go to Bev's to see her baby. Though she was curious to see it, her resentment of the Bitches still lingered, and to be brutally honest, she was also afraid she'd feel some envy.

Not that she was unhappy. She had the children at the school. Overall, she was very pleased with her work at Andrew. Though she hadn't made any progress with the Reilly twins, she had convinced their parents to dress them in different clothes. It hadn't stopped them from continuing to pull the switcheroo, but at least now they had to go into the bathroom or gym and swap their outfits to do it. If there was a darker side to their masquerading, she would have to find it in September. But most of her other work had gone well. Tina Foster was no longer taking dares or launching herself out into space. Though she was still a tomboy and preferred to chase boys than sit with the girls, she didn't seem at all self-destructive.

As Kate put some papers into her backpack, Jennifer Whalen appeared in the doorway. Jennifer had stopped her exaggerated lying, and Kate smiled at the little girl. "Coming to say good-bye?" she asked. Jennifer nodded. "You know, I'll see you in September." Jennifer nodded again and then rushed into the room and hugged Kate.

"Thank you for helping me with my shelf-esteem," Jennifer said.

Kate looked down at her, suppressing a smile. "You're very welcome," she said.

Jennifer nodded wisely and gestured to all the empty shelves in the office. "Do you have shelf-esteem, too?" she asked.

Now Kate allowed herself to smile. "Plenty," she told the little girl, and Jennifer smiled, too, turned, and skipped out of the room.

"See ya next year," she called.

Kate had just knelt down to straighten the dollhouse when she felt someone else's presence behind her. Still on her knees, she turned and was totally surprised to find Billy standing in the doorway. He took a step into the room and closed the door behind him. His face was bruised, with a swollen patch on one cheek and a scratch over his eye. She jumped to her feet. "Are you all right? I kept leaving messages on your machine. Where have you been?" she asked, and moved toward him. He must have been hurt in the imbroglio at Jack's party, as she had feared. She wanted to hold him and touch his face, but he put up a hand to stop her.

"So who do you expect a proposal from?" he asked. His face was pale, and the bruise seemed even darker against his livid skin.

"What do you mean?" she asked.

"What kind of game were you playing with me?" he demanded. "Don't try to deny it, because I heard all about it at the bachelor party. Those assholes called me Dumping Billy for most of the evening. And when one of them finally told me the score, I couldn't believe it." Kate realized she was holding her breath but couldn't seem to do anything about it. "Bina got that jerk-off Jack. Who are you expecting to get?"

For a moment Kate considered saying, "You. I want you," but she knew this certainly wasn't the time for an admission like that. She moved toward him and tried to take his hand, but again he extended his arm, silently telling her to back off. She could see the anger on his face, but beyond that she could see real pain in his eyes. He must truly care for me, she thought.

"It's not what you think," Kate began, and then tried to figure out how she could possibly explain all the machinations and manipulations that had gone on since the fateful day of Bunny's wedding. Before she could launch into an explanation, Billy spoke.

"Did you all do research? You know, to find out about the women I'd dated in the past and what happened to them after we broke up?"

"I didn't," Kate said.

"Don't become a lawyer," Billy snapped. "If it wasn't you, it was someone in your posse."

Kate looked away. She should have seen this coming, but somehow she had just thought things would continue as they were going or that Billy would tire of her the way he had with so many other women. She wanted to wiggle out of this, but she couldn't lie. The problem was, she also didn't want to tell the truth.

"My friend Elliot . . . ," she began.

"Is he the one you expect to propose to you after we break up?"

"Billy, he's gay, hooked up, and my best friend. He's a mathematician, and, well, he noticed . . . he discovered that after you left girls they immediately got married. He thought there was a cause and effect. And he convinced Bina that —"

"And you convinced me to go out with her. Repetition compulsion, my ass. The whole thing was a setup. And I have no goddamn idea why it worked, but Bina is marrying Jack and I figure you've got someone on the hook. . . ."

"Billy, you really have this wrong."

"Oh? I had three hours of bullshit from every guy at the party, all of them blaming me for their marriages."

Kate felt herself begin to lose her own temper. "I think you made a reputation for yourself long before I came on the scene," she snapped. "I just didn't know when you were planning to dump me."

"How about right now?" he asked. "And best wishes on your upcoming nuptials. I hope whoever your victim is richly deserves you." He spun around, opened the door, and virtually smashed into Dr. McKay.

"Am I interrupting something?" Dr.

McKay asked, his eyebrows raised and his eyes darting back and forth between Kate and Billy.

"No," Billy told him. "We're finished." Kate could only watch his back as he strode down the hallway.

Chapter Forty-four

Kate cried for an hour in her office. Then, when Elliot found her and bundled her in his arms to take her home, she cried in the taxi all the way back to his apartment. She cried when Brice got in, and she cried over the dinner he made. At last Elliot took her to the sofa, sat her down, and put his arm around her. "Kate," he said, his voice warm and compassionate, "I know how you hurt. And I hurt for you. But are you sure this isn't just a Bina Horowitz impersonation you're doing?"

Despite her pain, Kate almost laughed, and that made her choke, snorting tears up her nose.

"You also have to consider my rug," Brice added, sitting beside them. "It's a faux antique Tabriz."

Kate took a shuddering breath. She couldn't go on crying forever, though she felt as if she wanted to. But what was the point? She'd ruined her life. She'd hurt the man she loved, and now he despised her. Still, she might as well stop crying. She managed a wet grin. "There's my good girl," Elliot told her.

"Why don't you try to pull yourself together?" Brice suggested. "Go on into the bathroom and clean up your face?"

Kate nodded and stood up.

"Do you want me to help?" Elliot asked, but Kate shook her head.

"I'll brew up some teabags for your eyes," Brice told her, and patted her arm in a comforting way. "It will take down the swelling. Believe me, I know."

Looking at herself in the bathroom mirror, Kate couldn't help it: She began to cry again. Her face was a ruin, her eyes red and minuscule in the puff pastry around them. Her nose, especially around the nostrils, almost perfectly matched the color of her hair. God, she was ugly! She filled the sink with cold water, took a deep breath, and lowered her face into it. The shock felt good, and she stood, bent at the waist, her face in the sink, for what seemed like a long time. Maybe, she thought, she could drown this way.

She thought of Billy in bed, his arms around her. She thought of him from the back, moving shirtless as he cooked breakfast. She remembered every book and picture in his apartment, their walks around Brooklyn, and his garden. Without ever admitting it to herself, she had hoped that garden, that house, would be one they would share and fill with their children someday.

Kate's body shuddered for air, and she lifted her face out of the sink. She looked back in the mirror as she gasped for breath. She knew this breakdown was more than just about Billy. She had been crying because she'd hurt him and because she herself was hurt. But she felt she had also been crying for her past as well as her future. All the tears she had held back in grammar school, on lonely holidays, in high school, through the struggle of college and graduate school, all of the unshed tears seemed to be leaking out of her now. She filled the sink again and immersed herself. She opened her eyes under the water.

She could see now that Billy had been a chance to regain the good part of her background, to heal a lot of her wounds. She had changed her style, perhaps, but despite the education and the move to Manhattan, her roots were showing. She blinked. Underwater, with her eyes painful from crying, she could see that Billy had been a unique opportunity to love and be loved by an equal, by a partner who would truly know her.

Kate burst up out of the water like a submarine exploding onto the surface of the sea. She was about to begin crying again when she heard her cell phone ring. She ran out of the bathroom.

Brice framed her with two hands. *"Ophelia, Drowned for Love and Answering a Phone,"* he said. "Pre-Raphaelite school."

"Want to stop running the marathon and help clean up dinner?" Elliot asked.

She paid no attention. She got to her purse and began scrambling through it. Her phone was still ringing. Billy had changed his mind. Somehow he had realized that it had all been a mistake, that she loved him and wanted him, and that everything else that had happened was nonsense.

She was on her knees, her makeup bag and change purse and wallet spread all around her on Brice's carpet. But when she finally managed to find the phone, the caller had hung up. She quickly punched in the request for received calls, but she didn't recognize the number. It was a 212 area code, not the 718 of Brooklyn. It didn't matter. It had to be Billy. He had come looking for her. She pressed the call button and waited, literally holding her breath. It would all be all right, she told herself. It *had* to be all right. In a moment someone answered the phone.

"Hello, Kate?"

It was a man's voice, but her stomach lurched when she realized it wasn't Billy.

"Yes?" Kate said, though she wanted to hang up and throw the phone into the sink of cold water. If Billy didn't call, what did she need a phone for?

"Kate, it's me. Steven."

"Steven!"

At the sound of his name, both Elliot and Brice nearly dropped the plates and silverware they were clearing from the table.

"*That* Steven?" Brice whispered.

"Drop the phone into this soup right now," Elliot said, holding out a full bowl. "I mean it, missy."

Kate motioned for them both to shut up.

"Did I get you at a bad time?" Steven asked.

Kate almost laughed aloud. She couldn't remember ever crying for this long in her whole life. "A bad time" was a massive understatement. "No," she said. "I can talk."

Elliot shook his head wildly, but Kate paid no attention. She remembered how she had lived for his calls. And now the deadness she felt talking to him was new and curious. Maybe in two years I could feel this way talking to Billy, she thought. Maybe I can learn eventually not to care about anyone. But where was the benefit of that?

"Look, if you're not busy, would you consider meeting me for a drink?"

"Now?" Kate asked. She looked down at her watch. It felt like midnight, but it was only eight-fifteen. Typical Steven move: calling with no warning and expecting her to jump. But she felt no resentment. "I don't think so," she said.

"It's really important," Steven told her. "I'm sure you have other things to do, but I have something I have to tell you."

Kate couldn't think of a single thing that Steven could tell her that would be of any interest, unless he had taken a job distributing Publishers Clearing House lottery checks and she was a winner. And even then, what would she do with the money? Buy a big apartment to be alone in? Thinking of her empty apartment made her say yes. "Where?" she asked while Elliot shook both his head and his finger at her.

"Can you come downtown?" Steven asked.

Typical. He wanted a favor, but she had to go out of her way. She looked like shit and she felt like shit and she told him yes. What did she care? He gave her an address and she hung up.

"Kate, don't tell me that you're going," Elliot said.

"I am," Kate told him. She fumbled through her makeup bag, took out a mirror, and smeared concealer under her eyes.

"Rebound therapy is not a legitimate approach to this," Elliot told her.

Kate stood up, threw her scattered things back into her bag, and looked at Brice and Elliot. "I'm not going to rebound. I'm not a damn basketball." She walked to the door, then turned back to them, a happy couple in a world of couples. "I've already ruined my life," she said. "You don't have to worry anymore."

Chapter Forty-five

Kate sat beside Steven, her purse on her lap, her legs crossed. One foot was perched on the bar rail. She was actually grateful he had asked to meet at Temple Bar because it was probably the darkest boîte in Manhattan. It was so cool that the entrance didn't even have a name. It was the kind of place that Steven would know about and frequent. It was all dark velvet, elegant uplighting, murmured conversation, and $7 cosmopolitans. Nothing at all like the Barber Bar. It was pure Manhattan.

Steven hadn't seemed to notice her disarray, or if he did, he had the good grace not to mention it. But as she sat there and looked at him, she realized that he was more about being noticed than about noticing other people. There was something in the way he flipped the dark wing of his hair away from his face, the way he held his head, even the way he gestured, that made Kate think he was always performing for an audience, real or imagined. How had she missed that? She simply sat there, tired and sad, and tried to listen to him. It was a long harangue and had gone on for some time now.

". . . and I deserved it. I really did," he was saying. "I know I hurt you, and I know now that I was a fool. I guess I just wanted to prolong my childhood." He looked away from her, but she could see his expression across from the two of them in the mirror behind the bar. She wondered, in a kind of disinterested way, why he was bothering to go through this again. Elliot didn't have to worry. The good news was there was no way she was going to sleep with this player, no way she was going to let herself be hurt again. The bad news was she was so numb that nothing could ever hurt her again.

"I've done a lot of soul-searching," Steven continued. "I didn't really like what I found." Join the club, Kate thought, but she only nodded. "I've been irresponsible," he said. "The fact is, I've behaved like a boy, not a man."

You and five hundred thousand other single men in Manhattan, Kate thought. But again she just nodded. How could she have put up with him? The idea of beginning to date again, of having to meet new men and sit in bars like this and listen to their ruminations and take them seriously, seemed not just more trouble than it was worth, but a kind of torture that no one should be subjected to. Where was Amnesty International when you needed them? Kate supposed she could get used to going out again or she could simply give up, wait until the rest of her friends had babies, and make a career of being a dedicated aunt.

Surprisingly, Steven reached out then and took her hand. Kate jumped a little but managed to keep her purse on her lap and her perch on the bar stool. "I know you're not listening, and I don't blame you," he said. That brought Kate's attention back to him. Perhaps Steven was more aware of others than she'd given him credit for. "Kate, what I'm trying to say is that when we were dating we had different goals. At least I thought we did. But I've had a long time to think about it, and I spent most of that time regretting losing you."

Kate looked at him, face-to-face, for the first time. What was he doing?

Steven sighed. "I can't believe how stupid I was when we met for coffee," he said. "It was arrogant of me to think that an apology would be enough to put us back where we left off." He looked away for a moment. "Sometimes I lack . . . well, there's probably a lot that I lack. But because I lack you, I'd like to try, slowly, to prove I've changed."

Despite her pain, Kate tried to remember if he'd been more stupid than usual. She supposed asking her out at all had been arrogant, but nothing she would not have expected from him. The problem with Steven, she realized, was that everything came too easily to him. He had never had to suffer or work to get anything he wanted, so it was only to be expected that he believed he could get whatever he wanted simply by asking for it. Kate took her hand back from his. He looked down at the bar for a moment, recognizing her rebuke.

"Kate, you shouldn't waste your time on any man who doesn't value you. Who isn't willing to commit to you."

Tell me about it, Kate thought, and idly wondered whether Steven had decided to become a counselor for single women. Maybe he wanted her as a client. But, once again, he took her hand in his. Kate felt nothing. But because of her purse and her unsteady seat, she couldn't easily pull back.

"Kate, I'm asking for your hand."

"You have it," she said.

"No. I mean . . . I mean I'm asking for your hand in marriage."

Kate couldn't — didn't — believe what she'd just heard. Was she having an aural hallucination, projecting this onto Steven, or was he making some bad-taste joke? But, to her utter amazement, he reached into his pocket and took out a ring. Before she had a chance to do anything, he slipped it onto her finger. Kate stared at the diamond flanked by two smaller emeralds, her favorite stone. "Do you like it?" Steven asked.

She stared up at him. What in the world was he thinking of? His audacity, his presumption, were enough to infuriate her, but then she stared down at her hand. The diamond seemed to wink at her in the reflected light of the bottles behind the bar. And then she began to laugh. Once she started, she couldn't stop. Her foot slipped and her purse fell to the floor, but she couldn't silence herself. She wasn't trying to be cruel — she had lost control.

At first, as she began to laugh, Steven looked at her with a smile. Then, as her laughter continued, he stopped smiling. Patrons' heads began to turn and look in their direction. She didn't want to humiliate him, but he had already done it for himself. Why is life like this? Kate thought. When you really wanted something, you didn't get it. Then when you did get it, you didn't want it anymore.

With a tremendous effort she got herself under control. She stopped laughing and thought about all the things she could say, all the things she could tell Steven. In the end, she decided his education and therapy were none of her business. She simply took her hand from his, pulled off the ring, and handed it back to him. "I'm afraid not, Steven," she said. "It wouldn't be good for either one of us."

His face immediately took on the stricken look she knew all too well. For a moment she felt sorry for him. Pain was as hard to inflict as it was to bear. But she knew Steven. In a few days he'd find some other woman who would comfort him, trying to get that look to change. Good luck to her, Kate thought. Then she stood up and patted Steven on the shoulder. "I have to go," she told him. Her empty apartment suddenly seemed like a haven.

"Be well," she told him. Then she turned and walked down the long bar to the door. It wasn't the best exit line, but it would have to do.

Chapter Forty-six

Kate lay on her bed. The oppressive heat had closed down on New York. The temperature and stagnant air made it feel more like mid-August. Kate was unprepared for this kind of heat. She felt unprepared for everything in her life right now; she had an air conditioner stored in the basement but hadn't asked Max to help her bring it up to her window; she hadn't folded and put away her school clothes and refilled her tiny closet with her light summer things; she hadn't made plans for the July Fourth weekend. In fact, summer had come and Kate felt as unprepared for her whole life as she did for her vacation. Somehow, without planning any of it, she had wasted too much time with Michael, revisited a ridiculous relationship with Steven, inappropriately fallen for and been blown off by Billy. Meanwhile, everyone she knew was moving forward with their lives. Brice had gotten a promotion, Elliot was teaching a course at the New School, the two of them had rented a share on Fire Island, Bina was endlessly preparing for her wedding, Bev's baby was keeping her busy, and — the latest news flash was that Barbie had announced that she was pregnant. It seemed as if everyone had a direction and only she was rudderless.

Kate thought about the reasons she should get up. She had laundry piling up, she should go to the gym, she ought to try to get the air conditioner in somehow. There was a pile of books she had been saving to read over the summer. The plants in the living room needed watering. Still, she couldn't force herself to move. She tried to think of something she had to look forward to and failed miserably.

What came to her mind instead were thoughts that didn't bear thinking about: Both her parents were dead, she had no sisters, no brothers. Elliot would be gone for the whole summer. Her friends were married. She'd cut off Michael and was glad of it, but the proposal from Steven had thrown her. She didn't want Steven — but she had once. And she didn't want Michael, but she'd once thought she might have. She obviously didn't know what — or whom — she wanted. Maybe she never would. She was becoming more and more convinced that she would always be alone.

Something must be wrong with her, something deep, no doubt caused by the traumas of her childhood. Her mother had died; her father had been emotionally unavailable, and then he'd died. She had chosen abandonment or abandoning as a way of life.

She threw the sheet off of her and was exhausted by the effort. Why had she moved to Manhattan? Why had she struggled through school? Even her work with the children, over now for the summer, seemed hopeless, useless, and second-rate.

But it was the scene with Billy that made her inconsolable. Thinking about it was almost unbearable, but she played the scene over and over in her mind. Now she thought of the day they had gone skating in the park and his easy leadership when the crowd became unruly at the ice-cream store. She wondered if his garden was still so cool despite the day's heat. Thinking of the grass, the fish glimmering in the water, the canopy of leaves, she felt again how special Billy was and what a perfect idiot she had been. She had sent him two notes: One was a simple apology and the other a longer explanation. She hadn't gotten a reply. It wasn't possible to know if he had really loved her, if he'd read her letters, or if — regardless of the nastiness — he would have dumped her anyway; but falling in with Bina's crazy superstition and Elliot's plan had been madness. She thought again of his face when he had confronted her at school. She had seen real pain there and couldn't bear knowing that she had caused it. And she had hurt Michael. And she had hurt Steven, though he had deserved it. Still, she had never meant to hurt any of them and certainly didn't want this pain she was in.

Her loneliness was too big for her little bedroom. She felt it expand out the door and into the living room, until the place felt like a vacuum of love. Kate turned on her side and thought again of Billy. It was always Billy. She began to cry, and the tears were absorbed by her already damp pillow.

When the bell rang, Kate awoke with a start. She felt sticky and disoriented but managed to rise from the crumpled bedclothes and move toward the door. Who would be visiting her, unannounced, at one o'clock on a weekday?

She opened the door, and Max stood there with Bina beside him. Both should have been at work. It was Monday, wasn't it? Her terrible weekend had seemed endless, but it couldn't possibly still be Sunday?

"Katie, we have to see you," Bina said.

"Can we come in, or did we get you at a bad time?" Max asked.

Kate was too sad, dispirited, and confused to tell him that any time was a bad time for her. She just stood aside and let them walk past her into the living room.

"God, it's hot." Bina sighed and took a seat on the sofa.

"Oh. I should have remembered to bring up your air conditioner," Max said. "Why didn't you ask me?"

"I've been busy," Kate told him, but the sarcasm was lost on both of them. She must look awful, but neither of them seemed to notice. Instead of looking at her, they seemed to be either exchanging looks or avoiding her glance. She thought of the Reilly twins and their bad behavior, but what did Max and Bina have to be guilty about, and what naughtiness could these two possibly be up to together? Kate sank into her wicker chair. "What's up?" she asked.

"It's just that . . . well, I can't . . ."

Bina's mouth began to tremble. Kate wasn't sure that she could sit through one

514

more of her friend's cloudbursts. After all, she was getting everything she wanted and needed. She'd have the Vera Wang knockoff dress, the bridesmaids, a wedding with all her family there, the down payment on a house, a husband who might now appreciate her, and, no doubt, babies on the way. And, as always, after the flood of tears Bina would be cheerful and sunny again. It was Kate who would be drained.

Before she could manage to say anything or get up from her chair, Max put his arm around Bina. "It will all be okay," he said. "I promise. It will all be okay." He looked up at Kate. "Tell her it will be okay."

"What will be okay?" Kate demanded. "Bina, stop crying and tell me what's wrong."

"Everything. Everything is wrong," Bina sobbed. "I don't want to marry Jack. I can't marry him. But I have to."

"No, you don't," Max told her.

"Omigod!" Bina said. "What will people think?"

Kate tried to keep her mouth from dropping open. Why in the world would Bina . . . Then a hideous thought occurred to her. Could she be pregnant? Pregnant by Billy? "Bina, you have been using birth control, haven't you?"

Bina looked up for a moment and wiped her eyes. "Yeah. Sure. Why? Do I look like I'm bloated?" Max handed her his hand-kerchief, and she wiped her eyes. "My mother sent out three hundred invita-tions," she said. "A calligrapher wrote the addresses."

Kate leaned forward and took one of Bina's hands in her own. "You shouldn't feel guilty. Just because you slept with somebody else doesn't mean you can't marry Jack. It's not like you had a real rela-tionship. Or that you loved him."

"It is a relationship," Max said. "A se-rious one."

"And I do love him," Bina said, and began sobbing again. "I love him with all my heart." Now Max took Bina's other hand, which left her none to wipe her nose with.

Kate turned away, feeling sick to her stomach. She and Bina both hopelessly in love with Billy Nolan. It was ridiculous. "Look, it's just an infatuation. It's a phys-ical thing. It isn't real love," she said, trying to convince herself as well as her friend.

"It is real love," Bina said, and looked at Max. "It's real, isn't it, Max?"

"Of course it is," Max said.

Kate was wondering where the hell Max got off encouraging Bina's delusional behavior when, to her utter amazement, he leaned forward and gave Bina a deep, soul-searing tongue kiss that left Kate reeling. Then he turned and looked at Kate.

"It isn't just an infatuation, Kate. We're sure of it. I love Bina and she loves me. We didn't mean to do anything behind Jack's back. I mean, after all, he's my cousin. But he was, well, playing around and telling me all about it, and —"

"Wait!" Kate wasn't sure she was hearing this correctly. "You slept with Billy Nolan and now you're sleeping with Max?" she asked Bina.

"Billy Nolan? Why would I sleep with Billy Nolan?" Bina asked. "I just needed him to dump me. Then he did and Jack proposed, and I said yes, and you said it was all right even though I slept with Max, but . . ."

Kate tried to think back. When Bina had told her about her "indiscretion," she hadn't been talking about Billy. Kate had misunderstood. And she had spent all of this time tormenting herself about Billy's promiscuity while he and Bina had never . . . "Oh, my God!" Kate said.

"See. I told you. Omigod!" Bina echoed.

Max smoothed Bina's hair and kissed her on the top of her head.

"Look," he said, "I don't mind telling Jack, and I don't mind telling Bina's parents, but she's afraid that it will cause a big to-do and that they'll hate me."

Kate felt so hot and so confused that she was actually dizzy. The room was airless, but her mind kept working while she struggled for a breath. If she could possibly feel more regret about the end of her affair with Billy, she felt it now.

Billy had never slept with Bina. Her doubts about his character, all her suspicions, had no basis in reality. Billy had gone out with innocent Bina and had seen and respected her innocence. She could barely take it in. "But the towels. The night in the rain when he dried you off."

"Bina told you about that?" Max asked, and looked at Bina. "Did you tell her what we did afterwards?"

"That was you and Max?"

"That's the point," Bina said. "I want it to be me and Max, not me and Jack. But I have Jack's ring and the rabbi is scheduled and we picked out the flowers and hired the band . . ." She began to cry again.

"Do you two want to get married to each other?" Kate asked.

"Of course," Max and Bina said simultaneously.

Kate took a deep breath. She looked at the two of them and remembered the way Max had looked at Bina after her makeover, and the time she had once met them sitting together on her stoop, and the night she had met Steven and seen Max with a woman, and even the noises she had heard upstairs. "How long has this been going on?" she asked them.

"Shortly after Jack left," Max told her.

Kate thought back. She realized that virtually the entire time that Bina was dating Billy she had been interested in Max, and Kate had been jealous and . . . Oh, the whole thing was too ridiculous. She looked across at her friend. "Not the same old Bina."

Bina shook her head.

"Okay," Kate continued as the reality sank in. The truth was, she had never liked Jack. She had never thought he was good enough for Bina. And Max was perfect. All of this was a good thing — just because she had totally fucked up her life didn't mean that Bina had to follow in her footsteps. "Max, you take care of Jack and your family. I'll take care of Bina's side. And it's best to do it right away." She looked at

Bina. "But you'll have to give him back the ring."

Bina nodded.

"I'll get you a bigger ring," Max told Bina.

"I don't want a ring. I just want you," Bina told him, and they kissed again.

Kate reached for her phone. She dialed the number she knew so well. "Mrs. Horowitz, it's Kate." She was greeted with the usual effusive hellos, invitations to come over for a meal, and questions about her health, her job, and her dating life, all without a pause or the opportunity to answer. "I'm just fine," she finally managed to say. "But I have some news for you."

Chapter Forty-seven

"God, it's hot," Elliot said, as if they didn't already know that. He and Brice were in formal dress again, and once again they were in Brooklyn. But this time both of them were tanned, and the contrast of their sun-burnished skin with the blazing white of their shirtfronts made them even more attractive than usual. Kate, wearing a lilac silk strapless gown, was roasting.

Outside the Brooklyn Synagogue, dozens of friends and relatives milled around, greeting guests in voices as shrill as the call of mynah birds.

"Howahya?"

"Waddahya doin'? We haven't seen ya in three Passovers."

"So she's finally getting married. I tell ya, her mother was *plotzing*."

"Are the Weintraubs here? You know the story, don't you?"

The crowd began to move up the steps and into the building. Kate hung back while Brice moved with the press of people. "I'll get us good seats," he told them.

Kate stood alone with Elliot. She took a deep breath. "Another wedding," she said, and tried to keep her voice cheery. "At least this is the last. I'll never have to buy an ugly bridesmaid's gown again."

"Hey, you're not a bridesmaid," Elliot told her. "You're an old maid of honor."

"Thanks for reminding me."

Kate sighed. She knew that both Elliot and Brice were trying to keep her cheerful, but this was really hard. She was still unable to pull herself together about Billy. Although she knew that there was no such thing as just one person for any other person, she felt that for the rest of her life, she would be comparing Billy to every man she met. And the others would suffer by comparison. She had been stupid and she was being punished, and there was nothing she could do about it except pretend she didn't hurt as much as she did and wait for time to take the sting out. Having to participate in this wedding, however, wasn't helping her to have a sense of proportion.

As if he knew just what she was thinking — and he usually did — Elliot took her arm. "Okay, Katie," he said, making her grimace at the name. "It's show time."

They began to move up the stairs together. "Look on the bright side," he told her. "It's not a three-hour Catholic mass." He lowered his voice as they entered the sanctuary. "It actually looks more like a Jewish mess. Check out the outfit on the old lady with the walker."

Kate glanced in the direction Elliot indicated and saw the old woman with a fur piece draped around her neck. "Is it living or dead?" Elliot continued. "And I mean the lady, not the fur."

"Shut up," Kate hissed. "That's Grandma Groppie. She's Mrs. Horowitz's mother and bakes the best *mondelbrot* in Brooklyn. She used to send me care packages when I was away at school."

"And for that you're grateful?" Elliot asked.

Brice called out to Elliot before Kate had a chance to smack him. People were talking, waving to one another, and having mild disagreements over where they should sit. Behind her, two old yentas were busy gossiping. ". . . so, *takka*, he changes his mind, but he doesn't know she's going to change hers." The woman, her hair fifty years older than Heather Locklear's but the exact same shade, nodded. Her companion, short and dumpy but wearing a regal beaded dress, shook her head and tsked.

"After all those years, you would think Jack Weintraub knew what he wanted."

"Oh, the Weintraubs. For them it's a crisis to pick towel colors."

"These kids today. What a *shanda*." Heavily, she took her seat. But the elderly blonde wasn't finished.

"Don't judge like that, Doris. I lost Melvin after forty-one years of marriage, and if I had to do it over again, better I should have eloped with Bernie Silverman like he asked."

"Bernie asked you, too?" Doris asked in a shocked voice.

Kate was fascinated, but she, of course, was part of the wedding party and had to join them. "Can I leave you here?" she asked Brice and Elliot. "Or will you misbehave?"

"You can trust us," Elliot said.

Brice nodded. "I've never seen a Jewish wedding, except in *Crossing Delancey*. Will they really hold Bina in a chair in the air and dance around her?"

"This isn't *Fiddler on the Roof*," Kate snapped, and left them. By the time she found Bina and her mother, the hysteria had already begun. Somehow Bina had forgotten one shoe. "I must have left it on the dressing table," she was telling her mother.

"Omigod! What are we going to do?" Mrs. Horowitz whimpered.

"Myra, it's not a tragedy," said Dr. Horowitz. "If it was a foot she lost, it might be a tragedy."

"Arthur, what is she going to do? Hobble down the aisle like a cripple? And do you know how much we paid for these shoes? You have to go back to the apartment and get the other one."

Kate looked at Bina and figured she was about to begin crying. But today she saw a different Bina. It was a cliché to say that the bride was glowing, but between Bina's obvious joy and the heat, her face looked beautiful and incandescent, almost as if a candle burned within her. "Forget about it," Bina said. "I'll just go barefoot."

"Are you *meshuge?*" Mrs. Horowitz asked. She turned to Kate. "My daughter, the bride, has gone crazy. Talk to her, Katie."

"I think it's a great idea," Kate said. "After all, Julia Roberts did it."

"Another *meshugene,*" Mrs. Horowitz said. She looked at Kate. "You look beautiful, darling," she said, and kissed Kate on the cheek. Just then a sweating man in a shirt opened at the neck came in.

"We're ready to go," he said. "The cameras are set up, and we've put the lights on. You better start before the congregation melts."

"Where are the girls?" Mrs. Horowitz asked.

"They're in the ladies' room. Where else?" Dr. Horowitz asked.

"Go get them and I'll get the flowers. Katie, you keep an eye on Bina so she doesn't decide to marry a third guy."

Kate and Bina were left alone. "You look beautiful," Kate told her friend. "Are you as happy as you look?"

"Omigod! I'm so happy. And it never would have happened without you. Thank you, Katie." Bina's eyes filled with tears. "I love Max so much. I didn't know it could be like this."

Kate knew exactly what she meant but said nothing. Just then the girls arrived, looking like a bunch of tangerines that had rolled out of a broken bag. "Katie!" they called.

"Shh," Mrs. Horowitz said. "They'll hear you. With decorum."

"And the bouquets," Dr. Horowitz called. "Refrigerator fresh." All the bridesmaids received the same nosegay of orange orchids with glossy lemon leaves. Kate got a larger bouquet of lilacs, lianthus, and white roses.

"That's not the only thing that's fresh," Mrs. Horowitz whispered into Kate's ear. "I made kugel just for you. Just don't tell the caterers." She pushed back Kate's hair and then looked up at Bina. "Time to go," she said.

"Exactly," Dr. Horowitz told her. "Now go sit down where you're supposed to, Myra. I walk her down the aisle."

"See you at the *bima,* Bina," Mrs. Horowitz said, and cackled. "I waited thirty years to use that line," she told them as she went to take her place.

Kate stood under the traditional canopy in front of the whole congregation with the Bitches arrayed behind her. There wasn't a lot of room, and the brims of their picture hats were bumping into one another as well as into the back of Kate's neck. She had her hair up and was actually grateful for the tickling because it kept her distracted. Max and Bina stood on either side of the rabbi. Kate couldn't take her eyes off Bina. She looked so happy and stared adoringly at Max. He was a little pale, but he returned the passion of Bina's looks. In fact, it seemed to Kate that they were unaware of the rabbi, the wedding party, or the couple of hundred guests before them. Kate looked out at the crowd. She wondered how many of the couples sitting in the rows loved one another. She also wondered if Jack was feeling desolate on this day. Along with his family, he had decided to boycott the wedding, and Kate couldn't help thinking that he had no one but himself to blame if he had lost the most precious thing in his life.

Most of the ceremony was in Hebrew, and Kate was clueless as to what it meant. But she did know that it meant that Bina had gotten the man she loved and that Max was a kind, loving, and dependable man. Kate supposed that she would never find a man she could look at the way Bina was now looking at Max. When the wedding vows were repeated in English, Kate couldn't keep the sadness at bay any longer. Bina would now join the sisterhood of young wives and mothers. . . . How ironic that just when Kate had merged her old friends with her newer ones, she would lose Bina to housekeeping, motherhood, and preschool.

"Do you, Max, take Bina to be your lawfully wedded wife . . ."

Kate heard the words, and this time it was not Bina's but Kate's own lips that trembled. She thought of Billy, now lost to her, and the way he'd looked at her when her face had rested beside his on the pillow. Had his eyes shone with as much warmth as she now saw in Max's eyes?

"I do," Max said.

"So do I," said Bina, jumping the gun. People throughout the temple laughed, and Kate, who had been on the edge of tears, had to laugh as well. Same old Bina.

The heat and the noise at the reception were almost overwhelming. It didn't help Kate's mood that the reception was being held at the same banquet hall where Bunny had been married and where all of the Billy Nolan nonsense had begun.

Elliot and Brice were doing their best to keep her diverted, but it wasn't an easy assignment.

"When do we Elders of Zion do the blood ritual with a little Christian baby?" Brice asked.

"That's *after* the appetizer," Kate told him.

Unfortunately, the two of them couldn't keep up the bodyguard act because Kate had to sit on the dais with the wedding party. That left her open to the women who kept accosting her, wanting to know, "When is it going to be your turn?" Kate wanted to tell them she was a lesbian and had already had a civil union with a lady gym teacher performed in Vermont, but she wasn't sure there was oxygen and an EMS team nearby. As soon as the bandleader announced that the dancing was about to begin, she stood up because she couldn't bear to sit there like a target any longer.

"And now, ladies and gentlemen, for the first time on the dance floor, let us put our hands together for Mr. and Mrs. Max Cepek."

The room was filled with the sound of applause, shouts of *"Mazel tov!"* and the dinging of forks against glasses. Max stood up, put his arm around Bina's waist, and swept her onto the dance floor, where the two of them began to waltz. Kate applauded along with the rest, despite the tears in her eyes. Over Max's shoulder, Bina threw Kate a kiss and mouthed, "Thank you." Kate nodded.

To the end of her life Kate couldn't remember how she got through the next couple of hours. Part of the time she hid in the ladies' room, part of it she spent woodenly smiling, feeling like a target at a carnival shooting range. Occasionally she danced with Elliot or Brice but could barely acknowledge their jokes. She did remember how tired her face got from holding grimly to the smile she kept plastered on it. Finally, the cake was served and she saw that there might eventually be some escape. At last Bina came over to her. "We're going to go soon," she said. "Get ready to catch the bouquet because I want you to be the next one married. Meet us downstairs." Kate nodded.

Then, because she could bear no more, she stepped off the dais and, as unobtrusively as possible, opened a door to the terrace.

Chapter Forty-eight

Kate slipped out onto the terrace unnoticed and leaned against the closing door. She was dizzy and having trouble catching her breath. She knew that most likely she was having what psychologists would term "an acute panic attack," but at the moment she was more woman, less psychologist. She took a moment or two to calm herself. Behind her in the hall, she heard the band begin to play "If I Loved You." Kate walked through the heat to the end of the terrace, but there was no escape. It was a corny song, and she didn't like ballads from musicals. That was more in Brice's department. But there was something undeniably poignant about the unexpressed fear and longing in the song. She felt her own loneliness welling up inside her.

She'd never get married, and even if she did, she had no parents to throw her a wedding. Not that she wanted a wedding thrown for her any more than she wanted the damn bridal bouquet that Bina was conniving to have her catch. She sighed, a catch in her throat.

Then, just a few feet away, there was a shaking of the ivy along the balustrade. Kate stepped away, expecting to see a squirrel or a chipmunk. Instead, the trembling became wilder, and the vines beneath the ivy actually jumped back and forth. Kate watched, fascinated, until a hand grabbed the railing. It was followed by a second hand, and then Billy Nolan's head and shoulders appeared. He hoisted himself up by his arms, then threw his long legs over the balustrade.

Kate couldn't tear her eyes away from him as he stood there, breathing heavily, recovering. He was wearing jeans, a white shirt, and loafers — obviously not wedding attire. Finally, after what seemed like an eternity of staring at him in silence, Kate found her voice.

"What are you doing here?" she asked, working hard to sound perfectly at ease, as though something like this happened to her all the time.

"I might ask you the same question," Billy said.

She blushed. "I'm here to see Bina celebrate."

"Out here on the terrace?" Billy asked.

It was too much. She didn't need to be teased by the man she'd loved and lost.

"I just . . . I have to go back now," she told him. "Nice seeing you."

She got as far as the door, her hand actually on the knob, when his arms came around her and his hand rested over hers. "Don't touch the dial," he said.

Kate watched, her face reflected in the glass of the terrace door. Her lips were trembling. It wasn't a pretty picture. Inside, everyone was on the dance floor, celebrating with Max and Bina. Why was Billy torturing her like this?

In the reflection of the glass, she saw him lean forward. She felt his face beside hers. "Kate," he whispered in her ear, "want to dance with me?" Without turning around, Kate shook her head. "Oh, come on," he said, the familiar coaxing tease in his voice. "You know you want to."

Kate turned to look at him. They were face-to-face, an inch or two of space between them. She could feel the stream of air from his nose on her forehead. She might not be able to have him, but for now she could inhale the same air he breathed. Then he took her in his arms and they began to move to the music.

Kate was stiff at first but soon couldn't

help but relax into his body. God, she missed his smell, his skin, his clean heat. This was breaking whatever was left of her heart, but she couldn't help it: She moved her arms up so that they draped over his shoulders.

"Kate," Billy said, pulling back slightly, "tell me you missed me."

"Missed you?" Kate echoed. Could she — or should she — describe the ache and emptiness and regret she'd felt since . . .

"Look, I don't know how the whole thing started, or whose idea it was, or whether it started as a joke," Billy began, "but I heard about your proposal."

She looked up at him. How did he know about Steven? She'd told only Elliot. But then, she reflected, he'd probably told Bina, and she'd told . . . well, everybody. "It was ridiculous," she said. "It had nothing to do with you."

His shoulders, under her arms, shrugged. "Maybe yes, maybe no," he told her. "You know what happens after you date Dumping Billy."

"Stop," Kate told him. "I never dated you because of that. It's a stupid nickname."

Billy shrugged again. "Everyone called me that. And everyone knew its truth but me."

"You don't think you've got some kind of . . . power, do you? I mean, to get people married?"

Billy laughed. "Don't worry. I'm not delusional. At least not in that way. I watched as one by one, all the guys I knew got married. And I wondered, What was I waiting for? What was wrong with me?" He looked down at her. "I had a prolonged adolescence. And I knew how much my dad loved my mom. I . . . I had fun, but I didn't want to settle. You know what I mean?"

Kate nodded up at him.

"You were different. You had the courage to leave, to raise yourself above what you came from. You, well, you're accomplished." He paused. "And I probably shouldn't say this, but I think we have a lot in common. I'm not saying I have your education or anything. But we both overcame a lot of early loss. You know what I mean?"

Kate nodded again, speechless, listening. His body against hers, moving to the music through the heat, felt like some kind of delicious dream. She didn't want to think about waking up.

"I think people who haven't suffered, well, good for them, but they're different from those of us who have," he said. "I

536

don't know all the psychology, the way you do, but I know that people like us, we're always going to be scared that we're going to screw up, that we're going to make the wrong decision and wind up where we started. You know?"

Kate nodded. She knew too well. She felt her heart begin to beat faster. Was it possible that he wasn't just forgiving her, but . . . She couldn't think. The heat and her excitement seemed to close in on her.

"I don't know why I had higher ambitions than the guys I know. Or why I went to France. I don't know why when I came back I wouldn't settle for a job working for someone else. Why I took over the bar and changed the clientele. I just wanted to be . . ." He paused. "It seemed like I wanted something more than Arnie and Johnny did, not that . . ." He took a deep breath. "I mean, how do you pick a partner not just for a few months, but for life?"

Kate nodded. Steven had done for months, and so had Michael . . . but for life? How did one know?

Billy continued. "It's not like I'm a snob, or I look down on the guys I know or the women I dated. We had fun. When we broke up I didn't hurt them. I liked them."

"I know you didn't hurt them," Kate said. "They all like you."

"Good. And it seemed to help them resolve things." He smiled. "I mean, they did all get married. My magic touch?"

Kate felt her face get hot again. "You know I never believed that nonsense. . . ."

"Until it happened to you."

"It didn't happen to me. I had known Steven for years. And I wasn't interested in him."

"Really," Billy said. And at that moment the band inside began to play the hokey-pokey.

Kate pulled herself away from him to stare into the room. "How did you do that?" she asked.

Billy just looked at her and smiled. "Coincidence."

Kate wouldn't accept that. Had he timed this? Did he know the band? He seemed to know everyone. She continued to stare at him. "How did you get them to play that just now?"

Billy shrugged. "Magic?" He leaned forward and nuzzled her ear. "You put your left foot in, you put your left foot out. You put your left foot in and you shake it all about," he murmured. "You do the hokey-pokey and you turn yourself around."

He swung Kate out away from him but held her hand tightly. Then he pulled her back into him, this time closer than ever. He stopped dancing and put his arms around her. He kissed her, and she let him. She kissed him back passionately, even if this was the last kiss he gave her. Even if he'd shown up only to punish her for her deceptions. "This is what it's all about, Kate," he said. Tears came to her eyes. Billy kissed her again.

"You're not angry at me?" she asked.

"Well, of course I was angry with you. I was furious." He paused. "You know how it is. The truth hurts. But I figured the entire thing out, and the parts I didn't know, Barbie and Bev were happy to fill in."

"They were?"

"Sure. And you know what the French say: *Tout comprendre c'est tout pardonner.*"

To understand all is to forgive all. Kate, for the first time, began to feel flooded with hope. "But we, well, we tried to use you for Bina, and I, well, I . . . I didn't mean to hurt you, it was just . . ." She didn't get to finish. Billy put his hand over her mouth and then kissed her again.

Kate looked through the terrace door to see a large crowd of women gathering around a barely visible Bina and Max. She knew the couple planned an early escape to get the last minute flight they'd booked for their honeymoon.

"Kate," Billy said, and she turned back to him. "I know I just own a bar in Brooklyn, that I'm not as educated as you are, but I can't stop thinking about you. From the first time I saw you, I —" He was interrupted by a hubbub below them.

The wedding crowd was streaming out the front doors. Billy and Kate watched from above as Max covered Bina's face. The two of them were pelted with confetti and flower petals. (Mrs. Horowitz had not allowed rice. She said it was too dangerous and could put somebody's eye out.) The driver of the wedding limo was holding the door open, but the guests and family were shouting and blocking the couple's way. Billy looked down and grinned. "Ah. The usual gauntlet."

Kate watched her friend. Bina was laughing and struggling to get into the car. "Throw the bouquet! Don't forget the bouquet!" yelled Barbie.

Bina looked around wildly. "Where's Katie? Where's Katie?" she yelled back. "*She* has to catch it."

Same old Bina, Kate thought. She knew she should be there seeing Bina off, but she'd never make it downstairs and outside in time — and most of all, she couldn't bear to leave Billy.

"Let's go, Bina," Kate heard Max urge. "We'll miss the plane."

Meanwhile the crowd was getting rowdy. Arnie and Johnny were "decorating" the limo with shaving cream and streamers. Mrs. Horowitz was giving a bag — probably full of kugel — to the driver, while Dr. Horowitz tried to confiscate the aerosol cans.

"Throw the bouquet! The bouquet!" Bev screamed.

"Katie!" Bina shrieked.

At that Max took the flowers from her hand. With all his strength, he wound up to pitch and tossed the bouquet in a wide arc high into the blue, blue sky. All eyes followed it.

With a somewhat violent *whoosh,* Bina's bridal bouquet hurtled through the air toward the terrace. Kate stepped back in time to avoid being seen by the crowd below. To her amazement, the bouquet fell with a splat at her feet. Startled, she and Billy stared at it silently. She felt paralyzed with embarrassment and . . . fear. Her longing was almost too much to bear. Then Billy broke the moment by stooping gracefully, picking it up, and offering it to her. Kate accepted it as if in a dream. She stared down at the bouquet in her hands, then at Billy, then back to the bouquet. She said a silent prayer that this moment wasn't just a coincidence. That it meant something real and lasting. She knew she was blushing, but she forced herself to look at Billy Nolan, even if it gave her away.

"How did you manage that?" Billy asked. "Was it magic?"

Kate, no matter what the cost, nodded, because it was.

"Kate, will you marry me?" Billy asked.

And, of course, she did.

About the Author

Olivia Goldsmith, novelist and journalist, was the bestselling author of *The First Wives Club, Flavor of the Month, The Bestseller, The Switch, Young Wives, Pen Pals, Bad Boy*, and, most recently, *Insiders*. Her articles appeared in the *New York Times, Cosmopolitan, InStyle*, and the *Observer*, among other publications.